About Jude Hayland

Jude Hayland is a writer, teacher and tutor. She spent many years writing commercial short fiction under the name Judith Wilson before completing an M.A. in Creative Writing and publishing her first novel. A Londoner by birth and upbringing, she now lives in Winchester, but spends as much time as possible at a family house in North West Crete. *The Legacy of Mr Jarvis* is her second novel and she is currently working on her third.

Follow her blog and latest writing news on:
www.judehayland.co.uk
Facebook: Jude Hayland – writer
Twitter: @judehayland

Also by Jude Hayland:

Counting the Ways

Reviews of this book:

*It made me think, it made me feel. It has everything
that a good book should have*

★

*The writer presents the characters in all their vulnerability,
with compassion and hopefulness*

★

*The characters are so real they become part of your everyday life –
always a great sign of something very worthwhile*

★

Well-developed characters steeped in emotions and strength

★

A lovely story with intriguing twists and turns

THE
LEGACY
OF
MR JARVIS

A novel

BY JUDE HAYLAND

Matador
9 Priory Business Park,
Wistow Road, Kibworth Beauchamp,
Leicestershire. LE8 0RX
Tel: 0116 279 2299
Email: books@troubador.co.uk
Web: www.troubador.co.uk/matador
Twitter: @matadorbooks

ISBN 978 1838591 564

British Library Cataloguing in Publication Data.
A catalogue record for this book is available from the British Library.

Printed and bound in the UK by TJ International, Padstow, Cornwall
Typeset in 11pt Aldine 401 BT by Troubador Publishing Ltd, Leicester, UK

Matador is an imprint of Troubador Publishing Ltd

To my late parents – with love – so much love

Acknowledgements

As always, grateful thanks to my family and close friends for their interest, enthusiasm and constant encouragement. In particular, to Carol Randall, Linda Anderson, Jane Robertson and Marie Armstrong. To my sister, Jane Gaudie, for always being there, willing to read, comment and offer constructive advice. Thank you to my patient and supportive partner, Alexander Innes.

Last, but never ever least, thanks to my son, George. For everything.

"For the fragment of a life, however typical,
is not the sample of an even web."

George Eliot – *Middlemarch*

"The truth is rarely pure and never simple."

Oscar Wilde – *The Importance of Being Earnest*

I visit every other Monday. By the time I arrive, apologising for being late, smiling at the staff as if needing their forgiveness, she's usually downstairs from her room. She likes to sit by the window in the blue chair, looking out at the garden, noting the sparrows, the occasional squirrel. She smiles at me, lets me kiss her cheek. And each time I visit, I am astonished, appalled even, at finding her old. My mother has become an old woman, vulnerable and helpless, and I am constantly shocked at the transformation. It even angers me a little, as if she is being wilful in choosing such a state, in allowing it to happen.

Ida tries to say something, my mother, Ida Foster, tries to speak, but words do not come easily, as if language has become foreign, remote from her grasp. She searches in her mind, grovelling in a cupboard that has become disordered, muddled. I talk, recite a sort of monologue and too rapidly cover the immediate topics: my journey, congested roads and traffic delays. The dead bird the cat sneaked in through the back door just before I left. Sad remnants of a garden sparrow. I pause and look around the large room, at the dozen or so old people in varying stages of decline, beached in their chairs, entirely dependent upon the whims and indulgences of others. Others like me, who are fortunate, so very fortunate not to be them, but are disturbed by such proximity because it is a stark reminder of our place, our position in the line. I turn back to Ida, take her hand as she fumbles for sense, letting words come out singly and in the wrong order so that I try to pick up the clues, piece together the idea she wants to share.

"Him… he… what's… what's his name?"

"Dad? Jack, you mean. He's all right. Coping well, really. He came to see you yesterday, didn't he? I spoke to him last night. He'll be in to see you tomorrow, I expect. He doesn't like to miss more than a day or two."

She shakes her head quite vehemently and I feel as if I have insulted her, assuming her meaning, suggesting a senility that is not hers.

"No, not… not him. Not… no, the other one…"

I prevaricate. Shuffle and dodge. I cannot be sure of the implication of her words, but I feel suspicious and suddenly wary. Her memory of long gone events is, after all, still intact. Past histories are brought easily to mind whereas recent days and weeks are knotted and confused. So, intentionally, I try to confound her, head her off from the direction in which she might be leading us. After all, we have waded through several decades with certain knowledge suitably crushed and suppressed. Maintaining the habit seems obligatory.

"Felix? He's fine, growing so fast. You wouldn't believe how tall he is. Busy with school, of course, and his football club and he's playing a lot of tennis these days." My son is an easy distraction for her for a while, her only grandchild, and a name she can fix upon, even if I feel unkind for thwarting her attempt to direct the conversation. It's as if I am the cowardly parent steering my young child away from an unsuitable exchange. The subject of Felix provides me with endless material that seems to divert her and provides a content of sorts. She smiles as I talk of him, even manages to focus on a photo I find in my bag. It would not be kind, after all, to venture into the dubious past with her, to somewhere that would offer at best, embarrassment, at worst, profound distress.

The day is too cold to take her out.

Sometimes we go for a drive, find a garden centre where we look at bulbs and annuals and perennials, sit in the café eating cake until she grows anxious and wants to leave. But today rain threatens and even this far inland the breeze off the sea seems to penetrate and is bitterly sharp. I've brought magazines that I know she won't read, but I prop one on her lap, turn the glossy pages and feign interest in lives supposedly glamorous and enviable. This is not Ida, my mother, sitting next to me, fingering the garish photographs, passively listening to my empty talk. It is some other woman who has covertly stolen her identity, crept into her skin and infiltrated her mind, her temperament. This stranger bears some fleeting facial resemblance to my mother, but she is nebulous, a blurred image of a person, a bland reproduction. I glance at my watch and she sees.

"Go? You… must be… late."

"Soon," I answer, "I'll go soon. I like to be back for Felix if I can and he'll be home from school in no time." I am ashamed of my own thin excuses. Ashamed of my intense desire to be out of this place, driving away, feeling with each mile covered a confusion of both guilt and relief. She closes the magazine, leaves the others untouched on the table in front of us. Later, the staff will come and take them, read them over their lunch break, their sneaked cigarette by the back door, then put them in the hall for visitors to see.

"Just want… can't remember…" Her hands are conducting a small invisible orchestra in their attempt to substitute for words. She laughs thinly at her own inadequacy and perversely I wish she would show more frustration, a rebellion, however pointless, against her regressed state. I put on my coat, pick up my bag, ferret for keys and kiss her cheek, attempting to hug her narrow, shrunken frame. Her eyes are unsettled, roaming as if in search of focus. Halfway across the room, I stop for a moment to say something to a care assistant, then turn to wave and see that Ida's face is suddenly animated and her voice, when it calls out to me, is sure and firm.

"Fred," she says, "Freddie… Freddie Jarvis. That's him. He's… it's… did he… die?"

The answer is simple.

"Yes," I reply, "yes. Mr. Jarvis is dead."

1

This is where I have to begin.

This is where the story of the past has to start.

After all, before we moved to the house at 8, Sea View Parade, to live close to the sea, our lives were blithely ordinary with nothing of note to recall. We were simply Ida and Jack Foster, my normal, predictable, faintly dull parents, and me, their only child, Mary Elizabeth, whose dark brown wavy hair refused always to lie straight and with skin that was prone to freckles. And we were living normal, inconspicuous lives in our semi-detached, pebble-dashed house with a bit of garden at the front and some more at the back in a suburban slice of North London.

But then the tea chests arrived.

I was eleven years and seven months old. Precisely. To the day.

Yes, if I am rash enough to go back, wilfully choose such a task, it's those tea chests that abruptly hook me to that morning in late August and the business with the huge removal van outside our house and the men with their tattooed arms, the sort I had only ever seen on fairground people guarding the dodgems and helter-skelters.

So here I go. Stepping recklessly back some forty or more years out of curiosity. Out of a need, at last, to know.

Remember, I am Mary Elizabeth, and eleven and a half years of age. Or thereabouts.

★ ★ ★

And it was the summer in between.

Primary school was over and a secondary of sorts lay ahead and my best friend, Anne Thompson, and I were spending most days in the memorial park, endlessly watching the canaries in the aviary, carefully avoiding the loud boys smoking and swearing from the seesaw and swings. Anne Thompson was off to the county grammar across town in September and had been boasting about her smart grey hat and blazer with a Latin motto all summer. She'd managed her mechanical arithmetic paper in the 11 Plus while I'd hazarded guesses, left gaps. She'd breezed through the intelligence test and sat with folded arms, sucking the red ribbon on her plait in the desk next to me. I had only been interested in the composition exam and consequently was down for the secondary modern two streets away, along with the smoking, swearing swings and seesaw boys and destined for a navy tunic and scratchy cardigan that would make my skin look sallow.

But this morning, the huge removal van and the tattooed men halfway down the path were suddenly of more importance.

"You're in the way, love," the man said to me, as I stood with my skipping rope in one hand next to the bed of dahlias. The man had a snake's head inked from wrist to shoulder on one arm and the words, *sexy Sue,* on the other. He was carrying armfuls of cloth, large grimy dustsheets like the ones my father used when he decorated. He pushed past me down our path, between the two squares of neat grass, and others followed him as if our house had suddenly become a place of enormous interest. Obviously, there was some mistake and I waited to see the men retreat, sent next door to Mrs. Owen or down the road to people like the Parkers, my mother cursing and railing at their inefficiency. We were not moving. Nobody had told me we were moving.

And it was not the sort of thing you forgot to mention like you might the visit of an irritating aunt or an appointment at the dentist. But the men did not leave. My mother's face did not appear at the window, exasperated and annoyed. I forgot Anne Thompson, I forgot the shilling in my pocket intended for Woolworths, threw my skipping rope into the dahlias and went inside.

The house felt invaded, disturbed, as if a rather cheeky kind of burglar had decided to chance his luck. Upstairs, the floorboards groaned and creaked. My mother was in the kitchen, kneeling on the stone floor of the larder, scrubbing bare shelves. She smelt of bleach and disinfectant.

"There you are, Mary," she said, glancing up at me as if she'd just remembered who I was. "Now you can give us a hand by starting to pack all those books of yours in your bedroom. There's a lot to do, you know, if we're going to clear this place by tomorrow morning." She turned back to her cloth and rubbed hard so that the veins in her hands stood out. Upstairs, men's voices and the shove and push of furniture seemed to threaten the ceiling. I stood there, my hands stuck out on my hips, watching my mother wring out her cloth in a pail of scummy water. I waited for her to tell me more. After all, yesterday, things had seemed quite ordinary. She'd been busy, one of her brisk days when she was forever vacuuming or rubbing down the paintwork or cleaning the bathroom tiles. But there was nothing particularly strange in that. My mother often behaved as if Princess Anne was about to come to play and stay for tea and get picked up by her royal mum and dad later. I crouched down, wedging my back against the larder door so that her face was only inches from mine. She stopped rinsing her cloth, found a handkerchief in her apron pocket and sneezed into it.

"Too much dust," she said. "I haven't cleaned properly in here for months."

"What's going on?" I said in a quiet voice, as if asking the question loudly would make something unpleasant become real. She looked at me for a moment then stood up and went to the sink to empty the bucket of dirty water. Her blue apron was wet, clinging to the pleats of her grey skirt like glue.

"We're moving, Mary, surely you've grasped that," she said sharply. "We're off to the seaside, which will be nice for all of us. A new start down on the south coast. Everyone wants to live at the seaside, don't they? Now take yourself off and start being useful, there's a good girl."

Upstairs, the removal men had already begun to attack my bedroom, shoving the furniture into the middle of the room, an island surrounded by a sea of pink carpet with a stain where cough mixture had once spilt when I'd had bronchitis. Out of the window, in the back garden, I saw my father mowing straight lines in the grass, which seemed a reassuringly ordinary sort of occupation. Except that my father should have been at work at the tax office on a Wednesday morning, not dilly-dallying with grass cuttings and the wheelbarrow as if it was Sunday afternoon before tea. He caught my eye, staring out of the window at him, half waved then shifted swiftly back to his mowing. I turned to my shelf of glass animals, looking shipwrecked on the wall instead of sitting comfortably above a bit of furniture. My bookcase was bare and my animal bookends stood deserted on the windowsill. I looked for my bed, planning to throw myself under the candlewick bedspread and bury my head in the pillow and hide. Hide until everything had returned to normal, until this odd nightmare had dissolved and disappeared from sight. But the removal men had got there first, stripping my bed of its sheets and cover and pillow and standing it up on end against the wall, its steel springs looking like lots of hedgehogs in a row. I rescued the glass animals, shoved my seahorse, the polar bear, the Dalmatian dog and the starfish into the pockets of my skirt and went into my parents' bedroom. Two very large men were emptying the wardrobe, gathering handfuls of my mother's clothes, her camel hair winter coat, her skirts, her best grey dress and her sensible shoes. My father's three dark suits lay under a polythene cover on the bed, a tangle of ties, snake-like, at their side. I went next door into the box room, the room at the front of the house where I'd slept when I was small. I'd had whooping cough and chicken pox and the measles in quick succession when I was two and my father had stuck a frieze of nursery rhymes around the wall so I could watch Bo-Peep and Humpty Dumpty as I scratched and itched and grew hot. Curtains were gone from the window, a solitary curtain hook remaining. Outside in Ash Gardens, boys were playing football in the road, taking it in turns to be Geoff Hurst and Gordon Banks, and chanting *They think it's all over… it is now* over and over again while two girls at the other end of the cul de sac were racing scooters along the pavement. One of the boys kicked the ball into someone's front garden by mistake and a window opened in protest, causing them all to scatter, disappear down side alleyways and through front doors. The game, it appeared, was over. For that morning, at least.

★ ★ ★

Yes, this is the start of it although, of course, I didn't know it at the time. Years later, once I realised how pivotal that moment had been, leaving Ash Gardens for Sea View Parade, and how easily the lies had then begun to thrive amidst such change, I wish I had insisted on some sort of explanation, asked more questions, for then, perhaps, the fabric of deceit might have failed to weave its way quite so seamlessly into our lives. But, of course, I was a biddable child of my time, pliable, acquiescent, demanding and expectant only of what was likely to be given to me. Children occupied a very different place in the hierarchy then and I was entirely used to toeing the line that my mother, Ida, firmly drew, conditioned and comfortable with conformity, finding any other behaviour too inconvenient to consider. Even at the age of seventeen, once I began, at last, to see the levels of deception, I was still too naïve and ingenuous to respond adequately. I judged the lot of them, of course, despised them, but then simply withdrew into hostile, entirely tacit condemnation. Inevitably, my evasiveness had its consequences. For later, when my attitude began to wane, thawing slowly like a clod of snow losing its hold, the absence of an angry, vocal confrontation at the moment of my discovery made it somehow easier to pretend that nothing extraordinary had actually taken place. As if it was possible to erase it from knowledge, from the fabric of our past. It was what the three of us did, a sort of familial herd instinct, perhaps, choosing a complicit silence, a cowardly kind of appeasement.

But that was then. Not now.

Now we are in another century where we play by such different rules and the idea of perpetually suppressing truth and choosing to live alongside distorted memories seems absurd. I blame Ida. Blame the blatant way she called out across that beige, insipid sea of carpet on my last visit to her at the nursing home. *Fred Jarvis.* The name like a litmus paper for family secrets, scandalous deceptions. Perhaps even Ida needs some final blazon of truth. Or her muddled mind no longer censors itself so effectively so that his name slipped out brazenly, as if trying its syllables on the air after decades of silence. So I am pulled back, along with my ailing mother, for whom speech is now an elusive and precious commodity, frustrated by ignorance, by a lack of understanding.

I want to talk about the man. About the late Mr. Fred Jarvis and his place in our lives.

★ ★ ★

Early the next morning we left our semi. The night had been spent lying stiffly on a mound of old blankets, floorboards sticking into my backbone each time I moved, so that it was almost a relief to climb into the car. I sat in the back of our loaded blue Austin Cambridge, wedged in between paisley eiderdowns and a box of bone china dinner plates we never used, as we drove sedately out of Ash Gardens. Mrs. Salter from across the road stared from her front window. The boy who'd once stolen my bike for an entire day watched from his garden wall. I pulled a silly face at him and stuck out my tongue. We turned into Bridge Street and drove past the Langham Cinema, where they were showing *The Heroes of Telemark*. Past the expensive greengrocer's that we never went to and the cheap one that we did. On into Marsh Road and the draper's that sold buttons and elastic and ribbons and darning wool from glass drawers that were pulled out to reveal their neat, orderly rows. The station went by on our right, men in suits, one or two with hats, stopping to buy newspapers at the kiosk and a few women with handbags and skittery heels hurrying into the underground. which was actually overground until it passed Wembley Park. Bus queues trailed along the pavement, people waiting for the 183 and 209 in the thin sunshine. I watched it all pass, lose its solidity, become a faint outline through the rear window then a smudge before dissolving entirely from view. My father in his tweed jacket, that always smelt of petrol and peppermints, drove resolutely on.

"We've made a good early start," he said, "although I expect we'll meet the usual jam on the South Circular."

My mother glanced behind her.

"All right, Mary? I shouldn't read if I were you. It'll only make you queasy." She passed me two glucose sweets even though I'd grown out of carsickness when I was seven. They talked about the traffic, about something in the news they'd caught on the car radio, in normal kind of voices, just as if this was a normal day. A day like any other instead of one snatched crazily out of nowhere with no right to attach itself to us. They talked until suddenly silent, as if having run out of things to say. and then the quiet of the car seemed worse than their chatter. My head ached. I tried to sleep then I tried to read, wanting to do what my mother had told me not to do. But even Noel Streatfeild and Lalla and Harriet in the skating competition failed to hold me and the words jumped around the page, refusing to stay together in sentences to make sense. I gave up and shut my eyes and let my mind play a pretend sort of game. What if we weren't moving at all, but simply heading for a day trip to Brighton? Yes, that was it, just a day out. Every now and again, we'd do it, on a hot summer Sunday. There'd be a picnic of paste sandwiches and hard-boiled eggs, still with bits of shell attached, then some dabbling in the icy cold sea, water as far as my thighs. Pebbles would pierce through my sandals as I went in search of shells and graze my shins. My mother would complain about blood on my white ankle socks, find a plaster and stick it unsuccessfully onto wet skin. Sometimes, there'd be Roll a Penny on the Palace Pier with my father and maybe even a fish and chip supper in newspaper on the way back. There was a place near Kingston that gave you more chips than you could eat and the smell of vinegar would hang around the car for ages after. A day's trip to the seaside was what we did, all we did, coming home late to our house in Ash Gardens with pockets full of sand and seashells, hair matted with saltwater.

Then I opened my eyes and let myself remember.

They'd packed it all up, our house, emptied it, boxed it up, left it vacant and tidy for other people who would sleep in my room and play in my garden. Find my best marbles lost last summer in one of the flower beds. Laugh at my growing chart my father had pencilled against the hall wall. I turned myself round, knelt up on the back seat and stared out of the window as familiar places slid by and out of grasp. Longer stretches of green appeared and fields with cows and big houses hidden behind high hedges. After a while, I grew sleepy, the way I always did on long car journeys, dozed a bit then woke with a jolt when we pulled up at a level crossing. My mother and father were talking again, saying something about keys and electricity switches and my mother sounded excited, talking in the rapid way she did whenever she was particularly pleased about something. Like the time she bought an ugly, old chair off a rag and bone man and could not believe her luck in finding what she called an antique. The chair had sat in the living room until its smell of tom cats and seedy old men became too overpowering. I must have slept again for when I opened my eyes, there was a thin line of something very like sea on the left, a long stretch of promenade with empty benches and then we turned sharply right, another right and finally the car was still, the drone of the engine gone. We had, apparently, arrived.

The house was old. It was the first thing I noticed when we pulled into the kerb in front of the long terrace of houses. Number 8, Sea View Parade was an old house. The estate agent's board, stuck into the overgrown pretence of a front garden, shouted out SOLD in bold letters as if not quite believing the fact. If the faintest glimmer of anticipation had begun to stir in me when I had first spotted the sea, it was instantly extinguished. Like a firework that finds itself placed in damp, sodden ground. Besides, it was a cheat. There might have been a sea view when the terrace was first built a century or more before, but a couple of roads of squat bungalows now sat barring its claim to the name. My mother fished for keys buried deep in one of the many bags gathered around her feet while I sat firmly entrenched in my back seat. Although my legs were stiff from three hours in the car, my head thick with the stifled air, I was determined to be stubborn. It was the only thing I could think of to express my fury.

"It's quite a project, you know," my father said, rolling down his window so that a breath of sharp air flooded the stuffiness of the car. "Take a bit of time to get it into shape, of course. But then…" He got out his pocket diary, found his propelling pencil and made a note of the mileage. He always did that on long car journeys, a bit of routine I usually found comforting, but on this occasion, foolish, since we were clearly not going to be making a return trip.

"It's just what we need, a real find," my mother said, grinning a little alarmingly and looking out at the tall, thin house as if at an extravagant mansion. "I can't believe this has just fallen into our laps. You'd think it would have been snapped up instead of being on the market for over a year. But then, people are so short-sighted these days, snapping up new, ready to move into places. It's all this silly trend for modern houses since the war. Whereas we've got a real investment here. And space. Just think of it, Mary, a big house at the seaside!" She turned round to look at me, her eyes bright like a thieving bird. She made the whole thing sound like an adventure from one of my precious books. Five go to the Seaside, The Secret Seven's Sea Venture. Summer Term at Soppy St. Clare's. Seaside White Boots. I was not so easily convinced.

"But it's so far away. So far from everyone we know," I said in a voice that was quieter than I intended. I had only ever lived in Ash Gardens. My parents had started their married life in two rented rooms in Kentish Town and had moved to our cul de sac soon after I was born. I'd heard all about how thrilled they'd been to buy their first house, a house with an upstairs bathroom and a back garden and their own front door and a bargain because of the fixed prices for house developments in the decade after the war. I could not imagine living in a place without a station that swiftly delivered you to Finchley Road or Baker Street, without red double-decker buses heading for Hendon or Harrow. Besides, people who moved got new houses. Shiny red brick houses with porches and garages and driveways. Like my friend, Anne Thompson, who was going to the grammar school, in her four bedroom and downstairs toilet and parquet flooring detached house in the new estate near the memorial park. That was why people moved. For something smarter. Better.

My mother was already out of the car and moving down the stone path to the front door of Number 8. She moved a couple of old tyres out of her way, stepped over an ancient mangle, turning round to grin at us as if this were all part of some entertaining obstacle game. My father seemed to be my last hope, my only chance of escape from this madness. I leant forward from my back seat, positioning myself to speak close to his ear. Surely, he'd listen, he'd understand how impossible and idiotic this whole idea was.

"If we don't like it, we'll go back, won't we?" I said quietly but insistently into his ear. "Promise me if it's horrid, we'll go home to Ash Gardens?" I locked my arms around his neck, felt the soft fabric of his shirt, smelt the coal tar soap smell of his skin. His Old Spice cologne. An angry batch of seagulls squawked overhead, startling both of us, jerking us apart. I replaced my arms, held tight. He said nothing for a moment and I waited patiently for the reassurance I felt sure of finding.

Then slowly, he disentangled my hold around his neck, turned round to face me, smiling falsely in the way people do when they are about to deliver unwanted news.

"It's a new start, Mary. You'll get used to it, tuppence. After all, everyone wants to live at the seaside, don't they? You're really a lucky girl, you know, very lucky indeed." He opened his car door, closed it gently and stood on the pavement, looking up at the old, skinny house. So that, apparently, was that. My throat felt strangled, my eyes stung and I jammed the nails of one hand into the palm of the other, the way I always did when entirely at a loss for whatever else to do.

In the road ahead, a huge removal van had started to unload, filling the pavement with our furniture. There seemed something shocking in seeing it all sitting there, homeless and forlorn. Our mahogany sideboard with the water-marked surface, the big radiogram that I used to sit on when I was small for *Listen with Mother*. The sludge-coloured three-piece suite that suddenly looked shrunken and thread-worn. I watched my father trying to give instructions to the men who were drinking tea from thermos flasks, lighting cigarettes and laughing loudly. Then my mother came out of the house and the men threw the contents of their cups into the curb, stubbed out cigarettes and began to shift the furniture strewing the pavement. It suddenly seemed an ideal moment for me to disappear, to jump out of the car and run. Run down to the sea and drown myself, run to the main road and hitch a lift to London, run into the arms of the first stranger and risk my life at his hands. That would make them sorry. That would put worried looks on my parents' smug and satisfied faces. The fantasy occupied me pleasantly for a while, although my imagination stalled at thinking of sufficiently grim and grizzly outcomes as I tended to read books about poor vicarage families and boarding school feasts rather than desperate kidnaps and abductions.

Then, unexpectedly, I was rescued. I saw the girl.

Sitting on a low wall the other side of the road, in front of the row of bungalows, she was first watching me, then watching the removal men, as if deciding which was the more interesting. She was dressed in shocking pink shorts and an orange top that clashed gloriously. My grey pleated skirt, white blouse and white socks felt grubby and dull in comparison. I was glad she couldn't see the stain of spilt orange squash on my sleeve. Suddenly, as I stared, she got up, the girl, yanked a bike from where it had been left on the pavement and pedalled away ferociously fast as if remembering somewhere crucial she needed to go.

A flash of pink and orange disappeared swiftly around the bend, accompanied by the cling-cling of a bicycle bell.

★ ★ ★

Of course, it was probably not entirely like that. Those shorts might have been purple. Or even dull beige. Memory distorts, plays games, invents what it fails to recall in an effort to paint as authentic a picture as it can.

But I am being stringent in viewing all this through the prism of the child, Mary.

Not with the interpretation of hindsight or through some clumsy analysis that the adult Mary could so easily substitute. That's not the point of this at all.

I want to go back to see it as it was then.

The young are not interested in the past, of course. It's a bore, an embarrassment even, full of tales of far more fallible and flawed generations. It's the future that engages them, hooks them to their own unmapped stories of success.

But the coin flips.

There is a point when what lies ahead holds too little to excite and the years already stacked up behind become unexpectedly compelling, potent for dissection. So I am finding Mary, in the grey pinafore dress or that red tartan kilt she used to wear, with short summer socks or fawn winter ones, who suddenly feels not so much four decades away, but simply a small stretch so that, with a little effort and careful reminiscence I can bring her faithfully to mind. And Eva, too. For Eva, the girl in the pink or purple shorts, was certainly there from the start too.

★ ★ ★

That first night, I was given the attic bedroom. My mother warned me that the arrangement might not be permanent, that it was very likely to change in the coming months, but I forgot to listen, too glad to escape up two flights of stairs to the top floor where my white chest of drawers from Ash Gardens and my bed were already waiting for me. Even my winceyette nightdress and candlewick bedspread had been unpacked and a box of my books was splitting out onto the thin carpet. I picked up my battered paperback of *A Dream of Sadler's Wells* and my hardbacked *Little Women,* its cover hanging on only by a hinge, and felt reassured, as if my books confirmed that I was still me and had not been exchanged for some changeling child once we had left the south circular. There were two skylights and I stood on my bed and peered down into the street far below and looked over the bungalows towards a band of grey, like a pencil margin drawn against the sky. My mother had insisted on an early night and sent me upstairs soon after tinned tomato soup at seven, saying I must be tired, although I'd done little more than sit in the car all day then helped her hang some old curtains at the big windows that spanned from ceiling to floor and rattled every time a slight breeze blew. I could hear my parents now two floors down, low murmurs of sound rather than words, furniture pulled over bare floorboards followed by footsteps and doors closing clumsily. It was barely dark, the late August evening light filtering so easily through the skylights, and I lay in bed listening to the new noises outside. The sea swallowed up and smothered sounds of cars so that it was the to-ing and fro-ing of waves I heard instead of engines, the tide drawing in or out, heaving and tossing pebbles, rearranging them in its path, like some gigantic harvester. I lay on my back in bed and traced the ceiling cracks into sea monsters and horses with long flying manes.

It was the gulls that woke me in the morning, screeching loud and piercing outside, so that I stood on my bed to watch fans of white wings flying past. And the girl was there again, the girl in the shocking pink shorts, her top bright yellow now instead of orange, wearing black plimsolls that looked like large ink blots at the end of her thin bare legs. She crossed the road, dropped her bike on the pavement outside Number 8 and started to walk down our path.

2

My elderly father, Jack, spends a lot of time in his shed these days. So often when I ring he's out there, sorting things, mending, measuring bits of wood that might, as he says, come in useful. I gave him a mobile phone at Christmas, tired of leaving messages on his landline answering service that he never checks. He wasn't keen on the idea, of course. It took ages to convince him it's only a sensible, safety measure, not intended as a constant intrusion.

"What do I want with one of these things?" he said. "Not as if I go many places these days."

In fact, he's still remarkably independent, still driving the car and looking after himself quite adequately in the small house they moved to ten years ago. The burden of the big house, of 8, Sea View Parade, had been absurd, but it had taken years to persuade my mother, Ida, to leave. She had clung on stubbornly, her usual pragmatic approach apparently dormant when it came to that house. Eventually, however, they left and settled several miles inland in a quiet street away from the onslaught of sea storms and the excessive traffic that had transformed Beach Parade.

Now it is just Jack here alone, adjusting.

Once he finally agreed that Ida would be safer, happier in the nursing home, he set himself a daily routine as if to justify a good reason for getting up each morning. Consequently, the house is neat and clean, the cupboards always stocked and his meals taken regularly. I've seen the lists he pins to the back of the kitchen door, ticking off his household tasks as he completes them each week. Washing, ironing, bathroom cleaning, vacuuming. It's his way, no doubt, of keeping going, and he's always been an endlessly practical man. A man, some would say, without imagination, with his feelings and passions kept firmly in check. You could say this has been the saving of him. Or, alternatively, see it as his failing. There was certainly a time when his placid attitude enraged me and I came close to despising him for it. But that's all a long while ago now, feelings hitched to another time, another stage in our lives. My father, Jack, is here, living out a pleasant enough existence, coping with being alone, managing his awareness of the limited span remaining to him.

A week after I visit Ida, I call in, ostensibly to collect a few more things she may like for her room. A footstool she was fond of, her photograph albums, a warm dressing gown. Jack's made me tea, strong tea that he's forgotten I dislike, and arranged small fondant iced cakes on a plate. We carry the tray into the living room, look out at his garden that's dense with white and purple crocuses, early daffodils and a scattering of primroses. He's always been a dutiful gardener, never allowing weeds to thrive, roses to go unpruned. I remember the order he so swiftly imposed upon the back and front gardens at Sea View Parade so that there was always a healthy profusion of shrubs and seasonal flowers. He used to let me pick bunches of marigolds for the kitchen table, sweet peas and lily of the valley for the hall. Ida said it made a good impression on the lodgers, flowers welcoming them into the house. Or rather it's what she said when they first arrived, when Miss Mackie moved into the basement room next to the kitchen and Mr. Jarvis took over the attic. Later, when Miss Mackie left and only Mr. Jarvis remained, Ida said he was too much like a member of the family to bother about such touches as flowers.

I drink my tea, eat a pink cake, refuse a second and head upstairs to the main bedroom – orderly, a precise tidiness as if ready for snap inspection. I quickly find the dressing gown, a spare pair of slippers from the bottom of the wardrobe, the cardigan I bought her last birthday. I pile them up on one of the twin beds, open the drawers of her dressing table. For ten minutes or so I'm looking, sifting through old powder compacts, lavender linen bags long absent of any scent, hairbrushes and combs, a small leather ring box, a bracelet with a broken safety chain. Jack comes up the stairs and I shut the bottom drawer guiltily as if caught pilfering.

"Got everything you want, love?" He sits down on the chair in the corner as I fuss over the articles I've collected, slip them into a bag. He looks suddenly tired, old, his thin face a little more gaunt, and I wonder if I should offer to take him home with me for a couple of days. "What was it you were looking for?" he asks, seeing my eye dart around the room, glance at the chest, the bedside cabinet. "The photo albums are downstairs, I've got them out for you."

"Thanks, that's fine, then, I've got everything she needs. I thought the albums would be nice to share with her when I next visit." I follow him downstairs, feeling thwarted, interrupted in my search. Yet I have absolutely no idea what I am looking for. Ida is hardly the type to have kept a diary, written a memoir. And the idea of stumbling over a bundle of letters, pulling open a drawer to discover a romantic correspondence neatly bound in red ribbon is ludicrous. I insist upon washing the teacups and Jack parcels up our leftover cakes to take back to Felix. He won't come home with me, shows me the ham salad he's prepared for his evening meal. Wafer thin slices of cucumber, an egg hardboiled and quartered, beetroot already staining the yolk purple. He's planning to grow tomatoes this summer, he tells me, and radishes and Cos lettuces if he can find a way of preventing the slugs. His face comes alive, talking of his garden, and he shows me the seed catalogues that he's asterisked and circled in black ink. He thinks he might plant another rose bush, a fragrant climber that he can train around the front door. I leave him standing there, contemplating the brickwork, load the car with the items I've collected, sensing something not found.

It's driving home later, switching on the radio to the six o'clock news, that I realise what I have been looking for. I have been looking for Ida. And I am exasperated by the futility of my task and even its arrogance, as if I have some extraordinary prerogative to know her ultimately. I remind myself that the best I can hope to gain is some sort of clarified understanding, an acceptance, if you like, of her actions, of Jack's apparent complicity. Of the part played by Fred Jarvis in their lives. It's one of the reasons for going back, after all, for trawling through those years, starting with Mary on the cusp of discarding her Alice bands and socks for tortoiseshell slides and stockings. (It took quite a time for tights to reach our south coast backwater, for cumbersome suspender belts to lose their utilitarian function and reinvent themselves as underwear of allure.)

In the meantime, though, I need to concentrate on the dense traffic of the A23, the nightmare of the intersecting M25, and turn up the volume on the radio to flood my thoughts more glibly with international atrocities and global disaster.

3

She seemed deep in conversation with my mother when I arrived downstairs in the hall. I'd shoved my white cardigan over my nightdress, the only thing I could find without digging into suitcases.

"This is Eva Mason," my mother said and I felt infuriated that she'd got to her first. She was, after all, my discovery, spotted from the car the day before and then from the skylight in my attic bedroom. "She wants to show you around a bit. Show you the beach and that. What do you think, Mary?"

My mother seemed about to agree and I saw that Eva was the kind of girl good at winning over adults. The kind who knew the things to say, the things to leave out in order to get, more or less, what she wanted. Her name probably helped. People listened to a person called Eva, thought her worth attention. I looked at her pink shorts, at the bright yellow top just beginning to show signs of things growing underneath, small pert swellings like buns proving, and felt very aware of my creased nightdress and white cardigan.

"She'll be ready in an hour, Eva, you can come back then," my mother said, starting to close the door on her. I was worried Eva would disappear, but she just shrugged and lifted her eyebrows, the way I'd seen people do in films and had tried unsuccessfully to copy.

"I'll just hang around then," she said. "Ma doesn't want me back until this afternoon. I'll just wait here if that's all right."

She perched herself on one of the old tyres in the front garden as if it was a perfectly acceptable garden seat and the sort of thing all desirable gardens possessed.

We headed down towards the sea to the coast road. I'd managed to find some navy blue trousers, but my mother had insisted upon an ugly old anorak in case it rained. I envied Eva her bare arms and legs. She hopscotched very fast along the pavement and I had to skip to keep up with her. I'd tied clumps of my hair back from my face with an elastic band, but it was so wavy that strands of it kept escaping and blowing into my face in the strong breeze that tasted of salt. Eva's hair, thin and flat like bands of pale silk, stayed obediently hooked behind her ears. The main road ran the stretch of the coast in both directions as far as the eye could see. I followed Eva across the road and down a couple of steps onto the seafront. Facing out towards the grey English Channel were a series of benches every twenty yards or so, most of them occupied in spite of the cool wind. Old men sat with their heads buried in newspapers, trying to control the pages from buffeting away. People with dogs sat and talked to each other, pulling at leads to separate their barking hounds. Other people were all alone, simply sitting and staring straight out ahead of themselves at the sea.

"What do you think people find to look at?" Eva said, leading us to the only empty bench further along the seafront. We sat down and I copied the way Eva was sitting, pulling my feet up onto the bench and resting my chin on my knees. "It always looks the same, doesn't it? The sea, I mean." I followed her gaze to the dreary horizon, solid sky merging with the dank, dark sea. "Their lives at home and their houses must be pretty dull and boring if they think it's better to spend their days sitting here all alone."

"Perhaps they're dull and boring people living in boring houses so they're only happy doing dull and boring things all day long," I said, and was very pleased that Eva found this funny. She turned it into a kind of song, snatched a tune out of her head and sang my words to it out loud in a silly sort of high voice like someone trying to be in an opera. When we stopped giggling enough to talk clearly again, I told her how brilliant she was at singing.

"Oh don't you start, my ma's always going on about me being able to sing. Thinks I should join a church choir or something. Maybe become a professional singer when I grow up."

"That would be all right, wouldn't it?" I said. "You could become famous and earn lots of money and stuff." Even if I had any talent at singing, which I hadn't, I knew my mother would never suggest it for a career. Eva's mother sounded promising. Very different to mine.

"Anyway," she said, "I'm going to be an air hostess when I grow up. And fly to lots of hot places and stay in expensive hotels. What about you?" She wrapped her arms around her legs, neat and tidy like a cat. I hesitated. I had no idea what I was going to be when I grew up. I imagined, on the rare occasions when I thought about such matters, that I'd have to be a shorthand typist or a nurse. Or a secretary in an office. I hadn't really heard of anything else that normal, ordinary girls like me were allowed to do. Girls called Mary who had failed their 11 Plus. Eva appeared to have lost interest in her question.

"How old are you?" she asked.

"Nearly twelve," I said, "very nearly. In January."

"I'm already twelve. My birthday's in July. But it doesn't matter." She stood up, stretched her squashed legs and produced a sixpence from the pocket of her shorts.

"Got any money? We could go to Beach Parade, if you like. It's freezing just sitting here."

I followed Eva back across the coast road and we walked to a small row of shops with a bus shelter at one end and a pub called the Black Boy at the other. She led me slowly past each one, as if conducting a guided tour. There was Kennarths, the grocer's, with a pile of wire baskets outside and a sign on the door in large green letters saying SELF SERVICE NOW! Next door was Balls, the chemist, with a window full of elasticated stockings and corn plasters and teething rusks. Eva pushed us on, past the newsagent, past two boarded-up shops plastered with peeling old billboards advertising an end of pier summer variety show. She stopped outside Beaumont's.

"This is the best place. The man lets you spend ages in here. He's a bit deaf, actually, and ancient, so I think he forgets how long you've actually been in here."

Inside, a smell of cough candy and plasticine and tobacco smoke hung in the air. At the front of the shop, there were tall jars of boiled sweets and a counter selection of chocolate bars and gobstoppers and bubble gum and sherbet dabs and penny chews. A fat man sat on a high stool, reading the *Racing Times*, dropping ash from his cigarette onto boxes of liquorice allsorts. At the back of the shop, down two steps and conveniently out of view of the counter, was a section for toys. Jigsaw puzzles, Fuzzy Felt kits, dolls' clothes, toy cars, packets of jacks, bags of coloured marbles, Meccano sets, were higgledy-piggledy, stacked from floor to ceiling, like a playroom that no-one's ever tidied. In an alcove, that could only be reached by climbing over a miniature train set and a small rocking horse, was a jumble of buckets and spades, dusty beach balls, sand rakes and plastic sand shoes, all marked REDUCED – END OF SEASON.

"It always says that," Eva said, "it's been the end of the season here forever."

We settled down on the floor to play a game of jacks then inspected the dolls' clothes then the toy cars. Eva's interest in such things was a comfort. I'd spent much of the past year worrying that, at nearly twelve years of age, I was supposed to forget toys and think only of pop music and boys. But a girl with long, straight blonde hair and thin, straight up, straight down legs with no obviously awkward sticking-out knees could naturally be relied upon as a guide in such things. And at that moment, Eva paused, a Fairy Glen box of dolls' clothes in hand.

"It's all right just to pretend we're still babies, you know. It's all right when we're in Beaumont's. Have you still got your dolls?"

"One or two," I said vaguely, thinking of my family of plastic-faced, stiff nylon-haired dolls with staring blue eyes, lying buried deep in some packing case.

"Me, too," said Eva, "just one or two."

Eva spent her sixpence on a Milky Way and some penny chews. I'd found a threepenny piece in the pocket of the ugly anorak and bought a bar of Fry's milk chocolate. We sat in the bus shelter at the end of Beach Parade for a while, eating and chewing, and looking at the list of destinations on the timetables.

"Perhaps we'll be allowed to go to Brighton together when you're twelve too. Or Eastbourne. They've got piers and slot machines and amusement arcades there, you know," Eva said. "Not like this place at all."

"Do you think we'll be allowed? I mean, to go on our own?" I was still head over heels and dizzy with confusion over leaving Ash Gardens to feel confident about venturing any further. Besides, the buses here appeared to be green, not trustworthy, reliably red buses like I knew. Anything could happen to you on a green bus.

"Of course," said Eva, "we'll be teenagers in no time and then we'll be able to go anywhere we like." We began to walk back towards Sea View Parade where my mother would be expecting me. I had been allowed out for exactly two hours. Anyway, it had started to rain, slicing, soaking rain that was sinking through my sandals and would end up staining my ankle socks red.

"You can be my friend if you like, Mary," Eva said when we reached Number 8. "I had a best friend called Rosemary, but she's gone to live in Canada. Her whole family, I mean, 'cos her dad's gone and got a job there." She picked up her bike from our front garden where she'd left it beside the rubber tyre turned garden seat. "I don't suppose you know anyone else living here."

I saw my mother waving at me from the front window, and then pointing to her watch as if I were late for some urgent appointment.

"No," I said, "we only arrived yesterday and…"

"That's settled then," Eva said, climbing onto her bike. It was too small for her and her feet wildly overshot the pedals so that she had to ride with knees nearly up to the handlebars. "We'll be friends, Mary Foster. I'll come round tomorrow because we haven't got much time left."

"Time left for what?"

Eva raised her eyebrows and did her shoulder-shrugging thing.

"Time to do things before school starts again, silly. It's nearly the end of the summer, after all."

★ ★ ★

It was my father who first mentioned the idea of the lodgers. The first week at Number 8, Sea View Parade slid by in a mess of emulsion paints and turpentine and white spirit and he was forever at the top of a ladder or on his knees sanding bare floors. There were too many rooms for the amount of furniture brought with us so most of them were bare or only half filled. The high ceilings meant large windows and my mother's attempt to fill them with our old curtains, releasing their gathers so they looked like reused wrapping paper, was hopeless. She'd even resorted to hanging the old blackout curtaining left over from the war that had lurked spectre-like in a corner of the loft at Ash Gardens. It had always worried me, that curtaining, as if the war was something that could return at any moment and my mother was determined to be prepared.

"Just a temporary measure," she said briskly, giving up on trying to make curtains meet in the middle, "until I find some cheap material and make some new. And of course we'll start to pick up some more furniture in time."

The three of us sat in the basement kitchen round the Formica table that only took up a quarter of the room. I'd spent two hours helping her scrub the old dresser and walk-in larder in the hope she'd let me go out later with Eva. Eva had called every day and I was beginning to know Beach Parade, the bus shelter and Beaumont's stock nearly as well as she did. She'd promised to ask me to tea at her house, but I knew I would not be allowed to go. Not yet. My mother would need to know a lot more about Eva and a considerable amount about Eva's mother before I would actually be permitted to visit her house. I already knew quite a bit about Eva's house, which was modern and detached with fitted carpets and two toilets and a big garden with a rabbit hutch and two baby rabbits. She'd drawn me a picture of her bedroom on the back of an old bus ticket we'd found in the shelter. Eva had a white dressing table with a gathered skirt made of floral material and a mirror on top and a fitted wardrobe with gold curly handles.

"Of course, there'll be some good second-hand sales in these parts, I shouldn't wonder," my mother went on, pouring creamed mushroom soup into three bowls. "And jumble sales! Just the kind of thing you need when you move house, Mary. Isn't that right, Jack?" My father agreed and the two of them started talking boringly about what they'd bought when I was a baby and they'd moved out of their two rooms in Kentish Town into Ash Gardens. The idea of buying brand new rarely occurred to my mother and she seemed never happier than when reinventing a use for something, cutting down, sewing up, making do. I'd even detected the way our meals tended to have a connection with the one before, a left-over in some sly disguise finding its way sneakily onto the plate. I dipped my slice of bread into my bowl.

"Now, Mary, I want you to show your father around a bit this afternoon," she said, "all these places this new friend of yours has been showing you, the local shops and that." I was about to protest that the coast road and the Front and Beach Parade hardly needed a guided tour from me. Eva was bound to call and I didn't want to let her down. But my father winked at me across the table and smiled.

"Give me a chance to put my paint brush down for a change, Mary, and get some sea air into these poor lungs of mine. Only a couple of days until I start work and I've hardly seen outside the front door." He peered out of the basement window, which showed little more than a sideways view of the stairwell. A filter of light was, however, trying to steal its way down. "And it looks like there's a bit of sun out there, too, for a change."

And there was. We walked down to the Front and saw that the sea was not entirely grey and murky, but had a sort of tinge of dark turquoise mixed with purple blue. The sky was bright and although clouds still scudded thickly across it, they looked unthreatening and almost friendly, cotton wool clouds rather than matted blankets. We sat down on a bench and my father produced his packet of strong peppermints that he always kept in his jacket. His pockets were like a lucky dip; stick my hand in and it was rare not to find a dusty square of milk chocolate, the last sweet at the end of a tube, a toffee in its cellophane wrapper. The tide was slowly pulling out, revealing more and more of the pebble beach and leaving behind strands of seaweed that looked like long dark tresses of wavy hair a bit like mine. Seagulls squawked and swooped across the sea's surface.

"Searching for a fish dinner," my father said, popping another peppermint into his mouth. I sneaked a glance at him, wondering what other people thought, what other people saw of my father when they looked. He was a thinnish kind of person with grooves down the side of his face as if he could perhaps do with a bit more padding. His brown hair was thin, too, and his eyes were small and dark, warm brown buttons that took a bit of finding. He worked in an office, the way people did. A tax office, and he'd got a transfer down to another one, he'd told me, a tax office at the seaside. He'd made it sound as if things would go on exactly as before once he started working there. At Ash Gardens he'd left the house each morning just before eight and had been home just after six. In summer, he'd go upstairs to change out of his suit then go outside into the back garden and see to the weeds or the rose blight or the climbing ivy for an hour. My mother handed him his cup of tea out of the kitchen window then later called him in for our meal at seven o'clock. In winter, it was the shed, where he mended things or emptied seeds into small pots or cleaned brushes and tools. I used to go out to the garden with him every now and again, help a bit with the beds or the seeds until I got bored and went back inside, upstairs to my bedroom, closing the door firmly so I could read my book in peace. Sometimes, I used to wonder whether it would have been better for my father if I'd been a boy. A son would have been more like a dog, really, someone to take on walks or play with a ball in the park. Someone to go fishing with or to share the cricket scores.

Suddenly, he yawned, sitting on the bench next to me, stretched out his arms.

"It's a tiring business getting this house together, you know," he said, "but well worth it in the end. And your mother's got… she's got such plans for us." I had a feeling he was building up to tell me something. He was the kind of person who seemed nervous about making surprise announcements and liked to give small clues, creeping up cautiously to any news.

"Plans?" I said. "Are we going to move again?" The packing cases were still littered around the rooms so the possibility that we had not reached a final destination still hung in the air. Since this move had been entirely unexpected, the prospect of a series of them had begun to feel quite likely.

"No, Mary, of course not," he said, with a laugh that seemed awkward. "We're going to take in lodgers. Just a couple of them, I expect. Possibly three at a pinch. We've so many rooms to spare that just you, me and your mother will be rattling around the place if we don't fill it a bit."

"Strangers, you mean? People we don't even know will come and stay with us?" I was unsure whether the idea was very exciting or absolutely dreadful. The thought of having permanent visitors, sudden strays like the bedraggled cat that had once arrived at Ash Gardens, sounded so peculiar.

"It's an ideal way of making some extra cash, Mary," he went on rapidly, not sounding like himself at all. It sounded more like my mother's way of putting things and I was suspicious that she'd had to do a bit of convincing to get him on her side. "Investing in property is always sensible. It's what people are doing these days and this way, with the lodgers and that, we can afford to run a bigger house."

I said nothing, just dug my hand into his jacket pocket and found two cellophane wrappers, a dusty Refresher sweet and a sixpence. I wondered if he'd let me spend it at Beaumont's all at once as a treat, a Mars bar, perhaps, or a quarter of pineapple chunks that we could share. A dog was barking loudly on the beach in front of us, chasing a bit of driftwood, backwards and forwards it went, snarling and whimpering in between each throw until it grew tired of the game and headed instead for the cold water. The owner ran, snatched it back just in time and tethered it to its lead. I squashed up close to my father on the bench, wound my arm around his and eventually said, "If we don't like having the lodgers, we'll get rid of them, won't we? We just won't have any. That would be the best plan."

My father said nothing, slowly moving his arm away from mine and searching for the shopping list in his trouser pocket. He seemed to spend a bit of time reading it before getting up, handing it to me as if for safe keeping.

"Now show me this Beach Parade of yours, Mary, and we'll get these bits and pieces of shopping for your mother. Kennarth's for groceries, you say? And then we'll be getting back. There's a lot I need to do this afternoon and clearing that front garden while the weather's still dry is at the top of my list."

★ ★ ★

It was months before anyone mentioned the lodgers again. It was as if the entire idea had been abandoned, simply a random thought that was swiftly forgotten. At least I quickly forgot about it. Instead, there was my new school and Eva Mason to occupy my time.

Eva was already at Court House School for Girls, a school year above me, whereas I was heading for the first year at the local secondary modern. After a couple of days of trying to persuade my parents to send me to Eva's private posh place where you got to wear grey flannel skirts and velour hats and regulation maroon woollen gloves and learn lacrosse, I resigned myself to Churchill County Mixed and a bottle green tunic. It was what I'd earned, after all, what I deserved for failing my 11 Plus exam and being utterly defeated by bewildering arithmetic sums, pointless money puzzles. There were days when I still painfully missed the neat cul de sac of Ash Gardens and red double-decker buses and the silver overground trains heading for the underground and the thought of Baker Street only a few stops away. I still missed the familiar shops in the High Street and the memorial park and the huddle of black taxi cabs around the station. There were some nights when, lying in bed, I had to hold my hands over my ears to shut out the violent rush of the waves and the force of the tide on the shore, and on mornings when thick sea mists swallowed everything so hopelessly, I felt afraid to go outside in case I disappeared into it too.

But otherwise, the dull routine of things was consolingly, reassuringly normal. My father went off to work at the tax office in his grey suit and white shirt, my mother cleaned the big house and shopped and cooked the same sort of meals we'd always eaten. And I went off each day to Churchill County Mixed Secondary School. At first, everything terrified me. The older boys with their impossibly long, lanky legs and huge lace-up shoes and untidy, heavy mops of hair that half hid their faces. The older girls with their green skirts hitched up showing their thighs and stocking tops, hanging around the school gates at the start and end of the day. I knew I would never be as old as them, as daring as them, and I tried to disappear into my beret and oversized blazer as I slunk past. I wasn't alone, of course. The other First Years mostly slipped their way timidly into school alongside me each morning and filed into form rooms to fill in names in new exercise books. We were still primary school children at heart, of course, but trying to grow up fast into sharp secondary school kids. By half-term, it had all became a little less foreign and frightening. I'd got used to shoving my way past the huge, sprawling boys and the girls who hung around the gates. And at the end of the day, there was always something to look forward to, the bell at fifteen minutes to four and a quick dash out of school to the corner of the road where Eva would be waiting for me, her velour school hat and regulation gloves already removed and shoved to the bottom of her satchel.

★ ★ ★

Just before our first Christmas at Sea View Parade, my grandmother died.

My mother seemed to treat the whole matter as wilfully selfish of her.

A telegram sat on the kitchen table next to the brown teapot and after swiftly scanning it, she picked up the bread knife and calmly continued to cut slices, smearing them with a bit of butter before removing most of it with the back of the knife.

"I'll have to go up there, of course," she said. "If I leave in half an hour or so I should get to the hospital for evening visiting. Unless it's already too late for that," she added in a more cheerful tone. "It's surprising she's lasted so long considering the way she's neglected herself. Living on gin and cigarettes for years and dreadfully overweight." She tightened the belt of her skirt as if to draw attention to her sensible waistline. "Such a foolish woman. No sense of responsibility at all." She sat down at the table, poured out the tea. I watched her face from over the rim of my cup. Surely she should be upset, a little tearful at the prospect of losing her mother. I had never, of course, heard her speak of her with any love or affection and my grandmother had certainly been a remote figure for the whole of my life. An obligation, it seemed, rather than a family asset. Even so. "We can take you to the station," my father offered. "If we drive you into Bampton you can pick up the main London line into Victoria."

"No need for any of that," my mother said briskly. "The bus from Beach Parade will drop me right outside the station and you've got enough to see to here. I really don't need anyone holding my hand over this, Jack, see sense. It's just one of those inevitable things, given her age and the state of her. But it couldn't be at a worse moment, what with Mary breaking up from school in a day or so and Christmas just around the corner."

My grandmother's choice over the timing of her final collapse was clearly thoughtless and inconsiderate. My mother swallowed her tea, ate half a slice of bread and jam and was on her feet again. She seemed to have forgotten the mince still sitting in the saucepan on the stove.

"I need to make a couple of calls before I go, arrangements and that, so I'll just pop down the road to the phone box." She grabbed her purse, took the change that my father was offering her for the call box in case buttons A and B swallowed up too much, and left us speedily.

"If only we'd got connected by now," I said to my father, pleased to find an excuse to complain. "Everyone has a phone in their house except for us."

"All in good time, Mary, we're on the waiting list, you know that." He poured us second cups. Number 8 still had no phone line and my mother had become well acquainted with the red telephone box down on the coast road near the

Black Boy pub. She seemed forever nipping down to make some calls and there was a pot of change kept in the hall for her purpose. Eva's house, of course, had two phones, one cream, the other a daring bright red, and I was beginning to feel embarrassed by our lack of any at all.

My mother was back within ten minutes. I followed her upstairs and sat cross-legged on the floor of the bedroom as she changed out of her everyday skirt into her olive green suit usually saved for smart occasions. I imagined that visiting her dying mother in hospital must somehow count. She took her black attaché case from the top of the wardrobe and filled it with bits and pieces while I rushed to the bathroom to collect her toothbrush and flannel.

"There's a bus in five minutes," she said, "and it connects with the London train at Bampton. Hairbrush, Mary? It's on the shelf next to the bathroom cabinet." Downstairs in the hall, my father was holding out her winter coat, but she brushed him aside, buttoned up her suit jacket and slipped on her gloves. I hung onto the bottom of the banister, threading my feet through the rails, as she rapidly gave us our instructions.

"Now, Jack, I'm bound to be away two or three days whatever happens. At least I can stay at her place, although I hate to think of the mess I'll find. And goodness only knows what state her affairs are in. I doubt if there's even any money left for a decent funeral. And how am I supposed to arrange that before Christmas?"

"Well, let's not get too ahead of ourselves, love. It might not even come to that and anyway, Mary and I could come up and give you a hand at the weekend, you know," my father said, but my mother appeared not to hear. I knew this mood of hers, her top gear of activity when she was too absorbed and focused to notice anything else. In fact, she seemed remarkably excited, considering the reason for her sudden departure to

London. Rather like a wild animal gearing up to pounce on its prey.

"Now once your school holidays start, Mary, I don't want you just hanging around the streets with Eva. I'll rely on you to keep things clean and tidy here, you know. Although perhaps Mrs. Mason would be kind enough to ask you over for lunch one day."

I assured her I would be fine, that Eva's mother said I was always welcome and that the two of us had Christmas shopping to do. But I knew she was only pretending to listen, her face a picture of distraction. She opened the lid of the hall chest and found her best black handbag, dusted it with the back of her hand.

"Now there's enough mince left from last night, of course. I was just about to warm it up. And if you're careful, you'll leave yourselves enough for tomorrow night too. Especially if you peel some potatoes to stretch it out a bit, Jack, even add a tin of tomatoes if you must, that will do the job." She opened the front door, stood for a moment on the bottom step as if checking whether anything had been forgotten. Then, almost as an afterthought, she stepped back inside to give me a hug, pulling me close so that I could smell her face powder, her pale pink lipstick that she wore on special occasions.

My father and I walked to the end of the path, waved and watched her disappear down the road into the darkness of the midwinter late afternoon. And suddenly I wanted my mother back. I hoped desperately that she'd change her mind and decide to leave her visit until the next day because I had never known her not to be here with us. It felt as if without her naggings and constant chorus of reminders and mild scoldings neither of us would know how to behave. As if the foundations of our lives would fracture, disintegrate without her support. The house seemed even bigger, colder without her, as if she'd left a gap by her going that neither of us knew how to fill. And when we tried to heat up the brown mince for our supper, the old gauge on the gas stove stuck and neither of us could remember her knack for urging it into action.

4

When I arrive today Ida is not in her usual place by the window. One of the carers, a plump woman whose patience is saintly, finds me looking lost and hesitant among the white-faced residents.

"Your mum's poorly," she says, "nothing to worry about, we don't think. Just caught a bit of a bug so we thought it best she stay in her room for a couple of days." I am ashamed, very ashamed, to see a window of release. Perhaps my visit will be unwise in the circumstance, risk of infection or germ contagion in her lowered state, and I can go back to my car, resume listening to the programme about women in Iran and drive away. "But it will cheer her up no end seeing you," the carer goes on and I smile broadly to compensate for my thoughts.

"Good, I'll go up then. As long as I'm not disturbing her."

She's dressed and sitting in a chair next to her bed, I'm relieved to find. It's shameful to admit, but the sight of her in bed distresses me more. Her decline seems so blatant when her hair is uncombed, her loose flesh undisguised by clothes. At such moments, my own mother seems completely absent and the old woman in her place a disturbing substitute. Miss Havisham without the mice and decaying wedding cake and Dickens' joyous prose. I go in and kiss her on the cheek. She smells faintly of urine. Her smile seems strained, as if she is unsure whether it is appropriate.

"It's... good... good..."

"How are you?" I ask foolishly. "Not been so well lately?"

"I... I'm not so... fuss – lot of fuss." She touches my hand and tries to say how good it is of me to come. I feel guilty and start gabbling about anything, everything, including the colour of the paintwork, the floral blouse she's wearing that I don't recognise as hers. My mother has never worn turquoise and it doesn't suit her. One of the staff comes in with a drink for Ida, weak coffee in a green cup, and offers me the same. I refuse, hope I don't sound rude. The room is hot and I wonder if I can open a window, wonder if it's allowed. I am cowed by this place and am anxious to comply.

With relief, I remember the photograph albums I collected from Jack, retrieve them from my bag and place the three volumes on a table in front of her. Mostly, they're rather random, disorganised collections that span several lives, not always in chronological order. We were never a family given to carefully compiled records and these are testimony to a certain carelessness in pinning down the past. But there's a small album, its cover stained and torn with age, that I've forgotten or not seen for years and this is far more orderly. It is Ida's work. Something that she apparently began at some point in earnest, although the final few pages are bare, as if enthusiasm waned, her interest shifted. A quick glance at the clothes shows that the album spans her mother's life over five decades or so and I settle down on a chair next to her with genuine interest. Ida turns the pages slowly, with something curiously akin to tenderness. At times she needs help to negotiate the procedure, as if even this page-turning action confounds her co-ordination.

My maternal grandmother, Ida's mother, Sylvia Louise Sullivan, a selfish, opinionated woman according to my parents, occupies the early pages: a 1918 wedding photograph of a pretty, petite, very young bride who stares straight out expectantly at the camera as if blithely certain of the good fortune that life is about to provide. Her soldier bridegroom is Harold, on leave from the French Front where he returns a few days later for the final weeks of the war. Turn the page and here is Sylvia again, her confident smile already checked, as she stands at the side of her husband who has returned to his bride, disabled by the loss of a leg and subject now to depression and chronic nightmares. If he was expectant of finding solace and comfort in his young wife, he was to be disappointed. According to Ida, she begrudged him his disability, his tentative grasp on the business of the greengrocer's shop he inherited from his father. Even the shop itself she saw as a burden, intended as it had been for the older son, killed two weeks before the armistice. Quite without irony, evidently, she always talked of herself as a casualty of that war. She had not imagined herself as a greengrocer's wife, her sights more set on Harold placed in insurance or accountancy and the two of them installed in a red brick villa in Hampstead or Chiswick. Instead, she found herself in the flat above the shop in Barnes, poring over the books that Harold could not balance, squabbling with the shop assistants she suspected of stealing, attempting to make meals out of the stock they could not sell. Ida, their only child, was born several years after their marriage and there's a christening photo then a studio pose of the little girl dressed in white, about four years of age. I draw Ida's attention to it and she smiles and tries to say something then loses the thought or cannot find the words and shakes her head, confused and suddenly anxious. I turn over the page. Poor Harold Sullivan, my maternal grandfather, died in 1941, caught in nighttime bombing over London. His widow, resentful of his failure to reach an air raid shelter in time, abandoned the greengrocer's shop in Barnes, sold it for next to nothing, and deposited herself and her daughter on Harold's only sister in south Devon. The two of them spent the rest of the war on the dairy farm where Sylvia began to get fat on clotted cream. Grudgingly, she sewed a bit, cooked a bit and tried to avoid the light cleaning work that was pushed her way. Returning to London after the war, she'd attached herself to various relations and remote friends until their spent patience forced her to take a couple of rooms at a fixed rent above a betting shop in Streatham. Ida, she had always told me with pride, took herself off at fifteen to learn to type and soon acquired a job and a bed in a girls' hostel in Camden Town. She'd had enough of dependence on others' goodwill, of her mother's indolence, and instead was determined upon self-reliance. Whereas Sylvia sat passively waiting for life to impress her, Ida saw the need to manipulate circumstance, to chivvy and connive for an existence shaped to her own liking. We used to visit Sylvia, my grandmother, when I was small. I remember crossing London on a series of Tube trains and climbing up steep steps to a stone hallway and her front door. I remember her as enormous, flesh seemingly seeping into an armchair where she appeared to sit all day, eating quantities of cheap cake and jellied sweets. She ignored me mostly as I sat tight at my mother's side, watching the clock on the mantelpiece tick away the minutes until we could leave. A discontented woman who lived a wasted life, Ida would say dismissively, dispatching Sylvia Sullivan as if she were someone she'd been misfortunate enough to stumble across. A brief encounter best forgotten.

The album has moved on. Now it is Ida's wedding, post-war frugality still entrenched as she stands in her borrowed dress, make-shift veil and my father, earnest, serious in his ration-squandering suit at her side. Their youth astounds as if it is something not quite real, acquired just for the occasion.

But she's tired. This Ida folded into her chair next to me here today is tired. Like a toddler, she rubs her eyes, loses interest, fiddles with the cuff of her cardigan.

And I cannot bear it.

For a moment or two I think I am going to start to cry and I know that if I start I will sob uncontrollably in a way that I have not done for years. And I am uncertain whether my sadness is caused by the reminder of such stunted lives, Harold and Sylvia, the two of them mismatched, unfulfilled, thwarted. Or whether I want to weep for something more inexorable. I look at Ida now, entirely oblivious of the tasteless turquoise floral blouse she wears, see her powerlessness, her slow sinking into a state where her individuality, her very self, is gradually being overwhelmed by her disease.

By the passage of time itself.

I shut the album firmly, put away the unfortunate Sylvia, unlucky Harold, my youthful, fledgling parents, return them to the lives they were anticipating rather than the ones they led. I wonder if Ida considers that, somehow, it has all added up to less than was intended. Perhaps it always does.

"I should go, you haven't been well and I don't want to tire you out," I say. Ida reaches for my hand. She holds it firmly. "It's... it's... just good... so good to have you... next to me," she says. "It's all... I..." She gives up, trusts I understand. I look around me at her small, neat room. The single bed with the institutional pink blanket, the narrow wardrobe with her handful of clothes, the hard-backed visitor's chair. A life reduced to essentials. I kiss her cheek, hug her even. We have never been a family for demonstrative gestures.

"I'll see you soon. Perhaps we'll look at more of the albums next time." I move over to the wardrobe, place them inside next to spare slippers. Ida stares at me then props her head on one hand as if trying to puzzle out what she needs to say.

"Yes, good, I'd – not that it… you never know, maybe… you know, not Jack, but who knows if… I'd like to. See him…" she tries. I cut her short. For sometimes, her meaning is clear regardless of the inadequacy of her words or the muddle of her mind. And she's wrong, of course, quite mistaken in thinking that any pictures of Fred Jarvis ever found their way into an album. Jack would have made sure of it. At least, I think he would.

"Yes, we'll look at some more next time," I interrupt, "pictures of you and Dad and me as a baby. Some of Felix too, I expect. Next time."

5

iss Mackie moved into the room next to the basement kitchen of Number 8 on New Year's Day. My mother told me that once, when our old house was first built, it would have belonged to a servant, the housekeeper or cook, no doubt. That confused me at first, thinking we were going up in the world and employing staff rather than gaining a lodger, but my mother told me not to be so foolish and didn't I know anything about social history and progress in the 20th century. The room had been solid with packing cases for months, full ones at first until gradually emptied, so I'd almost forgotten the room existed at all. My father had painted it one early December weekend and my mother had dyed some old white bed sheets to navy blue, whirred away at her heavy Singer sewing machine and turned them into curtains. The room, already dark, looked like the murky bottom of an inkwell. However, with a single bed found from an ad in the local paper along with a jumble sale wardrobe, it was, evidently, ready for its occupant.

Christmas, our first at Sea View Parade, was dull and dismal, sandwiched in between my grandmother's death and her funeral that took place two days after Boxing Day. At the last minute, just before the shops closed on Christmas Eve, my father brought home a reduced price tree, a wispy, drooping effort that we wedged into a bucket with damp soil and then wound some old tinsel around to disguise its skinny branches. My mother said it was not a year to go spending money wildly on presents after the expense of the move and that my grandmother's death was further reason for restraint out of respect. Consequently, on Christmas morning, I unwrapped a pair of navy blue tights and some woollen mittens in school uniform green. My father gave me a selection box that I was not allowed to open until after lunch. There had been stockings in the past, at Christmases in our last house, with a lucky dip of small gifts spilling out on my bed when I'd woken early. Nothing extravagant, but even so the sort of things that I loved to unwrap and line up on my window sill: pencil sharpeners, a small packet of crayons, a pack of cards to play Happy Families, perhaps a puzzle book and always a balloon and a tangerine. But my mother said that, even without the need to hold ourselves back this year, surely I was too old to want such childish things now I was as good as twelve. I pretended to agree with her. The three of us ate roast chicken and sausage meat and watched The Queen and a variety show. Then we played Monopoly and my mother swiftly bought up Old Kent Road and Whitechapel and The Angel, building several houses on them, whereas I spent too much money on Pall Mall and Piccadilly and Mayfair, bought hotels and became bankrupt. My father ended up in jail and had no money left to buy his way out.

We drove up to the funeral service on a morning when the ice was so thick on the car windscreen that my father had to chip away at it for ages before we could leave. I wore my pleated grey skirt and warm fawn jumper, my mother was in her worsted black wool that she'd had since her office days, she said, and my father wore a black tie against a very white shirt that made him look sinister and unlike himself. I was quite looking forward to the funeral, expecting a graveyard, ancient tombstones and a deep, muddy pit, an old church smelling of damp and women in black veils sniffing into cotton handkerchiefs. So it was a huge disappointment when we turned off a busy main road in south London, down a short drive to find ourselves outside a large, bleak building with an enormous car park. There were a few people huddled together, two or three old men smoking cigarettes, one a pipe, and half a dozen or so women, equally old, chatting and fiddling with gloves and scarves and heavy coats and hats. Sleet and icy gasps of wind tugged at our faces as we left the car and my mother led the way decisively towards the group, said something to them that I couldn't catch and then, as if on some sudden joint impulse, we all scuttled swiftly into the red-brick building, the crematorium, chased by the biting nips of air so it must have looked as if we were rushing with enthusiasm into the Oxford Street winter sales instead of to a funeral service.

My first funeral and it was a considerable let-down. A man stood up and read something out in a quiet voice. He seemed to be the person in charge yet he managed to get my grandmother's name wrong, calling her Sandra instead of Sylvia. No-one corrected him even though my mother sighed and tut-tutted loudly. Everyone sat staring straight ahead, ignoring the presence of the wooden coffin as if it was awkward and a little inconvenient to the proceedings. There was a reading of sorts, something sounding biblical, mumbled rapidly as if the person doing it was embarrassed, then some prayers and a very short hymn, since we were told in a stern tone only to sing the first and last verses. One more prayer and then, when we all looked up again, it had gone. The coffin had slid noiselessly into some netherworld with Sylvia, rechristened Sandra at the very end, tucked neatly inside. My grandmother, hardly known to me, had now been dispatched forever.

No-one had sent flowers. I'd expected at least wreaths of flowers.

Afterwards, we went back to someone's flat in Balham, a woman called Edith Dixon who claimed to be Sylvia's closest friend, although my mother said a little too loudly that Sylvia had never gone in for that sort of thing. "My mother," she said firmly, as too many of us were squashing into the Austin Cambridge, "was sufficient unto herself, the more's the pity," but I don't think anyone quite knew what she meant. We spent an hour or more in Edith Dixon's small front room, cramped alongside four elderly ladies who spoke in shrill, piercing tones. One of them stared at me for a long time and then said, "Of course, I always say a funeral's no place for a child," and went on staring. Fumes from the honeycombed gas fire overlaid with the odour of mothballs and too-sweet scent of lilies of the valley filled my head and stuck down my throat. My mother chatted brightly at first, helped pour cups of very strong tea into parchment-thin floral tea cups, but even she soon grew silent and darted looks of panic towards my father. The prospect of snow, a forecast he fished suddenly and threw as a convenient lifeline, eventually got us out of the place and on our way back home.

★ ★ ★

And then Miss Mackie. There had been no snow, but by the first day of January, the weather was still bitter with cold, bleak air and a sharp stinging wind off the sea. It even bit through the unfortunate brown balaclava my mother insisted on me wearing and my fingers were numb inside my bottle green Christmas present mittens. Even the prospect of five shillings to spend at Beaumont's, a sum I'd carefully saved up from meagre pocket money in my tin moneybox, was not enough encouragement to drag me out to Beach Parade. Anyway, Eva was still away in Scotland doing Scottish New Year things with Scottish relations and evidently learning how to ski. Beaumont's was not nearly so much fun without her. My mother found me slumped over a fifth reading of *Pony Jobs for Jill* in my attic room, curled up on my bed under the blanket, the last bit of chocolate from my Christmas selection box stashed under the pillow.

"Oh Mary, there you are," she said, as if she was surprised to find me there. I was worried she'd found me a useful job to do around the house. Sorting out the airing cupboard, tidying the threads and buttons in her wooden workbox. "We've a lady moving in today," she went on. "The first of the lodgers. She'll keep herself to herself, no doubt, but you might come across her in the kitchen from time to time." She started to pick up stray knickers and vests from the floor, tucked them into the top drawer of the chest. Lodgers, it appeared, were back on the horizon. Not only that, but the number of them had swelled.

"The first of them? You mean, there's more than one? More than one person coming to stay at a time?"

"Live, Mary, not stay. These people aren't visitors, they're lodgers. There's two of them at least, possibly a third, and this house is to become their home." She sounded so annoyed that I wondered for a moment if I'd got things wrong. Perhaps these were lonely orphans we were sheltering, abandoned children in need of our food and care. I'd read *The Silver Sword* and was quite prepared to welcome people like Ruth and Edek and Bronia into our house. But the picture was soon made clear. Miss Mackie, who was arriving after lunch, was certainly adult, and a secretary at the local hospital in Bampton. She'd been lodging a couple of roads away with people who had just decided to emigrate to Australia so was in a panic to find somewhere else close by. Evidently, she'd visited one day while I was at school and had arranged to move in after the Christmas holiday. Naturally, no-one had bothered to tell me this. Whilst my mother had the habit of explaining in unnecessary detail the most insignificant activities in life, like how to squeeze the last bit out of the bottle of Vosene shampoo, how to iron used wrapping paper on a low setting, the topic of another human being coming to live in our house apparently attracted no need for conversation at all. I felt suddenly cold. I shivered and pulled my blue blanket closer so that its roughness rubbed my chin.

"Anyway, Mary," my mother continued, sitting down on the end of my bed, "you knew about all this ages ago. Your father explained it to you. About why we got this big house in the first place. I really don't know why you're looking so surprised."

"I thought it was just one. One lodger at a time, I mean. Like… like a hotel. Like people who stay in a hotel and then go home after a few days."

My mother laughed. She laughed rather too wildly to be comforting since there seemed to be no particular cause for it and laughing was not a daily event for her. She straightened the skirt of her apron over her knees, fiddled with a bit of dirt that had become attached.

"Silly girl. Think of these people more as… well, almost part of our family. That's the way to see them. Miss Mackie and Mr. Jarvis. Mr. Jarvis will be here next week. On Monday, I think. And he'll need…" She stopped, looked around her at my bedroom, at my desk under the skylight with its neat rows of pencils and ruler and fountain pen. She looked at the orderly bookshelves with my Puffin paperbacks and *Girl* and *Bunty* annuals. She stared at the picture of the ice skater I'd cut out from my *Jackie* comic and stuck crookedly on the wall. My dolls, reluctantly now living on the top of the wardrobe, gazed down at her with their brittle blue eyes.

"He's an artist, you see," she went on eventually. "Mr. Jarvis is rather a talented artist. And he's a teacher as well. He's just got a new job teaching students at the college in Bampton which brings him down from London. But he needs to spend a lot of time on his own painting, of course. He needs – well, a lot of space. For his easel and canvases and that. A sort of studio, in fact. Somewhere with good light." I could not imagine why my mother was suddenly bothering me with any of this. I wanted her to go. I wanted to get back to Jill and the rosettes and rivalry at the Chatton show ground. "So there might have to be a bit of rearrangement, you see," my mother said, standing up and moving towards the door. "The rooms and that. To make the best use of the space in the house. I think I made that clear at the start, didn't I? That things might change. You'll be all right with that, Mary, won't you?"

I mumbled something agreeable sounding so that she'd leave me to my next chapter.

If Eva had been at home I'd have gone round and asked her what she thought about things. About things like lodgers. I needed her. I wanted to be able to will her instantly to leave her grandparents in Aberdeen and skit back swiftly to her house. The pale pink carpet on her bedroom floor was where we usually sat and talked, digging our fingers into its pile. With our backs against her divan bed, legs stretched out so that our feet were toasted under the radiator, we did our homework and swapped stories about school. Mrs. Mason, Eva's mother, always gave us biscuits, chocolate biscuits, sometimes even ones covered in foil, and tall glasses of coloured fizzy drinks. The sort that my mother would say were only good for causing teeth to rot. Mrs. Mason always came up the stairs and knocked at Eva's door, actually knocked, waited to be asked in, then put a tray down on the bedside table and disappeared. But then Eva's mother, Jean Mason, was nothing like my mother. She wore scarlet court shoes and straight black skirts that sat above her knee. She wore soft, low-cut sweaters that showed the edge of her lacy black bra and she painted her nails bright red. Her hair was a dark shade of blonde and had no streaks of grey in it like my mother's hair, although Eva told me that she paid a lot of money to her hairdresser to keep it that way. Mrs. Mason cooked meals that had French names and she sat reading foreign-sounding recipe books, pouring herself glasses of sherry from a decanter she kept near the fridge. The first time I'd gone round to their house, she had been sitting on the sofa in the lounge, smoking a cigarette and reading a thick, glossy magazine.

"What do you think of these evening dresses, girls?" she'd said, flicking her ash into a turquoise glass bowl. "Revealing just a little too much, don't you think? And hopeless if you don't have a good bosom." I'd waited for Eva to be shocked, to blush deep red and rush me out of the room. But she'd wandered over to her mother, glanced over her shoulder and made a face.

"Revolting," she said. "I wouldn't be seen dead in anything like that." And Mrs. Mason had laughed and said she'd change her mind in a few years and would we fancy spaghetti bolognese for tea. Then we'd gone up to Eva's bedroom and she'd shown me her collection of foreign dolls. A Spanish girl with miniature castanets in her hands, an Indian lady with dark plaits and a sari. An African woman with gold hoops in her ears.

"My dad goes abroad for his job, you see," Eva told me, "all over the place he goes. And we get presents when he comes home. My ma gets perfume and rings and stuff. And I get my dolls. It's really exciting when we go to meet him at the airport 'cos we know we're going to get presents." Eva had a brother called Hamish. An older brother, much too old to be of any interest to us, who was away at university studying something with a scientific name. We had crept into his room along the

50

landing from hers, behaving like robbers in danger of being caught.

"He never lets me in," Eva said in a whisper, as if her brother was suddenly going to appear from out of the wardrobe. It had been disappointing, though, giving away nothing about Hamish with its bare walls and table and stripped bookshelves. But there had been a different sort of smell, I'd noticed, a smell that was a mix of soap and toothpaste with a touch of damp clothes after a shower of rain. "He never comes back for long now, even in the holidays. So you see, I'm sort of an only child like you," Eva had said, spinning the globe that sat on her brother's empty desk and stopping it with her thumb on the Atlantic Ocean. "He's now more or less left home. More of a grown-up, really. And anyway, he was always pretty horrid to me. I really wouldn't recommend brothers at all."

Miss Mackie appeared in the kitchen that evening, cradling an egg in one hand. I'd caught sight of her when she'd arrived earlier, a small suitcase in one hand and a carrier bag in the other apparently being the extent of her luggage. Now she stood looking at us in some amazement as if she'd forgotten she was living in the same house as other people. She hesitated and seemed on the point of scuttling back to her room.

"I was just going to cook myself a bit of supper," she said in a nervous voice, "but if it's a nuisance I can easily go without."

She was quite the smallest person I had ever seen. For an adult. A bit like a bird with a long nose in place of a beak and sharp eyes that darted constantly around the room. I couldn't help wondering if my mother had selected her as a lodger because she'd be so hard to spot around the place.

"Nonsense, Miss Mackie," my mother said, gathering together a pile of ironing that was draping the chairs. "The kitchen is for your use too. You mustn't think you have to keep yourself to yourself in your room the whole time.

Although, of course," she added swiftly, possibly concerned at sounding too welcoming, "we've spent a lot of time making your room as comfortable and homely as possible. I really do think you'll find you have nearly everything you need in there."

Miss Mackie stared down at the egg in her hand then her eyes flitted across to the gas stove.

"Just a light boil, perhaps. Four minutes would do it. Three, at a pinch."

We produced a saucepan and then, since Miss Mackie appeared not to have considered one, an eggcup.

"So kind of you," she said, her gaze fixed on her wristwatch as if terrified one of her egg-boiling minutes would skip by unnoticed, "so kind. I don't want to be a burden. Never that, you know. And I get a proper midday meal at the hospital. Very nourishing and well balanced as you would expect from our wonderful NHS. So I want very little of an evening. Very little."

I slid off my chair, intending to disappear upstairs to the attic, but my mother's eye stopped me.

"You've not met my daughter, have you, Miss Mackie? Why don't you sit down and eat your meal with us for once? We do need to get to know each other a bit, after all."

The bird woman looked uncertain, as if suspicious that this was some kind of test set for her. She looked towards the door of her room and then at my mother who had started ironing again.

"Of course," she said, perching awkwardly on a chair and placing the eggcup on the edge of the table so it looked in danger of falling, Humpty-Dumpty like. "There are mice to consider." My mother lifted the hot iron from the pillowcase, looked at me, looked back at Miss Mackie. "Eating in my room, I mean, it might encourage mice. Or rats even. You wouldn't want that in this lovely house of yours, would you, Mrs. Foster?"

"We could get a cat," I said instantly, pleased with my own inspiration. I'd wanted a pet for years. "Cats are brilliant for keeping mice away, you know."

"But the fur," Miss Mackie said, her face a picture of disgust. "All that fur. Not all of us can cope with it."

She tapped the top of her boiled egg several times. My mother went back to her pillowcase. I grudgingly accepted defeat on the cat.

"Mary's just settling into secondary school, you know, and doing very well indeed," she said after a few moments of silence. "Aren't you, Mary?"

I was unused to handling compliments and particularly wary of them if they came from my mother. Nor was I aware of doing anything spectacular at Churchill County Secondary Modern except for keeping quiet and out of trouble. Miss Mackie, however, beamed across the table at me, as if I'd just completed three somersaults in midair and landed on tiptoe.

"Splendid!" she said. "A clever girl! Just what I like to see! So many opportunities for young people these days. Don't let the men get away with all the jobs, that's what I say. What a man can do, a woman can do. Isn't that right?"

"Quite," said my mother, sifting through the linen basket to find a pile of my father's white handkerchiefs. I liked to watch the way she ironed them swiftly, one side, the other, in half, in quarter, then folded over diagonally so they looked like a ship's sail.

"Just look at the war!" Miss Mackie went on. "We women played our part there all right. WAAFS and WRENS and so forth. Where would the men have been without women in support? Of course, that's all a long time ago now, but it does no harm remembering once in a while." She punctuated her words with her teaspoon so that a slither of egg yolk headed in my direction. My mother went on while her mound of neatly ironed and folded handkerchiefs grew.

"We expect Mary to do well on the words side of things. Her father and I think her talents lie in that direction. Arithmetic is not her strength, but we don't all need to work in tax offices, do we? And someone who is able to put one sentence sensibly and clearly in front of another is always going to be of value."

I thought about this and suddenly felt hugely grateful to my mother. I had rather assumed that, since I had failed my 11 Plus, there was little to be hoped for in my school career. People who passed and went to grammar school were clever. People who failed and didn't, weren't. It was that simple. So the idea that I was not an entirely lost cause was very reassuring. My mother collapsed the ironing board noisily, set the iron to cool on the stone floor that had cracks and burns caused by coals occasionally falling from the solid fuel boiler.

"Goodness, I'm overstaying my welcome," the bird said, leaping up and heading in the direction of her room. She darted back for a moment, collected her empty eggshell as if she had some serious purpose for it before making for her room again. "You see, I never want to be a burden on anyone, never that. Never a burden. No need for that at all."

And then Mr. Jarvis.

He arrived the following Monday afternoon. A stranger's car, heavily stacked with bags and boxes, sat outside Number 8 in the place usually occupied by our Austin Cambridge. I'd half forgotten about the expected arrival of our second lodger in the bustle of going back to school after the Christmas holidays. If I'd thought about him at all, it was with the idea of ignoring him. After her first evening, Miss Mackie had disappeared back into her room, hardly to be spotted again and I assumed Mr. Jarvis was going to be just as invisible. It suited me, ignoring these other occupants of the house as if they were wildlife behind the wainscoting. Eva slung her satchel down on the pavement, peered through the windows of the small black car.

"Easels and stuff. Do you think he's famous?"

"Course not. Why would he have to live with us if he was? Famous artists don't live in one room. That's just starving ones. Anyway, he teaches at the college or something."

"Perhaps he'll become famous. Then you'll be famous too. Famous for giving a poor artist a home and a place to paint his masterpieces. People will come and look at your house, you'll have to have a notice on it, a plaque thing to say he used to live here."

I ignored Eva and picked up her satchel to hurry her inside. The January wind off the sea whipped straight through my gabardine coat and the radiators at school had been only tepid all day.

"Won't your mum mind? Me coming to tea today when you've got this new lodger man here?" Eva said, trailing behind me up the path. She'd speedily switched on to the fact that whereas her mother was always welcoming to any unplanned arrival, mine liked to have an arrangement in place at least a week in advance. Eva's mother was modern whereas mine still occupied the 1950s and refused to move on a decade.

"Let's sneak you upstairs to the attic," I said, finding the key we kept under a brick near the front door. "She'll probably be too busy with this Mr. Lodger man to notice us."

We slid quietly in through the door, tiptoed across the hall, ignoring voices coming from the basement kitchen, and giggled in whispers up the two flights of stairs to my bedroom.

Except that it wasn't there.

The attic was there, of course, the narrow strip of six stairs to the top floor, the slice of landing at the top. But the room we arrived at was no longer my bedroom. My chest of drawers was gone, my bookcase, my neatly arranged desk had been removed. My candlewick bedspread had been replaced with a grey quilt. No ice skater picture and no cat calendar hung on the wall. My clothes, left on the back of the chair the night before, had been taken. Instead, someone else's coat hung on the hook on the door. Someone else's shoes, a man's suede lace-up shoes and an enormous pair of black wellingtons, were lined up against the wall. The room seemed empty, absent of me yet somehow full of someone else. A stranger who'd stealthily stolen his way in while I was at school, inhabited the place so that I was removed from it. I shivered, noticed the two skylights were wide open. Some papers, lying on the floor, flapped in the draught. Behind us, suddenly, we heard footsteps, and I turned to see my mother rapidly climbing the stairs, a bit out of breath, followed by a dark-haired man, with a beard that had a touch of ginger in it, wearing a maroon jacket. His feet, I noticed, seemed extraordinarily large, encased in black a bit like the giant in Jack and the Beanstalk.

"Mary," my mother said, her face flushed and smiling in a way unlike her usual self. "I didn't realise you were home. And Eva, how nice to see you, Eva." She fiddled with the buttons on her brown cardigan and I noticed that one was missing, a strand of spare thread hanging loose. The dark-haired man leaned against the wall, crossed his arms and looked first at Eva then at me. I'd grown so used to the attic that I'd forgotten the noise of the gulls as they swooped low over the rooftops. Now I heard them, as their screech and shrieks filled the silence in the room. Eva coughed twice. Eventually, the dark-haired man went across to the flapping papers on the floor, picked them up, placed them on the bed then reached up to close one of the skylights. He took off his maroon jacket, hung it round the back of the wooden chair, my chair that we'd brought from Ash Gardens and where I always put my school tunic and vest and tie each night before I went to bed. Then he turned to me and held out his hand. I fiddled with the fraying cuff of my bottle green cardigan and didn't move.

"You must be Mary," he said. "You look a little like your mother, you know. Definitely a resemblance there. I'm Fred Jarvis. So good of you to give up your room for me. It's for the light, you see. An artist must have good light."

Eva stepped forward, speaking very loudly so that the man looked surprised.

"Girls too, you know," she said, "girls like Mary who read loads of books need lots of light as well. Otherwise their eyesight goes bad. They might even go blind."

My mother gathered both me and Eva up with her eyes as if a trawler was attached to her pupils.

"We'll leave Mr. Jarvis in peace to settle in now, I think. Downstairs the two of you," she said.

Eva and I fled speedily down the staircase ahead of her.

★ ★ ★

It was my twelfth birthday four days later. My father gave me a watch. A narrow, rectangular box sat next to my breakfast plate on Saturday morning and I left it to open until last, hopeful. My mother had given me a new propelling pencil and an atlas she said would be useful for school. Even Miss Mackie had wrapped a small parcel, using so much tape to fasten it that it took ages to find the pencil sharpener inside. There was a card from her, too, a picture of lambs in a vivid green field, and inside she'd crossed out the word 'Easter' after 'Greetings' and shoved 'Birthday' in instead. I had not really spoken to either my mother or my father all week since Monday afternoon. I'd managed to get through most meals in near silence and had spent as much time as possible after school at Eva's house. My father had come into my new bedroom on Monday evening, trying to be jolly. My bookcase and desk and a chair were cluttered into the smaller, narrow space. My ice skater picture had been stuck up crookedly above my bed. The corner of it had torn.

"You look very cosy in here, Mary, very snug, I must say," he said. When I said nothing, had simply stared out of the window, he'd said something about how much nicer it was to have me next to their bedroom instead of on another floor above. Then he said something about needing to watch a television programme on British birds and retreated fast. At least Mr. Jarvis had not pretended that nothing had changed.

"You must tell me how to encourage that electric fire, Mary, which switches to press, you being an expert on the attic," he'd said at supper that first evening, when Eva had gone home and I had reluctantly slumped down to the kitchen and crawled into a seat.

"It doesn't work properly," I said in a voice louder than my normal one so that I hardly recognised it. I kept my eyes steadily on the table. "One bar flickers a bit, that's all. It's quite cold up there, you know." My mother had insisted that he eat with us, saying there was far too much cold meat and potato for the three of us. I hated cold lamb left over from Sunday's roast. Grey-coloured meat with a border of white fat glared up at me. I pushed my slices under a mound of potato and smeared it all with too much pickle.

"I must say the natural light up there is marvellous," Mr. Jarvis went on in his deep gravelly sort of voice, as if he thought everything he said was of huge importance. "I noticed it straight away. Even in midwinter you get that special quality that comes from being so near the sea. You were right, about that, Mrs. Foster, you said it was the kind of room an artist would appreciate."

My father passed round a bowl of limp lettuce and cucumber.

"What kind of painting do you do, Mr. Jarvis? I think my wife said something about landscapes."

"That's right," he said, picking up a fork in his right hand and seeming to manage without a knife, "landscapes by choice. I like to work with oils, you see. A bit like Turner. You know Turner? But of course if someone wants to commission me, I can turn my hand to portraits. I've done quite a few in my time. Life drawing, in fact, is also quite a strength of mine."

He looked around the table, grinning expectantly as if one of us was suddenly going to offer a hundred pounds for our likeness.

"You can see why we're so ideally situated for Mr. Jarvis," my mother said, cutting up a small piece of cold lamb on her plate into four smaller bits and then failing to eat any of them. "All these wonderful views and the sea storms and mists that we get. And of course so close to his college for his teaching."

"Yes, the paintings aren't bringing in enough on their own just yet." He helped himself to more potato without being asked. I noticed my mother had got out one of her best willow pattern dishes instead of just serving us dollops from the saucepan as usual. "But I'm hoping to get an exhibition together in a few months and that should be good publicity. It's a case of getting known, you see, letting people know about my work."

"And you're just with us during the week, I understand," my father said. "Back to London on Fridays?"

"Yes, sadly, back to Greenwich in the Friday evening rush hour traffic. I'm going to be something of a commuter. My mother's on her own now so I like to spend as much time as I can with her. Being her only son and all that business. I have to be a bit of a mummy's boy to her, you know how it is." He looked around the table at us, smiling for approval. "Weekends and holidays and so on, I have to give up to her. She gets very low, being on her own too much. In fact, I have to say she wasn't too keen on me taking this new job, being quite so far away from her during the week."

"I've heard good things about the college," my father said, "very good facilities, they say. A chap in my office says his daughter's doing very well there."

"It's a great opportunity for me," Mr. Jarvis said, leaning back in his chair so that it balanced on its back legs, folding his arms even though his plate was still half-full of food. I almost expected my mother to tell him off the way she would have done if it had been my father or me. "That's why I jumped at the chance. It'll be so good teaching students instead of dead end kids without an atom of talent. Not that I mean any offence to you, Mary, of course, I'm sure you're quite a prodigy in the art class!" He darted his grinning smile in my direction.

"Mary has her own talents," said my mother firmly, looking across the table at me for a moment before looking back to Mr. Jarvis. "We're waiting to see in quite what direction they'll lead her." And in spite of my fury with her over the attic, I was grateful for that. At least it meant I didn't have to answer Mr. Jarvis and he was silenced for half a minute.

He'd left me a birthday card before he'd driven off to Greenwich and his elderly mother on Friday afternoon. Intentionally, it was the last card I opened on Saturday morning, a large square shape wrapped in tissue paper instead of an envelope.

"One of his own works, Mary, that's special," said my father as I looked at the picture of a very red sunset with streaks of black and yellow running into it. It looked quite an easy sort of picture to do, I thought, with no firm features or lines required. A bit, in fact, like the sort of thing I used to do at infant school. On the back he'd written, *To Mary, with very best wishes for your twelfth birthday, I hope you have a miraculous year ahead of you, from Fred Jarvis.* Except that you couldn't really read his name as it had been scrawled in long, thin letters as if a centipede had landed in the ink and done a dance.

"You want to keep that, Mary," said my mother, placing a birthday breakfast poached egg in front of me. "It could be worth something in a few years or so. You never know."

"Impressionist, is it?" my father said, picking it up from the table and peering at it closely. "I think that's what you'd call it, the style and that."

I turned to my rectangular-shaped present at last, slid off the wrapping paper, opened the black box and found my watch. I had never had a watch. I lifted it carefully off its red satin throne and fastened it around my wrist. I stared at its clean white face and clear black numbers.

"Thank you," I said, "it's just right. It's perfect."

My father patted my head.

"That's all right, then, tuppence. I wanted you to have something a bit special this year. You've been a good girl, you know, such a good girl with all these changes and such like."

Suddenly, there was a noise, a clatter like a loud bell ringing over and over, startling us all and coming from upstairs in the hall. My mother headed in the direction of the stairs, climbing them two at a time.

"Did we forget to tell you, Mary?" my father said. "Those telephone engineers finally got round to us yesterday. We're on the phone now. Quite like other people at last, you know."

6

Eva's there first. I see her from the street before she sees me, punctual, early, in fact, as it's still a minute or two before one. For a moment, I'm surprised; for a split second of time I'm taken aback by the person I'm meeting in the restaurant. A middle-aged woman sits at the table by the window, the sunlight catching the slack softness of her face, the faint lines around her eyes. It's always the same. Eva and I do not meet often enough for me to be able to keep in the forefront of my mind the woman she is now. The woman I am now. As if such occasions should permit us to time travel back to become again our earlier selves: seventeen years of age, skin taut and flawless, indifferent to ravages of time. I cross the street, open the door and go in. She looks up, searches, then sees me, waves and smiles. And I am rescued by the shape of her mouth, by the way she calls my name so that a span of several decades dissolves in no more than the blink of an eye and we are as we were. Or we can pretend, anyway. I settle myself at the table opposite her and we order mineral water.

"So sensible! Why are we all so sensible these days?" she says. Her voice is still capable of scaling an entire octave in one phrase. "It's not as if we're even driving." So we think about ordering wine, look at the wine list, look at the choice and then forget to recall the waiter and settle for the water. After a moment or two of hesitation, a certain shyness, we start to talk effortlessly. We begin to trip over each other with so much to say. The waiter hovers, gives up.

It's three years since I've seen Eva. She comes to England every couple of years, but it's not always possible to meet. Her schedule is busy, obligatory relations, her brother, Hamish and his family to visit; her mother, a widow for many years. But we do try, both of us a little afraid, I think, that if we let too many years elapse we will drift apart, simply forget to bother. And too much connects us for either to be complacent about that. We share, tacitly, so much.

"You're looking so well, Mary, really you are. And you haven't changed a bit since last time. When was it now? Longer than it seems. Do you notice that? How it seems impossible to judge time passing accurately anymore? Do you think it's an age thing, our age, I mean? Not that I want to sound ageist at all, heaven forbid."

I smile, easily able to return the compliment.

"Thanks. You look… well, how is it possible you've three grown-up daughters, Eva? No-one could ever guess it, you know. You're exactly the same as your last visit and the one before. That time you came over with Don and we went to Stonehenge. Or was it Bath? Or maybe both."

Probably we're just pleasing one another. We've both reached a decade where it seems essential to defy time for fear of falling hopelessly into a downward spiral. The years now seem not so much to glide seamlessly away as to gallop ungainly towards some undesirable finishing post. Rows of unmarked years appear to be stacked up behind us like remaindered books, unlived, as if we forgot to get up and greet a few of them. Yet my flattery of Eva is genuine. There is a serenity about her now, a calm assurance that is in itself a kind of beauty.

Eva has lived in America for over thirty years. Her husband is American and, consequently, her three tall daughters, yet Eva has retained her English accent, polishes, I suspect, her long vowels. Only occasionally does a word slip negligently out of her grasp, her tongue slide too smoothly over a consonant. She married Don, a law student she met while waitressing in Spain, following him back at the end of his vacation on a fiancée's visa. I sent her a Wedgwood bone china teapot as a wedding present. It was late February and I was too poor and too exhausted from my first teaching job to attend. She sent me endless photographs. We used to write to each other for the first ten years or so, a normal habit then that now sounds woefully bygone. How did we have the time? Anyway, we found it and I would receive letters describing a life that sounded settled, assured, Don's career evidently a steady escalation to success and affluence. Three children, a large house, and a swimming pool in what Eva called the back yard and I insisted on calling a large garden. The photographs winged their way to my various doormats in rented flats in Croydon and Ealing and Earlsfield. My letters, I felt, were banal in comparison. I tried not to fill them with tedious detail about the infant classes I was teaching and resorted instead to faintly graphic, exaggerated descriptions of my inadequate personal life. But then we were both, possibly, creating a certain fiction about ourselves, writing vivid prose about our lives when the truth no doubt lay between the lines. Eva had embraced this other life so swiftly and wholly, her happiness too unconditional to entirely convince. As for me, my attempt to suggest something careless, delightfully louche and independent in my accounts of fraught and short-lived relationships, solitary Sundays in the city's parks and galleries, was a thin veneer for loneliness and confusion. Those neat pages of blue Basildon Bond that I sent off to Eva at an address north-west of Boston were more a reflection of a chosen alter ego than an honest communication to a close friend. I had no idea whether Eva was also indulging in a little subterfuge. Certainly, she had decided not to look back, to parcel up recent history and grab swiftly onto the chance that had nudged itself her way. I, on the other hand, still felt too timid and unprepared even to know what it was I really wanted. I remember privately envying her for the orderliness of her life at the time, her ability to blithely acquiesce to a future that contained nothing of her past whilst I was rudderless, hopelessly bewildered.

Our waiter returns to badger us and we look rapidly at the menu and order.

"How's the family?" I ask. "How's everyone? Don? Still running his marathons?"

"Only half ones these days," she says. "The girls tell him he's got to get a new sport more suitable to his age. Golf, perhaps, but I don't think he's got the patience."

"Emily must be… I've lost count."

"She's thirty next birthday. Can you believe it? How is it possible to have a daughter of that age?"

"You started young."

"People did. Or at least I did. It was what I wanted. And Don too, of course."

"Of course. I didn't mean…"

"No, I know. With you, it was…"

"Different. Late. Not really by choice, but just the way these things…"

"How is Felix? Do you have any photos?"

Our salads arrive, large white bowls of greenery with various worthy ingredients decoratively, sparsely arranged. I prise an anchovy from amongst a scattering of seeds. By the time we've plunged through the depths of watercress and curiously-coloured lettuce, we've each produced photographs, admired and smugly received the compliments. And we find it hard to tear ourselves away from this subject that obsesses us, steals our hearts above all other. Our children. Our inordinately, overwhelmingly precious children. Everything else seems comparatively insignificant and we give only scant regard to economic depression, political turmoil, environmental disasters. Shame on us. Eva wears her hair short these days. In fact, she cut her hair so long ago that it's hard to remember those long, straight blonde curtains of silk that I so envied. I have never been quite so bold, clinging still to some length, irrepressible waves that turn to tight tangles at the first touch of humidity. Eva always was the braver of the two of us.

We sit on amidst an emptying restaurant although we've barely been aware of anyone else, mutually absorbed, our focus narrowed by our concerns. We decide on coffee to delay us further and at last there's a pause in our conversation as we unwrap miniature biscotti nestling in small saucers. The sound of a street musician singing something faintly familiar reaches us.

"My mother died last year," Eva says suddenly, as if it is a confession and she has been waiting for the appropriate moment. "It was very sudden. A heart attack. My brother was visiting her and – well, you don't want to know the details."

"I'm sorry," I say automatically, the way one does. "You should have told me. Sent an email or rung me or something." And then I worry that I sound ingenuous, insincere. I try harder. "I am so sorry, Eva, it must have been a dreadful shock."

She shrugs, looks out of the window.

"Well, it happens, doesn't it? We're that age. We shouldn't be surprised to find ourselves orphans at last. Everyone has to die of something. And at least she didn't suffer. I don't think Ma would have been very good at a slow decline. All that indignity. I came over for the funeral, of course, but I was so busy with everything and I just didn't manage to let you know. There wouldn't have been time for us to meet, anyway." She sips her coffee, plays with the bowl of brown sugar, heaping it into small hills with her teaspoon like miniscule sandcastles.

"I'm sorry," I repeat, unsure quite what my sympathy is addressing although Eva seems to know.

"You didn't like her, Mary, I'm aware of that," Eva says, "but I know that she was doing everything for the best all those years ago. As she saw it, anyway. It was such a different time, like another world, when you think about it – and people were not so easy with... with things like that. People's attitudes were so fixed and judgmental. You have to see it from my mother's point of view."

I have not seen Jean Mason for years. For well over thirty years, in fact, so she has not grown old for me, but has petrified into the face and figure of a woman of forty, forty-five or so. Or rather the way some women of forty or forty-five looked decades ago. Women like Jean Mason with her weekly shampoo and set and lacquered hair style, already heading to become something of an anachronism, her powder compact and black patent handbag and leather court shoes. It is hard for me to think of her any other way. The few glimpses I have had of her over the years have been photographic, Eva's wedding party, a silver anniversary, babies' christenings and have shown a woman considerably changed. Thickened, fleshy even, hair the colour of steel wool. It is not the memory I hold of Eva's mother and I have found it impossible to make the substitution. And now, hearing of her death, sitting in the restaurant, coffee cooling in my cup, I find I am trawled back to a specific moment. Jean Mason comes into the kitchen, in their detached, modern house so unlike ours, so different from 8, Sea View Parade. She looks across sharply at Eva and me as if coming across a scene that she is unwilling to tolerate. Eva is crying, I am crying, bewildered, even a little frightened by what I have just heard and Jean Mason stares at the two of us with something close to contempt.

"No," she says loudly, aggressively, in a tone I have never heard her use before. "I know what this is about. And no, this is not how it is going to be. Do you understand? Have I made myself clear? There is going to be none of this. There is simply no need for it." And she stands up, opens the back door and tells me to leave. Commands me, in fact, as if I am an intruder, blatantly unwanted, and I go, frightened by her manner, that tone, confused by Eva's news, deeply hurt by her secrecy. And I run down their driveway, past Mrs. Mason's white Triumph, out to the road, running rapidly all the way until I reach Beach Parade and finally stop, breathless, nauseous.

If Eva had not gone to live abroad, I suppose it would have been inevitable that we would have met again, Jean Mason and I. There would have been those occasions the photos capture for a start. Occasions sufficient, perhaps, to thaw my attitude to her, to attempt a kind of rapprochement and some understanding. But as it happened our falling out became permanent, my judgment of her that day, absolute. Within months, Eva, unable to settle, had taken herself off to London then to France and Spain (and the fortuitous meeting with Don) before America, her parents eventually retiring to a cottage in Cornwall. I never met Jean Mason again.

"It wasn't so much that I didn't like her," I say to Eva, after a silence in which the waiter has hovered with the bill, retreated. "I just didn't understand her. I didn't understand how she could act the way she did. And, even worse, the way she refused to talk about—"

But Eva immediately turns away, fumbles with her mobile phone, her cell phone, as she calls it, says randomly that she is expecting a message from Don. Her brother, Hamish, might be in touch.

And I know that absolutely nothing has changed.

I want to say to Eva that this is all absurd. You are being absurd. It's the 21st century, Eva, and people don't think like that anymore. Those attitudes are now bygone, remote, clinging on only in extraordinarily unenlightened minds. Surely this is something we can now talk about. But apparently not. I watch Eva texting a message to Don then deciding to ring him instead, slipping outside the restaurant for a moment to get a clearer signal. She stands there in her smart tailored navy trousers, her silk scarf wound elegantly around her neck so that it nestles neatly just below her string of real pearls. And wonder why she chooses still to be coerced and controlled by the outmoded prejudice of her late mother. By Jean Mason's repressive, heartless resolution.

And I realise that I feel let down. Just as I am embarking on this obsession of mine to methodically, incisively, unpick the past, the events that have been carefully censored and removed from family view, Eva is as intent on concealment as ever. Who would have thought it? So clearly I am on my own here and as she comes back inside, slipping her phone into her bag, I launch into a trivial conversation about her shoes, shoes in general, heels in particular, to prove I am still playing by her mother's rules.

We tussle over the bill and once outside stand in the spring sunshine for five minutes or so, check watches, wonder how to spend the two hours left of our afternoon. I leave the choice to Eva, the visitor, the tourist, indulged only with her one day in London slotted into her busy ten-day schedule. We walk slowly along the narrow pavement, loitering in front of windows, stopping to stare. A young man sits on a thread-worn blanket, a skinny dog at his side, and he almost blocks our path as he gestures a hand rather helplessly towards us. We walk on quickly, shamefully, as if his presence is an embarrassment.

"Don't you feel as if you always want to give them something?" I say to Eva. "I mean, you find yourself thinking that it could be one of ours. One of our children, I mean."

"But it wouldn't be," says Eva reasonably, "we wouldn't let it come to that."

"No, of course we wouldn't, not out of choice. We bend over backwards to do everything for them. To protect them. But what if?"

Eva interrupts me sharply.

"Oh, what if nothing! You can't base your life on what ifs. It's the immediate that matters, what's straight in front of you." And I pretend to agree and we start to walk down to Trafalgar Square, along the Strand, crossing Waterloo Bridge until Eva remembers she wants to find a bookshop. We buy pots of tea at the Festival Hall and sit watching river barges and pleasure cruises and talk about the idea of me visiting Eva in Massachusetts one day, the visit that has been mooted for years, but has never quite managed to take place.

"Promise me, Mary," she says, "promise you'll visit."

"Of course," I say glibly, "one day. Of course."

Then Eva has to go and I watch her walk away, soon disappearing into the late afternoon crowds, the first surge of the rush hour battling its way to stations, crowded trains, homes and families.

I sit on a little longer. And wonder if it's sensible to be like Eva. To push away the past and refuse to examine it, to see it as an irrelevance that is best regarded as a tedious, unfortunate interval belonging in another life. A life tethered to habits and rules that now feel entirely alien.

But I'm not as sensible or pragmatic as Eva.

I never have been, finding it hard to push away entirely that litany of what ifs that hangs perpetually at the margins of the mind. The other lives that could have been mine to live.

I think it's what my mother does a lot of these days, elderly, frail Ida Foster, sitting in her chair, filling the vacuum of her days with her thoughts in free fall. Alighting, perhaps, with some relief on what has been suppressed and buried for so long out of expediency. No wonder Fred Jarvis seems to be preoccupying her. No wonder she appears anxious to want to talk about him at last.

7

Mrs. Mason poured out two glasses of limeade and pushed a plate of small chocolate cakes across the kitchen table.

"You two girls will be all right on your own, won't you? I've got a meeting to go to this afternoon, but I'll be back by five. You can easily amuse yourselves, I'm sure. Just don't get up to anything naughty while I'm away, will you?"

She snapped open her squashy handbag, found her powder compact and studied her reflection in its oval mirror, fiddled with an eyebrow. Then she rummaged at the bottom for a can of hair spray and quickly zapped her head with lacquer. Eva coughed extravagantly.

"It's not fashionable any more, you know," she said, as Mrs. Mason slipped her red blazer over her fluffy twin set and tied a scarf at her neck. "All that bouffant stuff."

"Hardly bouffant," she said, "just a bit of back-combing to keep the set in place. And you can't expect me to wear my hair in straight curtains like a shapeless teenager. Mary, now, you've got lovely hair. All that natural wave, you lucky girl."

I turned up my nose.

"Wish it was straight like Eva's. I'd give anything to have straight hair."

"You'll change your mind when you're older, you know. Save you a fortune in semi-permanents and fiddling around with rollers, although my heated Carmens are cutting down time spent on all that marvellously." She kissed Eva on the cheek, hooked her car keys over one finger and disappeared out of the back door. We heard her rev her little white Triumph in the drive and shoot off down the road. My mother didn't drive. She always said one driver in the family was sufficient.

"Where's she going?" I asked Eva, removing the cellophane cover from my cake. Eva stretched along the pine kitchen bench opposite me and shrugged.

"Who knows? Her meeting, she calls it. But I bet it's not just any meeting. Bet it's a man."

"A man?" I said, slowly licking the chocolate from the sponge to make it last longer. Eva Mason's kitchen cupboards were full of shop-bought cakes in smart boxes. My mother baked a dozen rock buns and a plain almond Madeira once a week. "What man?"

Eva sat up, rolled her eyes at me, the way she did when she wanted to display how much more she knew than me. And she did, of course. For a start she was eight months older and a whole school year ahead. And she had parents who told her more things and talked to her in a grown up kind of way.

"The man she's maybe gone off to meet. Her lover, you know. Perhaps my ma's got a lover." Eva sat up and drained her glass of limeade in one gulping swallow. I stared at her.

"You mean your mother's got... you mean... but what about your dad?"

She lay down again on the bench, shot her legs up in the air and pointed her toes at the ceiling. She'd sneaked the varnish from her mother's dressing table and painted two toenails a brilliant red.

"My dad's away a lot, you know. For his job. Perhaps she gets bored, my ma. There's certainly an awful lot of this going off to 'meetings'. Perhaps she goes off and meets someone and does things with him. This other man."

"Things?" I said, wishing this whole conversation had not started. My knowledge of such matters was too scanty and inadequate, random facts and information that I had not quite managed to sort into a sensible pattern. My mother had given me a very brief talk in a low, subdued voice in the bathroom one evening just before we'd moved house. She'd said that things started happening to girls' bodies so they could get ready for having babies later and that I was to tell her if I noticed anything strange happening to me. If I found anything odd in my knickers one day. *Tell me on the quiet though,* she'd said, *certainly not when anyone else is about. Certainly not your father.* As if it was all a bit shameful and unfortunate and best hidden, a kind of punishment meted out to girls for simply being girls. I'd been utterly bewildered and kept taking sneaky glances inside my knickers in case anything unusual had found its way in there. Then I'd read the problem page in her weekly women's magazine, just the back page with anonymous letters from people and I'd only half understood about the girls who found themselves expecting babies when they weren't married. Girls who said they'd let their boyfriends *go too far.* Eva had rescued me from entire ignorance. She had quickly explained such matters and more to me although I had taken some persuasion to believe she wasn't making the whole thing up as it all sounded so foolish and not the sort of thing anyone would bother taking at all seriously if they had something better to do. Like reading books, for example. I tried to shift Eva onto the idea of going up to her bedroom and trying on her clothes, but she had other ideas for our afternoon.

"Let's follow her. Ma, I mean. See if we can find out where she goes? After all, we haven't got anything else to do this afternoon." Already she was slipping shoes onto her bare feet and standing by the back door impatiently waiting for me to finish my cake and limeade. Reluctantly, I followed her lead.

It was late May. A week's half-term holiday from school and it had rained and blown cold gales off the sea so that it was hard to believe it was almost summer. Except that there were small gaggles of people on the beach, sheltering behind windbreakers and testing the waves with bare toes. Some of them even attempted swimsuits and straw hats, as if adopting holiday clothes would somehow convince the sun to shine. Several bed and breakfasts and boarding houses had NO VACANCIES signs outside their front doors. Eva was scornful of these summer visitors and I was learning to become so. It was, after all, my first summer at Sea View Parade and I was still acquiring the rules.

"Fancy thinking this is the sort of place to come to on holiday," she had said one day when we saw a couple attempting to set up deckchairs on the pebble beach. "I mean, it's just where people live. Hardly exotic, is it? Hardly palm trees and foreign food and garlic and stuff unless you count the Italian ice cream place in Bampton."

"Perhaps they're Scottish, these people, so this is a sort of foreign country to them," I said. Eva considered it, nodded.

"Suppose so," she said, "or Welsh. Or Irish. Still not properly abroad, though, is it?"

Eva and her family were going to Spain in August. They'd been the year before and I'd seen photographs of a swimming pool and a big white hotel with balconies and Eva and her mother in strappy sundresses with their noses burnt red and her brother, Hamish, in a snorkel and flippers that made him look sinister. I'd never been abroad. Holidays for us, for my mother and father and me, had always been occasional, chance, rather than the booked, organised affairs that Eva seemed to have. We'd been to Devon a couple of times when I was small. We'd stayed on a farm without running water where each morning the farmer's wife brought up large jugs that we poured into china bowls sitting on washstands. We'd been to West Wales and stayed at a guest house for a few days, spending them sheltering from winds in the sand dunes, picnicking in the car when the rain grew too heavy to ignore. But now that we lived at the seaside, the need to go anywhere else was, apparently, unnecessary. My mother had said as much only the day before to our two lodgers. I'd heard her, talking to Miss Mackie and Mr. Jarvis, as I'd hung around on the basement stairs.

"Oh, we'll not be going anywhere this summer or any other, for that matter," she'd said in her very definite way that always made me feel bleak. "Why drive hundreds of miles when we've the beach on our doorstep and all home comforts that anyone could ask for?" And she'd swept her arm around the room, gesturing the old gas cooker and the dripping fridge and the stone sink that still awaited replacement. So that was that, I'd thought. Holidays neatly dispatched and discarded as unnecessary. Even Devon and wet and windy Wales had suddenly seemed desirable. At least they were somewhere else, remote from the needs of Miss Mackie and Mr. Jarvis and the ongoing repairs and dilapidation of 8 Sea View Parade.

Eva peered both ways down the empty road, her mother's white Triumph well out of sight, took off her cardigan and tied its arms around her waist.

"Ma went this way, I just know it," she said, turning left and hop skipping quickly along the pavement. I followed her to the cross roads that led either into another crescent of houses like Eva's or out towards the main road and, eventually, the sea. Eva shrugged.

"We'll have to be quicker off the mark next time," she said. "She's obviously given us the slip. Gone off to her fancy man, leaving us no clue."

I didn't know whether to believe Eva. She seemed surprisingly calm about the possibility of her mother's unfaithfulness to her father so I suspected it to be made up. An entertaining bit of fantasy for us. Eva was always good at inventing things to fill an empty, dull moment. I had begun to think of her a little like a bossy, but resourceful, older sister, someone to rely on for support.

"So what do you think he's like?" I said as we walked towards the main road which seemed to offer more than the crescent. "This other man of your mother's. Her... her fancy man."

"Tall, dark and handsome, of course," said Eva. "He'd have to be, wouldn't he?" She sounded very sure of her facts. We'd watched *Gone with the Wind* together on television the previous Sunday afternoon, nearly four hours curled up on her living room floor with a packet of bourbons and the latest delivery from the Corona man and I was pretty sure who she had in mind for her mother's lover. In fact, Rhett Butler seemed ideal for Mrs. Mason and I began to picture him standing on their front doorstep, hands on hips, curling his moustache and saying, *Frankly, my dear...* Eva strode on towards the coast road and soon we were heading for Beach Parade in the full onslaught of the sea wind. I shadowed close behind her as she looked as if she had a clear destination in mind. It wasn't, however, her mother's love nest with her fancy man. Which was both somehow a disappointment yet also an overwhelming relief.

In the bus shelter, two boys sprawled across the wooden bench leaving no space, another lounged against the glass, long limbs crowding the space so that I felt there was no room for us. They looked enormous to me, as tall and gangly as the fifth formers who hung around the bike sheds at school smoking at break time. I expected Eva to walk swiftly past, pretending not to notice them. But she didn't. Instead, she behaved as if she knew them. As if she had arranged to meet them this particular afternoon. She stepped in, sat down on the seat, pushing her back firmly against a pair of legs so that their owner swiftly drew them underneath him. I hovered on the edge, half in, half out of the shelter, rain dripping down my neck, waiting for Eva to tell me what to do. She appeared, however, to have forgotten that I was even there. For a moment, no-one spoke, although one of the boys blew bubble gum and another drummed his fingers against the window. A motor bike sped past. Then another as if they were in some sort of race. An elderly man walked by, stopped to stare in at us for a moment, then walked on.

"So anything interesting happening?" Eva said eventually. "Parties and stuff? What's going on around here?"

The boys stared at her as if she had addressed them in an unknown foreign language. After several seconds of silence, one of them muttered, "What?" Fair, floppy hair half hid his face so that I was unsure whether he had eyes at all. His mouth snarled so that one lip seemed stuck to the bottom of his nose.

"Parties," Eva went on, "or dances. You know, with groups and things. Or with a disco." She was beginning to sound less sure of herself. She licked her lips the way she always did when uncertain of her next move. Someone jangled coins in a pocket, someone else sniffed several times. Eventually, the boy who'd been drumming his fingers behind his back, spread-eagled against the window, thin as a pin with pale hair hanging lankly around his shoulders, shrugged. Said in a very loud voice, "What's it to you, anyway? You're just a kid. The two of you. Just kids."

All three of them laughed as if something extraordinarily amusing had been said. Eva rolled her eyes, gathered her long, straight hair up with one hand and held it on top of her head.

"Actually, I'm fifteen," she lied. "Actually, I'm nearly sixteen and nearly leaving school. So that's how much you know," she said, dropping her hand from her head, letting her hair settle around her shoulders then shaking it so that it hung straight down her back. Eva's birthday had been in March. She'd had a party with twelve friends invited and I'd bought her a manicure set with pink and white beads embroidered on the case. We'd given her thirteen bumps and I'd eaten too many cheese and pineapple on sticks and chicken vol au vent cases because I'd never had either of them before. Eva was decidedly not nearly sixteen and I couldn't imagine why she wanted to pretend that she was. The boy on the bench stood up, stretched so that his fingertips brushed the top of the bus shelter for a moment before he buried his hands deep into his pockets.

"We're off now, anyway," he said and the other two made as if to follow, unfolding themselves, gathering limbs together like scattered possessions that they had forgotten belonged to them. "You could come with us if you were older."

"That's right," said the one near to me, bringing his face uncomfortably close to mine so that I felt I could smell his breath, his skin, the grease on his hair. I tried not to shiver. "Come back in four years and we might be interested. You might have something we're interested in!" And they all laughed explosively, like the crack of fireworks, and they kept laughing as they left the shelter, crossing the road, darting dangerously between cars, their long limbs like spiders' legs as they headed onto the beach front.

"Well," said Eva, after a moment or so in which I'd fervently prayed that she wouldn't suggest we follow them. "Which one did you like most?"

I sat down next to her and looked at her face, which had two bright red blushes on either cheek. Like a couple of splashes of crimson poster paint on a white sheet.

"Why did you say you were nearly sixteen? Why pretend?" I said. Eva laughed loudly, sounding just like Mrs. Mason.

"You have to pretend, you know. Like you have to pretend to like them even when you don't. It's how you get to have a love life, you see. That's what's next for us. A boyfriend. We'll have to get boyfriends before too long." She sounded very sure of herself and very unlike the Eva who went with me to look at the toys in Beaumont's and could even be tempted still to lift her discarded dolls down from the top of the cupboard in her bedroom and tell me their names.

"But we're too young for all that," I said. "We don't have to think about all that stuff for years yet. Do we?" I thought of the older girls at school with boys' names scrawled across their satchels, hearts with arrows drawn on their wrists. Their behaviour and their habits seemed remote from me. As remote almost as my parents' lives with their jobs and duties and responsibilities. Eva said nothing, just scuffed her sandal on the floor, a squeaking noise a bit like a mouse cornered by a cat. Drizzle turned into a full-scale onslaught of rain, pelting the bus shelter noisily.

"Well, we can't stay here all afternoon," Eva said eventually, "and we might find Ma on her way back. We ought to look for tell-tale signs, you know. Signs of her lover man."

"Like what?" I said, buttoning up my cardigan hopelessly against the May rain.

"Oh, you know, smudged lipstick and messed hair and stuff and like… sort of a man smell about her. You know the sort of thing."

I didn't know at all. But it was easy to pretend I did. Far easier than pretending to care about lanky, greasy-haired boys with enormous spots and giant's feet who hung around bus shelters and smoked.

I followed Eva's helter-skelter dash back to her house, arriving with sodden sandals and rats' tails of hair that would soon turn into springs of tight, tangled coils. The drive was empty. Mrs. Mason was, apparently, still being occupied by her lover. Eva turned on the hotplates of the electric cooker and we toasted our chapped hands.

"You see," she said, as if she had been thinking about the subject during the dash back in the rain and felt I would benefit from a bit of careful instruction, "when we're fifteen, we'll get boyfriends. That's the age for it. So you have to sort of practise now so you'll know what to say later. Sort of get prepared."

"You'll be fifteen nearly a year before me," I said with relief. "There's not so much hurry for me. And anyway, you've got a brother. You've got him so you must know how to do the talking to boys thing already."

"That doesn't count," Eva said, "and besides, Hamish's horrid and he's hardly ever here. Of course, you could always have him, Mary. You could marry him if you like. Then we'd sort of be sisters."

Eva opened a kitchen cupboard and found a square packet of orange jelly cubes. She broke it in two, handed me half and we went upstairs to her bedroom. The idea of marrying Eva's brother seemed both appalling and also an immense relief. I'd only seen Hamish a couple of times, in the Easter holidays when he'd been home from university, and he'd appeared not even to notice me. I had a very vague impression of someone with curly brown hair on top of a face with glasses, large lips and very long legs.

"Wouldn't he be too old for me?" I said, settling myself cross-legged on Eva's pink carpet. I decided not to reject Hamish Mason outright. After all, it would save me the agonising bother of having to get to know any other boys.

"It's not an ideal age gap," Eva said, combing her wet straight hair straighter still. "You're supposed to marry someone five years older, you know. That's how it's done. And Hamish is almost twenty already. Still, I don't suppose it matters too much. As long as he's willing to wait for you, of course."

"What about you? When are you going to get married?"

"I might leave it as late as twenty-five," Eva said after a long pause, as if she was trying to be as precise as possible, "so I can go round the world first. Because then it will be babies and things and there won't be time. And I'm going to have a very long train like Princess Margaret did because my ma said she looked really beautiful, the most beautiful Royal bride, she said, and you can be my chief bridesmaid and hold it up for me."

Eva wandered out onto the landing and I followed her into her parents' bedroom. We tried out the lipsticks sitting in a glass tray on Mrs. Mason's dressing table and Eva painted my mouth with Coty's Shocking Pink then turned hers scarlet with Revlon's Red Ruby.

"My ma married my dad when she was twenty-two and he was twenty-six," she said, blotting her lips with the edge of her dirty blue handkerchief fished from her pocket. "My dad was still in the Navy from the war and that. What did your dad do? In the war, I mean. He must have done something."

I was used to the question. I was still hopeless at answering it. Everyone else's dads seemed to have been in submarines or Spitfires or prisoner of war camps. They seemed to have fought in Burma or Egypt, on Italian campaigns or French beaches or flown daily into enemy territory and returned in time for tea. At least that's what children said. They had an answer, just one sentence usually, as if they knew nothing more about the matter and were claiming it for their dad like some sort of wartime job description. Sometimes I suspected they just borrowed ideas from one of the films they'd seen because they fancied their dads being like Steve McQueen or Gregory Peck. I lifted the lid of Mrs. Mason's glass pot of face powder slowly, to look as if I was trying to decide which part of my father's extensive war history to divulge. There was a large puff that I dipped and dabbed onto my cheeks so that they smelt sweet like overripe strawberries.

"Well, it was difficult for him. You see, he was sort of ill, very ill, in fact, so he could only do certain things. Sort of private things," I said, trying to sound a little mysterious and hesitant about divulging too much. "His lungs or something. Shadows on them. Yes, it was definitely his lungs. He'd had rheumatic fever when he was young, you see. Then he got TB or they thought he had. He had to go away for a long time into a sort of sanatorium place."

Except that this was later. This was not during the war, but after it, after my parents were married, in fact, and living in Kentish Town. My mother had told me so many times about how hard it had been for her while my father was away in the sanatorium, living alone in a fourth floor flat with no heating and no kitchen sink and a bathroom two floors down that you had to queue for in your dressing gown. A woman all alone, she used to say, as if my father had intentionally abandoned her instead of being carted off into isolation for months. This was all before I was born, of course, before they'd left Kentish town to move to the house in Ash Gardens. But as for the war, all my father had ever told me was that he had done his duty. I was not at all sure that Eva would be satisfied with such an empty answer.

But for the moment, she seemed to have lost interest, having started to look furtively through the drawers in Mrs. Mason's dressing table, tightly packed with unopened packets of stockings and suspender belts and nylon slips.

"We might find some clues, you know," she said, fishing out a couple of old, empty perfume bottles, "about Ma's lover. Perhaps she's put a picture of him in one of her lockets or maybe there's a love letter."

"Wouldn't that be a bit dangerous? I mean your dad might find it."

Eva rolled her eyes at me in her most exasperated way.

"As if he'd ever look in her dressing table. It's a private place, this is, for her private things. Surely you know that, Mary. No-one's allowed to look in here."

★ ★ ★

There was a library in Bampton. Not a new, shiny library with polished parquet floors like we'd had before in Marsh Road, just round the corner from Ash Gardens so that I could walk there in moments and spend hours amongst the stacked shelves. But a library at least and after a considerable amount of persuasion my mother started to let me go on the bus alone into town to choose and change my books. My mother didn't particularly approve of reading. Factual books were all right, children's encyclopaedias and dictionaries and Ladybird books of Transport and the Seashore and Science and the Observer books of Birds and Wild Flowers. Books were suitable for finding out information, she seemed to think, and she usually managed to find second or third-hand editions of something along these lines to give me each birthday. The smell of TCP seemed to spring off the pages as if they were books that had lived long in a sick room or had needed to be disinfected before sending to the local jumble sale. Fiction books seemed to worry her. Whenever she saw me stuck into a cheerful-looking paperback that I'd borrowed from Eva, she'd quickly find me something dull to do as if concerned that my imagination was running dangerously loose and wild.

Bampton Public Library was a small building squashed between a hardware shop and the fishmongers and the smell of wet, white fish seemed to filter through the walls to the elongated room with its shelves of hardbacks and alcove of children's books. But it was my discovery and I relied upon it for most of our first summer at Sea View Parade while Eva was on her fortnight in Spain and then at her grandparents' in Scotland. I waded through the limited children's section quite rapidly, rereading all the Chalet School books and working my way through the stories of pony clubs and ballet academies and vicarage families, envious of all these fictional children whose lives sounded so much more interesting than mine. Then I came to a bit of a halt. Leaving the children's alcove for the adult section seemed too bold. I was, after all, only twelve and a half and had failed my 11 Plus. But, unwilling to trawl again all those boarding school midnight feasts and triumphant, flower-strewn debuts at Sadler's Wells, I thought I'd have a sneaky peek. The librarian, loftily tall with hair pulled back into a French pleat and a string of pearls bobbing upon her large bosom, watched me from her desk near the entrance. Perhaps she thought I was going to deface a book with colouring pencils or stick chewing gum between the chapters. I didn't know what to look for. I stood there, feeling as if I'd entered a foreign place with names in a language that I didn't understand. There were no catchy, explicit titles like *The Swish of the Curtain* and *Masquerade at the Wells* with bright, colour-washed pictures on the covers ready to entice you inside. I knew she was still watching me, the librarian, twisting the gold bracelet on her narrow wrist as I wandered helplessly amongst racks and displays of people with cryptic names like C.P. Snow and A.J. Cronin and R.F. Delderfield. Suddenly, there was a waft of sweet scent and a pale blue twin set and narrow navy skirt were at my side.

"Can I be of any assistance?" she asked, not exactly smiling, but certainly not scowling. "I've noticed you're one of our regulars. Quite the little bookworm!" I should have been insulted. Eva would have been insulted, would have flicked her hair over her shoulder, thanked her coldly and walked away. But I simply stood there, overwhelmed with gratitude. For a recognition and acceptance of sorts. "Perhaps," she went on, "you're ready to progress to something a little more taxing, more mature. Our children's selection is very poor for someone with such an appetite for reading as you obviously possess." Blushing furiously, I followed her along the shelves, silent in case I said something that sounded foolish. At any moment, I was afraid she would ask which school I went to, discover I was at the secondary modern rather than the girls' grammar and send me back to the children's alcove where I clearly belonged. Instead, she spent some time flicking through shelves, glanced at a couple of books, discarded one or two and eventually pressed a couple firmly into my hands. Their cloth-backed covers, stringy at the edges, were not inspiring. But I made noises to make her believe I was thankful and as if this was exactly the kind of thing I had in mind, but hadn't known where to find it. I followed her to her desk, handed over my two scruffy beige Junior library tickets which she quickly discarded and replaced with three green Adult tickets. It made me feel there was no going back now, no return to the cosy children's corner and I was unsure whether to be alarmed or relieved. "Let me know how you get on," she said, date-marking the books, removing their square catalogue cards and flicking with her perfect pale pink painted nails through a long wooden box that stood on her desk. Then she turned away, switched her attention to an elderly woman who was moaning loudly that the local paper was not in its usual place. Discarded, I carefully tucked the books in my duffle bag, feeling a nervous sense of responsibility, and headed for the door before there was a chance she'd change her mind about my sudden promotion to adult reader.

The lack of light in the mid-afternoon was more October than late August and I caught sight of my reflection in the window of the fishmongers and noticed how scrappy and shoddy I was in my blue summer dress that was growing too short for me and my sandals that were scuffed and tight. I wandered down to Woolworth's, thought about a cornet, but bought a packet of Spangles instead, then managed to waste half an hour or so looking at the exercise books and pencil cases, although I only had enough money left for my fare home. At the bus stop, I hunched against the timetable board to wait for my ten past the hour back to Sea View Parade and opened the thinner of the two adult library books.

Last night I dreamt I went to Manderley again.

★ ★ ★

Miss Mackie approved. The bird woman picked up my book from where I'd left it on the kitchen table.

"Ah, Du Maurier! Well, a little bit of romance won't harm you at your age, Mary. Although don't go confusing it with real life, will you?"

I was tempted to say that I rather thought that was the point of novels, to make the story sound believable, but my mother was there rolling out her heavy pastry for the evening's mince and potato pie so I daren't risk it.

"Better reading than hanging out along the sea front to all hours at any rate," she said, as if suddenly discovering that books had some use after all, if only as a deterrent to wilder behaviour. She gave the white pastry a firm thump with the rolling pin. She always attacked her pastry as if it was a disobedient child that needed bringing into line. Miss Mackie hovered, flicking through the pages of *Rebecca* as if revisiting an old and rather flighty friend. She made little noises, small gusts of delight like a puppy yelping because it's seen its lead. I poured myself a cup of tea, waited for her to finish with my book and hand it back so that I could read more about the alarming Mrs. Danvers. I saw little of Miss Mackie on the whole. She left for work before I was downstairs on school mornings and in the evenings tended to retreat to her room with a cheese sandwich or bowl of tinned soup as soon as my mother started to clank around with cutlery for our evening meal. At weekends she generally disappeared with one of her 'groups', as she called them. Ramblers' groups, Local History group, Keep the Beach Tidy group, Adopt a Stray Cat group, she seemed to have endless enthusiasms for very dull things. She had a brother who lived in Eastbourne and sometimes he arrived in a Ford Estate and whisked her off for Sunday lunch or tea and scones at a sea front hotel.

Mr. Jarvis was more conspicuous.

Most days when I got home from school he was there, sitting at the kitchen table reading the paper and drinking black instant coffee and smoking a cigarette. At first it annoyed me, seeing his large black jacket hanging around the back of the chair, his long green scarf trailing on the floor, the smell of his smoke filling the basement room so that it lingered long after he had gone out. But after a while, I forgot to notice or even to mind particularly. He was simply there and even the cigarette butts and the smoky smell became just part of the place, the otherness that 8, Sea View Parade had been for me since we left Ash Gardens. If the weather was warm, he'd often be sitting out in the back garden instead, although it was still little more than a rubbish tip for everything that my father was pulling out of the house. Rotted window frames, stained lino, an old mangle we'd found in the downstairs cupboard. Even some ancient gas lamps that had still been hanging in the living room and an armchair that had been home to several extended families of mice. Sometimes he'd be sketching something remotely on the horizon, balancing a pad on one knee and drawing broad strokes with a lead pencil, stopping every now and again to flick ash from the cigarette in his other hand. He taught most mornings at the college and on three evenings a week went back for the night students, as he called them, coming in late after I'd gone to bed so that I'd hear him on the stairs, heavy, slow treads up to the attic. It was impossible to forgive him for taking my room, of course, but it was hard to ignore him when he insisted on talking to me, asking constant questions the way adults rarely did. He'd ask me about school, about the teachers, about my friends and although I'd give short, abrupt answers which told him very little, he didn't seem to mind or even notice. I took to mumbling at him in some sort of effort at mild hostility, keeping my head down or stuck in a book so that he could hardly hear me. But he seemed to be the sort of person so convinced of his own popularity, delighting at the sound of his own voice, that he preferred one-sided conversation, anyway. When he was in the room he seemed to take charge, as if the rest of us needed him to fill every silence. Still, thankfully he was only with us during the week. On Friday nights he disappeared in his little black car, a bubble of rust and scratches, driving fast down Sea View Parade, screeching around the corner towards the coast road and back to London, to Greenwich and his ancient mother. He'd be back late Sunday night or on Monday afternoon, saying he'd missed the salt air and the seascapes, breezing in with another jar of his instant coffee and four packets of Benson and Hedges, tipped.

But once I'd got used to the idea of small Miss Mackie in the back room, of considerably larger Mr. Jarvis filling the basement kitchen, the smell of his stale smoke never quite absent, I forgot to notice them a great deal. Really, they had so little to do with me and bothering to get annoyed with either one of them was simply paying them the attention they didn't deserve.

8

My mother is very tired today when I visit, apathetic, almost as if it's all a little too much bother. And perhaps it is. The nurse says she didn't want to eat lunch, though apparently she's well enough, given that now she exists permanently in a state of declining health. They all do, of course, the residents, for that's the point of the place. It harbours the vulnerable, those hovering at the edge, with bodies gradually becoming less obedient and conversant with the rules and obligations of living. I sit down next to her, take her hand. Ida's hands were always slim, oval-shaped with long fingers that could have been mistaken for a pianist's. She did play, of course, but only adequately, replicating notes learnt and scales practised that she'd drummed into herself at some early stage in her life. For a few years, at Sea View Parade, she played for the Wednesday afternoon and Saturday morning ballet classes at the local parish hall. Just the Babies and Beginner's classes with their litany of nursery rhymes, background music for their enthusiastic spring points and gallops and skips. For the other classes an accomplished pianist took over and the hall was filled with more serious classical strains. She didn't seem to mind the obvious inferior status this inferred, accepting her limited repertoire and grateful for the bit of money it brought in. I break open the bar of chocolate I've brought her, place a square in her hand. She takes it, eats it swiftly and I give her another. Milk chocolate treats for a child who refuses to eat her lunch. I joke with her about it, at the same time despising myself for the condescension. Why should she not choose to refuse lunch? Why should she not exercise a whim, a right to wave away the well-cooked meat, the fruit crumble and custard for once? So few choices remain to her now. Others direct the order and running of her day, the way a parent controls the routine of a very young child. I wonder whether she resents the imposition and her incapacity to express it or if there's a certain relief in being biddable, submissive.

I rattle on about this and that, tell her about Jack's magnolia bush that's just flowered, tomato plants he's bought from the local market ready for the early summer, bedding plants, the hanging basket he's planning for the front of the house. Seasons hardly touch this place. They make an effort, of course, the cheerful care workers, the devoted nursing staff, try to break up the year with appropriate gestures, celebrations. At Christmas there's a tree, presents and, of course, a compulsory Father Christmas in awkward beard. The local primary school comes in to sing carols under the assumption, presumably, that the old enjoy seeing the young. At Easter, there are cochineal-stained eggs for breakfast, chocolate ones for tea. Daffodils and tulips fill every vase. But otherwise, seasons are irrelevant. The weeks and months seem marked in a more melancholy way by arrivals, disappearances. The man who used to greet me in a surprisingly forthright voice no longer sits on the red chair near the door. His place has been taken by a large woman in a wheelchair who says nothing, but constantly looks around her as if ready to admonish anything untoward. She looks like an old-fashioned headmistress from the lost world of spinster teachers, gym slips and chalk boards. But Ida is remote today and silent. She does not make eye contact with me and soon I run out of conversation and just sit holding her hand. It is so thin, bones protruding like the sketch of a witch in a fairy tale. She turns away from me to look out of the window, but appears to see little of the sparrows, the squirrel who fidgets at the bottom of the oak tree. She stares blankly out at the indifferent day and I wonder where she is and hope that her mind has places of escape for her. Somewhere far away from the here and now of this place, the inevitable humiliations and degradations of being here. The past, her past in particular, is perhaps of consolation to her now if she can reach out and touch it. An illumination, spots of time, to warm her in this growing darkness. Abruptly, she grabs my hand, clasps it forcefully, suddenly anxious. She turns to me as if to speak, searches my face, then turns away as if she has changed her mind or has lost the impulse and energy for talk.

"How are you feeling today?" I say, to fill the void. "Did you have a bad night? Slept badly?"

Ida was always a light sleeper, went to bed late, up early. As if sleeping was an indulgence that wasted precious time for purposeful activity. I remember when I was studying for exams, at the age of seventeen, eighteen or so, finally becoming aware of what she did with those hours when most people were in bed. Sorting washing at one in the morning, ironing before six, peeling potatoes for meals that would not happen for another twelve hours. She'd bring me cups of milky coffee, glance briefly at the quotes from *Paradise Lost* I was trying to learn, lists of French vocabulary for the following day's oral test. And I was aware of her tacit approval of the midnight hours I was burning studiously and glad of it. Absurdly glad considering how I felt about her then. For that was a time of unimaginable tension when I could speak hardly a word to either of my parents, to Ida or Jack, for fear that the whole fabric of our lives would dismantle, leaving the three of us comfortless, hopelessly bereaved. I know I was aware then of feeling I was simply getting through the months, tolerating what felt intolerable until I could get out, away. Imagining a future free from the events of the recent past, as if by merely walking out of the front door of 8, Sea View Parade would remove them. Like walking out of a film that has not been to my taste, switching off something unpalatable on the television news. Glibly, at the age of eighteen, I saw the future as an entirely different place, neatly labelled, pristine and new into which I could step unblemished, fetter-free.

The trolley comes round. Tea and slices of homemade cake that Ida takes and begins to eat with some interest, spilling crumbs onto her lap that I try to mop up with a tissue. The oversweet pink icing sticks to my fingers. One of the care workers, Sally, I think she's called, comes over to chat.

"Your dad was in yesterday," she says to me. "He's so good, isn't he? Likes to pop in several times a week."

Ida looks at Sally sharply, without warmth. Sally's voice is high, quite shrill, and her hair is unnaturally bleached with dark streaks at a centre parting. She is only young, no more than twenty-five or twenty-six, and I wonder at her working in this place, at her acceptance for what she must have to see and do daily. "But he must miss her so, mustn't he?" she goes on. "After all those years, a lifetime of being married and then suddenly being without her."

"Yes," I answer, "it's not been easy for him."

"Devoted, you can tell. You can always tell the devoted couples, you know," Sally says firmly, "the ones who've had a really good marriage. It's so nice to see." She touches Ida's cheek as if fondling the soft face of a new-born baby. Ida glares at her. Sally moves away, crosses the room to help someone master their tea cup. Ida watches her go then says too loudly, "She's... she's... I don't like her, that one. How... how... what... what does she know?"

I crumble the remaining cake into four pieces.

When I get home, Felix is sitting in the kitchen, spooning cereal from an overflowing bowl and carrying on a monosyllabic conversation with someone on his phone, balancing it between ear and shoulder. I want to throw my arms around his youth, dabble in the wholeness and perfection of him. He appears to have grown since I saw him this morning, another inch or so added to his lanky frame. He looks up, half smiles, half waves a milky spoon in my direction.; I throw down my bag, scatter shoes and jacket in the hall and go upstairs to strip off my clothes, standing in the shower to remove the place, stepping away from the thought of Ida's face, her loneliness as she watches the garden outside her window grow dark. Guiltily, I banish her, consign her to a remote corner of mind. She tends to resurface unexpectedly, of course. In dreams, she crops up, forceful and looking as if she's still forty, telling me off about something, irritating me until I wake up and remind myself that she's no longer here. Not like that, not like she was. Felix lollops up the stairs, wielding a football.

"I'm just going to the park, just for a while. With Tom and maybe a few other people."

"Who?"

He shrugs. The way only teenage boys can shrug. Evasive, as if unsure quite how much he wants to divulge.

"Don't know. Maybe… don't know till I get there."

"Homework?"

He shakes his head.

"Haven't got any. Don't think so, anyway. Not for tomorrow. Or not much at least. A bit of geography, a sheet or something."

"Don't be long. It'll be dark in an hour, you know."

He's halfway down the hall when he calls back.

"Oh, and Dad rang when you were out. Before you got back from Grandma's. I'm seeing him Sunday. That's all right, isn't it? For lunch, I think, or something."

"Fine. That will be nice."

"He said would you give him a ring. Just sometime. Just to make arrangements or something like that." And he's out of the door, darting across the road, squeezing through the gap in the hedge that he's made his own unofficial short cut to the park. I watch him from my bedroom window. Watch him bounce his football on the pavement the way I used to tell him not to when he was small, fearing him running into treacherous roads in pursuit of it. I go to the phone, start to ring David's number then cancel it before it connects. Later will do, later, and I go downstairs into the kitchen, fetch vegetables out of the fridge, stare at them assembled neatly on the chopping board as if ripe for purpose.

For years, I had seemed skilled at selecting inappropriate men. I spent my twenties ticking off a list of patently unsuitable partners as if I was particularly gifted in the art. Feckless men, fickle men, faintly psychotic types, even, with whom the prospect of a sensible, grown up sort of a life was remote. A life with things other people had like mortgages and joint bank accounts and children. Which I supposed was what I wanted. Because that's what, on the whole, everyone else chose. I watched my friends get on with their lives in a far more purposeful sort of way, graduating from the engagement ring to the wedding list, from the first then, inevitably, the second child, in respectable, acceptable order. Ida and Jack looked on, quietly appalled by my failure to conform. Brazenly, I brought one or two of these dreadful men home to meet them, to 8, Sea View Parade, where the bed and breakfast business had eventually taken over from the lodgers after Mr. Jarvis. But I was inadequate to the task of shocking them for long, embarrassed by Ida's candid, blatant disapproval, wounded by Jack's bewilderment. I was not cut out to rebel, to hurt those I essentially sought to gratify. It was simply not in my nature. The compliance imposed by my upbringing, perhaps, or my own cowardice.

But then, eventually, there was David.

And I had to agree with everyone's view, Ida and Jack's especially, that David was quite a find. David, in fact, was pretty perfect permanent couple material. No worries about David's stability, probity, reliability, his exemplary intentions towards me. And since he genuinely loved me into the bargain, it seemed obstinate to object. What else, after all, was I looking for? Getting married was what people did. A more or less obligatory rite of passage, it appeared. Ida said as much when I told her about his proposal.

"This is what you want," she said firmly, her hands resting on my shoulders, I remember, as if attempting to anoint me with certainty. "This is what you need." And I assumed she must be right and felt curiously relieved to please her, to have my future so tidily defined at last. Eva, already married to Don for some ten years and mother to three, sent profuse congratulations as if I had finally satisfied expectation. It was only when I was sidling into the registry office a little late one very wet June morning, my cheap white hat from C and A's flopping over my forehead, my long, drooping broderie anglaise skirt tinged with mud, that I allowed myself to doubt. I looked over at David, his square solid frame in his dark grey suit, at my mother talking avidly to him, my father silent at their side, and knew I should turn back. This was their idea, a benign conspiracy of sorts, and I had vacuously, spinelessly simply gone along with it. I saw that I was marrying David out of some sort of convenience rather than true conviction. I was fond of David, of course. He was a notably kind man whose genuine deep love for me, however rationally and conservatively expressed, felt flattering. Consoling. The thought that I did not love him in return had seemed an irrelevance since I had long stopped believing in the possibility of faithful, enduring, monogamous love. And perhaps his excess of the stuff would be enough for the two of us, contaminating me, a pleasant opiate to which I would eventually, feasibly, succumb. Love as a habit, a practice and routine that would serve us to all intents and purposes. But as I joined him, took my place at his side and moved into the dreary wedding suite smelling of institutional polish with a faint trace of disinfectant, I felt suddenly frightened by my own fraudulence. I had stared down at the raindrops still clinging to my scant posy of hothouse freesias and tried to shift my deep unease, see it merely as nervous apprehension. David had put a finger under my chin to tilt it and had smiled at me with such evident delight, with overwhelming tenderness, that I had abandoned doubt out of expedience. This was, no doubt, how most marriages began, I told myself, and what I felt for David was sufficient, an affection, an easy tolerance that, like a small shoot, would grow steadily and eventually blossom.

So I married him and settled down to wait for this inevitable flowering. And nothing happened. Nothing came of nothing. Instead, as the months tipped into a year or two, I found myself utterly incapable of loving David or even feigning a semblance of love. I liked him, of course, everyone liked amicable, cordial David yet I felt an imposter as his wife and began to despise my own deception. Infidelity didn't even occur to me since I already felt weighed down by the guilt of failing to love him, which in itself seemed a betrayal. Instead, I cultivated a certain detachment towards him, a neutrality, you could say, which was cowardly and callous.

But then, in time, there was Felix. And my ecstasy was so extraordinary, my love so wild and excessive that I almost forgot about my unsatisfactory marriage. I could spare no time for negative thoughts when this perfect, beautiful miracle needed me, was entirely dependent upon me, for it had taken years to conceive and I had begun to abandon all ideas of a child. So effortlessly he earned his name, Felix, bringing only delight, unalloyed joy. I was content, rapturous at last to feel fulfilled, settled.

With my child, at least.

It's hard to remember the moment when I knew David was gone. Not absent from the house in a physical sense with his white shirts and dark suits and corduroy trousers still hanging in the wardrobe and the garden shed cluttered with his concerns for rose blight and slug control. But gone from me, politely sidestepping his way out of our marriage because I gave him so little reason to stay. In fact, I admired him for possessing the boldness to leave. For in the end, it was David who strayed, David who was brave enough to do something about our inadequate partnership and have an affair. He chose sensibly, of course, embarking upon a quiet liaison with his sweet secretary, Celia, who had always patently adored him. I'd watched her cautious envy at the office Christmas parties as David and I had left together, his arm possessively linked through mine. I'd noted her supreme secretarial duties when she'd waded through snow-bound streets to bring David papers to sign and glanced covetously around our family-cluttered Edwardian semi. When I confronted him with the facts, my awareness of his affair with Celia, I was embarrassed by his guilt, his profound contrition. He broke down, like a small child unsuited to deceit, and I felt obliged to console him, reassure him of my compliance. He moved out the same day, taking himself off to Celia's house in Wembley, where he lived initially alongside her elderly mother and bachelor brother until our divorce and their eventual marriage.

Felix was too young to be consciously affected. Or so I told myself. His father's absence from our home has been his only reality, but I've often felt guilt that my failure to love David sufficiently, to tolerate a state that was less than love, has deprived Felix of a conventional family life. The consolation of its unremarkable ordinariness. But David has remained close, a loving, affectionate father and I have grown far fonder of him in the years we have been apart than I would ever have done as his wife. I kiss him on the cheek as I would a kindly uncle, advise him to drive with care on icy roads, berate him for indifference to a bad cold. And Felix adores him, I know that for sure. He never asks why we are not together, David and I, when clearly we do not despise each other. I wonder whether Felix's reticence stems simply from lack of curiosity or if he is unwilling to know too much.

Perhaps it's a family trait.

David and Celia live only a few miles away. She is a shy, reserved woman, or at least she is shy and reserved with me on the few occasions when we meet, but they are content. Celia and David are a contented couple, happy even, and I am delighted. David deserves a loving, affectionate wife who can wholeheartedly give to him what I could not.

I stare out of the kitchen window, see the sun has gone, the sky has begun to darken. Felix will be back soon. We will eat dinner, he will slink off to his room to stare at his computer screen, message his friends, and I will ring my father, Jack. Check that he is all right, tell him that I have visited Ida. There is not a lot to say these days. I'll ask him what he's eaten for supper, if he's mown the lawn or if the grass is still too wet with spring showers. We'll string out a conversation together for five minutes or so, to entertain him, to reassure me. At least that's how I think of it, but perhaps I'm deluded. Perhaps I'm the one in need, clinging on to Jack, still lucid and suitably parental in his concerns for me. Ida, on the other hand, is alone, vulnerable to the care of virtual strangers who will undress her, put her to bed, stroke her thin hair from her pale, bewildered face.

On the hall table are some letters, bills mostly, a reminder of an overdue library book, some circulars. A bank statement. And a pale blue envelope addressed to me in an unknown hand, in thick, black ink. On the back, one of those little gold address labels that some people use shows it's come from somewhere in Lancashire. And before I even take in the name of the sender, I know. It's as if I have unconsciously been waiting for such a letter for years and have simply assigned the expectation to some recess in my mind. I gather it up, the pale blue envelope with the gold address label that has travelled a couple of hundred miles south, scrunch it into my hand with the circulars and stuff the lot into the rubbish bin along with carrot peelings and an empty carton of milk.

Felix, thankfully, is at the front door and he comes in, smelling of chill evening air.

Of cut grass.

9

"I've asked Anthea," Eva said, "Anthea Heaton. The one who's got a pony. You can ask someone from your school too, if you like. What's that girl you've told me about?"

I pulled my fawn socks up over my knees, wishing I was allowed to wear stockings like Eva. I pulled my wretched socks up at least one million times a day and my mother moaned that I made them thin and stringy.

"There are two of them," I said. "I'm sort of friends with two of them this year so which one do you mean?" Now that Eva was in the Third Year, she had exchanged a tunic for a school skirt. It made her seem almost as old as the fifth formers at my school who could go without their green berets. "There's Susan, of course. She'd come, I expect. In fact, she'd probably be really pleased we'd asked her. Or there's also Gail who's really nice, at least most of the time she is."

"Whichever one you like," Eva said, "but only one. Five wouldn't work on the bus. Someone would have to sit alone and that would have to be you because this whole thing is my idea."

We pushed open the gate of Number 8, which my father had repaired and painted with several coats of creosote months before, and the smell had never quite disappeared.

"I don't even know if I can come yet," I pointed out. "Anyway, why do we have to take other people? Why not just you and me? And why Anthea Heaton? She's so stuck-up."

101

"Safety in numbers," Eva said. "If one of us gets hurt or lost or something, there'll be three others to get help. Besides, I want Anthea Heaton to ask me round to her house so I can have a ride on her pony. Everyone in my class is trying to get an invite."

I stuck my key in the front door, turned on her before I let her through to the hall.

"Don't say that stuff to my mother about safety in numbers and one of us getting hurt. You've got to make it seem nice and safe or there's no chance of me being allowed. Don't say anything about the pier and the amusement arcade and roll-a-penny and stuff, all right? And nothing about Anthea being rich, because she probably won't trust someone like that."

Eva rolled her eyes, pushed past me and hung up her grey blazer on the coat stand in the hall.

"You worry too much. Your mother will probably think we're being enterprising, wanting to go off to Brighton for the day," she said. "Exploring the local area. Like a geography trip or something."

I had my doubts about that, but simply said, "I think I'll ask Susan Johnston. I'll see if she wants to come with us." Susan was sensible and reliable and kind and, on the whole, quite dull. Other girls thought her too fat. They also thought she was boring as she was homework monitor and wore her school tunic down to her knees and sang in her church choir. She sat next to me in most lessons and seemed to like me because I never said anything rude about her bad eczema or told her to lose weight. "My mother would think Susan was all right."

"Susan? Oh all right," Eva said. "She's a bit quiet, though, isn't she? Not exactly an exciting sort of person. But I suppose we've got Anthea for that."

She went down to the kitchen, two stairs at a time, ahead of me.

During the summer, my father had painted the walls of the room a bright custard shade of yellow, a surplus bargain he'd found at a shop closing down in Bampton. It had at least cheered up the basement and, with the red check curtains that my mother had made out of a jumble sale tablecloth, the room looked less bleak, if a little startling. Rather like fried egg yolks covered in vibrant ketchup. Mr. Jarvis was sitting at the kitchen table, his chin propped on his hands, newspaper spread out in front of him. He looked surprised to see us and glanced at the clock on one of the bright yellow walls.

"That time already?" he said. "I'd better get my skates on or the college will be wondering what they pay me for." Eva sat down on the chair next to him.

"Don't let us disturb you," she said, looking down at his newspaper. "You seem to be in the middle of the crossword. Anyway, we're looking for Mrs. Foster. We've got to ask her something. Something quite important."

Eva was doing this all wrong. She was drawing far too much attention to something I intended to drop casually into the conversation to make my mother think it was an insignificant request. Like going to the library in Bampton or down to Beach Parade for an ice lolly. If she thought there was something daring in the idea of a bus ride to Brighton and an afternoon spent there left to our own devices, she'd ban it instantly. I found the cake tin, broke the last rock bun into two halves and gave Eva the bigger piece. Mr. Jarvis closed the pages of his newspaper, folding it carefully before looking at Eva then at me.

"So are either of you going to tell me all about it?" he said. "This important matter you've got to discuss with Mrs. Foster. Or is it for her ears only?" He picked up his mug of coffee, peered into it as if wondering whether it was fit to drink. I sat down at the table and glared at Eva. This was nothing to do with Mr. Jarvis, with someone who was just the lodger and I despised him for trying to get involved. He fumbled in his jacket pocket for his packet of cigarettes.

"Smoking's not good for you, you know," Eva said. "I keep telling my ma. My dad's already given up."

"Sensible man," Mr. Jarvis said, sticking a cigarette between his lips and flicking his thumb down the side of his lighter. "That's something I'll think about doing in my old age. Being sensible." He lit the cigarette, puffed and slowly released a whisker of smoke into the air. Eva coughed extravagantly. I heard my mother's footsteps coming down the basement stairs.

"I didn't hear you girls come in," she said. "I'll put the kettle on. Does your mother know you're here, Eva? I wouldn't want her to be worried." She filled the kettle slowly from the obstinate tap that chugged out water as if it really resented the offering, set it on the gas burner.

"It's all right, Mrs. Foster, it's Ma's day for her Ladies Circle. She's never back before five."

"These girls have something to ask you, evidently, Mrs. Foster. I rather get the impression that a lot depends on your answer." Mr. Jarvis tapped ash into a green saucer.

"It's not like that at all," I snapped, desperate to sideline Mr. Jarvis and deflate the subject of our afternoon out, which seemed to have bloated into a helium balloon. I charged rapidly on. "It's just that me and Eva want to go to Brighton on Saturday. This Saturday. To… to look at things. That's all. Just shops and stuff and maybe the Pavilion. It's historic, you see. And probably geographic when you think about it. And Eva's mother – Mrs. Mason – she says it's all right because Eva has already checked with her. And we might take some others from school, just two others so it's not just me and Eva. There's safety in numbers, after all." I sat back, breathless. My mother's face said nothing, but then it rarely did. She kept her expressions as if under lock and six keys.

"Susan Johnston and Anthea Heaton, that's who we were thinking of asking to come with us," Eva joined in. "Someone from my school and someone from Mary's. That's fair, isn't it? And we'd go by bus. It's not far, you know, it doesn't take long to get to Brighton, you'd be surprised."

My mother opened the red and gold tea caddy and spooned four scoops into the brown teapot.

"I know where Brighton is, Eva. And the cost of the bus fare which is ludicrous considering it takes barely half an hour."

"We'd be halves," I said. "That's much cheaper."

"They've obviously thought this whole thing through, Mrs. Foster, you've got to give them that. And it's only Brighton. It's not as if they want to take themselves off to London and Carnaby Street or the King's Road and get up to who knows what. That's where the real scene of the moment is now, you know. There's not much to lead them astray in Brighton. Or only if you go looking for trouble and know how and where to find it."

Eva beamed at Mr. Jarvis and he gave her a wink as my mother's back turned to see to the tea. I was annoyed to have to feel gratitude for his support. I found myself thinking that for some reason my mother would trust his opinion. Or at least she wouldn't want to be seen disagreeing with him.

"Now who did you say, Mary? Susan Johnston? Well, she's a nice enough girl and her mother works all hours at that fish and chip shop down Paradise Road," she said.

"They live above it," I said helpfully, as if this information was relevant to our request. "They all live in the flat above the shop. Her school uniform often smells of vinegar and frying. And her books too, actually."

"And you'd really like Anthea Heaton, Mrs. Foster, everyone does," Eva went on speedily, "and she's nearly the oldest girl in the Third Year and she's really clever. And she's got a pony and a massive big house out near the downs."

My mother took the blue and white milk jug out of the fridge, set it steadily on the table with the tea pot.

"Let it brew," she said, as she always said. "Give it a minute or two," as she unfailingly added.

"Sounds like a good day out, if you ask me," Mr. Jarvis said. "Only wish I could go myself and give the lot of you a lift in the car. But of course, as this little jaunt is planned for Saturday afternoon, I'll be back in Greenwich then being the dutiful son. Now what do you say, Mrs. Foster? Are you going to trust these two young ladies and their friends to venture down the coast for a few hours? Such well-behaved girls deserve a bit of trust, don't they?" He stood up from his place at the top of the table, picked up his huge jacket from the arms of the chair, swung it over his shoulder and walked towards the stairs. My mother sat down in front of the brewing pot of tea. We waited. Eva played with the spoon in her saucer.

"We'll see," my mother said, in the way she always said when she knew she would eventually give in, "we'll see once Saturday gets nearer."

We got the front seats. Susan had arrived at Number 8 half an hour early and I'd bundled her out of the door to wait at the bus stop for the others in case my mother changed her mind. She didn't complain.

"It's nice to be away from the shop. Saturday afternoons I usually have to get all the papers ready for the evening trade. You know, the newspapers to wrap it all in. Saturday night's our busiest, of course."

"Don't you have other people working there to do stuff like that? I didn't think people our age were allowed to work,"

I said, skipping from one foot to the other to try to keep warm. I was wearing only my dark blue cardigan over my dress as otherwise it was my awful anorak or my best camel coat that was too old, too short and too dull for the day.

"It's my granddad's shop," Susan said patiently, "it's just family. We all help. My gran peels all the potatoes and makes the batter and my granddad is the fryer. My mum does everything else. The money and serving and stuff. And the ordering, of course. And I help out here and there." She buttoned up her school gabardine mackintosh and gave me a long stare. "You're not wearing enough, you know, you'll be freezing." Already the streets and gutters were solid with autumn leaves and there was little warmth in the sun. Summer had long passed without it actually ever having made an appearance. I'd been in the sea precisely three times and my fingers and toes had turned blue within moments. My father had taken a week's holiday from the tax office during August and he'd driven us to other beaches along the coast. Eastbourne had at least given us a bit of sand and Worthing was all right with its pier, so coming back to our pebbled bit of the coastline was depressing. But, as my mother kept on pointing out to us, we couldn't have afforded to buy a big house like Number 8 in places such as Eastbourne and Worthing. Let alone Brighton. Proper places, she meant, with a proper town where people actually wanted to live and even visit for holidays.

Eva appeared at the end of the road in her black and white shift dress and her yellow cape. She looked a bit like a large bumble bee. Anthea Heaton was by her side dressed in a red trouser suit with a cap to match and a white handbag with a long strap over her shoulder. I'd seen her before, of course, at Eva's birthday party when she'd complained of feeling unwell and had spent most of the afternoon alone in Eva's bedroom. Mrs. Mason had taken her in a piece of birthday cake which she'd somehow managed to eat and even asked for a second slice. I decided then that I didn't really like her and was not keen on her coming with us to Brighton. Still, there was the matter of her pony to consider. I'd never been on horseback and Anthea Heaton was likely to be my only opportunity. Eva ushered us upstairs on the bus, heading for the front seats with Anthea next to her and Susan and me across the aisle from them. We bought our half returns to the Palace Pier from the conductor and Eva and Anthea settled down to talk while Susan and I sat staring out at the road ahead of us. Anthea seemed to know everything about every pop star and each song in the hit parade and she claimed her father's secretary's brother's wife knew someone who was very famous and had promised to get his autograph and introduce her to him one day. Eva sounded very impressed. I knew she was thinking of the pony that was called White Shadow and the chance of a canter around the paddock. Susan and I sat in silence like two middle-aged women who couldn't keep up with the conversation.

"Do you like pop music?" I said to Susan quietly when Eva and Anthea had eventually stopped talking and were hunched up instead over a magazine Anthea had pulled out of her shoulder bag.

"No," Susan said quietly, "not really. But don't tell anyone at school I said that."

"I promise," I said. "It's easier to pretend that you do. That's what I do most of the time. It's easier to pretend to be like everyone else, isn't it? Then you sort of fit in."

Susan shrugged.

"Don't know why I bother. It's not as if anyone likes me."

"That's not true," I said, knowing that it probably was. No-one really liked Susan Johnston. It was just a fact and everyone knew it. "I like you. We're friends, aren't we?"

She shrugged again.

"You just feel sorry for me. But that's all right. It's better than nothing."

She was right in a way. It was easy to make friends with Susan as there was no competition. If I didn't sit next to her at lunch, ask her to partner me in science experiments, swap answers to mark in French tests, no-one else did. And she was grateful for so little that she made me feel a nicer person than the others who avoided her because of her eczema. Because her hair was usually greasy and her uniform never quite clean. Because she didn't seem to mind, take any offence or make the slightest effort to change simply to become more popular.

Anthea Heaton had her own ideas once we got to Brighton. We stood on the sea front and blocked the pavement so that people had to edge around us.

"We'd thought of the West Pier, actually," Eva said, when Anthea asked which shop we should visit first. "Me and Mary want to go there. We've decided." I was relieved I was back into her conversation and that her wish to ride White Shadow hadn't removed me entirely from our friendship.

"Piers? You didn't say anything about going on the piers when you asked me to come," Anthea said in her rather high-pitched, silly voice, making the idea sound quite infantile. "I thought this was a shopping trip, for the boutiques and all that. Surely that's what Brighton's about." She swung her white shoulder bag more firmly across her shoulder, catching a strand of her long hair and folding her arms as if prepared to be defiant.

"I'd like to go on the pier," I said quietly. In my red purse in my pocket I had precisely half a crown which seemed to me a substantial amount for the slot machines, but clearly inadequate for a visit to a Brighton boutique. Eva turned to Susan for more support.

"You want to go on the pier, don't you Susan? And maybe afterwards there'll be time for shops."

Susan nodded and then muttered something about not getting back too late. Anthea glared at her and then stepped back and bumped heavily into an old man with a stick who was trying to edge past us. He called her all sorts of names so we scuttled swiftly away in the direction of Hove and the West Pier with Anthea relieved to follow. We changed shillings into pennies and threepences and charged around the amusement arcade, winning some money back before losing it again. Eva spent ages trying to hoopla a fluffy dog with horrid green eyes and Susan seemed glued to the Roll a Penny. Anthea had disappeared behind a curtain into Gypsy Rose Lee's lair, spending a foolish five shillings on finding out her future. She emerged after a few minutes, inspecting her palm.

"It's all here, you know," she said, a pink blush on her cheekbones, "the whole of my life is here in these lines. It's amazing."

Eva grabbed her wrist.

"I suppose there's a tall dark stranger with pots of money ready to enslave you with his love. Bet that gypsy's promised you beauty and happiness forever."

Anthea retrieved her hand, inspected her fingernails at great length.

"Something like that," she said, "and lots more stuff. But she said I wasn't to tell anyone or it wouldn't come true."

"Then she wasn't a proper gypsy," Susan said in her flat, sensible way. "Real gypsies would say it was your fate that you couldn't escape, come what may. Your destiny."

Anthea looked furious. She tapped her black patent shoe on the wooden boards of the amusement arcade. Her shoes had small heels, I noticed, heels that my mother would have considered flighty for a girl of thirteen or fourteen.

"You don't know anything, anyway, Susan whatever your name is," she said eventually and stalked off on her own. We caught up with her and walked to the end of the pier, past the fishermen with their lines and bait and the candy floss sellers doing little business.

"We could buy some chips," I said, smelling from somewhere that sweet mix of vinegar and salt and hot fat and thinking how my mother would never buy me chips in the middle of the afternoon. It seemed too good an opportunity to miss. But Eva, of course, had a better idea.

"No, we'll go and find a Wimpy," she said, "or even an Old Kentucky. There's bound to be one near here. Susan doesn't want to eat chips on her day away from the shop, do you?"

Anthea seemed on the point of protesting about Brighton boutiques again, but she gave in rather sulkily and followed the three of us, keeping at a bit of a distance as if she wanted people to think she wasn't really with us.

In our Wimpy Bar booth, we waited for our food. Susan had only ordered a banana milkshake.

"If it's the cost, I'll pay for it, Susan," said Anthea in a deliberate and loud voice, causing Susan to glare at her.

"Or I could lend you some money," said Eva. "My ma always gives me emergency money when I go out so I could give you some of that and you could pay me back."

Susan turned her attention to the tomato-shaped ketchup bottle on our table, lined up the salt and pepper pots.

"I'm not hungry, thank you. I don't need anything to eat."

"Suit yourself," said Anthea and took out a small mirror and comb from her shoulder bag and stared at herself.

"You can have some of my food," I said to her quietly, knowing I would have to eat again when I got home. My mother considered eating out was something done from necessity rather than choice so I would be keeping my Wimpy a secret and eating my usual tea later.

"It's all right," Susan said fiercely and made the sugar dispenser spin off its axis across the table towards me. "It's not the money. I'm having exactly what I want."

We were silent. I traced spilled sugar with my fingertip into small pools. Eva borrowed Anthea's comb. Anthea stared at a group of boys sitting at the next table. I even caught her smiling at one of them. Our orders arrived. Susan sipped slowly from her tall glass of bright yellow milkshake as if to make it last longer than our food. Anthea pecked away at her Frankfurter Bender.

"So," she said, pushing her plate away as if appetite had suddenly deserted her. "What's it like at your school? I mean, you're the very first people I've ever met from Churchill Secondary Modern." She pronounced the name of our school as if it was some institution for deranged convicts. Eva kindly barged in.

"It's much better than our place. Much more fun. More normal."

"It's all right, actually," I said, feeling a sudden surge of loyalty to Churchill County Secondary that surprised me. "It's good, isn't it Susan? Some of the teachers are a bit strict, but then that's the same everywhere, isn't it?"

"And if you get 5 O levels, you can go on to the grammar school when you're sixteen," Susan said. "Or to the college. That's if you want to."

Anthea stared hard at Susan.

"So what are you going to do when you leave? What are your career plans? Run the fish and chip shop with your mum? Get behind the deep fat fryer with your dad?"

Eva kicked me under the table, managing to kick Anthea at the same time in the narrow booth.

"What's the matter? Have I said something wrong?" Anthea said loudly, her large pale blue eyes staring round at us.

"There's no dad. Just my mum and grandparents," Susan said and went on noisily sucking at her banana milkshake through a straw that had become clogged.

"You must have a dad," Anthea went on relentlessly, "even if he doesn't live with you. Even if they got divorced or he's dead or something."

"Maybe Susan doesn't want to tell us," I said, "maybe it's just nothing to do with us and it's very rude of people to ask questions about it." Of course both Eva and I were really longing to know. It was exactly the question I'd wanted answering ever since I'd known about Susan's family, but had always been too embarrassed to ask. And although I disliked Anthea even more for provoking poor Susan, I was secretly grateful for her insistence. Eva, Anthea and I turned to look at her.

"My mum didn't like him, that's all," Susan said, "she didn't like the man who was my dad. You can't end up with someone you don't like, can you?"

Even Anthea couldn't think of anything to say. I saw her start to form sentences which eventually resolved only into a weak sort of 'oh'. Eva was bolder.

"So she knew she was expecting you when she wasn't married to your dad and then she decided not to marry him?"

Susan shrugged as if the whole conversation was tedious. She looked at her watch and started to do up the buttons of her school gabardine mackintosh.

"But don't you mind?" I said, determined to make the most of this conversation in case I never had the courage to return to it again. "I mean it must be so peculiar not to have a father. When everyone else does."

"Not everyone," said Susan wearily as if I had not been listening to her.

"Everyone we know," said Anthea. "And your mum could have always married your dad and then got rid of him, divorced him afterwards if she didn't like him."

"What would have been the point of that?" Susan said reasonably.

"Or maybe your mum would have found that he wasn't quite so bad once she'd married him," said Eva, "she might have got used to him. And then at least she'd have had a husband."

"And you'd have had a father," I added. Susan said nothing. She looked steadily at the three of us, huddled in our booth with the remnants of our Wimpys and chips and ketchup congealing on white plates on the Formica table top. Suddenly, she seemed far older than me. Far older even than Anthea with her red trouser suit and white shoulder bag and her pony back home in its paddock.

"I need to catch the bus home," she said steadily. "We open at six. And there's always a queue on a Saturday night. Anyone coming?"

We pooled our shillings and sixpences and threepenny bits to pay the bill and followed Susan out as she threaded our way along the pavement to the bus stop.

The bus back was crowded and we got separated, me and Eva downstairs squashed into one seat, Anthea upstairs and Susan standing, clinging on to the ceiling rail.

"She's nice, isn't she?" Eva said in a whisper, looking at Susan as she balanced herself between some loud football supporters who seemed to be reliving their match. "Sort of nice, anyway."

"Much nicer than Anthea," I said. Eva did her eye rolling thing.

"If it wasn't for the pony, for White Shadow and the tack room and everything, I'd never speak to her again."

★ ★ ★

Eva didn't give up on the idea of her mother having a lover to occupy her time while her father was away on his business trips. Nor would she let us forget that it was our mission to follow her and uncover their secret meeting place.

"I bet he's called Hugo," she said to me one day when we were walking home from school. "Or Leonard." I was having tea at Eva's house and she had the front door key just in case Mrs. Mason wasn't back when we got in.

"Why Leonard or Hugo? Why not Alan or... Barry?" I said.

"Don't be silly, my mother wouldn't have an affair with someone who'd got an ordinary name. It wouldn't work."

"That's just stupid. After all, it's your parents who give you your name so this lover person can't help it if his parents just gave him a dull, normal kind of name. It might well be something like... like Gary. Or Mick."

Eva looked at me with scorn.

"There's absolutely no chance of Ma having a lover called Mick. She just wouldn't even consider it."

"But she might have fallen in love with him," I persisted, "and not be able to help herself having him."

"What's love got to do with it? She's in love with my dad, isn't she? This is just for an affair. Just for... well, sexy things when he's away. Black stockings and suspenders and stuff." Eva fished the key out from her pocket and let us in. The house was quiet. In the kitchen, there was a tray with two glasses and an unopened packet of chocolate biscuits sitting on a plate. Eva ignored the tray, headed upstairs.

"Where are you going?" I wailed. I was starving. My packed lunch that day had consisted of an egg sandwich that I'd shoved in the bin when it had started smelling out the classroom before first break. I followed Eva upstairs where

I found her going through her mother's wardrobe, checking out her dressing table.

"Just searching for clues," she said, "to see what she's wearing. If she's put anything special on. Or used her expensive perfume."

I sat down on the broad double bed, fingered the pink velvet pleated headboard with its deep buttons.

"Your mother always wears expensive perfume and wears nice clothes. That's no clue at all."

"Maybe," Eva said. "In fact, perhaps you're right. She probably goes in disguise to meet him. I mean in really tatty old stuff so no-one's suspicious. She'd take the sexy stuff with her in a bag."

I was beginning to get bored. Downstairs in the kitchen, there was an entire packet of chocolate biscuits and no doubt in the fridge fresh bottles of limeade and lemonade waiting for us which seemed far more deserving of our attention. Eva dilly-dallied a bit longer, checking out her mother's bedside chest, opening the little gilt-edged drawer cautiously as if she expected to disclose something extraordinary. But there were only a few pamphlets, a newsletter from some society and a gold watch with a broken bracelet strap. We'd just made it back downstairs to the kitchen when Mrs. Mason's car swept into the drive. Eva wasn't to be defeated.

"Watch out for any signs," she hissed as her mother opened the front door, calling out to us. We heard her toss down some carrier bags and hang up her coat. "Particularly check for... well, anything unusual, really. You know the kind of thing by now."

Mrs. Mason came into the kitchen, talking away to us as she always did. She'd had her hair done and was unsure whether she liked the colour. A bit too yellow blonde, did we think? She didn't want people to know she needed a little help from the peroxide bottle these days, she said, disappearing into the downstairs cloakroom to check in the mirror. Eva kept catching my eye, but this was hardly evidence for a wild, sexy affair, since Mrs. Mason was always having her hair done.

"I thought it was one of your meeting days," Eva said with heavy sarcasm, "not the hairdresser's at all."

Her mother paused on the way to filling the kettle.

"It was both," she said. "I didn't know you were so interested in what I get up to while you're at school, darling. Meeting first with the girls then onto Miracles in Bampton although I have to say I'm beginning to think that salon is falsely named. I'm going to have to think about finding somewhere new, which is never easy. Into the frying pan and all that. Now why don't you two young ladies take yourselves off for a spot of TV to relax your brains a bit? I really can't think of supper for you until at least six. Will that be all right with your mother, Mary? I'll ring her to check if you like."

In the hall, Eva grabbed Mrs. Mason's bags and led the way into the living room, closing the door firmly and turning the television up loud. I watched the *Blue Peter* lady explain how to make a tissue box holder for Mother's Day. Eva looked through her mother's handbag then through the two carrier bags and made four neat piles on the carpet, which she had to admit were disappointing. Slowly, she replaced the birthday card for Hamish with *To Our Dear Son* in swirly gold letters, two pairs of the sort of tights Eva wore for school, a jar of nail varnish remover, some talcum powder, a tin of hair lacquer and a packet of yellow dusters. Mrs. Mason's handbag was equally dull and predictable. Her large brown suede purse, her cheque book, a couple of coloured handkerchiefs, a letter about a parents' evening at Eva's school and a booklet called *The Society for the Modern Woman*. This was equally uninspiring with a list of monthly meetings with titles such as *Working*

Woman or Wife? and *House Wife or House Slave?* and *Do we really want Equality?* Eva shoved everything back carelessly and returned it all to the hall. We could hear Mrs. Mason singing along to the radio in the kitchen then the phone rang and we scuttled quickly back to the TV and the wretched tissue box holder. After a couple of minutes, the door opened and Mrs. Mason peered round, smiling.

"Eva, that was Daddy on the phone. He was ringing from the airport in Hong Kong. He's managed to cut things short out there and he's flying home tonight. So we'll have him back with us tomorrow. Very late, of course, as he has stop-offs all over the place. But isn't that lovely? Just as well I had my hair done today, girls, it's always important to look your best for your man, you remember that!"

And with a little giggle, she went back to the kitchen and turned the radio up again. We heard her singing along with Petula Clarke going *Downtown.* I looked at Eva. She looked at me. Then she leant forward to the television set and changed channels.

"*Magpie,*" she said, "let's have *Magpie.* It's much better than *Blue Peter,* you know."

Eva's obsession with her mother's adulterous affair was, thankfully, over.

10

he's decided to spend the morning in bed, the nurse says to me brightly when she greets me at the door. *She's having a bit of a lie-in,* says the care worker who fluffs her pillows and brings her tea. It's a clear, mild day and I'd hoped to take her out. It's growing increasingly awkward to shift her into my car, reassemble her into her chair after a short drive. So I've taken to wheeling her into the local village which is kind enough to provide a tea shop, a florist and a gift shop selling a bewildering array of pot pourri and scented candles and lavender bags. They're getting to know us in the tea shop.

"Will it be the toasted tea cake and a pot for two?" And they help me negotiate the tables and tuck her wheelchair into a quiet corner.

"Nice," Ida always says, "nice." And she looks at the jars of homemade preserves stacked on the shelves, jams and jellies and lemon curd and pickles and chutneys and says, "Busy. Someone's… someone's been… yes, busy. Nice."

Usually, we sit for so long, filling the slow minutes of an hour over a pot of tea, one solitary tea cake between us, that I feel obliged to buy something. Now my kitchen cupboard contains more jam than I shall ever use and I've switched to leaving a generous tip. But today, Ida has decided to stay in bed and I feel foolishly thwarted of an outing.

I hardly remember her being ill when I was young. Other people got flu and bad colds and had bilious attacks and laryngitis, but my mother seemed faintly disparaging about such weaknesses. Perhaps now her body is giving in after years of repressing disease. Her bones, her muscles, her limbs seem to be allowing a disintegration to seep swiftly through her as if tired of keeping illness at bay. Whereas Jack, always prone to bronchitis and chronic coughs in the past, weaknesses from his early TB, now seems relatively robust, untouched by little more than slight arthritis in one knee.

"I'm thinking of asking Dad to stay for a few days," I say, as Ida smooths the edge of her blanket over and over with her thumb. "It's always hard to drag him away from his garden, but I think the change would do him good. Some company, especially." She smiles at me, turns to look out of the window. There's a magnolia tree that's just come into bloom in the middle of the lawn. Ida points to it then lets her hand drift to the curtain instead. In truth, I'm feeling guilty for not having Jack earlier over Easter. He's an easy guest, happy to sit reading the newspaper, ponder over his crosswords, but our house always seems a little hectic for him and I think we puzzle him. I am not as orderly, no doubt, as he would expect, as he has been used to with Ida. Mealtimes tend to be irregular and I work variable hours that he cannot quite understand.

"This teaching you do these days," he says, time and time again, "it's not like in a school, is it? Not like you used to do." And I have to explain about the adult education centre where I work and the classes in cold halls and badly lit meeting rooms. Remind him again how I moved on from teaching infants a long, long time ago. Nowadays, it's literacy and basic English skills, an adult literature course and the catch-up examination classes for people suddenly discovering a need for a qualification. Even so, I know Jack always enjoys being with Felix, likes to talk football with him, cricket, rugby, and the companionship makes a break from his solitary days.

"Yes," I say firmly to Ida, as if assertion will make me firm to my word, "I'm going to ring him tonight and suggest he comes next weekend. Perhaps the weather will be good enough to sit in the garden. It's about time it warmed up." I get up, open the window a little as if to prove my point, but really, it's to ease the stale smell of the room, the bed, the sheets. The faint suspicion of urine. I continue with endless pointless chatter for half an hour until Ida seems restless, tries to get out of bed. I help her to the chair, wonder whether I am expected to try to dress her and know I am feebly inadequate to the task. It is years since I have seen my mother without clothes and the prospect appals me. I am partly ashamed of my scruples, but mostly accommodated to them. Give me babies any day. Give me small children, messy and helpless and utterly vulnerable and I will envelop their new, fresh limbs with love and affection. I have wiped many a running nose as an infants' teacher, dealt with the tears and inevitable accidents found in small, sodden pants in the Reception class. But Ida, sitting shrunken and hesitant in her chair, her body like a discarded chrysalis, is beyond me. I am both too moved and too remote to help. The door opens abruptly and I greet the care worker with absurd alacrity.

"Well, up at last! We'll soon have you dressed and fit for company, won't we?" She ushers me out of the room and I gratefully follow her lead. There's a text message from Felix. Something about an invitation, but his abbreviations elude me and I ring his mobile instead. He's been invited for a sleep-over at his close friend Ollie's house, he tells me, can he stay on, come home in the morning? Yes, I tell him, that's fine. Yes, of course. There's still a few days until the end of the school holidays when order and some attempt at reasonable hours have to resume so there's no problem. See you tomorrow morning, I tell him, arrange a pickup for ten as we both have the dentist at eleven.

Ida's sitting in the chair by her bed when I go back in. She's wearing a bright pink sweater and grey baggy trousers that expose very white ankles. Again, in spite of painstaking care with name tags, she is wearing someone else's clothes. Still, she is neat and clean, her hair is clearly brushed and she's even wearing large clip earrings that the care worker has found in a drawer. I am certain they are not hers.

"You are looking smart," I say and take her hand. She wears her wedding ring still and her engagement ring sits in a box in a dressing table drawer. She was never a woman to wear jewellery beyond a single string of fake pearls and a tortoiseshell necklace that Jack bought her for her fiftieth birthday. As a small girl there was little for me to dress up in beyond a pair of high-heeled patent shoes long discarded at the bottom of her wardrobe and a red felt hat with a black veil that she'd bought for a wedding before I was born. I'd envied friends who had mothers with net petticoats and sleek black evening gowns stowed in old trunks. She looks at my hand now, my fingers wearing a couple of silver rings and a large blue turquoise stone.

"Married him, did you?" she says, "you… no, I've forgotten. So long ago." She smiles as if resigned to her memory loss and almost amused by it. "Better not to… he was… the right one."

"David?" I grapple. "Felix's father, you mean. Yes, he's a nice man. A kind man. You always liked David, didn't you?"

"Always liked David," she echoes. It is her easiest, most fluent form of speech these days. Repeating the phrase I've said, even the inflection. Like a very young child learning to speak by imitation, repetition. Except that Ida is at the other end of the spectrum, clutching at speech before it eludes her entirely.

"It will be lunch soon," I say inanely. "What do you think you're having for lunch today?"

She ignores me and I am grateful that she still has the capacity to judge evasiveness when she hears it.

"The house," she says, "it was… the house. The big house."

"Number 8? Yes, it was a big house. How many rooms did it have? Shall we count?"

We go through the rooms. Or rather, I begin to list them and Ida nods and smiles. The hall, the big basement kitchen, the living room that was too large ever to heat adequately. It had two fireplaces that Jack would occasionally attempt to light. At Christmas time, perhaps, or on particularly bleak winter days when he and I might go down to the beach, gather some kindling and come back and try to chivvy the fires into catching. The smell of wood smoke and burnt paper would linger pleasantly for days, filter into the rest of the house, although only effectively offer warmth if we sat inches from the flames. Ida always considered our efforts futile.

"There's the electric," she'd say, chasing black soot and spots from the mantelpiece, chivvying stray sparks from the rug. "The electric does the job far better. You've more time than sense, you two," she'd say, as we tried to starve the flames of air with a sheet of newspaper, blow encouragingly at the wilting embers. She smiles now as I nudge her memory, remind her of our efforts, praise her for being the sensible one although for me those struggling wood fires that my father and I tended are inexplicably significant. Why is it that ordinary, ostensibly commonplace events take on an importance in recall? As if, in fact, what we cherish in retrospect is the mundane rather than the extraordinary. My father, Jack, and me, twelve or thirteen or fourteen-year-old Mary, taking ourselves off to the beach on a particularly desolate day in winter, gathering driftwood that no doubt splintered into our numb fingers, carrying armfuls back and carefully, cautiously placing sticks onto our burgeoning, tentative fire suddenly seems an occasion loaded with joy. Yet at the time, I no doubt moaned about the cold, about the awkwardness of holding onto the damp driftwood, about the smoke in my eyes as the kindle tried to catch the flame. Sitting here now with Ida, sifting the past for incidents that are devoid of treachery, of betrayal, it seems there is a rich store of simple memories that are clearly clogged with love. With easy, familial affection. I have to remind myself of that.

The attic room at 8, Sea View Parade never lost its smell of oils, paints, pastels. At least to me. Even when Mr. Jarvis was gone, his possessions boxed up and dispatched, the room still held onto him, as if he refused entirely to leave. Certainly, there was no thought of me reclaiming it. For a while, it became a dumping ground, a place where things were put when there seemed nowhere else for them to go. A rarely used picnic hamper with fiddly plastic straps and plastic cutlery that broke instantly on use. My scratched school satchel, a hockey stick, my junior tennis racquet in its wooden press. Then the bed and breakfasts started. And Ida, apparently re-energised, recovered from that appalling interlude of apathy, had the attic cleared for twin divans, bedside tables and a Teasmade. I had taken little interest. Desperate only to get away, I began flicking through college prospectuses, determined to put distance between me and my parents that would, I convinced myself, offer another life entirely undefined by the events of recent years. Cardiff, possibly, Leeds or Leicester, or even Hull would do the job. At the age of seventeen or eighteen, I was so sure that getting away was easy, a mere matter of geography, as if county boundaries somehow conveniently removed what one no longer wished to confront.

There's no reason for me to drive straight home. Felix is at Ollie's house and a quick phone call to his mother, Rose, confirms he's to stay the night. Unusually, I am entirely free. I leave Ida to her cottage pie lunch, kiss her twice, promise to see her very soon and drive out of the care home's car park. I think of calling in on my father, Jack, just a few miles away, but instead, I drive south, take the road towards the coast, pulled inevitably to the direction of Sea View Parade after my morning with Ida. The traffic's heavy and the road is slow. There are too many roundabouts and only brief stretches of dual carriageway so that I get stuck behind vans and container lorries heading for channel ports. I've been back before since they left, but only once and then I was not alone. Driving with a friend to Brighton a few years ago, I asked him to take a detour and he obligingly drove me past. We'd hovered for some moments while I took in the changed façade of the place in silence and he'd asked swiftly and with only partially concealed irritation if I'd had enough. Other people's pasts are like their dreams recounted, tedious and desperately self-indulgent. I'd waved him on, feigning indifference to the house, to any sense of turbulent feeling it might hold, yet I'd begrudged the man's curtness. It had not been a good start to the day out and our friendship had dwindled swiftly.

But today I can be as sentimental as I choose. I have no need to pretend and when I eventually turn into Sea View Parade, I feel a sense of anticipation, as if this return visit is long overdue. There is nowhere to park. One side of the street is reserved for residents. *Residents' Parking Bays*, the sign says, *Between the Hours of 8am and 10pm*. The other side of the road is meter controlled and all are occupied. I drive on and belligerently park on a single yellow line outside the entrance to the parish hall. Except that it's gone, that pebbledash squat building that used to be at the end of the parade. The home of the Brownies followed by the Cubs on a Thursday evening, Whist Club on Wednesdays, Girl Guides Fridays and where Ida played the piano for the beginners' ballet classes. In its place, there's a very large detached, belligerently ostentatious house, mock Grecian columns, elaborate gates, an attempt at topiary, a sweeping driveway with a handful of parked cars. As I sit staring disparagingly, a man comes out of the house and gets into one of the cars, revs the engine while he waits for the roof to retract, the gates to open on his cue. I see him spot me in his driver's mirror, glance several times with suspicion. Once he's gone, I get out, leave my car on its illicit single yellow line and walk back towards Number 8.

Sea View Parade is now smart, clearly affluent, immaculate, in fact, each house painted in discreetly fashionable shades. The right kind of cream, of taupe, stone, porcelain or old white, as if the owners have completed some kind of interior design course before being permitted to purchase and decorate. There are no old mangles in the gracious front gardens. Not even a spontaneous weed or dandelion encroaches on the carefully landscaped rectangles that lie behind wrought-iron fencing. Burglar alarms are blatantly visible. Sea View Parade is now desirable, no doubt about it. And I ache to think that Ida was partially right in what she said about these houses all those years ago. Victorian and Edwardian homes had far more market longevity, potential esteem and value than the shiny modern boxes frantically thrown up and temporarily desired. Like some celebrity of transitory fame or regard. Like Eva's uncompromisingly square red-brick, Lego-like house that I'd so envied. In truth, the required renovation of Number 8 never really took place. My father, Jack, did his best, fixing things, refurbishing things piecemeal style. He painted walls and ceilings, filled in mouse holes in the skirting boards, saw to the dado rails, mended leaks, sealed draughty windows. But it wasn't like the serious renovation jobs they do these days with their formal planning applications and hired architects and project managers. He and Ida didn't know about tasteful sanded bare floorboards and minimalist white walls and subdued downlighters and kitchen islands and integrated appliances and ceramic floor tiles. But then no-one did. Or at least not ordinary people like us back then. We were still crawling our way through the 20th century, gratified to have moved well past the halfway point without encountering another world war to be excessively aspirational, and home improvements seemed limited to a dozen or so paint shades on the Dulux card. The 1960s was wild and psychedelic for the selected few, but for most of us the tentacles of the 50s still had us in a firm, tedious and repressive hold. And although the last twenty years of the century managed to shift most of us into avid consumers and spenders as if material affluence had suddenly become our birthright, my parents, Ida and Jack, remained impervious. Post-war austerity and a make and mend attitude still triumphed as if they chose to inhabit some kind of time capsule carefully set down for posterity's enlightenment.

Number 8 looks silent, unoccupied. There are drawn shutters at the front windows and upstairs blinds or curtains are pulled across. The front door is painted the palest of pale mushroom and a pair of miniature potted bay trees sits either side of the narrow path, like custodians. I am surprised by the nostalgia I feel, conspicuously standing outside on the pavement and peering through the high gate towards the house. After all, it's not as if I am returning to some site of unalloyed happiness; rather, a place, an address that has always attached to itself matter too potent to examine. So I turn away hastily, cross the road and walk briskly towards Beach Parade, sea gusts, threatening rain, biting into my face, nipping my fingers.

The shops are gone. Those few shops where Eva and I wasted endless time have entirely disappeared. In fact, the whole parade is so remodelled that it's hard to imagine

Beaumont's and Ball's, the chemist, the newsagent's, the grocer's and the Black Boy pub. In their place are an assortment of three-storey apartments, a nail parlour, a hairdresser's and a small gym called Breezes. Through smoked glass I watch people on treadmills, aping cycling, running, striding, intense faces mostly transfixed on a large screen showing west coast surfers and pop videos. I stare in for a while until someone catches my eye and I move on guiltily as if caught at a peep show. Across the road, things are far more familiar, seemingly rooted in time past, for the benches are still there. Or possibly they're different benches, but still assuming their same positions, staring out to sea, spaced thirty feet or so apart, all along the seafront. Today they're deserted, the gym and the nail parlour, the hair stylist, perhaps, favoured in their place. I sit down, feeling unprepared without a newspaper, a bag of sandwiches, a book to occupy me and the overcast day hardly justifies sun-seeking. Once he'd retired, Jack came here most mornings with his newspaper, he told me. *Out from under your mother's feet,* he used to say, *important still to have a bit of a routine, you know. What with your mother being so busy with the house.* For Ida had the bed and breakfasts to see to, the full English to prepare, sheets to wash and iron, rooms to clean. Or so she claimed. For although they never complained of lack of business, I knew that the popularity of Number 8 shrank rapidly over the years as people's standards sharpened and they began demanding something more than Ida and Jack knew how to provide. Ida, in particular, was unprepared to service her guests with more than she considered adequate and that did not include private bathrooms, breakfast muesli and duck down duvets. Gradually, Number 8 was overlooked in favour of places more alert to the changing times.

There are white horses as far as the line of the horizon and a seagull swoops low then dives under the waves. Another lands on the railings in front of me then squawks and flies away. Eva and I sat here the night before I went off to college. She was wearing a very short white skirt and a tight black ribbed sleeveless sweater that made her small breasts look larger. I was wearing my long blue floral Laura Ashley skirt that dragged on the ground so that the hem was ingrained with dirt. (At least I think I was – it's the skirt in the photograph that Jack took the day I left and I associate it with the summers of 1973 and 4 and 5 and more.) Eva had already completed her year's secretarial course at her prim college in Kensington. We had hardly met all year, a brief and rather embarrassed exchange of token gifts on Christmas Eve and a couple of letters being the extent of our communication beyond one weekend visit. She seemed so different, so grown up, and I was aware of the distance between us now, but was too naïve to know how to broach it.

"Do you want me to come and visit?" Eva said, pulling her tight white skirt down a little so that it covered her thighs more convincingly. She had returned from London with her hair cut very short. It encircled her face, gamin-like, emphasising her neat features, her large pearl blue eyes. I felt I hardly knew her any more.

"If you like," I said coolly, wondering what she wanted me to say. "It's not that far, you know." After all my talk of heading to remote regions, I'd cowardly settled on a teacher's training college near Oxford. Oxford, after all, sounded impressive and I'd heard it was, geographically, about as far as you could ever possibly get from the sea, which illogically made me feel suitably removed from my parents' conflicted lives. "You could sleep on the floor of my room," I went on cautiously. "I've got a room in a Hall. That's just if you want to."

Eva said nothing for a while, scrambling around in her bag for a packet of cigarettes instead. She lit one and blew the smoke out in an extravagant long train.

"Actually, I won't be around for a year or so. I'm going to be an au pair for a while. At least that's what Ma has in mind for me. She thinks I ought to go off to France or Switzerland or somewhere and improve my French before I get a proper job."

"Do you want to go?" I asked, surprised. "You always hated French lessons at school and you were always hopeless, you said."

Eva shrugged, puffed again and flicked ash unintentionally onto my skirt. She made a fuss of brushing it away.

"I don't mind. Might be better than being in some secretarial pool and stuck behind a typewriter all day long. Maybe if I get really good at French, I could be a bilingual secretary rather than a dull, ordinary one and get lots of fun trips abroad." She sounded unconvinced, as if she were repeating words someone else had said to her. Words that her mother, Jean Mason, had said to her, no doubt. She stood up, unhooked her sling back sandals, tossed them aside and went down the steps onto the beach. She selected several pebbles and threw them slowly, one by one, into the waves, each reaching a little further into the sea.

Eva did come to see me at college, but just once, in my final year, during that long hot summer of 1976. After endless wet, bleak summers endured at Sea View Parade when the beach was best avoided and Bampton library my main refuge, real heat had finally arrived. And with it, the unfamiliarity of parched flower beds, scorched fields, early mornings heavy and thick with heat haze. Eva was back from her au pairing and morose about the prospect of signing on at temping agencies or finding a permanent job. She seemed restless, not particularly happy, although she easily drew attention from the male students whom she treated casually, even disparagingly. We went to the college disco and sweated in the steamy union building, our bodies pressed too close to others as we pounded our way through the music. She got very drunk on cider and vinegary cheap white wine and spent the night on the bathroom floor at the end of the corridor in my Hall. The next day we joined some others for a picnic by the river, trying to find shade in the long grass under the trees. Eva took her short skirt off and waded into the water up to her thighs in her purple bikini underpants and yellow t-shirt. I remember being grateful for her behaviour. I had been a very dull and biddable student by the standard of the day and Eva's fleeting visit did a little something to repair my reputation, as if I could be considered decadent and louche by association. My three college years had been something of a failure. Not in academic terms, but in my expectation of how I saw myself behaving, the construct of the person I planned to inhabit. After all, others had seemed to shake off their background so effortlessly. I had watched them the first few weeks of that bewildering first term, clearly forging new selves like former criminals adopting new identities. Actors role-playing characters prone to dissipation. But I had found myself so painfully shy, tiptoeing around, craving invisibility as if, suddenly, even basic social skills eluded me. And, perversely, I had been homesick. Not for the company of my parents or 8, Sea View Parade and the constant shrill of seagulls in particular, but for the seclusion and anonymity that the place seemed to allow. So little seemed to be asked of me there beyond quiet conformity. Here, suddenly, there was an obligation for behaviour far more flagrant and deliberate and I was too timid to indulge in it. Too frightened of the consequences. It was easy to blame Ida and Jack for my reticence, seeing it as an inevitable outcome of my mother's actions, my father's passivity. And I did blame them, of course, for it was the obvious thing to do, to excuse my own inadequacy. I retreated into my work, my neatly compiled notes and laboriously written essays and was not unhappy. In fact, I seem to have existed in a kind of limbo during my student years that was neither particularly painful nor ecstatic in the least, but merely a safe place that accommodated my books, my uncertain self. In the holidays, I had avoided going home, finding myself jobs ten miles away in the city itself, cleaning the colleges, waitressing in cafés, spending most of my wages on cheap rents of vacated student lodgings that unscrupulous landlords were subletting. Ida and Jack drove up once a term to see me, visits which seemed to take on the tone of obligation on both sides. They took me out to lunch at a pub in winter, offered a picnic of ham sandwiches in summer months. Ida would bring slabs of her dry almond Madeira cake wrapped in thin foil, those rock buns, and packets of Knorr dried soup, occasionally a tin of corned beef, that were supposed to supplement my student diet for the next few weeks. I talked to them mechanically about my course, my teaching practice in the infants' school, my friend, Felicity, who'd just got engaged. I was polite enough to them, pleasant enough, I thought, but knew that my father, Jack, was bewildered by my remote manner. My studied distance. Or perhaps he understood and accepted that it was the only way that the three of us, given what we all knew by then, could carry on.

I am stiff from sitting too long on the bench and walk briskly further down the seafront before turning around to retrace my steps. I'm not wearing clothes appropriate for a seafront walk and besides, I've had enough of the place, want to shake it off, get back in the car and drive home. Suddenly, the prospect of my quiet house, my pictures on the wall, Felix's untidy trainers on the floor, his unwashed dishes, is essential. But before I leave, I stand outside Number 8 for several minutes, inspecting the sash windows, the pristine repointed brick work, that pale mushroom paint, inviting attention as if craving to be asked inside. No-one takes any notice, of course. For no-one is the slightest bit interested in this middle-aged woman whose family lived here for a brief period in somewhat unusual domestic circumstances. It's a story of intense importance and significance to me: of utter, tawdry irrelevance to anyone else. At the end of the parade, just beyond where I have parked, I see someone approaching slowly, inspecting windscreen permits. I turn away from the house and break into a sprint along the pavement to rescue my car from the advancing traffic warden.

11

Eva decided she wanted to be an actress.

I am nearly fifteen, Eva is four months away from sixteen. Fourth Year and Fifth Year of secondary school respectively. We are still inseparable.

"I'm going to RADA," she said, setting up the ironing board in the kitchen and switching the iron on to 'steam'. "After I've left school, I'm going there and you learn how to be an actress. Then you get an agent and go on the stage."

"When did you decide that, to be an actress?" I asked, releasing my hair from its pony tail. I was about to undergo Eva's attempts to straighten its kinks and waves with a hot iron. Hers, of course, ramrod straight, even in humid conditions, required no such treatment.

"I've had it at the back of my mind for ages. Then there was a careers thing at school. Didn't you do one at your place? We had to fill in stupid, long forms and tick boxes and it turns out I ought to be an actress. Or something like that."

I lifted sections of my hair onto the board and let Eva cover it with a tea towel.

"It won't singe, will it?" Meg or Amy or possibly even Beth March before she died swiftly came to mind. *Little Women* had warned me about the dangers of burnt hair. Eva pressed firmly with the iron, steam spluttered and hissed.

"So I'm auditioning for the boys' school play this term. To get experience, you see. And you're going to as well. To keep me company. It'll be something for us to do on Friday nights because that's when they rehearse."

Eva lifted the towel. I inspected the strands of my hair, impressed. I shifted round, offered the other side a little more confidently.

"But I can't act," I said. "I'm hopeless at that kind of thing. And I won't be allowed because it's not for people at the secondary modern. It's for pupils from your place and Bampton Girls High. They're the ones who are always in the boys' school plays."

"No-one ever asks where people come from," Eva said, "and, anyway, you can pretend. Just come along with me after school one day to the audition and I'll put your name down next to mine and if anyone asks, we'll say we didn't know."

Eva released another section of hair. I was beginning to smell a bit like damp tea towels left on a radiator to dry.

"But I don't want to be an actress so there's no need for me to be in a play," I protested. "And I'd be too shy."

"Just a small, itsy bitsy part, that's what I'm talking about, Mary," Eva said, "hardly any lines to learn. The girls at the high school and my place only want the big parts so you'll have no competition. They'll welcome someone who just wants to be in the crowd, believe you me. We could ask Susan as well, if you like."

"I don't know," I said, running my fingers down the unfamiliar straight and sleek lines of my ironed hair. "I don't know if my mother would let me. I mean I have to work really hard now because of exams and stuff and I want to get enough passes so I can transfer to the sixth form later on." My mother seemed to have been impressed by my school report and satisfactory exam results at the end of the summer term. *You'll be able to transfer to the Grammar for the sixth form at this rate,* she'd told me. *It'll be A levels for you, Mary,* she'd said, as if the prospect was an unavoidable, bleak fate, *and a proper qualification of some kind. Providing you keep on the way you're going.* I was sure she would view a school play as a worrying distraction. Eva, however, was insistent.

"All that O level business is years away for you. Well, at least one year away. And, anyway, this boys' school play is really educational. It's Shakespeare, Mary, your mother's bound to like the idea of that."

"Perhaps I could be the prompt," I said, spying a get-out to performing.

"There's no fun in that," Eva said dismissively, "just sitting in a corner all the time. Although it might suit Susan, of course. More her sort of thing, in fact. But you want to dress up, don't you?"

I'd not thought about it until that moment. I'd never considered being in a play, not since I'd been a stable ass in the nativity play at my primary school. But Eva was persuasive as always. Besides, if Friday nights were occupied with rehearsals at the boys' school, it would dissuade her from her latest idea of wanting us to go to the local youth club discos. That was a far more alarming prospect. I'd been twice and had spent most of the evening hiding in the girls' toilets, claiming stomach problems to avoid anyone getting the chance to ask me to dance. Eva had danced all evening then spent the next day scorning the boys and their damp, sweaty hands and hopeless attempts to kiss.

"I'll ask my mother," I said. "I'll have to ask her first, you know that. You know what she's like."

Miss Mackie happened to hear. She was in the kitchen, spreading Bovril on toast for her tea. She'd just come back from a two-day coach trip to Bath with a friend of hers from the hospital and my mother seemed irritated by her insistence on describing the Pump Rooms and relating her fantasy about

Anne Elliot walking down Milsom Street and bumping into Captain Wentworth.

"*A Midsummer Night's Dream*, Mary! Well, that is splendid!" she said, waving a Bovril-smeared knife in the air in excitement. "And you will be playing… no, let me guess. Helena? Hermia?"

"Only a fairy," I said, "and not THE fairy, the one who does all that stuff with Puck. Just an ordinary one who flits around in the background. And that's even if I'm chosen. There's auditions and things, you know, and the high school girls get picked first."

Miss Mackie cut her small square of toast into four pieces then into four more. My mother poured tea, pushed a cup towards me across the kitchen table.

"But there'll be rehearsals," she said, "it will mean some late nights, I expect. And then you'll start neglecting your homework, Mary. I know what these things lead to, you know."

"Mrs. Foster," Miss Mackie said, "this is Shakespeare. Shakespeare!" She almost shouted the word and then turned pink and stared down at her plate of toast. My mother coughed.

"All I'm saying, Mary," she said, "is that you have to sort out your priorities. I'm sure a bit of acting, Shakespeare acting, that is, at the boys' school will do no harm. No harm at all. Just as long as you keep your long-term goals in mind. Wouldn't you agree, Miss Mackie?"

Miss Mackie beamed at both of us. A slant of sudden, late afternoon sunlight managed to penetrate the basement kitchen window, catching her face so that she looked almost illuminated. I hadn't realised quite how many lines managed to cram their way onto her small, pointed face.

"You are such a sensible woman, Mrs. Foster," she said, "so sensible. That would be my advice entirely. It's the long-term goals that count, Mary, at the end of the day."

Eva got the part of Titania. The high school girls who auditioned were awkward and lumpy next to her so even though she fluffed her lines a bit and didn't really understand her speech as she hadn't read the play, there was little contest. I got attendant/fairy/servant and we dragged Susan in as prompt. No-one else had offered and Susan didn't object. Besides, as Eva said, it was an excuse for her to spend more time away from the fish and chip shop and the temptation of all that batter. We rehearsed once a week on Friday nights until Christmas then on Tuesdays after school as well as our March performances got closer. The boys' school was large with a bewildering number of corridors that we enjoyed losing our way around, turning up in science labs and changing rooms that all smelled very unlike my school, a smell that was distinctly boys mixed in with old wood floors and dusty books and meat stew. I had hardly anything to do and only a couple of lines like, *"Here, master,"* and *"Your majesty,"* and things they'd added so they could include more girls in the cast. There were eight of us attendants altogether, cluttering up the stage rather pointlessly, but giving the mainly male cast more fodder for flirting. The director was a terrifyingly tall and assured sixth form boy who looked at least thirty-five. He was called Gerald Hetherington and everyone knew he was brilliant and was probably going to Cambridge University. I avoided him at all times and even Eva seemed wary of him.

"I don't understand what he's talking about most of the time," she said to me in a break from one rehearsal when he'd made her do her scene with Oberon in mime instead of words. "He's scary. How come he knows so much when he's only a couple of years older than me?"

Susan unscrewed her thermos flask that she always brought to rehearsals. The prompt corner at the side of the stage was distinctly draughty.

"An old head on young shoulders, my gran would say. I expect he'll be famous when he's older and we'll be proud to know we knew him."

"But we don't know him," I said, "or at least he certainly doesn't know us. He called me Servant 2 just now. He doesn't even bother to learn our names."

"Anyway, he's not very good-looking," Eva said, swigging from her bottle of Tizer. "If you're going to be famous you have to be nice to look at as well."

Susan popped two white sugar lumps into her tea.

"No, you don't," she said, "that's a silly thing to say. Think of… think of Picasso. And Winston Churchill. And Alexander Fleming."

"Who?" said Eva, pulling away the bottle from her mouth too swiftly so that Tizer dribbled down her chin onto her white blouse, an orange marmalade stain the shape of a question mark that seemed larger than her original gulp.

"Penicillin," said Susan. "He discovered it. You must know that."

Eva shrugged.

"Possibly," she said. "Or possibly not. Who cares?"

"You do when you get ill and need antibiotics. Then you care." Susan stuck the stopper back into her thermos flask, replaced it in her duffle bag. It struck me suddenly that Susan was quite clever herself. She was in all the top streams for subjects at school and teachers were always reading out her work as examples of how things should be done. But I'd never really thought of her as clever because she was so quiet. And, of course, really rather plain and pasty-faced and large and so the sort of person most people chose to overlook. Eva fumbled for her comb in the bottom of her bag and found her lipstick there too.

"Now Lysander's a different matter, girls," she said in a loud whisper and indicated with her eyes across the hall to where a group from the boys' school were gathered around the radiator. They seemed to be making an awful lot of noise for three boys, laughing very loudly and throwing bits of screwed up paper at each other. "Steven Milligan is extremely handsome. And not at all scary. What do you think, Mary? Shall we go over and talk to him?"

"You can if you like," I said, darting a surreptitious look over my shoulder at Lysander, tall and skinny with fair hair flopping over his eyes and curling up on his collar. "He wouldn't even know who I am. At least you can introduce yourself as Titania which makes you important. He's got to get to know you."

"I'm not going on my own. That would look so obvious. So horribly obvious that we all fancy him," Eva said and sat down cross-legged on the floor of the hall.

"Speak for the two of you, I wouldn't have him for breakfast," Susan said, finding her prompt copy of the play and heading back to her quiet corner. "You'll have to be quick, anyway. Looks as though the director's about to call everyone for Act 3."

Gerald Hetherington coughed very loudly and clapped his hands, the way our headmaster did when everyone was talking in assembly. Lysander and Oberon and Puck stopped chucking their bits of paper at each other and headed towards the stage. As he passed us, Lysander looked in Eva's direction and Eva, flicking her hair over her shoulder, gazed back.

Eva was a slow learner. As the performance dates grew close, she spent more time than ever at my house, insisting I take her through each of her scenes.

"If you're going to be an actress, you'll have to get better at learning lines," I complained, tired of testing her on the same speech. She was lying on the floor of my bedroom, on Sunday afternoon, staring at the cracked ceiling as if expecting to see the words inscribed there. She passed me a tube of Polos.

"It doesn't mean anything, that's the trouble, Shakespeare doesn't make sense," she said. "It's like learning Polish or Dutch or something."

"No, it's not. It's just different sorts of words making sense. Poetic kinds of words."

"You sound as bad as Gerald, our amazingly ugly director," Eva said, "all that stuff he goes on about. Or you're like our English teacher at school talking about figures or something."

"Figurative language," I said, "but you do that in English and you'll have to do it for O level so you must understand it."

Eva pulled a face. She rolled over onto her stomach and did a head stand against the wall, slowly stretching her legs and toes until they reached nearly to the dado rail. She had on odd ankle socks, one pink and one pale blue, which would have looked careless on me, but managed to look specially selected on her.

"Who cares?" she said. "When I'm an actress I'm only going to do plays and films written in proper English. Modern English. Then I'll have no trouble learning the words, you'll see."

But I was finding it easy. Not that I had more than ten words to learn, but I was picking up Eva's speeches simply by listening to them. And loving them, too, the words, the sounds, the patterns of them that seemed special and beautiful. I was surprising myself at how much I enjoyed simply listening to the play even though I was as shy as anything about acting in it and mixing with the cast.

"Actually," Eva went on, "I've decided just to be a film actress. And maybe do a bit of TV too. But probably just films. There's much more money in that, you know. Then I'd only have small bits to learn in one go." She uncurled herself from the wall. "Yes, that's the thing. Films."

She went over to the mirror and practiced smiles and waves for her fans as though she were on some red carpet or in front of photographers' flashlights.

"Like Faye Dunaway, I suppose," I said. We'd sneaked off to the Odeon in Bampton the week before to see a rerun of *Bonnie and Clyde* so it was the first name to come to mind. My mother had assumed we were at *Ring of Bright Water* which had been on the previous week and we'd had to go on and on to her about otters when we got back. I'd been terrified that the manager would ask my age and I'd got ready to lie about being sixteen in order to get into something X rated, but no-one had taken any notice of us.

"Yes, like Faye Dunaway," Eva agreed, "just like her." She had a picture of Warren Beatty stuck to the back of her bedroom door so I knew she would be happy with the suggestion. She began speaking her Titania lines in an American accent, still staring at herself in the mirror. Then she broke off abruptly.

"Lysander's asked me out," she said, and came and sat next to me on the floor. I gave up on the play and Eva's line-learning, chucking the copy across the carpet. "Steven Milligan has actually asked me out." She looked extremely pleased and even blushed a bit, running her fingers through her hair as a sort of distraction.

"When? I mean when did he ask you? I've never even seen him talk to you at rehearsals."

"He rang me," Eva said, "last night. He got my phone number from Gerald, he said, and just rang."

"Who answered?"

It was my greatest dread that a boy should somehow acquire my phone number and ring our house to have my mother answer. Or even my father, who would be completely bewildered and no doubt pass the phone to my mother, anyway.

"Ma answered, but that doesn't matter. She knows I have boyfriends these days. I mean I am going to be sixteen very soon, that's practically adult." Eva hitched up her bra strap which had slipped down her arm. It wasn't entirely true that she had boyfriends. She sometimes hung around with boys from the grammar at the bus stop after school. She knew the two who worked Saturdays in the record shop in Bampton and always made us go there and try for discounts. But she could hardly lay claim to any who would call themselves a boyfriend. Still, I knew there'd be no problem with her mother. Jean Mason was just the sort to encourage rather than be horrified by the idea of boyfriends.

"So where are you going? I mean, is this a proper date?" I was not in the least envious. The thought of having to make conversation with a boy who was a virtual stranger was terrifying. I could imagine bleak silences punctuated only with the sound of my heart beating far too rapidly.

"Course it's a proper date. It's not just hanging around the bus shelter or Beach Parade. He says I can choose. Either ice skating in Brighton or a film in Bampton. Ma says I've got to pay for myself so it'll probably be a film as I haven't enough money at the moment for skating."

"He'll be able to help you with your words," I said, "for the play. I'm resigning and handing over to Lysander. Mind you, if you'd fancied Oberon it might have been more convenient."

Eva ignored me. She seemed anxious to keep us on the Lysander topic now she'd finally confided in me.

"He's going to come and pick me up on Saturday at four. So you've got to come shopping with me earlier in the day so I can buy something new to wear. I mean, first date with him and all that. I've got to look as though I've made a big effort."

"I thought you said you haven't any money at the moment. And anyway, you've loads of clothes and he's not seen any of them yet. He's only seen the stuff you wear to rehearsals."

"My dad's going to give me an advance on my clothes allowance," Eva said. "Ma said she'll ask him. Two months in one or something."

I'd tried asking my mother if I could have a clothes allowance like Eva. All the girls at her school seemed to have one although I had to admit they were thin on the ground at Churchill Secondary Modern. My mother's attitude to clothes was functional. If I grew out of something, she replaced it. She had said as much when she had turned down my request, told me that my bit of pocket money was quite enough for a girl of my age. Eva stood up, went over to my bedroom window and stared out at the dull day. Clusters of daffodils were neatly bordering the lawn and a bed of crocuses at the bottom of the garden looked from a distance like a bishop's gown. The garden of Number 8 was more orderly these days, appropriate to the season and somehow more cherished and attended to than the house. It was certainly transformed from the rag and bone man backyard appearance it boasted when we first moved in, and my father devoted endless hours to his bedding plants and herbaceous borders.

"Do you want to go out?" I asked, bored of Eva's obsession with Lysander. Bored of hearing her grapple for Titania's lines and deliver them inaccurately.

"It's Sunday," Eva said, "everything's closed. What's the point?"

We walked down to Beach View Parade and window shopped in Kennarth's and Beaumont's and the Black Boy pub. We read the cards stuck on the back of Beaumont's door at least twenty times, advertising for a Tupperware party, a char lady, a babysitter for twin girls. I found a stub of pencil in my pocket and wrote down the babysitter phone number on the back of my hand. Eva raised her eyebrows.

"Well, I might as well be earning some money while you're out with Lysander," I said, wondering at the same time whether my mother would let me. She'd already dismissed the idea of me getting a Saturday job at Beaumont's, but perhaps babysitting would be acceptable. After all, I could do my homework once the babies were asleep.

"He'll probably chuck me after Saturday," Eva said. "I'm trying not to get my hopes up that he might actually like me. More than other girls, I mean." It was not like Eva to sound so unsure. Normally, I basked in her certainty, hoped to be infected a little by the supreme confidence she always showed. And she knew it. We dovetailed each other as if born to the task. We crossed the road and sat down on the Front. Eva found some chewing gum, folded her last piece in half and split it with me.

"Anyway, I've got my O levels soon," she said, "and Steven's got school summer exams so I don't suppose we'll be allowed to spend much time together."

"You could help each other with revision."

"Not really," Eva said, "he's quite clever. At Science and Maths and stuff like that. He's going to go to university, he says. Whereas I'm just going to be an actress."

An old man walked past with an odd-looking dog, wheezing and coughing and snarling orders to the creature at his heels. He glared at us as if we had perversely chosen to cross his path. Eva glared back.

"I hate that man," she said, once he was safely out of earshot. "He's ugly and nasty and cruel to his dog."

"Maybe he's had a sad life," I said. "Maybe his mother ill-treated him and his wife left him and he's taking it all out on the dog."

Eva shuddered.

"What a waste of a life. Fancy wasting a whole life being miserable. That's just silly. There's no way you'll find me doing that."

"Do you think Susan's happy?" I asked. "Maybe we should be kinder to her. Ask her out with us and stuff." I often felt guilty that we didn't include Susan more. We were her only friends and although I hung around with her at school we rarely met at weekends.

"Susan's all right," Eva said. "She's got the play now, hasn't she? We got her into that. And she's not a sociable type. Not everyone is, you know. And she's too busy with her fish and chips and her homework most of the time." Eva was reassuring. It made it easy for me to swallow my guilt. "Anyway, it's up to her. It's her life, isn't it? It's not up to us to turn it around for her."

★ ★ ★

Lysander became a fixed feature for Eva on Saturday evenings. At rehearsals, they virtually ignored each other.

"We don't think it's very professional to behave like boy and girlfriend in front of the rest of the cast," Eva said, smugly, "and old Gerald would be furious. He went mad when he caught Puck kissing Helena."

"Perhaps he's just jealous," Susan said, unscrewing her thermos flask and drowning her sugar lumps and searching for her two Garibaldi biscuits. "It doesn't look as if anyone's making any passes at him."

Eva and I looked at each other in surprise. We didn't think Susan noticed things like that. We didn't think she even knew the vocabulary involved.

"Anyway," Eva went on, "you can rely on me and Steven for being very… what's the word?" She looked over in the direction of the boys in their usual huddle by the wall.

"Discreet," Susan said. "Circumspect. How are the Titania lines coming along?"

"I'm word perfect now," Eva said, "nearly, at least. Actually, I wouldn't mind one of you testing me on that long speech to Oberon."

"*These are the forgeries of jealousy,*" I said, "surely you know that one by now."

Susan and I started to recite it to her in unison. I'd forgotten that her job as prompt meant that she knew virtually the entire play cover to cover. Eva limped her way through with us, tried twice more on her own and eventually more or less got it.

"So how many people have you got coming to see it?" she said, collapsing in a heap on the hall floor after her exertions. I shrugged.

"No-one. I mean I can't imagine anyone's going to bother to come and see me when I've only got about four words. What about you?"

Eva counted on her fingers and soon ran out of available digits.

"Well, there's Ma and my dad, of course. And maybe my brother if he's around. And then loads of neighbours. And my auntie and uncle from Kent. Mary, you've got to sell *some* tickets. It looks really odd if you've got no-one in the audience. Can't the two of you get a whole crowd from your school?"

Susan looked at me, pulled a face.

"It's not as if it's a professional production, Eva. Who's going to bother to come and see some school kids messing around with Shakespeare?"

Eva looked furious. Her face went pink and she stared at us contemptuously as if we were worse than useless. I muttered something about mentioning it at home. To Miss Mackie, perhaps, or even Mr. Jarvis, although in truth I really had no intention of asking him. Fortunately, Gerald chose that moment to call everyone over to practise the curtain call. By the time Eva had been placed centre stage and we'd rehearsed the ovations several times, she was looking cheerful again.

Miss Mackie, in fact, bought two tickets.

"I'd like to bring my friend from the hospital," she said. "We like to support amateur theatre."

"I don't suppose it'll be very good," I said, hovering by the door of her room while she searched in her purse for the money, picking out the coins painstakingly as if she could barely afford to part with them. I'd never seen inside her room since she had moved in and could not believe she stocked the entire contents of her life into it.

"It's the enterprise that counts, Mary," she said, handing over the ticket money, "it's the collective theatrical experience that we'll all share."

Over supper I said something about the performances the following week, vague mutterings about being late on three nights. I waited, a little embarrassed by my expectation that my parents might actually be interested in coming.

"Just as long as you get your homework done, Mary," my mother said, portioning out the fish pie. "And you'll have to have an early tea on those nights. Something light on toast would probably be best."

My father filled glass tumblers with water from the tap and passed them round the table.

"I'll pick you up afterwards at the grammar school. Can't have you coming home on one of those late-night buses, can we?"

I sprinkled too much salt over my pie and began to eat.

"Don't bother," I said, "I expect I'll get a lift from Eva's parents. Or her auntie. Or one of their friends. She's got someone there every night, you know."

My mother spooned pale cabbage onto my plate. I pushed it deliberately to one side.

"That's nice for Eva," she said. "But then they're that sort of family, aren't they?"

"What do you mean?" I said. "What's That Sort of Family supposed to mean?" Potato from the densely potato laden fish pie glued itself to the roof of my mouth so that my words were not clear. My mother looked across at me.

"Drink some water, Mary. And eat more slowly. You started your meal without asking and you know how rude I find that." I drank, dissolving the wodge of solid potato, wondering whether to press the point. Of course, the truth was that I did not really want my parents to come to the play. I wanted to feel aggrieved by their absence rather than embarrassed by their presence which would be, I knew, awkward. If I had parents like Eva's, it would have been different. Mr. and Mrs. Mason knew how to behave. They seemed to be of a different generation, as if they had allowed themselves to adapt and change along with the times. My parents still inhabited a twilight world where you only asked for what you knew you could get. They seemed to me to be the sort of people who set out to avoid rather than seek pleasure, to see life as something that needed to be simply waded through stoically. I wielded my fork in search of some fish amongst a sea of sauce.

I hadn't expected Mr. Jarvis to show any interest. Or at least to make a claim on support.

"Of course, I have all my evening classes, otherwise I'd have been there cheering you girls on," he said, as Eva and I left for the first night, costumes tucked under our arms and already wearing far too much make-up. For once, I had an indisputable right to layer on the eye shadow and my mother could say nothing. "Break a leg, isn't that what they say?" he went on, and offered to drop us off at the grammar school on his way to his college classes, but Eva had arranged for us to meet up with Lysander and Theseus at the bus stop. I was relieved to have an excuse to refuse Mr. Jarvis even if it did throw me into the path of Theseus. Eva seemed to think that if he was constantly in our company, I'd grow into the idea of having him for my boyfriend and then the four of us could go out on double dates. I, in turn, obstinately resisted her match-making attempts by remaining silent whenever he was around.

We crept a little uneasily through the first performance then edged more certainly through the second. By the final night, I was beginning to enjoy myself and regretting it was all nearly over. Suddenly, I felt sorry for Susan stuck in her prompt corner in her brown trousers and old Fair Isle sweater while I wore pale pink tights and a skimpy costume of nylon and net. Eva had made white paper flowers to stick in her hair and she'd let me have a couple for mine. She'd tied rags round her strands of ramrod straight hair, slept in them for days, so that it fell in long ringlets. For once, I was grateful for my bumpy dark waves that did the job effortlessly. Miss Mackie had praised us endlessly after her visit. She'd insisted on ringing Eva and telling her she was a born actress with a special feel for Shakespeare's language. She hovered around the kitchen as I ate my early tea on the final night. Cheese on toast that was charred at the edges because the grill's thermostat only did lukewarm or burnt.

"I've a good mind to come again," she said, "but I'm seeing my brother this evening. And although very cultured in his way, not terribly into the drama."

My father, drinking tea at the table with me, looked guilty for a moment as if he was aware of being neglectful. But he soon recovered.

"I'll be outside the grammar school at ten, Mary, straight from my bridge class. No staying to after show parties or any of that malarkey, of course!" He laughed rather loudly as if the idea were his joke when, of course, there was to be a party. A party that Eva would be allowed to go to, and Lysander and Theseus and everyone else in the cast who had parents who would consider such a thing as normal. I knew there had been no point in even asking. The whole notion of a celebration party would have been impossible for them to grasp and they would have been so suspicious and cautious about me going that it would have taken all pleasure away. At least I wouldn't be leaving alone. I'd promised we'd drop Susan off at the shop so she could help with the post-pub lot who always came in for their chips and batter bits around eleven.

It went very well. Only Helena forgot her lines and picked up her cue from Susan, spoken clearly and instantly, in a moment. For the first time, Eva didn't wobble in her dance and the mechanicals got laughs in all the right places and didn't laugh themselves. At the curtain call, Gerald Hetherington made a little speech, sounding ridiculously calm and confident for a seventeen-year-old, as if he'd been making speeches for the past fifty years. He thanked us, his wonderful, dedicated cast, and I thought how well he lied, suddenly saying such complimentary things when he'd shouted insults and abuse at us constantly for the past four months. I didn't like him at all and could imagine him growing into a horrid, overweight and objectionable man in his later life. Reluctantly, we trooped back to change in the classroom that had become our girls' dressing room for the past few nights. At least I changed back into my ordinary clothes and Susan swept the floor that was dusted with face powder and bright pink rouge and picked up discarded socks and cardigans and hair clips and ribbons. The other girls in the cast, heading, of course, for the after-play party in the gym, stayed in their costumes and plastered on a bit more make-up, redid their hair and became very giggly and silly. I felt like Cinderella with the absence of a fairy godmother. Susan stoically swept on, methodically filling her dustpan several times and emptying it into the classroom litter bin. Eva barely noticed us go, attached to the group of girls passing around the green eye shadow palette and the mascara and just flicked her eyes briefly in our direction as we left the room.

Outside we waited for my father. He was late. We stood for twenty minutes in the sharp night air until he finally arrived, flustered and bothered to find that he'd been waiting at the wrong side of the school.

"Sorry, love, I left the bridge class in good time, but it's hard to recognise buildings in the dark. And it's such a big place, isn't it? Got its own playing fields and everything."

Susan and I said nothing. We dropped her at the shop, still thriving with business, a small queue snaking out of the door and along the pavement. The smell of vinegar and frying fish flooded the car as she got out. I thought of suggesting a bag of chips, but knew my father would not risk my mother's disapproval at anything so indigestible late at night. There'd be a mug of hot milk or Ovaltine and two digestive biscuits waiting for me on the kitchen table at home.

"She's a hard-working girl, that one, and her mum, too," my father said as we drove away, heading towards the coast and Sea View Parade. "It's no joke having a business like that. Long and unsociable hours and not great profits, I wouldn't have thought." I mumbled something, not thinking at all at that moment of Susan and her family's welfare and the cod and chip business. Because I was thinking entirely of Eva and the others, Helena and Hermia and Hippolyta and my fellow fairies that I'd left behind. They'd be eating the sausage rolls and the crisps and the twiglets I'd seen earlier in the gym and dancing to the records the boys had brought in, laughing and joking and talking endlessly about the play.

We pulled up outside our house and my father turned off the engine. At first, absorbed with being bad-tempered and morose, I didn't notice anything unusual. Then, as I got out of the car, clutching my carrier bag of now redundant fairy costume and fake flowers and my very first tube of pink lipstick bought from Woolworth's the previous Saturday, I saw Miss Mackie. She was waiting on the pavement outside Number 8, looking up and down the road, a small suitcase in her hand. At that moment, a car drew up from the opposite direction, a beige car that I recognised vaguely and Miss Mackie darted towards it, wrenching open the door as if in a frantic hurry. My father called out to her, but it appeared she didn't hear because she continued to get in and the beige familiar car pulled away so rapidly that we caught only a glimpse of her face through the side window, her suitcase piled awkwardly on her lap. My mother was at the front door. She looked at us in surprise as if she had forgotten we were expected.

"What was all that about?" my father said. "Is Miss Mackie going away? I don't remember her saying anything about it. And who was that man in the car?"

"I think it was her brother," I offered, remembering now the car that picked her up on her occasional Sundays out. We went inside to the hall and my mother firmly closed the front door and led the way downstairs to the kitchen. Predictably, two mugs were set out on the table. There were no biscuits, however, on the bare plate next to them. And no sign of milk or Ovaltine.

"Miss Mackie's left," my mother said abruptly. "She's moved out. She'll be back for more of her things at the weekend. At least, that's what she said. But she suddenly took it upon herself to go." She folded her arms and leant against the draining board then turned her back on us and started rinsing a couple of plates under the tap.

"Moved out? But why?" my father said, directing the question first at my mother's back then at my face, as if I were supposed to supply an adequate answer. "Whatever's got in to her to go off all of a sudden? At this time of night?"

My mother turned, stared at us as if wondering quite what we were doing in the kitchen, then moved to the fridge and wrenched open the awkward, ill-fitting door.

"I've always thought her very odd," she said in a loud voice, as if speaking to a larger number of people than simply me and my father. "Haven't I always said that about her? That she's an odd kettle of fish. Quite the eccentric, in fact." She found the jug of milk and poured some into a pan, lit the gas.

"Well, I'm not sure about that," my father said hesitantly. "I've always found her quite a pleasant sort, but... well, yes, I see your point now, Ida. This is all a bit strange, I must say."

My mother opened the biscuit tin, picked out four digestives, returned to the gas stove and poured the barely-warmed milk into the two mugs.

"I mean, the woman is a lonely, solitary spinster and it's obviously turned her mind in some way," she said, "packing up and leaving virtually in the middle of the night! That's not what normal people do, now is it? If you ask me, we're well rid of her. And I'd rather none of us ever had anything to do with her again. Do you understand, Mary? There's no need even to mention her name. Let's just forget Miss Mackie ever came into our lives."

My father and I looked at each other then we both sat down at the table and shared the digestives. A thin skin scudded across the surface of my mug of milk and I hooked it off with my dipped biscuit. Footsteps came down the basement stairs. Mr. Jarvis appeared, filling the doorway, bringing with him his smell of cigarettes and a shudder of cold night air. My mother turned to the fridge and fiddled with the stubborn handle that resisted a gentle approach.

"It's not the door at all," she said, as if we'd been discussing its obstinacy, "it's the handle that's the problem."

Mr. Jarvis hooked his jacket around the back of a chair and sat down at the table, smiling broadly at me.

"Well, Mary, tell me all about the last night. Was it standing ovations all round? Bouquets for the principals and all that?"

My father muttered something about checking he'd locked the car door, what with all the commotion over Miss Mackie, and disappeared upstairs.

Mr. Jarvis took a new box of cigarettes out of his jacket pocket, slid off the cellophane, tipped one out between two fingers and lit it.

"Something like that," I said.

12

Chronology now eludes Ida. Order in time and events have been replaced by something more chance and random. There's no longer a clear sense of before or after so that she may as well recall my fifth birthday as my visit the week before last. It's comforting, in a way. She's like a young child who cannot cope with the complexities of time and distance. I remember when Felix was small it was no use telling him that we would be going to his friend's party in half an hour. He needed concrete explanations.

"In the time it takes us to drive to the big shops," I'd say, perhaps. "That's how long it is until we leave to go to Sam's party." But of course, Felix soon grew out of such narrow understanding whereas Ida is hopelessly tunnelling her way deeper into bewilderment.

Jack comes to stay for a few days. Only two days, in truth, arriving Monday evening and leaving first thing Thursday. I cook him careful meals, take him the newspaper in the morning and sit with him for some time over pots of tea in the lengthening afternoons. I love this time of year. I love the promise of light in chill April evenings. There will be a summer to inherit despite the relentless frosts of early mornings. He seems content enough, Jack. Felix is kind. He passes him the sports pages of the papers, flicks onto sports news and tells his grandfather about cricket in South Africa, rugby in New Zealand.

"Don't mind me," Jack says as I hover around, proffering coffee yet again. "I'm quite happy here with the crossword and such. You take yourself off and do what you have to do, Mary." And he means it. He's happy to potter in my small garden, wrenching the odd weed and planting the abandoned house hyacinth he's found by the back door. He fixes things I've overlooked for months. The toilet roll holder in the bathroom now has two screws and hangs horizontally. Batteries have been replaced in the kitchen radio. The door to Felix's bedroom receives a much-needed coat of paint. I know he is content to feel useful, used.

"Takes me back a bit," he says as we sit over dinner. "Finding things to do all the time. Like at Number 8. That house was a full-time job, I can tell you."

"Endless," I say swiftly, and pass the vegetables.

"So many rooms to keep up with, that was the trouble," Jack says, spooning a conservative portion of potatoes beside his chicken breast. "Just thought you'd got to the end of the painting and the bit you'd done first began to look shabby." He smiles as if the memory is fond rather than an irritant. Felix eats swiftly. He's already halfway through his food, shovelling it in as if it might disappear before his eyes, while we're still dealing with carrots.

"So why did you buy such a big house?" he asks between hasty mouthfuls. "I mean, there was only the three of you, wasn't there? It's not as if Mum had brothers or sisters." He sounds genuinely interested. I don't wait for Jack to answer.

"An investment," I hear myself say rapidly, "it was an investment. No-one was buying big houses like that at the time. Old houses, I mean. They just weren't fashionable. Yet obviously fashions would eventually change. As indeed, of course, they did." I sound like my mother, Ida, as if I imbibed those convictions of hers, and look at Jack who sips tentatively at the small glass of wine I have poured him.

"It was all your grandmother's idea, Felix," he says, "she was the one with the ambition, the big ideas. She could see the way things were going. And, of course, we thought it would be nice for your mum to grow up by the seaside. All that healthy sea air and such. Nice for children to have a beach to play on." Jack turns his attention to his chicken. He seems a little suspicious of the red pepper nestling beside it. I top up my glass. Felix's enormous trainers strike against the table legs.

"I remember going there when I was little," he says, "at least I think I do. With Dad. And we went onto some hill and flew a kite."

"That's right," I say, a photo of Felix about five years of age wearing a blue and red t-shirt coming to mind. I had forgotten about kites and how David had bought countless numbers of them for Felix. Kites that had got stuck in high trees or had strangled themselves on knitted strings.

"Well, it was certainly a windy spot, Sea View Parade. And you and your dad would have gone up onto Hill Head just beyond the Front," Jack says, "that's where everyone went for kite flying." There's a sudden loud explosion of noise from somewhere near Felix's chair. Jack looks startled whereas I am used to such abrupt interruptions.

"Sorry," Felix says, pushing his chair away from the table and retrieving his phone from his pocket, "Do you mind if… or I could… it's just it's probably Harry about meeting up tomorrow. If I could… sorry."

He disappears out of the kitchen and I hear him in the hall, talking to Harry. Talking to him in an entirely different accent than the one he has used with us for the past hour, devoid, mostly, of consonants and with a monosyllabic, staccato kind of delivery. I marvel at how spontaneously he switches. Jack and I plough on with our Spanish-style chicken.

"Course, it was a job to keep the place warm. What with those high ceilings," Jack says. "A devil to reach them to decorate, too." He seems to want to return to the subject of Number 8 as if the thought of the house is of some comfort, warm nostalgia attached to the place rather than livid memory. Perhaps now that Ida can no longer have such conversations with him, he sees me as an effective substitute.

I see my chance and I know I have to take it. I put down my fork and plunge right in before I lose my nerve, interrupting his description of decorating the basement kitchen.

"Was it really all her decision? I mean, didn't you have any say in whether we moved from Ash Gardens to Number 8?"

"Your mother's always known her own mind, Mary," he says swiftly, admiringly even. He cuts a small piece of chicken then seems to forget to eat it, glances out of the window as if for distraction. Eventually, he goes on, "And I've always admired her for that. Always did. From the moment I first met her, you know. I was a bit too cautious for my own good, she used to say. And she was right, of course. You've got to have a bit of drive if you're going to get anywhere in this life."

Jack has always liked his platitudes, suitable smokescreens for original thought. I push further.

"But how did you feel about the whole idea? I mean, when did you understand what was really behind the sudden…"

Then I stop because I see Jack's hand shaking as he tries to prod some food on his plate, drop peas from his fork onto the table. His face has grown even thinner, strands of his grey hair lie flat, inadequately masking spots of sun and age across his head. He has always been a slim man, but now I see that his frame is shrunken as if flesh finds it too hard to cling to his bones. I have been too distracted by Ida's physical decline to note Jack's, but now I see that he, too, is growing less resilient, his eyes no longer so keen, a weariness loading him down.

And I wonder what I am doing in my pursuit of some absolute truth.

As if the events of a few years really matter so very much in the setting of an entire lifetime. This elderly man is, after all, my father. Ida, my mother, is now alone and extraordinarily frail, dependent upon the kindness of strangers for her most essential of needs. Jack has, perhaps, chosen to construe another version of the past, has rearranged and tilted memory so that it is acceptable, tolerable. Victims of appalling accidents, even the perpetrators, it is said, find their recall muted, recast. Felix is talking in the hall then his voice becomes more distant as he carries on his conversation going up the stairs and into his room. The door closes firmly. I get up abruptly, scraping my chair on the wooden kitchen floor, clear plates from the table and deposit them by the sink. Somewhere inside the fridge there's a lemon mousse I've made and I clamber my way through packets of cheese, left-over pie, knock over tins of beans to retrieve it. I put white china dessert dishes down on the table, spoons. Jack looks at me for a moment as if he has almost forgotten where he is. Then he gazes out of the window at the growing darkness. The neighbour's black cat streaks across the grass.

"Tell you what," I say with conjured enthusiasm, spooning out a portion of pale mousse and placing it in front of Jack, "shall we go to the nursing home tomorrow? Go and see my mother – Ida? Drive down there? It would only take us about an hour and it would be nice for her to see us together for once. A really lovely surprise. What do you think?"

Jack sits forward in his chair, picks up his spoon, keen, suddenly, to eat, to think ahead.

"Now you're talking," he says. "Do you know, Mary, you're just like your mother. When you put your mind to it, you're so full of good ideas."

★ ★ ★

Ida is wearing a purple cardigan over a pair of turquoise stretch trousers. The effect is bold, even a little chic in a bohemian kind of way. She sits by the window, staring out as if to admire the well-tended beds. The care nurse is our advance party.

"Look who's come to see you!" she says. "Two in one, today, Ida, now whose luck's in?" She looks startled for a moment as we walk towards her across the patterned carpet. Jack bends down to kiss her and takes one of her hands in his.

"Mary's brought me in to see you today," he says, "aren't I lucky? I've been staying with her for a few days and with Felix, too, of course. They've been spoiling me rotten, they have. It's been just like the old days when I had you waiting on me hand and foot."

As far as I could recall, Ida had never been over-indulgent towards Jack. She'd cooked the meals, kept the house tidy, but her services towards him had always appeared rather rationed if anything. She was never one to squander gestures of affection or indulgence unnecessarily. Still, Jack appears to choose to remember otherwise. He produces the large bar of milk chocolate he's brought her, the pot plant we found at the garden centre close to the nursing home.

"Something to cheer up your room," he says. "Cut flowers just wouldn't last a moment in the central heating, you know. Wilting before we'd left you, no doubt."

He's much better at this than me. Jack chats endlessly, it seems, even extends the conversation to the woman sitting on our right, a sad-looking, very large woman who always wears a white hat a little like a cloche. I've seen her many times, but have always ignored her, as if trying to suggest I have not even noticed she is there. Now she stares at the three of us and is unresponsive even to Jack's efforts to involve her. Ida looks first at Jack, then me, then at Jack again, laughs a little at things he says. It's hard to know whether her response is chosen or chance.

"Just... like old times," she says suddenly in the middle of Jack's tale about the new vacuum cleaner he's bought. He breaks off, smiles and strokes the back of her hand with tenderness.

"That's right, just the three of us, you, me and Mary. Like it used to be years ago."

"She doesn't... ride her bike," Ida says slowly and then repeats herself with irritation. "That bike... Mary doesn't ride it."

Jack and I look blankly at each other for a moment, then I grasp where Ida is, decades in the past, at Sea View Parade. I'd nagged and nagged my parents for a bike so that I could go on rides with Eva. I must have been thirteen or fourteen when subsequent birthdays and Christmas presents had failed to produce one. Eventually, Ida had found an old and unattractive second-hand affair, brought it home and suggested that I could pay her in instalments from my pocket money. I'd hardly ridden it. It was awkward and uncomfortable and by the time I'd acquired it, Eva and I had outgrown bike rides anyway, and were keener on catching buses into Brighton and Worthing. It had sat for years rusting in the back garden, a source of occasional reprimand from Ida, until it had disappeared, probably stolen, one summer in the early 70s.

"You're right," I say, catching Jack's eye, "I hardly rode it at all."

"You and me used to have bikes," Jack says, leaning a little closer to Ida to catch her attention. Her eyes wander constantly as if focus is tiring. "When we were first married. Remember? Great heavy things that we got on coupons somehow. I think I knew a fellow at work who got them for us." Ida smiles, but does not seem to remember or at least is detached from the thought. Jack perseveres. "We had them for years, even when you were first born, Mary. Until I got our first car, that Hillman, remember love? Not everyone had cars those days, of course, it was still a bit of an event when a car arrived in the road." I don't recall the car in particular, but there's a black and white photograph of me, a scrap of four or so, sitting on the bonnet of something that looks extraordinarily old-fashioned and cumbersome. Ida turns towards me, frowns as if for a moment she has forgotten what I am doing here. Or even, perhaps, quite how I fit into her life. If I could suddenly transform myself back into my awkward fifteen-year-old self, I may be more recognisable to her. She stares at me blankly and I find myself foolishly close to tears. I say something pointless about the arrangement of tulips on a far table, the smell of warm food that's coming from the kitchens. I am more distressed than I wish to admit.

"Terrible… just… terrible… that business," Ida says slowly. "Such a shock," she says, and fiddles with the neckline of her purple cardigan. Jack looks across the room. We both do, as if waiting for the other to come up with the best response. But Ida is less hesitant today. "Too young, too… too… just like that," she says, her expression dark, grief-stricken, almost. "Just like… so sudden. So…" Jack stands up, starts across the room as swiftly as his slightly arthritic knees allow.

"Just need to find the… just need to spend a penny, Mary. Won't be a moment."

I wait until he disappears through the door, his slight figure heading across the reception hall, nearly colliding with a care worker carrying a pile of towels. I pull my chair closer to Ida. She doesn't seem to have noticed Jack has gone, still seems riveted by her thought.

"Who was too young?" I ask, "who do you mean?" It's

pointless asking her such a blatant question, attempting to demand bare facts when for months she's inhabited somewhere remote from such clarity. Yet I can't resist doing so. Her troubled expression softens, turns to something of a smile and she even laughs a little and says a few words too quietly for me to catch. I ask her to repeat herself.

"Lovely… lovely," she says, "quite the… quite… who would have thought… who would…" She closes her eyes, her hand goes to her face and she looks suddenly quite exhausted, as if the effort of our visit has overwhelmed her.

"Who are you talking about?" I say, and repeat the question pointlessly. Even if she gives me the name I am expecting, I will have gained so little. Hardly a confession, the explanation I crave. She looks at me now, bewilderment, even fear, clouding her eyes. She grabs my hand firmly, almost hurts it in her grasp.

"Home," she says. "Let's go… please. Home."

It's what she used to say when she first arrived here. She'd ask repeatedly to go home. She cried each time we left her. She would make noises, keening, it could be called, and the two of us, Jack and I, had to placate both Ida and ourselves with inane phrases. *It's for the best, they can look after you here. They're lovely people,* we'd say, and I'd even find myself saying it aloud in the car on the way home, aiming to convince myself that it was the truth, that there was no other way. But it's been months since she's spoken like this. Perhaps Jack and I coming here together has been a mistake. I try to release my hand from her grasp.

"It'll be your lunch time soon, won't it? The food is good here, isn't it?" I say. "Imagine what a big job it is, cooking for all these people." And I sweep my hand around the room as if encompassing a coterie of food critics.

"Fred," Ida says. She states the name clearly, almost too loudly. I look towards the door and see Jack returning. He meets my eye across the large lounge. "Fred," she says again, even louder. The very fat woman in the strange white hat looks across at us sharply. "Why doesn't he... I want to see Fred. So long now."

Jack joins us. Ida looks at him coldly. He kisses her cheek. Quickly, she puts her hand to her face, touches her cheek as if uncertain whether anything has been left there.

"Don't upset yourself, love," he says to me quietly, "it takes her like this sometimes. All of a muddle, she is. I've seen quite a bit of it lately. It's just not one of her good days."

On the contrary, it is one of Ida's better days. At least in terms of her ability to talk coherently, construct sentences which convey sense. Jack is saying something to her about a holiday they took in Bognor when I was very small. He's trying to hook her memory onto a donkey ride on the beach, the boarding house where we stayed, run by a woman called Mrs. Higgins. Ida stares at him, unamused.

"I think there are some photos in one of the albums," I offer. "Me in a soppy sunhat sitting by a sandcastle that someone else must have built."

"She always had us out by nine in the morning, Mrs. Higgins," Jack says. "Come rain or shine, there was no loitering after breakfast. And we weren't allowed back until five for high tea. Remember that, Ida? The things we put up with in those days!"

"Fred," Ida says, and looks out of the window at the garden. The rain has started to fall, sudden shafts of heavy rain spiced with hail. "Lovely man. No... no good, though. Lovely man. Loved him. Such love."

She rubs her eyes, the action of a baby in need of sleep or of someone disguising tears. Jack stands up.

"We'll go now, Ida, me and Mary. It's all a bit too much for you, having the two of us together, isn't it? Too much of a good thing, perhaps."

And he moves towards her, tries to kiss her, but she turns her head away. He squeezes her shoulder instead.

We stop for petrol at a service station just along the road from Ida's home. I buy a newspaper for Jack, hoping to occupy him so that there is no need for conversation. But he spends so much time alone these days that when he has a chance of company he tends to want to talk.

"You wonder what's going on in her mind, don't you?" he says, having glanced at the paper briefly and folded it politely, neatly, onto the back seat. "I mean she's got no sense of time any more. I just wonder whether I could have kept her at home longer. She's gone downhill so quickly in that place."

"That's ridiculous," I say, almost snapping at him. "No-one could have done more. You were making yourself ill."

"Yes, but it's what it's all for, isn't it? Marriage, I mean. What's it say? For richer, for poorer, in sickness and in health."

We're pausing at traffic lights. I take a side look at Jack's face, see his sadness, his sense of having failed Ida in the dullness of his eyes. He mutters the vow over again under his breath like a mantra. The lights turn green.

"You have been so tolerant, you know," I say, pulling away too sharply and causing a slow pedestrian to scarper. "No other man would have put up with what you did. And even now you…"

Jack's pressing buttons on the car radio, haphazardly darting along the row so that snatches of opera, rapid French, lazy saxophone notes tumble over one another until I take over control and guide us towards sense and stability.

"Ah, the news, thank you, Mary," he says. "I always like to catch the midday news to see what's what in the world. No doubt more about this credit crunch business. All sounds very complicated to me."

"Yes," I say, driving steadily on, "all very complicated."

13

Eva had a part time job at Beaumont's in Beach Parade that summer. She finished her school term as soon as her O level exams were over and her mother found her five mornings a week and every Saturday for the whole of July. I had started babysitting most weekends for a neighbour with three small children who lived at the end of our parade. At last, I had some money of my own and enough to buy a few cheap clothes from Martin Ford's in Bampton. My mother didn't seem to notice that I wasn't only wearing the things she found for me in the children's section at Littlewoods or C and A, but I often took the precaution, anyway, of covering up with one of her awful bargain buy jackets until I was well out of her sight.

On her second Saturday at Beaumont's, Eva already seemed disenchanted with work. I went in and found her yawning and rubbing her eyes behind the counter. Blue eye shadow and dark black mascara smudged her cheek.

"It's pretty boring," she said, propping up the counter, elbows leaning into the Bounty bars and Milky Ways. She fished me out a small bar of chocolate. "I get a percentage reduction on everything, but I can't do percentages so just give me some coins to shove in the till."

Mr. Thompson, the owner, was smoking in the back room only just out of earshot. I wondered if he'd given Eva any training or if he just liked the idea of a pretty, thin, long, blonde-haired girl at the counter. We'd long had our suspicions about Mr. Thompson's interests, but Eva's mother had just laughed about what she called our wild imaginations when we'd mentioned it. I handed Eva the scant change in my purse. She shoved it in the till without ringing anything up.

"Anyway, what are you doing later?" Eva asked. "I finish at five, so maybe I could come round to your place. Or you to mine. As long as you're not looking after those children or anything."

I shook my head. "The family's away in Cornwall for a fortnight. But what about Lysander?"

Eva shrugged, examined and nibbled at a thumbnail.

"He's got a driving lesson, I think. He's doing a course of twenty or something to get him ready for his test. And anyway, we've decided not to see so much of each other." She turned and started to fiddle with the pyramid display of Quality Street behind her, removing a thin film of dust with one of her pink-painted finger nails.

"You mean he's chucked you?" I said, staring at her back. It seemed about time. Susan and I had taken bets on the unlikelihood of them surviving the summer.

"Certainly not!" Eva said angrily. "That's such a stupid thing to say. Whatever made you think that?" She turned round abruptly, abandoning the Quality Street, which began to topple and tip over. Box after box slowly descended to the shop floor, hitting Eva on the head and shoulder as they went. I started to laugh, but then saw how upset she looked, and went behind the counter to help her retrieve the boxes and slowly we reconstructed the pyramid between us.

"I don't know why I said that – about him chucking you," I said, evasively. "I just mean that if you're not seeing each other so much it usually means that things are sort of over."

I knew absolutely nothing about such matters on a personal level, but I'd listened to other girls at school talking about the significant signs and wanted to sound informed.

"Well, you're talking nonsense," Eva snapped. "It doesn't mean anything. It's just that he's going away with his parents for the summer. Or most of it. To France or somewhere so he can speak French all the time. Or maybe it's German. I can't remember, but it's to do with his A levels and stuff. And you know I'm going to Canada in August with my parents. So we've got to get used to being without each other. Until September, of course. That's all it is."

I went back to the customer side of the counter and watched her start to sort out the tubes of Spangles into more orderly rows, as if it were suddenly the most urgent job of the day and time was against her. It was unlike Eva to lose her temper. It was unlike her not to turn something unexpected I'd said and she'd done into a joke. I felt as if I had offended a stranger, not Eva.

"So tell me about this Canada thing," I said after a while. Neutral ground seemed the best option. "You're so lucky. I shall be stuck here all summer and it'll probably rain every day and I'll have no-one to be with."

"There's Susan," Eva said. "The two of you can go to the library and talk about books. And I'll send you masses of postcards, I expect. Then when I get back I'll be all grown up and in the sixth form."

"Like Lysander," I said, "except that he'll be in U6 by then and talking about university or careers and jobs and stuff. He'll be eighteen next year, after all." I hadn't meant to return to Lysander. I couldn't imagine why I had. Perhaps Eva was annoyed I always called him that rather than his real name, but it had become a habit that was hard to drop. Eighteen sounded awfully old. I'd noticed that the boys at the grammar school started to look almost like middle-aged men by the time they left, with rough chins and huge hands and some of them driving their mothers' cars. I couldn't imagine Eva going out with someone like that. Eva was more like me, really, however much she pretended otherwise, and simply worked hard at seeming sophisticated and mature. Mr. Thompson suddenly stuck his head out from the back room, blowing cigarette smoke towards us. His shirt was partially unbuttoned and a huge stomach spilt over the waistband of his grubby trousers. His white hair was uncombed, too long, and he had two large warts on his forehead. I shuddered involuntarily every time I saw him.

Eva said, "Can I interest you in some Milk Tray?" adopting her polite shop assistant tone and starting to shove big boxes in my direction. Mr. Thompson wheezed a bit, hitched up his trousers, did up a couple of shirt buttons, then looked suspiciously straight at me and edged his way beside Eva so that his arm touched hers. She flinched, visibly. Then he reached underneath the counter for a moment and re-emerged with his copy of the *Daily Mirror* under one arm.

"Holding the fort, eh?" he said, shoving his nose close to Eva's cheek. "That's the way. Let me know if we're overrun. You never know at this time of year." He took himself off again and we heard him fill the kettle and settle himself down in his armchair in his back room. Two small children came in and spent at least ten minutes filling a small paper bag with penny chews and gobstoppers and Lucky Dip. Eventually, Eva grabbed the bag from them, threw in a couple of jelly babies and they handed over their money and left the shop speedily.

"Beaumont's books won't balance," I said, and she shrugged dismissively and looped her hair behind her ears.

"When I'm famous I'll talk about my first job in a dead-end shop in a dead-end place," she said, "working for a dirty old man who smoked his life away and was found dead one morning collapsed under a pile of Vanilla Walnut Whips."

I sat down on the shop floor, leaning against the glass cabinet that housed liquorice and loose chocolate slabs and Eva came and sat down next to me, handed me a sherbet lollipop.

"So you're still going to RADA?" I said. "You're still going to be an actress?" We hadn't talked for a while. Not properly. There'd been Eva's O levels when she'd had to go straight home from school each afternoon to revise. Or at least to pretend to. Then there were my school summer exams and, of course, most weekends Eva went out with Lysander while I was babysitting my family along the parade. I couldn't remember the last time I'd been to her house and sat on her bedroom carpet talking and drinking limeade. Recently, I'd seen more of Susan on Saturday afternoons than Eva. We'd been to a couple of films in Brighton and helped each other revise French verbs and learn quotes from *Cider with Rosie*. Susan worked most of the time except when she was doing late nights behind the fried fish counter and even then, she had a text book in her overall pocket. She'd get her transfer to the grammar school with no problem. But I had to work really hard to keep up and I was worried that if I didn't do well in school summer exams, they'd shove me into CSE classes for the fifth year and that would be that. My mother had warned me that girls who were only allowed to do CSEs had to work in shops or just do filing in offices all their lives. *Then you won't be able to stand on your own two feet,* she'd said more than a dozen times when she thought I was neglecting my homework. *I'm not having you leaving the secondary modern and going out to work at sixteen.*

Eva sucked at her sherbet lolly then stuck the wooden stick between her bare toes, where she twiddled it back and forth.

"I don't know," she said, "about RADA. I mean, probably. But I'm not sure any more. My dad wants me to go into the

BBC, he says, start at the bottom, as a typist or something, and work my way up."

"Up to what?" I said. Girls at school were planning on being typists. If they weren't going to be nursery nurses, they were going to learn shorthand and typing and get jobs in typing pools or such places. It didn't sound like the sort of thing that would content Eva.

"Oh, you know, BBC sort of things. Television sort of things. Like... like making programmes. Being a producer or an announcer. Or on *Blue Peter*, maybe. Oh, I don't know."

Eva began to plait her hair, thin wisps of plaits so that in no time she had countless straggly strings of them hanging around her face. She looked pale and thinner than normal, with dark rings under her eyes. I always had dark rings under my eyes, even if I went to bed at seven o'clock in the evening, but Eva usually had the kind of complexion that my mother described as peaches and cream. Perhaps she was missing Lysander more than she admitted. Perhaps she was working too many hours in Beaumont's under the unpleasant, smoky gaze of Mr. Thompson.

"I think you should go to RADA," I said. "I want a famous friend. Then I can boast about you and you can take me to amazing parties and introduce me to film stars and stuff."

"When you're a boring teacher, you mean. Surely you can think of something more exciting than that to become." I pretended to agree with her, but in fact, I'd felt flattered when the careers lady who'd interviewed us all at school had suggested primary school teaching. I hadn't realised that girls who failed their 11 Plus exam were later allowed to become teachers and my mother had latched onto the notion, leech-like, so I knew there was to be no turning back. She'd pointed out that teachers earned just enough to rent themselves reasonable rooms and had the holidays available to supplement their income and so the subject of my future career had, apparently, been swiftly settled. And I had to admit that nothing else appealed particularly. Unlike Susan, I didn't want to be a nurse and so teaching small children who knew less than me seemed a solution. The shop door opened and Eva got up hastily from the floor and retreated behind the counter. A woman I vaguely recognised as a neighbour from Sea View Parade made her way towards the back of the shop and the dwindling supplies of toys. Mr. Thompson said he was scaling down that line as children's tastes had changed and no-one was buying dolls' miniature dresses and Dinky cars any more. The truth was no-one was buying them from Beaumont's any more. A spanking smart proper shop had opened in Bampton the previous winter, with two floors of shiny toys and games and dolls that did not smell of cigarette smoke once you got them home. Susan and I had been in one Saturday just to look and I'd found myself wishing I was a few years younger and still eligible to buy a skinny, fashion-conscious Cindy doll.

"Of course," Eva said, "we might all just get married."

I stood up and stared at her across the Bounty bars and Wagon Wheels.

"What's that got to do with it?" I said. "Of course we'll get married. Eventually. Everyone does. But we've got to have jobs too."

Eva fiddled with an elastic band she found in the pocket of her skirt. She stretched it between her thumb and forefinger as if testing it to see how soon it would snap.

"Not if we get married soon," she said. "I mean, when we're still young. I mean, some people do, don't they? Like when they're seventeen or eighteen or something. It is legal, after all."

The customer at the back of the shop seemed to have dropped something. There was a tumble of boxes followed by a slow trickle of noise that sounded as if the woman had nudged a pile of jigsaw puzzles into a slow, downward spiral, distributing their contents across the floor. Eva closed her eyes. We heard Mr. Thompson mutter one of his colourful blasphemous phrases which started off one of his coughing fits that had a life of about five minutes. The woman made a furtive dash for the door, disappeared out onto the street.

"No-one does that anymore," I said, "marrying that young. At least not many people and only if they have to. And anyway, you'd still need a job. You've got to train for something, haven't you? Everyone does, these days. It's not like it used to be when women just stayed at home all the time."

"Like Ma," Eva said, "she hasn't worked for years. Not since she met my dad and got married and left her office place. I could be like her, couldn't I?"

Eva was being awkward. I knew from her pouting expression that she was in one of her moods to be intentionally difficult. I'd seen her like this before with Susan, with her mother, with her brother, Hamish, on the rare occasions he was at home. Only never with me. That was the difference.

"We're the next generation, though, aren't we?" I persisted. "We're supposed to want more. We've got more choices. We can be independent." I was alarmed to realise I was sounding a bit like my mother. And like Miss Mackie, who'd disappeared from our lives so abruptly on the last night of the play. "At least we can have choices if we pass our O levels and you'll be all right with those, won't you?" I was tired of sounding so serious. I was tired of Eva being quite so awkward. "So anyway, are you coming round to my place tonight or am I coming to you? If you're not seeing Lysander and your exams are finished, we could do something. Like we used to."

"Like what?" She sounded disenchanted.

"We can decide later," I said. The whole point of Eva and I spending an evening together was that we never needed to arrange anything. Susan and I would require a film or homework or the shops to occupy our time together whereas Eva and I could just loll in her bedroom or mine and talk. Talk for hours. Endlessly. About everything. At least we used to. "You can style my hair if you like," I offered. "Try straightening it with the iron again."

Eva stared out of the shop window as if looking for something to interest her.

"I don't know," she said eventually. "Maybe Ma will have something in mind. Or maybe I'll just stay in and sleep."

"Suit yourself," I said, affecting indifference, "it was your idea in the first place." I unfolded myself from the floor and removed dust from my legs. I wondered if Mr. Thompson ever cleaned the place and whether dirt could penetrate the wrappers of the sweets and chews and chocolate bars and boxes he sold. If so, Eva and I must have dirt-congested organs and bones and blood after years of spending pocket money here. I waited for Eva to say something, to show some enthusiasm for us meeting later after she'd finished work. When we'd first become best friends, my mother had been sceptical about our friendship lasting. *Don't be upset if Eva changes her mind and chooses someone else to spend so much time with, will you, Mary?* she had said to me when Eva had come to tea for the first time. *She's such a live wire, after all, and you're the bookish, quiet sort. Not the obvious match for one another, I'd say.* My mother always liked to check the idea of happiness, put it back in its place as if it was too precocious an emotion. Now, however, watching Eva fiddle with her chipped nail varnish, examine her hair for split ends rather than give me a satisfactory answer, I thought for the first time in years of my mother's bleak prediction. Mr. Thompson appeared again from the back of the shop. He looked at me suspiciously and with no obvious recognition of the fact that I'd been into Beaumont's with Eva several times a week for the past four years.

"We're closing up a bit early tonight," he said to Eva, edging so close to her side that his beige, ash-spattered cardigan nudged her white t-shirt at chest level. "It's the dogs at Brighton, you see, Saturday night and all that, so I want to be shot of this place by five."

"Good," Eva said crisply, "I've a lot to do tonight." She stared straight at me then reached behind her for one of the tall jars of loose boiled sweets. "A quarter of Pineapple Chunks, did you say? Certainly. Will that be all?"

★ ★ ★

She did come round that evening. About seven o'clock, I heard her in the hall of Number 8, talking to my mother, who was always a little deferential towards Eva as if in awe of her prettiness, her confident air with adults. It annoyed me. If I'd shown a shred of her assurance my mother would have instantly deflated it with one of her favourite put-downs such as *I'd leave your elders to say things like that.* She seemed to have forgotten her afternoon mood of lassitude in Beaumont's. We did our usual things and didn't mention Lysander at all. We tried on all my clothes and Eva chopped a length off a dull skirt of mine and turned it into a scarf. She cut the sleeves from an old purple dress, took off the Peter Pan collar so that suddenly it looked fashionable, original, rather than dreary and neat. She trimmed my fringe and removed as many of her split ends as she could find. We went down to Beach Parade just before it grew dark and walked the other way, away from the row of shops, into the force of the strong evening breeze that carried goblets of sea water or perhaps it was rain and soon my hair was a mass of dark, tangled frizz.

"Why are you going to Canada this summer?" I asked. "Why not to Spain or Italy like you always do?"

Eva said, "We're visiting those people who used to live here. You remember when you first moved here and I'd had a best friend before you? When I said I needed someone to take her place?" I didn't really remember, but nodded anyway. "Rosemary Martin," Eva went on, "except she calls herself Rosie now. In her letters and stuff."

"I didn't know you wrote letters to her," I said, then wished I hadn't sounded quite so petulant, like a jealous, suspicious lover. "I mean it's not the sort of thing you do, letter-writing." Susan wrote letters. Susan was the letter-writing sort. She had a pen friend who lived over a hairdresser's in Glasgow and another who lived on an RAF camp in Germany.

"I don't really," Eva said, "not now, anyway. Just a few letters when she first went. Now it's only birthday cards and it's actually Ma who remembers them and gets me to sign. Ma and Rosie's mum were really friendly, you see. Really close. Known each other for years or something. Like from when me and Rosie were babies. I was supposed to call her Auntie Helen, in fact. Although I never did."

We'd dropped down to the beach from the Front and Eva stopped to pick up a large pebble and tossed it towards the sea. The tide was out and her aim fell far short. She started to pick up more and more, as if staging her own personal challenge. "Anyway, we're not with Rosie and her family all the time. We're doing outdoor things my dad's arranged. Going on rivers and camping, but Ma's not that keen on all that, so we're doing some normal stuff too. Going to Toronto, I think, and then staying at the Martins' place at the end."

I was used to Eva's extravagant holidays by now and didn't even bother to envy them anymore, since clearly they were events belonging in another kind of life. She picked up a pale brown pebble, smoothed it against her cardigan then, taking a long run like a bowler in cricket, hurled it towards the sea. It plopped satisfactorily. "That's all right then," she said, staring after it.

"What's all right? Anyway, you cheated that time with the run-up."

"Still counts," Eva said. "Everything will be all right now. See?"

"Of course," I said and we started to walk back in the direction of home. There was a thin bit of moon although the sky was still far from dark, more the colour of a deep bruise. "Of course everything will be all right. You'll get brilliant exam results and win a place at RADA and your dad will let you go there and you'll get famous. Just because your pebble reached the sea."

"That's right," said Eva. "You can trust pebbles, you know."

★ ★ ★

Surprisingly, for once, we did have a holiday away from Sea View Parade that summer.

For three days. In London.

My mother told me the day after Eva had left for Canada and I was about to go into Bampton to waste an afternoon window shopping and hang around at the library.

"We thought it would be a good idea, your father and I," she said as I was halfway up the stairs from the kitchen, "if we got away this summer, Mary. A bit of a break for all of us for once. I mean Mr. Jarvis is back with his mother for the whole of August, of course, and we've not yet got around to finding a replacement for Miss Mackie. If we even bother to do anything with her room after all the trouble that one caused," she added with a sudden bitterness to her voice. "Of course there's always a lot to do around the house, but what with no lodgers here and… for once, I think we could do with a few days away."

"A few days?" I said. For a mad snatched moment, I'd thought a fortnight like other people. Or a week at least. Eva was to be away for over three. My mother swiftly clarified.

"Three days is quite enough to see what we need to see in London. We can take the coach there and back, into Victoria, which is much cheaper than the train."

What we needed to see was, evidently, museums.

We stayed in a bed and breakfast place in somewhere called Turnham Green. A tall, Edwardian house unfavourably similar to Number 8, its city cousin, in fact, with only a few more creature comforts. Home from home, my mother happily announced when we arrived and found ourselves in a narrow hallway with walls covered in picture postcards of Buckingham Palace and the Tower of London. We climbed the three flights of stairs to our bedroom on the top floor, the vaguely respectable carpet of the lower floors gradually deteriorating as we climbed. And we were sharing. My parents were sleeping in a small double bed covered in vibrant florals and I was given a child's bed in the corner. I felt there had to have been some mistake. Even my mother looked dubious.

"She said on the phone it was a big room," she said, "the woman who owns the place. Irish she sounded or possibly Welsh. Always hard to tell with those sort of accents on the phone. And I did tell her you were fifteen, Mary."

My father looked nervous, probably suspecting that some action on his part was required.

"Don't I get my own room?" I said, and stood in the doorway trying to appear immovably obstinate and capable of causing trouble.

"I suppose we could see if there was something else. Or even go somewhere else," he said, peering out of the window through the lace curtains at the high street below. "If it's not up to scratch."

"Nonsense," my mother said decidedly, lifting the suitcase onto the bed and firmly clicking it open, "it's August, Jack. Be reasonable. We've probably got the last room left in the whole of London. We'll negotiate a reduction in the price in view of the child's bed. When you think about it like that, it's a godsend."

The toilet and very pink bathroom were two floors below. Queuing in the morning began around 7am and the hot water ran out soon after.

We went to the British Museum and looked at all the Egyptian rooms. I pointed out a little truculently that my history for the next school year was going to be all 19th century Poor Laws and reforming factory acts and Corn Law repeals and Gladstone and Disraeli and that pharaohs and mummies were left behind at primary school. My father smiled sympathetically and muttered something about all knowledge being useful and pressed on behind my mother. She set the pace, peering closely at each glass case, consulting the free guide and skirting us away from the gift shop and café. Finally, we were released out into the air of a Bloomsbury summer's afternoon. I felt dusty and dry-mouthed, my legs were tired, my shoulders ached from the slouched posture I'd decided to adopt as some sort of tacit rebellion. A man was selling ice creams and cold drinks from a van and a small queue had formed. My father looked enquiringly at my mother and began to feel for coins in his pocket. But she headed us firmly down the road in the direction of a pavement bench, unscrewed the flask she'd asked to be filled at breakfast time and produced a packet of biscuits. I refused the strong, sweet tea, felt embarrassed by the sight of my parents carefully sipping from their plastic cups and dipping biscuits as if on the beach in Broadstairs or Bognor in 1958 or thereabouts. Behind us a row of second-hand bookshops and sandwich bars looked worthier of inspection than the ancient exhibits that had dominated our day. I edged along the wooden pavement bench in an attempt to make people think I was apart from my parents, entirely separate and detached from the thermos flask and packet of custard creams. I hoped people would see me simply as a dark-haired young girl, a student even, in a pale blue skirt and ribbed sleeveless sweater, sitting casually alone in the middle of Bloomsbury. I searched in my bag for sunglasses and my book to improve the picture and pulled out a Catherine Cookson, wishing it was at least *Jane Eyre* that we'd recently read at school.

"South Kensington now," my mother said a moment or two later and made a fuss about cleaning the inside of the plastic cups with my father's handkerchief and stowing them away again. We followed her further down the road to the bus stop. "We've got a couple of hours left for the Natural History," she went on, scanning the bus routes displayed. "There's time for the dinosaurs, at least, and then we'll do the rest tomorrow."

And we did. At the Science Museum, I pressed numerous buttons in a clueless, careless sort of way whilst my mother consumed the contents of the displays with a sort of meticulous compulsion, as if fearful of wasting this free access to knowledge, but without any apparent sign of understanding or enjoyment. My father, however, was very different. He stared in admiration and in wide-eyed wonder. He loitered behind us as if entranced and began conversations with the occasional room guide, darted back to reread exhibits' details. I began to think he was wasted in his tax office, dealing with dull, predictable figures, required to produce dull, inevitably predictable outcomes. My mother and I waited for him in the enormous entrance hall. I thought she'd be pleased with his show of enthusiasm and passion for the place. But she didn't even seem to notice.

Turnham Green did not seem like London to me. I had been expecting us to stay in the Strand. Or near Oxford Circus, Marble Arch, perhaps, or Piccadilly. A smart hotel with revolving doors and a large restaurant and a shop with glass windows and impossibly expensive gifts. And porters ferrying people's suitcases and calling them taxis. That was how I thought of staying in London. I hadn't imagined a high street with ordinary shops, shabby front doors, stairwells leading to bedsits above betting offices and barbers and newsagents. That's what Turnham Green looked like to me as we went backwards and forwards on the number 27 bus each day. On our first night my mother headed us towards a Berni Inn attached to a pub that she'd spotted when we'd first arrived. I could not remember ever going out to eat with my parents. I'd been with Eva and her family for her sixteenth birthday treat and they were clearly restaurant kind of people who thought nothing of going most weekends to try out somewhere new that had opened. My mother, however, viewed restaurants as places of necessity rather than pleasure. She scanned the large plastic Berni Inn menu swiftly.

"The gammon and pineapple, I should think," she said as the waitress stood at her shoulder, pad in hand, "for all of us."

"Perhaps we could treat ourselves for once," my father ventured. "Perhaps Mary would like a steak?"

"Yes, please," I said swiftly, "rump steak, medium rare." It was what Eva had ordered on her birthday and I had swiftly followed. I repeated it to the waitress who scribbled it down swiftly and glanced at my father.

"Yes, that would be very nice, for me too, please," he

said, and we smiled at each other conspiratorially over the plastic menus. The following day, as if in punishment for our rejection of gammon and rebellious steak order, my mother managed to find a small supermarket on our way back from South Kensington and we ate pork pies and sausage rolls in Gunnersbury Park for our supper before it grew dark.

On our final day, with just a few hours before we were due at Victoria coach station for the journey home, I pleaded to be allowed to go shopping to spend money saved from babysitting jobs and was amazed when my mother agreed. I had just two hours to myself when I came out of the Tube at Oxford Circus and in spite of begging my mother to go alone, I felt suddenly overawed at the freedom in such a place. And I blamed my parents. If we had stayed in Ash Gardens instead of moving to Sea View Parade when I was eleven, it would all have been familiar to me. Oxford Street and Carnaby Street and Shaftesbury Avenue and Leicester Square and the rest would have been mere destinations instead of names that floored me with their glamour and excitement. I stood there, next to the newspaper kiosk selling the *Evening Standard* and the *Evening News*, resenting the nervousness and uncertainty I felt about where to go and how to behave. It would have been all right with Eva. Eva was used to coming up to London with her parents, who took her shopping and to Christmas shows at the Palladium. She would have taken charge. Then I saw a couple of girls about my age looking in the window of Peter Robinson's opposite and decided to follow them in. In twenty minutes, I'd spent most of my money on a plum-coloured midi skirt and had just enough left to buy some large flower-shaped clip earrings for Eva. There was a small café in a side street behind the store and, feeling considerably bolder by now, I went in and queued up at the counter for a cup of the sort of coffee we couldn't get in Bampton and sat in a small booth for half an hour, reading a paper someone else had discarded on the table. I hoped I looked like a regular customer, like the local I should have been.

I was relieved to be home in the privacy of my own bedroom, away from the bed and breakfast place in Turnham Green. The indignity and discomfort of sleeping in a bed that was one foot too short and had restraining side bars was only a little worse than seeing my parents asleep in their double bed. Summer morning light had slipped in early through the room's thin curtains so that I could not avoid the sight of them lying silently next to each other. Singly, in parallel lines, like a couple of strangers sunbathing on an overcrowded beach, carefully occupying a demarcated stretch of space. Although seeing them touch each other, kiss or hug would have been unbearably embarrassing, somehow their separateness was worse. As if marriage was actually mocking the idea of being close, for, in fact, people were still entirely alone. Isolated. Curiously disconnected. I shook out my new midi skirt from its carrier bag, hung it up in the wardrobe and thought about ringing Susan. Eva was still in Canada for another week or so. She was to be home just before her exam results came out and we'd already arranged to have a day together in Brighton.

14

Except that Eva didn't come back. The day after she was due home, I rang her house. There was no answer. I tried again the next day. Still the phone simply rang. I pictured their big hall with the cloakroom under the stairs, post neatly stacked on the black table by their cleaning lady who would have been in while they were away and the Masons' smart cream phone echoing through the empty house.

"Probably having such a good time they've decided to stay on a bit," my father said, as he saw me putting the receiver down in the hall. "Canada! Quite a trip, that."

I let the weekend go by. Susan and I went into Bampton on Monday and spent money in Woolworths on new pencil cases and biros and cardboard files ready for the new term that started the following week. I rang Eva's house again. Still no answer.

"She's going to be back by next week," Mr. Jarvis said. Presumably my mother had told him about my endless, fruitless phone calls. "Not going to miss the first day in the sixth form, surely. That's quite a rite of passage." He was back after his summer in London, tanned, surprisingly brown after the indifferent summer, which he put down to spending hours with his easel on Blackheath Hill. He sat at the kitchen table, a muddle of timetables and student lists spread out in front of him.

"Of course she'll be back for Monday," I said sharply, to convince myself as much as Mr. Jarvis. "There's loads of time before that."

"Unless they've decided to stay," he said, sipping from one of his endless cups of black coffee. "Emigrating to Canada is quite the thing at the moment, I've heard. Great opportunities, bigger salaries and so forth, that's what people are saying. Probably cheaper house prices too, I wouldn't mind betting. After all, it's a big country so land's not the premium it is here."

I took myself out of the kitchen and upstairs to my room to avoid talking further to him. I'd forgotten how much space he seemed to consume when sitting at the kitchen table. How he seemed to centre himself in a conversation, barge in on it with some remark even when the subject had little to do with him in the first place. As if he was part of the family rather than just our annoying lodger. Besides, he was entirely wrong. Eva was not emigrating to Canada. Her holiday had simply run over a bit and she'd be home good and ready in time for school on Monday.

Except that she wasn't. Term started and I saw girls from her school on my bus, smart and superior in their braided blazer and velour hats kind of way. When I came out of the gates each afternoon that first week, I half expected to see her waiting for me on the corner as usual. Jumping out to surprise me and tell me about their delayed or cancelled or missed flight or lost luggage or something. I gave up ringing the Masons' house. Instead, I began to have terrible visions of what could have happened to them. There were bears in Canada. Perhaps they'd gone into the mountains and been eaten alive and no-one knew of their demise. I kept these rather dramatic ideas to myself, of course, simply looking forward to entertaining Eva with them when she eventually returned and offered up some dull and bland explanation for their delay.

I was taking the fifth year at school seriously. It was, after all, an all or nothing year. All meant a coveted place at the grammar school for two years and a chance of a further education. Nothing meant leaving and heading down to the Employment Exchange or possibly signing up for a college course in Bampton. Every day after school I came straight home and went up to my bedroom to do my homework. I worked slowly, partly because I wanted to get everything right and partly to occupy the time. I wanted to forget that Eva had still not come home and apparently considered our friendship too trivial to bother to inform me why. I'd had one postcard during the summer and the ink on her message had smudged so that I could only make out a few words about the weather and the long flight. One day I went round to her house on my way home from school when I was in a particularly irritable mood, having got low marks in a history test about the Causes of Misery and Distress in 1815, wanting to confront her, on the off chance of choosing the moment that she was stepping out of a taxi home from the airport. But there was no-one there, even though the grass was cut, the curtains pulled back and no sense of an unusual absence or abandonment about the place.

Then I saw Mrs. Mason. One Saturday at the end of September, I'd just left Bampton library when I saw her car, her little white Triumph, parked outside the hairdresser's. I crossed the road to it and at the same moment she came out, a silk scarf loosely around her head as if expecting rain. She was wearing the yellow jacket that I'd often seen hanging in their downstairs cloakroom. I stepped into the small gap between her and the car.

"Mary! Goodness, you startled me! Popping up like that, out of nowhere." She started searching in her big patent bag for her bunch of keys, balancing it on one knee. There was a ladder in her tights splintering from knee to ankle where it disappeared into her black shoe underneath her heel. "You look very busy," she said, "all those books! Goodness, what a lot to get through." Her keys spilled out onto the pavement, the familiar bunch hanging from the green leather key case that I was used to seeing on the Masons' hall table.

"When did you get back?" I said, trying to sound indifferent rather than deeply hurt and disappointed that Eva had not rung me. I bent down to retrieve the keys for Mrs. Mason, dropped my pile of books on top of them so that the two of us were crouched on the pavement trying to sift the muddle. I imagined her ladder getting longer, turning into a large hole that reached to her toes.

"Back?" Mrs. Mason said, as if it were an odd kind of word and one with which she was not quite familiar. "Back? Oh, but we've been back a week or two now. Not Eva, of course. We were happy to leave her there. She's been offered such a wonderful opportunity that we just couldn't deny her the chance of it."

We stood up, *The Go-Between* and *Far from the Madding Crowd* once more wedged under my arm and Mrs. Mason's grasp on her green wallet of keys secure. I noticed that her scarlet nail varnish was chipped.

"So Eva didn't come back with you?" I said.

"Oh goodness me, no!" she said, her voice hitting a high note as if I had made the most absurd suggestion. She shoved the keys into the door of the white Triumph. "Our friends in Toronto have invited her to stay on for a few months, you see. Experience the Canadian way of life on a daily basis, as it were. Can you imagine it? She's having such a whale of a time. And there'll be the winter soon for her to look forward to with all that snow and... well, all that cold. It gets terribly cold there, you know. So interesting. Such a fascinating opportunity." She threw her big bag onto the passenger seat where it tipped and spilled its contents all over the floor. A coral-coloured make-up bag, a tortoiseshell comb, her black leather purse, a packet of cigarettes. I'd no idea that Mrs. Mason smoked.

"But... but when's she coming back?" I said. "I mean, what about school and the sixth form and stuff?"

"We plan on her staying a good six months," Mrs. Mason said, adjusting the knot in her silk scarf that had begun to slip up her chin, avoiding my face as if there was a mirror just beyond my shoulder for her to stare in. "After all, an experience like this, Mary, well, you just don't want to put a time limit on it. I mean, what could be better?"

"Can I have her address?" I said, surprising myself. Why did I want to have Eva Mason's Canadian address when she'd failed even to let me know where she was? What kind of friend, let alone best friend, failed to mention the slight detail that her summer holiday was turning into at least a six-month stay? The white Triumph started to rev. Mrs. Mason slammed her door, ran down the window.

"Oh, I can never remember it offhand," she said, "so many numbers and no proper road name like we have over here. But I'll let you have it next time I see you, Mary. Nice of you to want to keep in touch, but I doubt Eva will have much time for correspondence." She smiled broadly and I noticed her lipstick had smeared onto her front teeth as if she had applied it with too much enthusiasm. A crimson crescent against very straight, white ivory. She rolled up the window, shutting me out, flicked the switch of the car radio so that her last words to me were drowned.

Even my mother was a little sympathetic.

"Fancy not even writing to you," she said. "A proper letter to explain things. I call that rude, you know, and not the sort of thing I'd expect of Eva. A well-brought-up girl like her."

My father, as ever, attempted to be more positive.

"Well, the two of you will have lots of tales for each other when she gets back, Mary. And it'll mean you can concentrate on your studies and make sure of that place at the grammar. So an ill wind and all that. Every cloud with its silver lining." He was fond of his stock of proverbs.

Susan was blunt.

"Obviously not such a good friend as you thought. Why don't you ask Lysander – Stephen, whatever his name is, the boyfriend – what he thinks about it all?"

I nodded as if in agreement, knowing the last thing I would ever do would be to contact Lysander. The idea was too embarrassing even if I knew his phone number or any of his friends at the boys' school. I tried to think of something to do to anger Eva. Like finding another best friend and refusing to have anything to do with her when she eventually came home. Or deciding to dye my hair without telling her, letting her come back to discover me ash blonde, titian red, golden-streaked since hair dyeing struck me as the kind of lawful rebellion available when feeling powerless to do anything else. But I did neither, of course. I failed to find a replacement best friend, simply using Susan as a temporary and rather unsatisfactory substitute, and hair dyeing was out of the question with the prospect of my mother's wrath. Besides, I was developing an increasing tolerance for my own natural hair by this time. Even its relentless waviness had begun to seem less objectionable and people sometimes even admired it. Suspected I might be a bit Italian, a bit Greek. Possibly of Spanish origins. I allowed their illusion for my father insisted that my hair colour must come from my paternal grandmother who'd died before I was born. And she had been Welsh. *Just a girl from the valleys who came up to London to be in service,* he'd told me too many times to be of interest. *Very Celtic, that dark hair, you know, Mary.* There was only one small snapshot of my father's parents, blurred, creased, and offering little clue to hair colour at all. In fact, evidence of his parents was so scant as if they had never quite occurred and it was hard for me to believe in their lives with so little material proof attached to them.

★ ★ ★

I decided to copy Susan and work as hard as her. I didn't have the distractions of long hours behind the counter of the fish and chip shop that she handled so I reasoned that I could equal her and still have time for other things. Not that there really were other things without Eva. There was Bampton most Saturdays, the library then dawdling afterwards in Smiths or Boots followed by a cup of coffee and sometimes a Danish pastry in the new Café Suisse that had taken over the old tearooms. Even Bampton was beginning to realise that people were developing tastes for something more sophisticated than strong tea and currant buns. Most of the other girls in my class at school spent Saturday nights at the youth club or one of the dances held at the Town Hall. Monday mornings were devoted to their tales of gropes and snoggings outside in the cold. Susan always raised her eyebrows at them, sniffed and adjusted the National Health glasses she'd just had to acquire. She was quite happy to show her dismissal of them whereas I, cowardly, pretended not to hear them in the first place.

No-one had taken over Miss Mackie's room.

"I've a good mind not to bother about reletting," my mother said one day, opening the windows in the small square room and removing cobwebs that had gathered in dark corners. It was finally absent of Miss Mackie, months having passed since she'd left, so that even the faint odour of her clothes, the suggestion of iodine and moth balls that appeared to cling to her, had gone. "That woman was so much trouble, I really can't be doing with taking a chance with someone else."

I was surprised that the bird woman was considered now as a trouble-maker since she'd seemed docile enough, suitably small and thin so that it had been easy, mostly, to overlook her. Her occasional forays out of her room into the kitchen had been brief and insignificant in search of little more than Marmite toast or weak tea.

"A bit of a loss of income, though," my father said. "We'd always planned on the two rooms, after all. But of course, getting the right person isn't always going to be easy."

"There's my money coming in now, playing for the ballet school," my mother said, spreading her mixture of malt vinegar and lemon juice on the windows and rubbing them energetically with the dusters I'd been instructed to hand to her. Not proper yellow dusters like other people had, but disgusting scraps of discarded, ripped underwear that looked as if it came from the scene of some violent attack. "We hadn't counted on that before," she went on. "I think we'd do well to forget about another Miss Mackie for the time being."

I saw a chance.

"So can I have it? This room, I mean. Instead of my own. I'd move all my things down here myself and I'm sure I could work better. It would be really peaceful, you know. Sort of…" It was a pointless pretence. My bedroom next to my parents was hardly affected by throbbing pop music seeping through the walls. My mother, however, surprised me.

"That sounds like a good idea, Mary. Somewhere to concentrate on your studies. What do you think?" Over her shoulder she glanced briefly at my father as if genuinely seeking his opinion. "We'll sort it out at the weekend," she said. "Now there'll be no excuse for not passing all those exams with flying colours."

I liked my new room. Once Miss Mackie's traces had been entirely removed, I'd stuck my posters up and arranged my books, I was happier. The happiest I'd been since Eva had abandoned me for Canada. And I did work hard and began to get teachers talking to me more optimistically about transferring to the girls' grammar at the end of the summer.

One even mentioned the possibility of university and suggested I discuss it with my parents. But my mother soon silenced even contemplating such a thought.

"Goodness, no, a nice teachers' training college is what I want for you, Mary. No good claiming higher than your due," she said, so that I felt embarrassed at having even raised the subject.

★ ★ ★

The day after Boxing Day, a Christmas card arrived with a Toronto postmark, my name and address printed in capitals, although I could detect Eva's handwriting through the bold, black letters. I took it into my back bedroom and stuck it on the mantelpiece, trying to ignore it while I went back to bed for the warmth of the eiderdown to read *Jane Eyre* for the third time. Once Jane had run away from Thornfield and was forlorn and destitute, I turned to the card. Deep snow, reindeers and lots of glitter that spilled onto my pillowcase covered the front. Inside, Eva had written a couple of sentences. *See you in the spring – that's if I survive the cold here. Hope you get lots of nice things for Christmas.* Then Eva's squiggly signature with the very long 'v' and the daisy she always drew instead of a kiss. On the back, she'd printed her address. I shoved the card in the drawer under a load of socks and tights and tried to get back to Jane. St. John Rivers appeared and rescued her from his doorstep where she'd conveniently collapsed. His sisters welcomed the bedraggled stranger and tended to her feverish needs. I told myself I wasn't going to write. If Eva couldn't even be bothered to cover a side of a Hallmark card with a proper message, couldn't even concern herself to ensure the card arrived in time for Christmas rather than days after, a reply wasn't in order. That afternoon my father and I tried to make the living room fire light. We hardly ever used the room, but it was a good place for the Christmas tree, a silver tinsel version that my mother had bought with rare recklessness on Green Shield stamps. The kindling was damp and the fire went out five times before we managed to encourage a few flames that eventually gave out a weak heat. It needed feeding constantly, but I loved its smell and glow as the daylight disappeared before four. We watched an old film together on the sofa, pulled up close to the fire so that my legs felt charred with heat while my back stayed icy cold. At six o'clock, my mother brought us up left-over turkey and stuffing sandwiches and slabs of the cherry cake I'd made in cookery class in the last week of the school term. The cherries lay like a red carpet at the bottom of the sponge, having obstinately refused to scatter themselves through the thick mixture the way they were intended. We watched a Christmas Special. My father poured my mother a glass of sherry from the bottle that Mr. Jarvis had left before he'd gone back to London for the holidays.

"So you've heard from Eva?" my mother said suddenly, as if she was able to see into my mind and know that at that very moment I was imagining Eva in Toronto, in a snow-bound house that wasn't her own, surrounded by people who were now, probably, her closest and best friends. She sipped from her glass of sherry. My father got up to put the sound down on the television set as a loud, belting singer took over from the comedians. "You'll have to write back, Mary. You'll need one of those airmail letters you can get. You'll find that will be the cheapest way."

I shrugged, shoved a log deeper into the embers with the poker and felt the sudden soar of heat on my face.

"She'll be back in the spring," I said, "not much point writing now. And it's not as if I've any news to give her. Just school stuff."

"Even so," my mother said, and let my father fill her glass with another thimble of sherry, "it would be nice for her to hear from you especially as she's so far away from home. It's good to keep in touch with people, you know."

On New Year's Eve she came home with a thin slip of an airmail letter and left it on the desk in my room next to my French vocabulary book. It stayed there for a week or two until it got tea-stained and marked with my attempts at a new style of handwriting, sloping backwards with lots of loops that impressed me until my teachers told me it was unreadable. One day when I was in Bampton I went to the post office and bought a new airmail letter. That evening, I wrote it, filling it with flippant thoughts, to avoid writing the kind of things I really wanted to say. I wrote under headings, the way we did notes at school. Only instead of *The Chartist Manifesto* or *How to Make a Roux Sauce* or *Four ways of Finishing a Hem*, I wrote boldly under SCHOOL, then SUSAN, then MY NEW ROOM and filled the skimpy blue airmail page easily. Next morning, I posted it on the way to the bus, not really believing that such a thin and insubstantial slither of paper would make it all the way out of England and across the Atlantic to Toronto, Canada. And not particularly caring either. There were mocks in January. Practice exam papers to test how much we'd learned and how much we still had to learn before the real things in the summer term. Eva, I told myself, was really of very little significance to me anymore.

Mr. Jarvis began to take an interest in my future. Or at least began to nudge in when he saw me with books and files, which was most of the time.

"You could forget this grammar school talk, of course, and go to college for your A levels," he said, coming into the kitchen through the garden door. I didn't know he was home. I'd assumed I had the house to myself and was reciting quotes from *Romeo and Juliet* out loud. It was embarrassing to think he might have overheard me. "The Tech's very good, you know," he went on, "might see a bit more of life there, Mary, give you more idea of the real world."

"I know," I said sharply, "about the Tech, I mean. They've told us about it at school." It was partially true. There were lots of pamphlets around in Room 10 that you could go and look at during lunch times, but mostly you heard from someone who'd got a brother or sister already there. It was a huge place a bit like a high-rise block of flats, sticking up into the sky just outside Bampton. It looked worlds away from the girls' grammar and the idea of it seemed even more alarming.

"And after that, I suppose you'll be wanting to go off as an au pair for a year or two," he went on, filling the kettle and splashing water across the floor as the tap always gushed unless turned very slowly. Mr. Jarvis had never bothered to get the knack. "That's what all the girls are doing these days, brushing up on their French and learning how to cook Coq au Vin before going off to be students." It always annoyed me the way he talked as if he knew things, assumed to know me even more than I knew myself. I was delighted to disillusion him.

"I'd hate that," I said, "it's the last thing I'd think of. Living like a servant in someone else's house in a foreign country." I meant to sound strident rather than pathetic, but somehow it came out all wrong and I was annoyed to see him smile. I went on swiftly. "Anyway, I'm not thinking that far ahead at the moment. It's just silly planning things like that so far in the future."

"Absolutely, Mary! One day at a time, that's always been my motto. None of us knows what's around the corner, after all." He spooned his strong instant and stood waiting for the kettle. The exit to my room was partially blocked by his bulk and, besides, I was unwilling to let him think he'd succeeded in unsettling me. I spread out my file notes on the main characters of the play and sat mouthing and muttering away at one end of the table while he read his newspaper at the other.

★ ★ ★

I had a postcard from Eva in early March. *My trip's nearly over,* she wrote, *see you quite soon, Love Eva* and her daisy flower with a kiss inside it this time. Her large round handwriting meant the brief message took up the entire half side. I'd had no reply to my skinny odd letter so perhaps she'd never received it or saw no point in answering something so patently evasive and cold. Still, she'd be back soon and her absence had been so long that I was beginning to let my anger thaw, was close to forgiving her for it entirely. Eva had never written letters to anyone. We'd never needed to write letters to each other so no doubt the idea didn't even pop into her mind. And of course, phone calls from Canada would be impossibly expensive and probably indistinct given the amount of sea between us. If she arrived back just as the Easter holidays began, we'd have over two weeks of time to spend simply catching up.

It was still very cold. My father spent hours in the garden looking for definite signs of spring, but apart from snowdrops that had clustered in the front beds in late January there were only forced daffodils in the shops to give any indication that winter was ending. I'd long been convinced that our small slice of south coast was colder and bleaker than its near neighbours. As if Beach Parade had a particularly hostile position that left it exposed to the worst of the sea storms, leaving the rest of the sea fronts, to our east and west, blissfully unscathed. One Sunday night, the wind seemed to seep through the walls even more successfully than usual. I thought I heard the front door bang and assumed it was Mr. Jarvis back from his weekend with his mother in London. Sometimes he drove back Sunday nights, sometimes not until Monday morning, going straight to his college so that we didn't see him until tea time. So it wasn't unusual when he didn't appear next morning at breakfast. The dustbin had been knocked over in the night, spilling its rubbish across the front garden. Stones and pebbles, thrown up from the beach by the force of the wind, scattered themselves in the road like a particularly random kind of crazy paving. My mother was out at one of her piano playing children's ballet classes when I got in. I lit all the gas burners on the stove for five minutes to warm the place a bit, poked around in the larder for some bread and made toast. I thought of ringing Mrs. Mason to check on the date Eva would be back, but then shrank from the idea. I didn't want her to think I was desperate, entirely friendless without Eva. My father was home at ten past six as always and my mother five minutes later. I sat in my room learning the Sermon on the Mount for the R.E. test the next day and heard her next door in the kitchen say something about omelettes for supper as there was only fat and bone left from Sunday's lamb. She switched on the radio and clanked around with plates and pans with a background of the news and weather. Unseasonably cold for the time of year, evidently. Heavy overnight frosts. A risk of ice. *Blessed are the peacemakers, Blessed are the righteous,* I muttered, and hoped at least there'd be a bit of cheese to grate on top of the omelettes. *Blessed are they that hunger and thirst, For they shall inherit the kingdom of heaven,* I mouthed to my mirror and pulled bits of my hair down over my forehead and considered a fringe.

There was a knock on the front door.

"Get that, will you?" my mother shouted up the stairs to my father. "Whoever it is. Silly time to call when people are having their teas. Mary, come and lay the table for me, there's a good girl."

I threw the New English Bible onto my bed and went into the kitchen. I set four places, knives, forks, glasses of tap water, expecting Mr. Jarvis to come in at any moment. But he didn't. Instead, my father walked slowly down the staircase and stood at the bottom as if hesitant to come into the room. Behind him, his helmet held under one arm, stood a tall, dark-haired policeman.

15

The care assistant admires my jacket.

"Lovely colour, that," she says. "Duck egg blue, you'd call that, wouldn't you?" She watches me as I sign out of the visitor's book, noting that my stay has been less than an hour. I cheat, add six minutes. "You're your mother's daughter, all right, I can tell that," she says at my shoulder. I smile. Her bleeper goes. She chooses to ignore it. "I mean, you can tell your mum was one for clothes when she was younger. Must have had a lovely figure. So many of them run to fat when they get on a bit, but your mum... well, you can see she kept herself in check."

I wonder for a moment if she's mistaken me for someone else's daughter. I know this care assistant's face by now, remember that her name's Barbara, but it's quite possible she attaches me to another resident. The woman in the room neighbouring Ida's, perhaps, who plays her television very loudly. Ida's attitude to clothes could only ever be described as utilitarian. The few good things she's had have tended to be gifts from me, desperate for ideas for a special birthday. The pale grey cashmere sweater for her seventieth that she wore only for subsequent special occasions. The silk-lined gloves that resided for years in a chest of drawers. And as for taking care of her figure, Ida's always been naturally angular, over-indulgence of no appeal to her at all. I say goodbye to Barbara, find car keys and drive thankfully away. Not forgetting first, of course, to thank her, to thank all of the staff, these extraordinary every day saints, for their care and concern for Ida. Today she has said little. In fact, I am unsure whether she has even been pleased to see me. Sometimes I feel as if my visits trawl her unfairly back to a world in which she now can play no part. She looks at me, once in a while, as if she wants to object to the farce I am playing. I go on about Felix and what he's doing as if she has some imaginative grasp on the world of a teenage boy. I talk about work and the classes I have to prepare for, my students who are thankfully keen to learn. I talk, to occupy the time, to fill the void between us. Really, all I want to say, over and over again, is how has it come to this? How have you, in particular, come to this? Why do all of us celebrate life when its inevitable concluding phase is a downward trajectory full of suffering and sadness?

When I was about twenty-one or twenty-two, I suddenly realised that Ida was an attractive woman. Not in any obvious, eye-catching way, with her lack of vanity or preoccupation with appearance. But I saw that my mother had what people call a good bone structure and clear, strong features. And she was slim. Shapely, even. I'd envied Eva her mother's femininity when we were young, her cluttered dressing table with tubes of foundation and night creams and day creams and her lacquered hair. But later on, Mrs. Mason became stout, heavy, and her ample bosom suddenly seemed old-fashioned and matronly. Ida hardly changed for years. Eva and I grew up at a time when people were either fat or thin. None of us had figures. Figures had not been invented. Eva and I were skinny beanpoles, Susan had puppy fat. That was the way it was. A sort of acceptance with the given lot rather than obsessing and clamouring for something different. But Ida, I saw later on, had a certain kind of beauty that was possibly ahead of its time. Or at least not obviously hitched to its time, to be noted only by those who had an eye to see such things. No-one has ever noted a similarity between us. Barbara, the care assistant, is probably just making conversation, saying what she expects people want to hear. I have always felt I have few marks of my mother, either in temperament or appearance. And Jack, too, has failed to pass on his tranquillity, his even, steady temper that comforted me as a child. I shove a CD into its slot and drive home to the balm of light classics. I have work to prepare for the following week. There's my adult education group who are studying a selection of 20th century novels to fit in with the extremely vague and rather portentous course title of Women in Literature. It's what the Further Education college choose to call an Introductory Level – Continuing Education Class and it's proved popular, with fifteen signed up for the term. The idea is to look at novels with strong female protagonists as well as to introduce some of literature's greats. I've cheated a bit to produce a course that's reasonably user-friendly, by which I mean selecting some shorter novels accessible to adult students with busy, hectic lives. No-one, I am sure, will argue that Daisy Buchanan is a strong woman, but *The Great Gatsby* is a favourite and its brevity will balance out *Sons and Lovers* and *Howards End*. It starts to rain and the wipers hardly keep up with the torrents suddenly gushing from the early summer sky. Traffic gets heavy and I drive sheepishly on the sodden roads so that the journey home takes almost twice as long as it should. I park halfway down our cluttered road of early Edwardian semis, a road that does not historically accommodate the idea of cars.

There's another letter on the mat.

Somehow, I'm not surprised. It's the same thick blue envelope with one of those small gold name and address labels stuck on the back telling me it's come from Lancashire. No-one sends letters like this anymore. It smacks of another era when people made time for such niceties. I put it to one side, make a pot of tea and turn on the computer in the upstairs back box room that I elevate by calling it my study. The page won't format the way I want it to and Felix is out, his reliable skills remote from me on a tennis court. I gather together my old paperback editions of relevant novels and start to mark pages, passages for copying. But the envelope on the table in the kitchen is too distracting, its gold address label scratching for attention one floor down.

Her name is Eliza Jarvis.

I wonder whether she's never married or has just chosen to retain her maiden name. And whether she's really Elizabeth and has decided that Eliza is more of the moment. Less last century. I try to concentrate on other women, on Daisy Buchanan and her fixation with Jay Gatsby then become temporarily absorbed by Mrs. Morel, by resourceful Margaret Schlegel. But it's no use. Fiction suddenly seems insufficiently compelling compared with the pull of real lives and I go downstairs, find the letter sitting prominently on the pile of junk mail on the kitchen table and open it. It's just a single sheet, covered both sides in the same bold writing of the envelope. I flatten it on top of a flyer from the local kebab shop.

Dear Mary, she writes, in neat, very rounded and precise handwriting, *I expect you are surprised to hear from me and might not want me to be in touch. I managed to obtain your address from your father as I found his name in the phone book quite by chance.* The phrase is deeply unconvincing. As if Eliza Jarvis spent her time roaming the directories of south coast counties for such random enlightenment. *Please don't worry, I didn't explain to him exactly who I was, just said I was an old friend who had lost touch with you.* She couches deception as if I should be indebted to her sensitivity. *The past is the past, I know, but as the years go by, I can't help thinking about things and growing curious. Perhaps you too…* I stop reading properly and just scan the remaining lines, hovering here and there rather than absorbing the precise meaning, as if my refusal to give it full attention will lessen its implication. I put the single sheet back in the envelope, go upstairs and shove it deep into a drawer of winter sweaters in my bedroom. The phone rings. It's a nonsense call, a survey with pointless questions to which I start to snap answers until remembering that I can simply hang up. I go back to the computer and log off.

I feel as if Eliza Jarvis has caught me out at my own game.

As if she's heard me trying to stir things up with Ida, is following me on my meticulous trawl through that span of years for evidence, enlightenment, and has decided to confront me fully to test my resolve. How much truth am I willing to face, after all? There I go, mining for details, chipping away for scraps of something verifiable, disturbing Ida, poking at Jack's complacency, when I cannot even bring myself to digest the contents of a letter dangerously relevant to my search. For I have read enough to know that Eliza Jarvis is possibly even one step ahead of me. Thinking along lines that I've chosen always to step round, ignore. She wants an answer. She wants to know if I would like to meet. And in between her polite words, her ostensibly hesitant approach, I sense her determination. She's not going to go away easily. There's a sister, too, a younger sister, only three or four at the time, but the letter only refers briefly to her so this appears to be Eliza's mission. Lancashire is, conveniently, a considerable distance. I can leave her letter for a week or two, then respond in a vague kind of fashion as if she's in my long-term plans, but hardly head of the list. Stall her. Yes, that's what I'll do. Stall her rather than rebuff entirely her approach.

The front door bangs, surprising me, and I realise that I've been staring out at the scrappy back garden for ten minutes at least. Weeds are competing with the early summer border plants. I really need to do something about the lawn. Cut it, possibly. Feed it, maybe. I head downstairs. Felix is in the kitchen, shoulders in the fridge and I realise I should think about food. I want to hug him, enwrap his constantly growing frame in a huge embrace as if he is still three years old. I resist.

"Hungry?"

"Starving. There's nothing to eat."

"Of course there is. Tins and things. Stuff in the freezer."

He closes the door, moves to the cupboard as if expecting a fully prepared meal to appear in front of his eyes.

"It'll take ages. Freezer stuff. We could have a take-away. Chinese?" He's found half a packet of crisps at the back of the cupboard, eats them in two handfuls.

"It's Monday," I say, "take-aways are for weekends. Occasional treats."

"So?" Felix says.

"It's against rules," I say, opening the fridge again to find the open bottle of wine, "you know that."

"What rules? Why does it matter what day it is?" Felix helpfully hands me a glass and I splash wine into it.

"It just does. We're all governed by rules. It's like giving up if you have a take-away mid-week." But I'm weakening. Felix can tell. He's searching in the drawer for the *Oriental Star* menu.

"You don't want to cook," he says. "Why are you so hard on yourself? Rules? What's that about?"

"It's a generation thing," I say inadequately, "you earn treats so they're for weekends. After a week's hard toil." I don't know why he's bothering with the menu. He always orders us the same. They know us by now, the people at the *Oriental Star*. They hear my voice and join in with the sweet and sour Hong Kong style and the cashew chicken. I gulp wine. I can't help wondering what would happen if I simply went to the phone and rang Eliza Jarvis. Would she be cold and distant or adopt the tone of an old friend with much to share?

"So can we?" Felix says, expectant, looking suddenly deliciously young and anxious to be spoilt. Unconditional love overwhelms. "Can we order?"

"All right," I say. "We'll be good the rest of the month. Earnest home-cooked meals and lots of stews." He's about to pick up the phone when it rings as if summoned. Madly, I think of Eliza Jarvis. Felix gets there first and foolishly I find myself wondering how I'll explain who she is. But it's not her, of course. It's his grandfather. It's Jack. After a moment, he holds the phone out to me, looking concerned. Normally, there'd be some talk between them, a bit of banter about football scores, cricket even, and school. Immediately, I, too, feel alarmed.

"Mary? Sorry to worry you." He sounds remote, strained. My mind flies to Ida although it's only hours since I left her. Surely nothing could have happened in so short a time. Jack coughs, clears his throat then goes on in a voice a little too quiet to hear easily. "Sorry, Mary, but I've had a bit of a nasty turn, you see. Nothing, really, only they think I should let you know. The medical people here." I sit down at the kitchen table. "They want to keep me in overnight. Lot of fuss over nothing, but you know what they're like once they've got their hands on you. All these doctors taking a look and such. They say they want to do tests and... well, just to make sure."

I disentangle a few facts. Jack's in hospital. Evidently, his neighbour saw him in the garden, attempting some pruning one moment, slumped in the flower bed the next. He'd come round by the time the neighbour had made her way down the side path and through his back gate, but she'd insisted on calling an ambulance. He's been admitted overnight although there's no suggestion of anything particularly serious. At least according to Jack. "People faint, don't they?" he says, attempting to sound light-hearted. "Not a crime to faint every once in a while."

I can be there in less than an hour, I tell him, ignoring his protest which is mild. I am not sure who needs to see the other most. This is not what I have prepared for. Ida is the invalid, the one likely to cause a bleak phone call in the middle of the night, not Jack. Jack's supposed to have some years ahead of him of relative contentment and peace without the demands of caring for Ida. I am not ready for the loss of Jack. Felix is still standing across the room, still clutching the menu for the *Oriental Star.* He looks resistant to bad news as if failing to ask the relevant questions will repel the event.

"It's Grandpa," I say. "Probably nothing serious, but he's in hospital so we'll have to go and see him."

"Now?" Felix is visibly appalled. He's hungry, he's expecting sweet and sour pork and prawn crackers. He loves his grandfather, but everything has a time and a place. I pour wine from my glass down the sink, wish I hadn't already drunk half a glass.

"Yes, now. I need to see him tonight. We can't just leave him on his own."

"But you said it wasn't serious."

"No, but… but you never know. I mean he'll want to see us, won't he? We don't have to stay long." I push past him, still hovering in the kitchen doorway. "I don't want to leave you on your own."

"I'll be all right," Felix says, seeing a loophole, following me into the hall.

"No, you're coming," I say. "Please. I need you with me."

We stop at the *Oriental Star* on the way as a compromise. The journey takes us only forty minutes or so although the labyrinthine corridors of the hospital mean that it is nearly eight by the time we arrive at Jack's ward. Next to me Felix smells of soy sauce and his white t-shirt is stained orange, tie-dye style. Visitors are just leaving, but the nurses smile, wave us through, and we find our way to a bay at the end of a narrow unit. Jack looks shrunken in the bed, his head somehow too small on the stack of pillows. He's wearing a hospital gown, the sort that flaps ungainly open at the back as if designed to remove all dignity. Felix glances nervously around him, focuses on the floor.

"Goodness me, all this fuss!" Jack says as he sees us, but smiles broadly. He seems especially pleased to see Felix, flattered even, and sends him across the room to collect some chairs. "Don't remember a thing about it, that's what's so annoying," he says to me in a whisper, as if to spare Felix details. "You don't want to get old like me, you know, Mary. Start being a nuisance to people."

"You're never a nuisance," I say truthfully, "and you're not old. I won't have you thinking yourself old." I touch his hand. He has the hands of a craftsman who works in intricate detail, a wood carver or silversmith. Long, tapered fingers, a narrow palm. I wish we'd stopped to buy something for him. Some of his favourite boiled sweets, some fruit. I feel inadequate, sitting next to him without even a grape to offer. Visitors are supposed to bring grapes and barley water to clutter the bedside cabinet.

"What happened? I mean it can't just have been fainting. They don't bring people into hospital for fainting, do they?" Felix, bless him, is showing appropriate interest.

"At my age they bring you in for anything," Jack says. "They like to have a good excuse to examine you, especially the young ones who are still learning, and they're sure to find something wrong. A bit like an old engine in a car with all the parts rusting, that's me."

The ward is quite empty, only two or three other beds occupied and no doubt there for observation like Jack.

"How long will they keep you?" Felix asks. "Until they decide you're all right to come home?"

Felix is disposed always to be positive. To see the world only in measured, equable terms. Or perhaps it's that he's yet too young to suspect bleak consequences at every turn.

"Maybe I can have a word with one of the nurses?" I suggest, slipping easily into the parental role I play now for Ida. I leave Jack and Felix to talk about the cricket. Wickets and creases and ducks. At the desk I find a staff nurse who checks notes and says they were concerned that Jack might have had a stroke. A minor one, but nevertheless something they'd like to clarify in case there's to be a pattern. On the other hand, she says, it may have been nothing. Perhaps he was merely dehydrated. *Elderly people don't always drink enough*, she says, *none of us do, really, but Mr. Foster might be neglecting his liquid intake.* I notice how young she is and how pretty. Blonde hair swept back into a tight pony tail, large brown eyes and a long, graceful neck. She can't be so many years older than Felix yet I respect and trust her absolutely. She tells me they've taken bloods, will run some tests tomorrow then he'll probably be free to go. *We don't want to keep him unnecessarily*, she says. *People are so much better off in their own home, after all. Even if he has to take things easy, I'm sure he'll be happier to get back to familiar surroundings.* She smiles her young, radiant smile and goes to answer a phone. I think of Ida and remember the day I drove her away from her own home, her familiar surroundings, talking endlessly in loud, brittle tones to prevent myself from crying. Wanting to explain that the loss was mine as well as hers yet unable to find words to define this adequately. I had lied to her, of course, or at least had been economical with the truth, choosing to imply that the arrangement was temporary, something of an experiment. *You'll be happy,* I'd told her, *and so much more comfortable than at home, but we'll see how things go. How you get on.* Later, as I'd left her, I'd caught sight of her face across the large dining room, bewildered, hurt. As if she saw it as an appalling betrayal and I wished I'd had the courage to be more honest. Jack is telling Felix about the patient in the corner bed who's something of a gambler. Evidently, he's been passing on racing tips and is desperate to get on the phone to his bookie. The man looks across at us sharply and swears in a loud, voice. A nurse comes in and hushes him, plumps his pillows. A trolley rattles its way down the room, loaded with drugs.

"I'm a bit worried about the bungalow," Jack says, "leaving it overnight. I'm not sure the back door was locked. And I might have left the lawn mower out. It was all such a rush, you see, the ambulance business and feeling a bit under the weather." He seems more concerned about leaving the house in a hurry than about his own state of health. I assure him that his neighbours will keep an eye on things, but he looks doubtful. He doesn't want to be a bother to them, any more than he already has been.

"It wasn't your fault, Grandpa." Felix sounds exasperated. Jack's self-deprecation seems embarrassing to him. Something of another age.

"I'll ring them," I offer. "Rosa and Jeff, isn't it? They'll understand. Anyway, I want to thank her for calling the ambulance. If she hadn't been in and seen you, I hate to think…"

"That's the ticket," Jack says, "you give her a ring, Mary. That reminds me, a friend of yours got in touch the other day. Well, not the other day, of course, some weeks back now and I keep meaning to tell you. My memory plays such tricks with me these days."

I look at my watch. It's definitely time to go.

"We must make a move, there's school tomorrow for Felix and it's getting late."

"Has she rung you? She said she'd lost your number, something about moving around a bit, I think. Forget what she said exactly. Or was it your address she wanted? Sounded a nice person, very friendly and that, otherwise I wouldn't have given it to her, of course."

Felix is already across the ward, heading to the door. I kiss Jack on the cheek. Suddenly, he looks very tired.

"You take care of yourself. Have a good night's sleep. I'll ring you tomorrow and check with the hospital to see what's happened with these tests. See if you're going home or not."

"Has she been in touch?" he says patiently, as if I haven't heard him. "Her name's gone from my mind, or perhaps she didn't say what it was."

I find the car keys in my pocket. Suddenly I remember that I haven't eaten all day. Nothing since I left home this morning to visit Ida. I wonder whether there's any of Felix's egg fried rice left in the carton in the car or if the *Oriental Star* will still be open when we get back. Jack's still looking at me, questioningly.

"No," I say, edging across the ward towards Felix, "I don't think I've heard from anyone like that. Anyone unexpected, I mean."

Felix is quiet in the car. He roves around various radio stations and finally settles on one that's constantly interrupted by static. We find a late-night store and make do with stale sandwiches and a bar of chocolate that we share between us. It's barely dark and the moon is an enormous crescent that looks artificial, as if it's suspended by a wire.

"Grandpa's going to be all right, isn't he?" Felix eventually says, as we pull up outside the house. "I mean, I thought he was fine. He always seems really well. Like he never really changes. It's Nan who's ill, surely."

His face looks anxious in the half light of the street lamp. He wants certainties.

"Yes, I'm sure he is." I rest my head on his bony shoulder for a moment. When did he manage to grow so tall? "Hopefully, today was just a false alarm."

"That's all right then," he says and is out of the car in a moment.

Eliza Jarvis' letter, hiding away in the chest of drawers in my bedroom, suddenly seems an irrelevant absurdity.

16

My mother sat down at the kitchen table, a blue and white tea towel in her hand. The policeman looked across at me where I still stood in the doorway of my room. He looked away, into space above my mother's head.

"Dead on arrival at the hospital, I'm afraid," he repeated. "Pretty bad smash. Went into a lamp post, evidently. Poor bloke, but at least he wouldn't have known much about it."

My father coughed, cleared his throat.

"His college knows? Place where he works. He's… he was a teacher, you see, art teacher. Lecturer, I suppose you call it."

The policeman nodded.

"It was them sent me here, the college people. Got this down as his term-time address. Your lodger, I understand."

My mother said nothing. It was unlike her to leave conversations entirely to my father. She sat folding the blue and white tea towel into neat squares on her lap. I kept thinking that there was a mistake. This policeman must have come to the wrong house. There must have been an error identifying the man in the car crash. People didn't simply disappear, slip out of their life, our lives, the way the policeman seemed to be suggesting. At any moment, there would be Mr. Jarvis' heavy footsteps on the basement stairs, the smell of stale cigarette smoke on his black jacket. The radio was still on. In the background I heard one programme end, the theme tune to *The*

Archers start. I wondered whether I should slip across the room to the dresser to switch it off, but it seemed wrong to move.

"I presume his mother's been told," my father said eventually. "I hope there's someone there to look after her. She's quite frail, I believe, and a shock like this…well."

The policeman shifted, I saw him glance at the clock.

"Mother?" he said. "I wouldn't know about that. No family details apart from his wife."

My mother looked up sharply.

"Wife? Then you have the wrong person," she said, and stood up from the table abruptly, scraping her chair across the flagstone floor. "Fred Jarvis, our Fred Jarvis, the one who lives here, wasn't married. He isn't married, I mean."

"That's right," my father agreed, glancing towards my mother, "there's obviously been some ghastly mistake. Mr. Jarvis lives in London, Greenwich, in fact, with his elderly mother. At weekends and the holidays and such when he isn't lodging here."

The policeman looked at us as if trying to retain his patience. As if he felt he'd already gone beyond the call of duty and wanted to be back behind his desk at the police station worrying about meth-drinking tramps and stolen wallets and lost dogs. Slowly, he drew a small notebook out of his pocket, flicked it open and scanned notes on a page.

"Mr. Fred Jarvis lived in Croydon. 15a, Malpass Road, South Croydon. With his wife and family. They've been informed, naturally. On Friday night when it happened."

"Friday?" My mother's voice sounded like an objection. "This is all nothing to do with us. We would have known if anything… Jack, sort this out with the policeman. Tell him he's got it all wrong."

The policeman turned to go. My father took a tentative step towards him, looking as though he was going to grab his arm then thinking better of it.

"Really, we don't know what to make of all this," he said. "Is there any chance you can ring your station, check your facts? You can see how upsetting it is for us to think that we might… well, we need to be sure."

The policeman looked at my mother then straight at me. I pulled at the frayed cuff of my school sweater, feeling my middle finger find its way to a familiar hole. *The Archers* continued to hum away in the background. Someone seemed to be arguing about disappointing milk yields.

"He was just your lodger," the policeman said eventually, speaking slowly as if to young, rather dim children. "Perhaps you didn't know him as well as you thought you did. I think the college is going to be in touch about some library books. And his wife, of course, no doubt she'll contact you about his things. Personal possessions he might have had in his room here." He started to walk up the stairs, my father following him.

"I'm sorry," I heard him say from the hall, "it's never nice to bring bad news. And sudden death is always a shock. Although it's not as if he was a relative, is it? Just your lodger, after all."

We heard my father mutter something back, a few more words from the policeman then the front door opening and closing. My mother was shaking. She stood in the middle of the room, staring at the wall as if she'd forgotten that I was with her. I dashed across to the radio and switched it off. I felt frightened. I wanted to cry, not so much for the loss of Mr. Jarvis as out of a sense of panic at the random nature of his death. One moment sitting in our kitchen, annoying me with his big voice and forceful ideas, the next, nothing. An absence, as if he'd been swallowed whole into some pit of darkness. My father came downstairs and tried to take my mother's hand, tried to slip his arm around her shoulder, but she pushed him away, brushed past him and headed towards the stairs herself.

"Jack, you've got to sort it all out," she shouted at him. "It's just all a muddle. It's not him. They've got the wrong man. They've got it all confused. I need to know it's not how they say," she said, then she started to cry. Huge, loud gulps that terrified me, noises that seemed to come not from my calm, controlled mother, but from some wild and injured beast that had possessed her. My father tried to reach her again, but she rushed upstairs and we heard her all the way up to their bedroom, those dreadful noises, half crying and half yelping as if in intolerable pain. The bedroom door was slammed, the lock turned, yet still the sound of her reached us. Or we imagined it did.

Cracked eggs were sitting in a bowl on the table.

We both looked at them as if trying to remember their place in the evening. Neither of us spoke. I felt suddenly very cold.

"Shall I put the kettle on?" I said at last, wanting to fill the awful silence. "Make some tea?"

"Mary, what a good thought. You've got all the bright ideas." My father looked up at me as if he had quite forgotten that I was there and was very relieved to find that I was. "I think we deserve a cuppa."

I filled the kettle and fiddled around with cups and milk while he went back to staring at the kitchen's yellow walls as if expecting to see something significant. I poured three cups and sat down at the table. He came and joined me, but left his tea until it grew cold.

"Shall I take a cup upstairs?" I said, but he shook his head.

"Let's leave your mum for a bit, Mary. Nasty shock for all of us and you never know how these things are going to take you."

216

I wanted to go into my room and be on my own, but at the same time I wanted to pretend that things were normal. A routine, dull Monday evening with my mother's thin omelettes and her request that I help wash up. Suddenly, such ordinariness seemed utterly desirable since in its place was a senseless muddle that I didn't want to start to pick apart.

"We ought to have supper," I said, quietly so that my father could ignore me if he wanted. It's what my mother would usually say with her insistence upon order whatever the circumstance and I was surprised to hear myself echoing her. My father looked at me after a moment or two, as if trying to pull his mind back from somewhere else.

"Of course. Yes, that's what we'll do, Mary. You're quite right." He moved swiftly to the sink and poured away the contents of his cup. "Any ideas?"

"There's the eggs," I said. "We were supposed to be having omelettes."

"Omelettes," he said, "well, that's simple enough." Nevertheless, he watched me whisk the eggs with a fork, melt a bit of margarine in the frying pan, as if I was making a complicated gourmet dish. The egg mixture stuck to the bottom and when I tried to lift it out of the pan it broke into bits so that I had to try and reassemble it on the plate. Some bits were burnt, others were still puddles of raw egg. It looked dreadful.

"I don't think I'm very hungry now," I said, my face growing red with shame at my hopeless culinary effort. I'd meant to make things better and instead I'd turned the evening even more despondent. My father said nothing for a moment and I wondered if he was cross with me. Then, suddenly, he stood up, grabbed the two plates from the table and deposited the contents in the pedal bin.

"Chips, Mary, that's what we need. Let's go and get ourselves some fish and chips."

"Tonight? But we only ever do that at weekends. And what about… I mean, just for us?"

I was still frightened by the wildness of my mother's crying, but it didn't feel right to mention it. As if by ignoring it there was a possibility we could pretend it hadn't happened. My father was putting on his jacket, searching for his scarf from the dresser. He found the jam jar of silver kept on a high shelf to pay the milkman each Friday and shook out some coins.

"Yes, Mary, supper just for us, I think. Now get your warm coat. We'll have a bit of a walk and pick ourselves up something to eat. I think we could do with getting out of the house."

I scuttled into my bedroom, shoved my feet into my school shoes and got my coat quickly before he could change his mind. He was waiting for me on the step outside, jingling hands in his pockets. It was strange to see him so impulsive.

We walked down to the coast road and I had to skip a bit to keep up with him. It was bitterly cold and I shoved my hands up the sleeves of my coat to keep them warm. Rain, trying to turn itself into sleet, was in the air. When we got to Beach Parade, my father stopped, looked in both directions.

"We can go to the Flying Fish on the corner or walk further on, to your pal Susan's place. What do you think?"

Without waiting for me to choose the Flying Fish as the closer option, he turned left, saying something about the fresher fish and the dripping they used.

"We should have brought the car if we were coming this far," I said.

"Don't want to end up with it smelling of vinegar and frying," he said. "Besides, nice to get some air into the lungs. Nothing wrong with a bit of cold air and exercise."

Susan's mother was serving. Her grandfather was coating fish fillets in thick yellow batter and popping them into a vat of hot fat. Susan would be studying for the R.E. test upstairs in the flat, just the way I had been before the policeman arrived. During our walk I'd almost managed to forget the news he'd brought, dismissed it like an alarming dream. Now I confronted it again, standing in the fug and warmth of the shop, waiting for two cod and chips to be wrapped. We walked back more slowly, tucking the wrapped parcels of food into our pockets where they warmed our sides.

"Do you think it's definitely our Mr. Jarvis?" I said to my father, needing to ask, needing to know for certain.

"Yes, Mary, I don't think there's any doubt of that," he said, and we walked on in silence until we reached the edge of Beach Parade. "Police don't make mistakes about things like this," he went on eventually. "Identities, documents showing who people are, that sort of thing."

"But did you know he was married? Why didn't he tell us?"

My father took out one of the warm packets, opened it and handed me a couple of chips. I forgot to blow on them and burnt my tongue. He ate a large handful himself as if suddenly ravenous.

"Some things we'll probably never know for sure," he said between mouthfuls, "not so as you could swear on it."

I wasn't sure what he meant, but needed more answers.

"But his mother in Greenwich. Didn't he really go back and see her every weekend and all through the holidays? Was that all just stuff he said to us?"

"Truth and lies, Mary. Probably a bit of both all tucked in there. We only know what Mr. Jarvis chose to tell us, for reasons of his own, no doubt. And I'd say we'll be as well not to search too deep or worry about the facts too much. Not much point now," he added, more to himself than to me. We crossed the road, headed back to Sea View Parade to Number

8. Still I half-expected to see Mr. Jarvis' scratched black car outside. There was a space where he usually parked and I wished someone would come and fill it just to leave it looking less noticeably empty, drawing attention to itself.

The house was quiet. We took the rest of our fish and chip meal down to the kitchen and ate it on plates still dirty from the hopeless omelettes. I wished my mother would come downstairs. I wanted her to appear at the door, fussing about our extravagant supper and the bottle of malt vinegar we'd stuck on the table. Then I could simply forget her earlier behaviour, excuse it as some sort of overreaction caused by shock. Instead it lingered, a piece of unease surfacing every now and again like a crossword clue that needed resolving, an obstinate piece of ill-fitting jigsaw. My father found half a bottle of whisky at the back of the larder and poured himself a quarter glass. He caught my eye as I finished the last of my chips and the pickled onion.

"Just for medicinal purposes, Mary. It's been quite an evening. And when all's said and done, a man's died."

I wasn't quite sure why he was stating the obvious. He sipped steadily at his tumbler and refilled it before it was finished. I made an excuse about homework to finish and escaped to my bedroom, where I found my books, my revision notes about the Sermon on the Mount scattered where I'd left them hours earlier. I wanted to talk to Eva. I felt angry with her all over again for staying so long in Canada. If she was at home I could go round the next day after school. We'd sit on the floor in her bedroom and talk about death and she'd play her Leonard Cohen or Bob Dylan very loudly until we both cried and then we'd start laughing instead and feel considerably better. But it was still a couple of weeks before I could expect her back. I tried to read, but couldn't concentrate, thoughts of Mr. Jarvis and a wife we'd known nothing about jumping across my page. Eva would come up with all sorts of reasons why he'd lied about her, hidden her from us. There was the possibility that she was mad like Mr. Rochester's wife, of course, but somehow the idea of a mad woman stowed away in an attic in Croydon or even Greenwich was unconvincing. I lay awake, listening for sounds of my mother in the kitchen, half hoping she would come in to say goodnight and half dreading it. I would have liked her to put her arm around me and say something about how upsetting it had all been. I wanted some sort of explanation, a justification for his accident, along the lines of his bad driving or his ancient car, just to reassure me that it was unlikely to happen to any of us. A defence, if you like, against the odds. My father appeared to need whisky, my mother had taken to her bed, apparently distraught. I didn't know exactly how I was supposed to behave. It felt impossible to believe that Mr. Jarvis had been dead for three days whilst we'd been in ignorance, blithely getting on with our normal routine weekend, our ordinary Monday whilst meanwhile, in Croydon, he was being missed and mourned by his wife, his family, which amounted to more, so very much more, than one grey, elderly, frail mother in Greenwich. A family, after all, meant children.

Mr. Jarvis must have had children.

The next morning, I was relieved to hear my mother in the kitchen when I woke up. I took ages in my room getting ready for school, pretending I'd overslept, dashing into the kitchen and eating a bowl of cereal standing up at the table. My father poured me a stewed cup of tea while my mother seemed to be absorbed by a stubborn stain in the sink. The smell of bleach sank into my tea so I could taste it. I felt nervous of mentioning Mr. Jarvis in case, like a touch paper, it rekindled her sadness. Yet saying nothing made me feel foolish, as if I had failed to understand the tragedy of his death. There were no packed lunches on the kitchen table. Every morning without fail, my mother made a round of sandwiches for me, two rounds for my father, wrapped them in small squares of greaseproof, placed them in brown paper bags saved from the greengrocer's and left them by our plates.

But not this morning.

I had no chance to talk to Susan until break time, when I found her eating biscuits on the bench outside the science labs. The corridor always smelt of gas and chemicals and made me feel a little sick. She held out a choice of a ginger nut or a digestive. I took one.

"It's our lodger," I said. "He's dead."

Susan stared at me then started on the last biscuit, eating slowly. I noticed her skirt pocket was torn away from its seam.

"Natural causes? Heart attack, was it?" she said calmly, as if compiling a police report.

"No," I said, "a car crash. His fault, I think. I mean he didn't mean to, of course, but he kind of collided with a lamp post or something. It's terrible, isn't it?"

Saying the words clearly out loud for the first time suddenly revealed the enormity of it. The absurd and random horror of his death. I felt almost as shocked as when I'd heard the policeman first tell us in our kitchen. Susan became more responsive.

"Well, that's dreadful. Really, Mary, that's a terrible thing to happen. Are you all expected to go to the funeral?"

I'd not thought about a funeral. The policeman had not said anything about a funeral and I wondered whether my parents would think they should go. I finished my biscuit then remembered the other half of what I had to tell Susan.

"And he didn't live with his mother in Greenwich. In fact, we don't even know if he's got a mother, let alone in Greenwich. He lived in Croydon. He was married. He's got a wife and children, I think. Or rather he did have a wife. Now she's just a widow, of course."

After her initial reaction, Susan looked less interested than I'd expected and certainly less interested than Eva would be. But then she'd only met Mr. Jarvis a couple of times and was not the type to get imaginatively caught up in anything that wasn't of relevance to her.

"Well, people have reasons for saying the things they do," she said, "and for not saying things as well. I mean there was no reason why he had to tell you everything about his life. People are allowed to be private, you know." She spoke with a touch of defiance and I thought of her restraint over the subject of her father in the Wimpy Bar in Brighton that day with the dreadful horse-owning Anthea. The bell went. She ferreted in the bottom of her bag for her biology book.

"But are they allowed to lie?" I said. "It's one thing keeping quiet about something, quite another lying if you fail to mention you've got a wife and maybe a whole load of children back in London. I mean it's like pretending you're something you're not."

Susan shrugged.

"It's a bit odd, I'll give you that," she said. "Do you want to go and see a film at the weekend? My auntie's coming to stay so I haven't got to do the Saturday night shift at the shop."

For Susan, Mr. Jarvis' death was a brief curiosity over break-time biscuits in the science corridor and now dispatched from interest for all time. I left her and walked slowly to my lesson so that I arrived late for French. I thought of Mr. Jarvis' things in the attic room. His clothes, shoes, jumpers, his paints, the pillows and sheets and blankets covering the bed he wouldn't sleep in again. I hoped my mother wouldn't ask me to help her clear the room, clean it, remove his traces and prepare it for the next occupant. I assumed there would have to be another lodger for, after all, we'd lost Miss Mackie and now Mr. Jarvis. Losing lodgers seemed to have become a regular occurrence in our family as if we were unsuited to the task of containing them.

My mother was out when I got home and I was relieved to have the house to myself. I rang Eva's number. Hopelessly, I rang three times in half an hour. Later, we ate tinned macaroni cheese and peas for supper and neither of them were quite hot enough. My mother didn't eat at all. She put a spoonful of food onto her plate, picked up her fork then stared at it as if having forgotten its use. There was no pudding. My father and I sat for a moment, waiting for the usual custard and stewed or tinned fruit, the occasional jam tart, and exchanged brief glances. The fridge seemed to be making extraordinarily loud noises.

"I've got an essay to finish," I said, sliding out of my chair and shoving my plate in the sink. "In fact, I've hardly even started it so I'd better get on." My mother looked up in some surprise, as if she'd forgotten she'd just spent twenty minutes sitting opposite me for an inadequate meal.

"Of course, Mary," she said. "Such a good girl, you are, working so hard." She seemed to be attempting a smile.

"It's for English," I said unnecessarily, "comparing Mr. Rochester with St. John Rivers. Something like that. We're still on *Jane Eyre,* you see."

My father stood up, started to clear the table properly, carrying glasses to the draining board.

"We'd no idea we had a bit of a scholar here, Ida, did we?" he said a little too brightly. He touched my mother on the shoulder. She had dark rings under her eyes and her voice was low and subdued, as if she was too tired to talk.

"That's right, Mary," she said, "we're pleased you're doing so well, you know. You do know that, don't you?"

I mumbled something about lots of people being much cleverer than me. I reminded them of the terrible marks I kept getting in science. Neither of them seemed to be listening. Back in my room I wrote six pages in my English exercise book, which was more than was asked for. Then I curled up on my bed with my latest library book and read until past nine o'clock. I waited for my mother to come in and remind me about the time and offer a mug of hot milk. I read on until ten o'clock then, hungry after the inadequate bit of tinned macaroni, went into the kitchen and found some stale rock buns and made milky coffee. There were no lights in the living room upstairs so I supposed they'd both gone to bed. I couldn't ever remember going to bed without either my mother or my father saying goodnight. This, perhaps, was what it was like when adults were touched by tragedy. They forgot the normal things, the consoling ordinary gestures that you don't notice until suddenly they are no longer there and without them you feel rudderless. Bereft.

★ ★ ★

A week later, I rang Eva's number again.

"Mary!" Mrs. Mason said, as if she was raising her voice over a roomful of people. I imagined her pulling off one of her large clip earrings to accommodate the receiver. "Well, you're quite a stranger, I must say. How are you?"

"I was wondering about Eva. She sent me a card, said she'd be back soon," I said. "I just wondered if you knew when exactly." I felt bold, being quite so direct with Mrs. Mason. Our last encounter in Bampton months before had made me feel insignificant and irrelevant to the Mason family's movements. Ordinary little Mary in her scruffy house with her dull life, I'd imagined her thinking. But Mr. Jarvis' sudden death had splintered normality so entirely that I no longer cared what I said to anyone. Mrs. Mason appeared to cover the mouth piece of the phone, for I heard her muffled voice saying something to someone else about food and coffee cups and being as quick as she possibly could. Then she was loud in my ear again.

"You must excuse me, Mary, I've one of my ladies' groups here, you know. Sausage rolls and cheese straws warming in the oven as we speak."

"Eva," I said plainly. "I just wanted to know the exact date she'd be home. It's been ages."

"Hasn't it?" Mrs. Mason said. "What a time that girl's been having. I've been so envious. You know, your generation is so lucky with all these opportunities for travel. What did we have? The war, that's what. Hitler had an awful lot to answer for, you know. Now, Mary, you're really going to have to excuse me, I've got coffee to make for a dozen people here or near about. And the percolator is really a law unto itself if you don't know its peculiarities."

"So when exactly will Eva will be back?" I insisted.

"She'll ring you," Mrs. Mason said. "I'll jot your name down on this pad of ours and make sure she rings you the moment she steps over the threshold. How's that for a promise, Mary?"

It was all I was to get. My name placed upon a pad by the Masons' phone. I got the satisfaction of putting down the receiver while Eva's mother was still withering on about teaspoons and brown sugar. In my bedroom I started to make detailed notes for history revision. History seemed a particularly bleak subject to study as there appeared few topics that dwelt on happy, uplifting areas of life. It was all causes of war and effects of war or the need for factory acts or reform acts to dispel the dreadful conditions in which people were living their dire lives. I revised as far as the potato famine before I went to bed, leaving a few thousand Irish on the point of starvation. If my parents had decided that I was a bit of a scholar, I supposed I should prove them right by devoting myself to school work. At least it might cheer them up and out of the gloom and despondency into which they appeared to have been cast. Even the television was rarely on these days, as if it was indecent to seek out a bit of entertainment. My mother seemed to be spending an inordinate amount of time with her workbox, mending gloves and socks with beige darning thread. With the very earliest sign of lighter evenings, my father had started retreating to the garden after supper, prodding bare earth as if encouraging the hibernating tulips. I filled out the forms for the sixth form at the girls' grammar, forged a flamboyant signature to spare my parents. No-one had mentioned Mr. Jarvis' name in the house since the night of the policeman's visit.

★ ★ ★

One Saturday afternoon, about three weeks later, there was a knock at the front door. I was sprawled over the floor in the living room, reading a magazine, wondering whether I could be bothered to catch the bus into Bampton for an hour or two. If Eva had been home, we might have gone to Brighton, where we could have walked on the piers and wasted some money in the slot machines, but she wasn't and I was bored with Bampton. There was a second knock at the door, more insistent and certainly louder. Resentfully, I picked myself up off the floor and went to answer. A woman stood on the top step. She was small, barely taller than me, a narrow frame. Fair hair, with a touch of ginger in it, was piled up rather haphazardly on her head with a clasp so that it was escaping wispily down her neck. Her back was turned as if she'd almost given up and decided to go away. I waited for her to turn round and ask me for money for guide dogs or shake a tin with a picture of starving children on it, shove a leaflet at me about a local jumble sale. We got a lot of such callers. My mother usually sent them smartly on their way, my father would offer a coin or two. But this woman was different because she did none of those things. Instead, she turned round and simply stared at me, as if finding someone or something she hadn't expected. I waited for her to apologise for calling at the wrong house, ask for directions to where so and so lived. But she didn't. She just went on standing and staring, not at me now, but beyond me, into the hall of the house, as if searching for something she expected to find. There were footsteps on the kitchen stairs and my mother appeared, flushed as if she'd just boiled a kettle and held her face in its steam. I stood back, waited for her to say something, to ask what this stranger wanted, but she didn't. Instead, she looked hard at the small woman for several seconds then glanced behind her into the road, where a car was parked. Two small children, their faces flattened against the glass so they looked one moment comical, the next grotesque, were inside, kneeling on the front seat, clearly elbowing each other for space. One of them, the older possibly, started to roll down the window then rolled it up again quickly.

"No," my mother said suddenly to the woman, surprising me, making me jump. "No, I told you on the phone. I can't believe you've come all this way. There's no point in this, absolutely no point at all." And she started to push the front door firmly as if to close it against the woman. I was still thinking of the random callers we got with their collections boxes and causes, their envelopes and leaflets, and couldn't imagine why my mother was being quite so aggressive. But the small, fair, almost ginger-haired woman with a spiky fringe, those trailing wisps and skin the colour of pale speckled egg shell, shoved her foot in the door. I looked down at the flat sandals she was wearing, her bare toes, and thought how cold she must be. Her skirt was long, thin, more the sort of thing you'd wear in midsummer. Sprigs of fawn daisies on cream cheesecloth, the hem splashed with mud.

"I knew all along, really," she said, so quietly that I wondered if she was talking to herself, "it was what he was like, you see." She turned her head for a moment towards the car and when she turned back, I could see that she was crying. Or at least trying not to cry, her voice strangled and breaking as if it was difficult to speak. She pushed hair out of her eyes, but it matted onto her cheek. "It's just the way he was, couldn't seem to help himself. But we're his family, you know, and I want his things. Anything," she said. "There must be stuff here. It's mine by rights, you know."

I looked at my mother. She'd taken her hand away from the door for a moment and was fiddling with the cuff of her blouse. There was a brown stain covering the frayed buttonhole. I was waiting for her to say something sensible to me, something that made things clear.

"There's nothing for you," she said eventually, not to me, but to the woman. "Absolutely nothing here belongs to… I explained, didn't I? On the phone. I didn't know. I just didn't know anything about…" and it seemed as if she was going to cry too. It was only then that I realised they were talking about Mr. Jarvis. This must be his wife, his family of two young children, waiting in the car outside on Sea View Parade. And I waited for my mother to invite them all inside, Mrs. Jarvis and the children, ask them downstairs for some tea in the kitchen and imagined that everyone would break down and cry about poor dead Fred, ending up with their arms around each other the way people did. I thought they'd then all troop up to the attic and collect his things, his half-painted canvases, palettes of oil paints, the box of pastels. Some clothes, even.

But it wasn't like that at all.

Instead, my mother appeared suddenly to stop seeming sad and tearful and decided to be angry instead. I winced at the sharpness of her voice, embarrassed by the way she was treating this poor woman who looked so bleak and desolate, her eyes empty pools as if hollowed out by incessant crying.

"Go away, and don't come back. Ever. Do you understand? It's all over. There's nothing here for you. I never want to see or hear from any of you again." And she closed the door abruptly, slammed it, and leant her weight against it as if she thought the slight, pale woman capable of breaking it down with her thin, pale hands.

The hall clock chimed three.

I glanced out of the window and watched the woman walk slowly down the path as if uncertain whether to come back, try again. Just before she opened the car door, she turned, stared up at the house, then got in, her long skirt catching so that she had to open the door and slam it again. The children's faces continued to stare out, scrambling, it appeared, to the back seat until apparently told to sit back down, for they disappeared from view and eventually, the car drew away from the pavement, down the road and out of sight. A squirrel hopped across the lawn, froze for a moment then disappeared into a bush. I noticed a lone daffodil struggling to survive in a bare flowerbed. My mother suddenly looked at me as if she had just noticed that I was there. She moved to the hall table, ran her finger across it as if a layer of dust had abruptly arrived, rearranged a pile of keys. A stray stamp.

"Are you going out this afternoon, Mary? To Bampton, perhaps? We could do with some bread. And your father will forget, no doubt. As usual." She continued to stare at the keys for a moment, as if they posed a particular puzzle, then glanced up at me, smiling too broadly. My father was a meticulous man. He made lists. He did not forget milk and bread. I invented something about planning to catch the 3.30pm bus.

"A white farmhouse, then," she said, "or I daresay they'll have run out of those by now, being the weekend. You'd best just get what you can, Mary. Use your sense."

I went down to Beach Parade. I'd forgotten my coat in my speed to leave the house and it was too cold to sit on a bench to wait for the bus. I walked up and down, trying to decide whether to risk going home to collect it, but I didn't want to see my mother again until the incident of the woman was removed from the front of my mind. At the moment, she hovered between us, clogged the space so that I felt I could not look my mother in the eye without her intrusion. I could not understand why the visit of poor, bereaved Mrs. Jarvis and her children should provoke my mother so inexplicably, yet I knew seeking any explanation would be hopeless. I went to the phone box and tried to ring Susan, but the coin slot had been vandalised and refused to take the money I was trying to slide into it. In Bampton, I wandered around Woolworths and bought a new ruler and a packet of crisps. The baker's offered only empty shelves, but there was a tray of iced buns tagged half-price sitting in the window. I bought four. It was near to closing time at the library, but I managed to waste twenty minutes before being politely encouraged to leave by a Saturday assistant I'd never seen before. I hovered for as long as I dared, asked if there were often Saturday jobs available and was rewarded with having my name and address taken and placed on a waiting list. I let the 5.30pm bus back to Beach Parade slide away from Bampton High Street, started instead on the long walk back, stuffing chunks of iced bun into my mouth so that I soon felt suitably sick.

The farmhouse white sat in the middle of the kitchen table. My mother placed a dish of pilchards next to it. My father looked up from the *Evening Argos*, the racing page. He always read the racing page even though he never bet and I'd never known him go to a race meeting.

"Nice afternoon, Mary? I didn't know you were going into Bampton. Could have given you a lift myself."

"I wasn't meaning to go," I said, grabbing the loaf and slicing thickly even though I was still nauseous with too many buns. "But I just needed to get out." I tried to say it meaningfully, but my mother was attending to a tin opener and the Crosse and Blackwell vegetable salad and my father simply smiled.

"Know how you feel, Mary. Need to shake the cobwebs out a bit, that's what it is. Especially with you and all your books and school work and that."

He poured the tea. My mother sat down, spooned pilchards onto three plates, placed dollops of vegetable salad and put them down in front of us. I gulped my tea too hot, scalded my mouth.

"I'm going to be playing another class at the dancing school," my mother said. "Saturday mornings at ten o'clock. Too many beginners on Wednesdays so they're starting a new class. Miss Roberts rang this afternoon and she was very pleased when I agreed. Not easy to get pianists these days, you know."

"I'm sure," my father said. "It's all recorded music, isn't it? Records and tape recorders and such like. That's good then, Ida, keep you even busier."

I looked across at him, saw he seemed genuinely delighted, as if my mother had just been awarded a prestigious appointment at an internationally renowned concert hall. They began to talk about the possibility of repointing the front garden wall. I stared at the calendar on the wall ahead of me, noticed no-one had bothered to shift it on from February. I waited for my mother to tell my father about the woman. About Mr. Jarvis' poor wife and the car full of his children. But she didn't. I tried to convince myself that they'd already talked about her visit before I got in, when my father had dutifully returned from his shopping errand, loaf of bread and bottle of milk in a string carrier bag. But somehow, I knew they hadn't and that for some inexplicable reason my mother was choosing to keep silent, cleanly removing the event from the day. I stood up, swiftly swept my uneaten pilchards from my plate into the bottom of the bin, where they'd begin smelling in a day or so. I went upstairs to ring Susan, only to hear, of course, that she was working a Saturday night shift in the shop until late. Not that I particularly wanted to share with her the visit of Mrs. Jarvis, for I knew that her response would be inadequate and not what I needed at all, but at least she would have been some company, an excuse to get out of the house again. On the hall coat stand a long, dark blue woollen scarf hung, half covered by an old raincoat of my father's. It had belonged to Mr. Jarvis. I wondered whether his wife had noticed it when she'd stood on the step and stared fixedly behind me into the hall. Or if, in fact, it was the unframed canvas of a violent sea storm that hung at the bottom of the stairs that had caught her attention, her husband's initials, FJ, just about decipherable on the disturbed sea shore.

17

When I first separated from David, Felix and I moved to the country. I had the rash idea of an entirely new start for me and my small son. I conjured images of chickens and a smallholding with healthy vegetable crops and ideal self-sufficiency. Felix would be brought up with timeless values and knowledge about harvests and the cyclical nature of the year. I'd been reading a lot of Thomas Hardy. My child would collect a brown speckled egg for his breakfast each morning and eat bread he'd watch rise and prove. He would not spend leisure time in front of a television screen to become acquainted with the latest children's programmes and be in thrall to their merchandise. We would read books together, paint pictures, tend to our crops. Our hens. Possibly there'd be a goat. I'd heard they were good at eating the grass. And when the time came, I would home educate so that I could instil into my precious, beautiful child eternal values, essential truths. We would live cheaply, but richly.

We survived ten months.

I did acquire the hens. I swore unhealthy oaths at them each feeding time, threatened to leave their hatches open for the friendly local fox. I was either overwhelmed with eggs or worrying about a dearth and buying supermarket versions as substitutes. The cottage, spotted on an idyllic June day with a garden of stocks and hollyhocks, was damp, draughty, the windows small and ill-fitting. There was a visiting frog in the pantry. At night, mice scampered about in the attic above us and in the kitchen one floor below. I'd wake at three in the morning to check Felix in his cot, terrified vermin were tucking in next to the warmth of his small, sweet body.

And then I got flu.

And I yearned for a television to occupy Felix while I lolled, sick and weedy on the sofa. I wanted the convenience of a local shop where I could slope off and collect essential supplies. David had kindly encouraged my venture when I'd first told him about the country. He admired, he said, my pluck. My spirit. My mother, Ida, thought I was insane. But then my decision to allow David to leave had already rendered me incomprehensible in her view. She said as much. Frequently. A woman who didn't know a good thing when it was in her grasp and insist on tethering him, come what may, was either ignorant or a fool. My country venture she sniffed at with similar disapproval, vocalised bewilderment. My father, however, surprised me. Jack seemed positively envious. He spent a lot of time finding out about hens' habits and breeds and helped me paint the absurd rented cottage, dug me a rudimentary vegetable patch. He always looked rueful when a visit came to an end and he had to return to 8, Sea View Parade and the demands of the B and B guests. And when I admitted to the two of them, to Ida and Jack, that I was giving up and returning to something more urban, he was clearly disappointed. Ida, of course, was positively smug and seemed to take enormous pleasure in being proved right. David made no judgment. He has always been a gracious man.

I was less forgiving of myself. I felt foolish, self-indulgent, ashamed of acting like a naïve seventeen-year-old lurching from one whim to another in search of some defined identity. I'd tried being a wife to a good man and had clearly failed. My attempt at being a modern-day pastoral heroine had proved equally vacuous. I'd imagined that I could adapt and live a contented rural existence. I thought of myself as strong, independent and capable of taking on whatever tasks and trials I selected. But I was, of course, hopelessly deluded. The need for convenient shops and children's gym classes and pleasant cafés, the shelves of a good bookshop, the scent of a well-stocked library, the hard slab of pavement beneath my feet, the consoling anonymity of a crowd, pawed at me, brought me back sheepishly to something far less remote, to satisfy my undeniably urban instincts. These days, I tell Felix that once he ate breakfast eggs we'd collected still warm from their laying. He shows little interest.

I never really considered another marriage. I felt I'd been rash in agreeing the first time, giving in to something that seemed obligatory rather than a free choice. I was, after all, entirely sceptical about the arrangement, seeing it as too often a veneer under which lurked, at best, compromise, and at worst, livid treachery. And since the social climate had changed so radically from when Eva and Susan and I had sat as school girls, imagining marriage as the only possible outcome for our lives, I had little reason to try it again. One self-inflicted failure was enough to make me consider a second attempt unwise. Ida, of course, expected me to marry again. Jack wished for it, I know. As if a husband would provide some essential security, a little like an insurance policy that's there for the unfortunate eventualities of life. But I resisted. Mostly with ease, for the few men I met seemed either too dependent or too flippant to consider seriously and when, once, I grew close to thinking of something more permanent, someone tethered and attached to us, to me and Felix, I panicked, thrashed around like a trapped, desperate creature. It is all too easy to blame my parents, to see my truculent attitude towards relationships as a result of the behaviour of Ida and Jack. They have sustained their own marriage for well over fifty years, after all. But still, there's a residue of doubt in me that stems inevitably from the events of those years at Number 8. And from, possibly, connections and circumstances that I am only now just on the cusp of uncovering.

★ ★ ★

I don't remember the day Eva returned from Canada. The event is now distilled through too many impressions and inventions to be sure of it. I don't remember her ringing me up, arranging for me to go over and see her and yet there must have been some such first phone call. Or perhaps she simply knocked at Number 8 and I went and found her, standing expectantly on the doorstep. Glancing behind her, perhaps, at the growing clusters of daffodils and globe hyacinths and early tulips in the front garden. Mrs. Jarvis' visit would have only been a few weeks before, a month at most, so still vivid in my mind, late March or early April, Easter holidays, anyway, when the days can be as warm as August or as bleak and wet as November. No, I don't remember the precise details of our initial reunion for sure.

But what I do still hold onto is this.

I am at Eva's house, up in her bedroom and we are looking in her wardrobe. She's still in her dressing gown, the one that normally hangs on the back of her door and she says she slept late. *Jet lag, maybe?* I suggest, although she's been back some days, a week perhaps, and she just shrugs. Her room has been decorated. There's a smell of paint, of wet wallpaper glue and the walls now have smart stripes of purple and pale blue instead of floral patterns in pink. I can see a bright red dress with a white collar that she's evidently brought back with her. She's holding it out, holding it against her then she scrunches it up, clumsily shoves it in her wardrobe. I don't like the dress, but I don't say so. Instead, I say something about it looking very American and she corrects me by saying Canadian.

They're different, you know, she says rather impatiently, *why does everyone think Canada's the same as America?* I tell her I don't. And I sit down on her bed and notice that it's got a new cover. I tell her, resentfully, that I know very well where she's been for so many months. That I looked it up in the atlas. Toronto, Canada, Ontario. And I wait for her to apologise for not letting me know sooner about her prolonged stay. For leaving it to her mother to tell me, quite by chance, one day in Bampton. But she doesn't take the hint. And I, in my turn, cowardly choose to let the moment go, as if hesitant to create any discord between us. Instead, I let Eva talk, go on and on about accents and how most people can't even tell them apart, Canadian from American. She says it all in a rather superior way as if she's suddenly the expert, the mature, experienced traveller. Which in a way, of course, she is. Compared with me.

She's brought me back a sweater.

A present, she says, although it's not wrapped up, and she pulls it out of the open suitcase that's still sitting on her bedroom floor. I suspect she's worn it herself and dislikes it. It's orange, tangerine orange, with a pattern of white daisies around the cuffs and neckline. It's not the sort of thing I would usually wear. I try it on and the wool itches.

Mr. Jarvis is dead, I say abruptly and am gratified by her reaction. She sits down on the floor next to the case and listens, really listens. She wants to know all about the policeman, wants me to tell her the story at least three times. So I do, editing bits, elaborating pieces. I tell her my mother was upset, shocked. My father too. They were equally shocked, I tell her instinctively. She likes the part about the wife. She is suddenly like Eva again, fantasising that he possibly had two or three of them, wives and families, conveniently scattered around the country. She wants to know if his scarf is still hanging in the hall, his picture on the wall.

Yes, I tell her, *I think so. Or maybe not. I've stopped noticing, really.*

I relax, feel the past few months of her absence shrivel into insignificance. Then Eva decides to get dressed. She opens her wardrobe and pulls out her jeans and then changes her mind, throws them on the floor. She grabs a black skirt, shoves it on, fiddles with the zip which seems stuck.

You've probably caught the material in it, I say, *let me help.* But she turns away from me abruptly as if I am fussing and scoops a grey sweater from the suitcase.

I'm starving, she says, *let's get some food. It's nearly lunch time. And I was asleep when it was breakfast.*

I follow her downstairs. There's a strong scent of beeswax furniture polish in the hall and in the kitchen, the smell of ground coffee. I hear Mrs. Mason in another room, vacuuming, singing along to the radio that she has playing loudly. Eva opens the fridge door then begins fiddling again with the zip of her skirt. She's swearing at it under her breath, trying to jerk it up to reach the waistband.

You'll break it if you tug it so hard, I say and then she appears to rip the fabric, a button spins across the floor and Eva bursts into tears. She covers her face with her hands so that the skirt drops and sits in a pool at her bare feet. She goes on sobbing, apparently careless of the split skirt, her bare legs, her grey skimpy sweater riding up above her waist. And I look at her exposed stomach, white, soft, spongy, tiny lines crossing it like a snail's trail. She stares back at me. The vacuum cleaner in the next room stops abruptly as if the plug has slipped from its socket.

I had a baby, Eva says, *that's why I stayed in Canada.* But she's crying too much for the words to come out this clearly. It takes me longer to understand her. I have to ask her to repeat herself. To be sure of what she is telling me.

I knew I was pregnant before I went. Before we went off on holiday last summer. But I didn't tell anyone. Not even Lysander. Not till I was there. In Canada, I mean. Then I told them. Ma, I mean. And my dad. And… it was a boy. I mean it's a boy. I had a son.

And then suddenly there is someone else in the kitchen. The radio is still playing in the other room, but Jean Mason is here beside Eva. Eva is now crying inconsolably. Her mother looks at her for a moment, then looks at me as if I am the culpable party, the cause of her tears. She grabs the black split skirt from the floor, holds it out and tells Eva to step into it and pulls it up, managing to fix it with brute force around Eva's thickened waist. Her bracelet rattles as her hands roughly pull the skirt together. Then she appears to try and calm herself. She moves towards the kitchen table where a pot of coffee sits cooling and sits down.

No, Eva, she says, biting out her words, *there's no need for all this. You know what we decided. This is not how it is going to be.*

She is angry. I have never heard Mrs. Mason speak like this, as if she has lost her temper and is uncontrollably furious. She goes on, stressing her speech, enunciating as if she is speaking to someone whose grasp of language is insecure.

This is not the way. You know the rules. We decided. We are never talking about it again. There is absolutely no point at all. It's all gone. It's all in the past now. It has to be as if it's never been. Our rules, Eva.

And I wait for Eva to say something, to protest. I expect Mrs. Mason to smile now, to soften and say something about how we must be hungry and move to the fridge and take out food, fry us eggs, chips, set the table. I wait for Mrs. Mason to apologise for her outburst, to say that it's been a difficult time and that she'll leave Eva to explain it all to me and that she will be grateful of my friendship and support after what she has been through in the past months. But none of this happens. Instead, Mrs. Mason simply glares at me as if unable to believe I am still there. Still standing close to Eva, whose crying has turned now into suppressed gulps and hiccups. There's a box of tissues on a shelf and I'm wondering whether to reach out and take one for her. Her face is blotched, a mess of dried tears with dark rings circling her eyes.

I think it best if you go now, Mary, Mrs. Mason says firmly, *right now. Do you understand? I want you to leave. And you'll tell absolutely no-one about all this. It's forbidden. Just forget what you've heard – this… this silly little outburst of Eva's. It's family business and so it has nothing to do with you.*

And she gets up and moves towards the back door and opens it wide. I stare at her for a moment, noticing how set and precise her hair is, triumphantly lacquered to withstand all eventualities. Then suddenly, I am outside. I am running down the road away from Eva's house, towards Beach Parade, and walking fast along the sea front. I sit down for a while on a bench, out of breath, unsure whether I want to go home. Eva has had a baby. And if Eva has had a baby, Eva has had sexual intercourse with a boy. She has done something that only other girls do. Girls who get into trouble at school and run away from home. Girls who end up married at sixteen and living on the big estate on the edge of Bampton with four children and a stick thin boy-husband by the time they're twenty. I knew all about girls like this. Every year at least one pupil from the fifth form began to look large and podgy in her shapeless school summer dress and left early before the end of term. Later, there'd be a bold appearance at the school gates, a plump baby balanced on one arm like a trophy declaring a rite of passage. It was what happened to certain girls, of course. But not to girls like Eva. Not to girls who had mothers like Jean Mason.

After a while, I am too hungry to stay on Beach Parade, staring at the sea with only a bit of chewing gum in my pocket, so I go home, find some packet soup and scald my fingers on boiling water as I fill my mug. The phone rings as I hold my hand under the cold tap and I rush to it, expecting it to be Eva. Hoping it's Eva saying she's coming round to see me and cares nothing for what her mother says. But it's not, of course. It's a wrong number and the woman at the other end takes a long time before she believes her error.

And that's all I know.

As fact, as certainty. Eva stayed in Canada because she was expecting a baby. Lysander's baby. And no-one was allowed to know. I don't even know if she gave her son a name. If she held him, nursed him at all before he was whisked away and out of her arms. I have never felt able to ask her for precise details, which I see as my own inadequacy. A cowardice of sorts. But then I knew about the birth only by default, by accident, as it were. Over the years, I have got near to confronting her. That time when she visited me at training college in Oxford and got drunk. I thought about asking her for the whole story. What it was like to have a baby so far away from home, at the age of just sixteen or seventeen, in secrecy, a hushed-up shame that her mother swore her to maintain. But I didn't ask her. The moment must have presented itself, hovered then dissolved into drunkenness. Embarrassment. And I have never been sure whether Lysander ever knew. About his son. His child, adopted, no doubt, into a loving, caring Canadian family, an event so far removed from us now that even its memory seems gratuitous, something of an emotional indulgence. After all, it was just clumsy teenage sex and an unfortunate accident, a matter wrapped up and dealt with efficiently according to the habit of the time.

And yet there was a birth.

A child produced by some feeble, naïve fumbling that was probably impulsive, certainly unguarded. But new life, nonetheless.

I know I never forgave Mrs. Mason for her duplicity, her careful burial of the truth. As Eva says now, it was so different then. Another climate, another way of thinking about things. I envy her ability to dispose of the past with such ease, to mitigate its hypocritical judgments so blithely. To accept without question that it was, simply, like it was.

I don't think I ever went to the Masons' house again. It wasn't long before Eva began her secretarial course in London after she'd scratched around for a while at home, talked about going back to school, into the sixth form and perhaps she even tried it for the summer term. I don't remember. What I do know is that by the autumn she was learning shorthand and typing at an expensive secretarial school in Kensington and living in the students' hostel near Gloucester Road. She wrote me a few letters, I faithfully replied and I went up to stay at half-term. I remember being surprised by the stuffy, rather staid atmosphere of the secretarial college and its ladies' hostel. The other students were mostly rich, blonde, rather large and disappeared at the weekends to house parties in Norfolk or Suffolk, intent, apparently, on acquiring husbands as speedily as possible. Eva had been remote, subdued during my visit and I'd felt cowed, suddenly seeing our friendship as fragile, insubstantial. We shoved around Oxford Street and I bought a jacket at C and A's. We went to see a film at the Kensington Odeon and walked the length of the high street looking for somewhere cheap to eat. On Sunday afternoon I caught the coach home from Victoria. I waved to Eva, watched her turn and walk away, into the late October day, tugging her gloves out of her bag. We seemed to lose touch for a while then, but perhaps we wrote. Maybe there was an occasional phone call, but I doubt it. What I remember most was the enormous sense of betrayal that Eva had not chosen to confide in me. I went over the weeks we'd spent together that summer before the Masons went to Canada when she must have first suspected that she was expecting Lysander's baby. And although I tried to understand, I continued to see her silence, her secrecy, as an act of blatant disloyalty.

★ ★ ★

The letter is inadequately hidden in my top drawer. Eliza Jarvis' neat blue envelope constantly resurfaces. However much I try to bury it under endless piles of tights and underwear, it manages to squirm its way to the top and even jettison itself out onto the carpet. One day, rushing to get to work for a morning class with my adult students, my session on Gertrude Morel and her relationship with her son, Paul, I forget to shove it back and come home to be confronted with it lying expectantly between the bed and the chest of drawers. Like the cat meowing at my feet, it seems insistent that I pay it attention. I hesitate for a moment then pick it up, push it back in between a couple of scarves, and see to our plump demanding feline.

18

My Saturday job at the library was sublime. I loved leaving home before my parents were even awake, catching the early bus into Bampton, eating a slice of toast and drinking a cup of coffee at Café Suisse before turning up just before nine to start my day. I was always first there. Even in midwinter, I was the reliable Saturday staff girl who never needed telling off for poor time-keeping. The full-time staff exploited me, of course. I could imagine them spending their weekdays putting aside the dullest tasks, loading the trolleys down on Friday evenings so they could confront me with shelf stacking first thing Saturday. But I didn't mind in the least. In fact, the more they simply left me to get on with things on my own, the more I liked it. I even enjoyed making them their endless cups of tea and setting out the biscuits in the staff room. The first couple of weeks I made the mistake of working too fast. When I'd tidied Children's Fiction and Toddlers' Picture Books by ten o'clock and reported to the desk for my next job, I received scathing comments from Daphne, the senior librarian.

"I want Fiction alphabetically, you know," she said. "You can't possibly have done them properly already. I suggest a little less dash and a more thorough approach."

So I returned to the shelves, shuffling them first in order to give me the task to do again. This time I stopped to read the first page of every other book and managed to string things out until lunch time. Daphne seemed far more satisfied. She beamed through her perfect crescent of lilac lipstick that gave her a slight witch-like appearance.

"Far better. I run a tight ship here, Mary. Libraries need order, remember that. Now, I think we could move you onto tidying the magazines and periodicals this afternoon."

Susan came in most Saturdays and went straight to work in the reading room. She was usually the only person under eighty in there as it tended to be occupied by dusty-looking old men smelling of stale spirits and even staler tobacco. One man with a particularly unfortunate-looking scar on his face and his trousers held up by string arrived every morning as the library opened and left just before closing. He spent the hours wading through the telephone directories, working his way from A through to Z, tracing down each page with a dirt-encrusted fingernail. Daphne said he did the same thing most week days. Sometimes Susan and I spent my lunch hour together wandering round the shops, sharing a packet of crisps or a bar of chocolate, sometimes a pork pie. My mother assumed the library provided me with a snack meal since I'd said it wasn't necessary for me to take sandwiches from home. I'd seen Daphne and her deputy, Frances, retreating into the staff room with their plastic lunch boxes for their allocated break, carefully pressed napkins brought from home to shield their pleated skirts. I didn't want to get like them.

I hadn't told Susan about Eva, about the baby, the child she and Lysander had unintentionally made. I convinced myself that Susan would simply not be interested. I imagined her shrugging the way she did and saying something about things like this happening all the time and what was all the fuss about. Susan, I had to admit, had a far more grounded and informed attitude about the ways of the world than either I or Eva had ever shown. Anyway, Susan would be inadequate,

I was sure. And as the months went on, I knew I'd missed the moment. There was no point in informing Susan of an event that was now far in the past. Eva was in London, learning her shorthand and typing, of little curiosity to Susan, who rarely considered things not of immediate, practical concern. So I'd told no-one and would not have minded so much if I hadn't felt that Mrs. Mason was getting her way. Burying the knowledge of Eva's baby, pushing it down deep like some wicked deed that could not be allowed to see the light of day. Just so that she could go on with her life as if nothing had happened to tilt her perfect balance, disturb the set of her hair, the varnish of her nails. Telling my mother was, of course, unthinkable. She would condemn Eva, no doubt ban her from the house forever and tell me to find a more refined friend. It was a word she'd begun to use a lot lately. Teaching was a nice, *refined* profession for me. My job at the library was deemed an acceptably *refined* way to spend my Saturdays. And the sixth form at the grammar school she'd decided was a *refined* sort of place for me to spend two years. There was no possible way my mother would ever have allowed me to go near Eva again if she'd known the truth about her months in Canada.

★ ★ ★

One Saturday afternoon, Miss Mackie walked into the library. I hadn't seen her since the night she'd abruptly moved out of Number 8, driven off by her brother in a flurry of bewildering speed over a year before. I'd hardly thought about her at all except for being grateful that her departure had meant me gaining the back room for my bedroom. But suddenly, here she was, overdressed for the mild day and sifting through a large carrier bag for three library books that she placed upon the counter. She seemed to be trying to talk earnestly and at some length to Frances who, extraordinarily shy and diffident with customers, was becoming flustered and red-faced. I cowered in my corner in the History Section, intent on sorting The Middle Ages into better chronology since I had no wish to speak to her. But Daphne chose that moment to summon me back to the desk for some label sticking. I couldn't avoid her. For a moment she simply stared blankly at me as if trying to scour her mind for a memory then her eyes, more bird-like and beady than ever, sparked with recognition.

"Well, goodness me! It's Mary, isn't it? Mary Foster. You've grown up a bit since we… well, since I last saw you. What a surprise!"

Curiously, she looked ill at ease, embarrassed, even. As if she wished she'd ignored me, regretted even starting a bland conversation. Daphne had moved to the other side of the counter to issue books to a couple of borrowers and Frances had slunk away, leaving me exposed.

"I'm just here Saturdays," I said as she continued to stare at me, "a Saturday job, that's all."

"And I rarely come in at weekends," she said. "Normally, I'm a late Thursday evening person, straight from the hospital, but I've just been on a little holiday, you see. The Quantocks and Exmoor. By coach."

She continued to stand there as if she'd forgotten quite what she had come for. As if the function of a library was something that suddenly eluded her.

"Can I help you look for… well, a book?" I said, to fill the awkwardness she seemed to be creating, adding self-deprecatingly, "of course I'm only the Saturday Junior so I don't know much."

Miss Mackie didn't appear to hear. She darted her eyes around the near-empty library behind her, fiddled with the buttons on her beige, Fair Isle-patterned cardigan. It was a quiet afternoon. We'd had few borrowers all day, the weather suddenly fine after a long wet spell and people were no doubt grabbing the chance to be outside. Miss Mackie turned back to me, leant some way over the top of the high counter as if anxious for privacy.

"A bad business," she said, in a voice I could only just hear. "I suppose you know all about it, being the age you are. I mean it's just not what you expect. Even these days."

I drew back a little to avoid the smell of her, her breath faintly acrid and the suggestion of damp on her clothes. Naturally, I assumed she was talking about Mr. Jarvis. I was surprised that she'd heard about his death then remembered there'd been a small paragraph in the local paper about his accident under the heading *College Art teacher killed*, or something like that. Susan had cut it out and brought it to school to show me and I'd stuffed it carelessly into my bag, where it had got torn and shreds had festered at the bottom for months.

"Yes," I said, "it was terrible, wasn't it? We were all really shocked." I waited for her to drift away in search of her books, but she continued to stand there, peering at me as if puzzled about something. I clunked things around on the desk, started on my label sticking task, hoping she'd disappear, but I could feel her continue to stand there still, as if she felt our conversation was midstream. In the end, I gave in, hoping that more information would get rid of her. "It was a car crash, you know. No-one else was involved, though. Just Mr. Jarvis and... well, I think there was something about a lamp post. Railings, maybe. It was raining. Just awful."

Miss Mackie's hand moved to the thin string of beads she was wearing. She clutched them as if someone was about to grab them from around her throat. Then she coughed a couple of times and moved a couple of steps back from the counter.

"Well, it just goes to show, doesn't it?' she said. "That's Fate for you, Mary. Or would one even call it Karma in his case? Getting one's just dues, anyway, I'd say. Nemesis is out there for all of us, you know, so it's best always to be on your guard and live a good life just in case. And in his case, one can't help thinking of the Greek gods, of course. Or even the case of the tragic hero with that fatal flaw."

"Yes," I said. "I mean, it was an accident and..." Miss Mackie appeared to have grown even odder since she'd left us. Perhaps my mother was right in thinking of her as trouble and being relieved when she departed.

"And you such a clever girl," she went on. "I hope this isn't all going to affect your future. And your parents are... your dear father, he's managing to... well, live with it all? Carry on?"

"Yes," I said blankly, "my parents are fine. Upset at the time, of course, but they're both all right." She went on staring at me as if waiting to hear more so I pretended to drop something on the floor and made a bit of a fuss about retrieving it. When I eventually got up, Miss Mackie had wandered off to the Travel section, although out of the corner of my eye I caught her looking over her shoulder at me every now and again. Fortunately, Daphne then sent me off to the staff room to wash up the cups from lunch time and make tea for afternoon breaks. I lingered over boiling the kettle and arranging the custard creams and butter Osbornes as long as possible and Miss Mackie was gone by the time I was back.

★ ★ ★

The summer seemed endless. We took our exams in June and there were too many days spent at home revising. I disliked the loneliness of the house in the mornings, when I was in my room supposedly studying and my mother was systematically cleaning. Once she went off to her piano playing job in the afternoons and I had the house to myself for a few hours I was happy enough. I could escape from my bedroom and play music loudly on the second-hand record player I'd bought with some of my earnings from the library. A girl at school called Elaine had a Saturday job at the newly opened record shop in Bampton and she used to get me cheap LPs in return for doing her French homework. Most of our class was leaving school in July, going to work in offices or shops in Brighton or Bampton. A few were going on to the Tech to do nursery nurse training or the typing course. Susan and I, mostly the odd ones out, felt isolated, alienated as if we thought ourselves a cut above the others. I said as much to my mother as I sat long over a piece of breakfast toast one morning, putting off the moment of going back to my room to revise for history.

"I don't know if I should become a teacher, you know. I could be a librarian. They might just take me on at Bampton straight from school, after all."

My mother, pulling on her rubber gloves to attack her twice weekly wash of the kitchen floor, looked appalled.

"Nonsense, Mary, that won't do at all. It's all decided. You're going to be a teacher. And be grateful that you've got the brains for it."

I missed Eva. After our exams were finished, we went back to school only to hand in books and then there were weeks to fill before results and, with any luck, a start in the sixth form. Susan was working all hours now in the fish and chip shop, especially since her mother had put her onto the deep fat frying once she was sixteen. I babysat for the family down the road and got a few more hours at the library covering holiday leave. Other than that, the summer seemed to be moving in slow motion.

But there was to be a party.

It was called the Leavers' Dance for the fifth year, held the day after school broke up. Susan and I claimed to be uninterested and detached from the wild excitement that appeared contagious to others in our class. But privately I was relieved to have an event to anticipate and Susan eventually agreed to go too. I'd taken to sewing. Or at least my mother had unearthed her old sewing machine and thrust it in my room one day, suggesting I needed something to occupy my time after my exams. She even helped me a bit when I came home with a paper pattern and some material I'd bought cheap in a sale in Bampton. I'd managed to cobble together a couple of skirts although my inexperience and the temperament of my mother's ancient Singer meant results were haphazard. But it was my only chance of getting a new dress for the party. I chose a pattern and spent all my babysitting and library money on some pale pink fabric covered in vague floral sprigs. Even though the weather had now turned warm and humid I worked on the dress painstakingly for days on end and hardly left my room. My father had a week off work and spent it in the garden, the lawn mower competing with my sewing machine for noise. My right arm ached from the constant turning of the handle and the bad tension of the machine meant I kept snapping needles and piercing my fingers.

The idea of the bed and breakfast guests came up one morning as my mother was complaining about the crowds on the beach and the queues at the bus stops.

"You know, we could do worse than think about holiday accommodation," she said, standing at the sink, washing the lettuces my father had brought in from his small vegetable patch. It had never been very productive, most years yielding only a couple of cabbages and a handful of new potatoes. This summer he'd prided himself on a vaguely edible crop that he'd managed to pick before the birds and worms got there. "There's a shortage, evidently," my mother went on, "of decent accommodation. That's what I've been hearing. Not enough rooms to satisfy the demand." My father looked at his muddy palms, said nothing. "It's not as if we haven't got the space," my mother continued, watching a slug shiver its way across the draining board before flattening it. "There's the room up there, I mean."

I hadn't been up to the attic since Mr. Jarvis had been killed. It was the sort of thing Eva and I would have done together, stealing up there for signs remaining of him, slivers of the man still in occupation. But not alone. My father seemed to start a sentence then stopped himself. I decided to help him out.

"I didn't think we were having lodgers anymore," I said, "not after… not anymore."

"For goodness sake, Mary, don't you ever listen?" my mother said sharply, turning to me as she dried her hands on her apron. "Bed and breakfast guests are not the same thing at all. Use some sense."

"It would be like when we stayed in London, Mary, in Turnham Green," my father said quietly, "people just taking a room for a few days or so. Very different from lodgers."

"I think we might take a look at upstairs, Jack," my mother said, "see how quickly we could sort it. After all, this weather might not last all summer and you have to strike while the iron's hot with this sort of thing."

My father shrugged, said something about it all being quite a big job to take on. But my mother seemed suddenly energised in a way I hadn't seen her for a long time. As if she'd woken from rather a long sleep, sleeping beauty-like, only without the kissing prince, and was ready for action.

"Nonsense, Jack, we can get the place prepared in a day or two. There's the bed up there already and enough cupboards. We just need a B and B Vacancies sign in the window and we'll be off. You can organise that, I'm sure." She whipped off her apron as if expecting guests at any moment. "I'll just have a word to see how much we can charge. Find out the going rate for this sort of thing. Mary, you can take a card down to Beaumont's later this afternoon. Their board's as good a place as any to advertise."

"So soon?" my father said. "Ida, I really think we need to talk this through a bit. It's all very sudden, you know."

He moved past her to the sink, held his hands under the running tap and slowly scrubbed the mud from them.

"Mary? You're not busy this morning, I'm sure," my mother said, ignoring him. I indicated the mass of pink fabric in my lap, the tacking stitches I was carefully removing from a seam. The light in the kitchen was better than in my room and I'd taken to sitting there picking at the material like some Victorian sewing maid.

"Actually, I am," I said, "really busy. The dance is only a couple of weeks away and I've still got loads to do."

"Nonsense," she said. "I need you upstairs."

She kept calling it The Upstairs Room. Not the attic. The B and B guests were to have The Upstairs Room or sometimes The Top Floor Room. My father managed to slow her down a bit and it was a week before the postcard went up at Beaumont's. Within three days the phone rang and my mother announced triumphantly to us at supper that she had her first booking.

"A nice-sounding couple who've been let down. Supposed to be staying at one of those places on The Drive and the family's gone down with the measles. They'll be here Saturday morning for three days. Down here for a wedding, they are, and they're sure we'll suit them perfectly."

"Well, it's no good pretending the money won't come in handy," my father said. "And we've certainly got the space, that's for sure, with this enormous house of ours."

I looked at him across the bacon and egg flan my mother

had just put down on the table. It was the first time I had ever heard him say anything about money. About the size of Number 8, as if, after five years of living there, the idea of it being preposterous had suddenly occurred to him. My mother, appearing not to hear, cut three slices of flan and handed them round to us.

But I was far more concerned with the Leavers' Dance and my pale pink dress. Some girls were taking boyfriends although they weren't really allowed. It suited me and Susan, naturally without anyone to take, that the event was intended for fifth year pupils at our school only, but it was well known that certain girls were going to smuggle particular boys in by the back gate, meet them down by the cycle shed with bottles of cider to spend their alternative evening. Susan was going to wear an old evening dress of her mother's that had been altered and chopped around to fit. I pretended to admire it. My dress was nearly finished and I was proud of my achievement. Although the stitching was very ropey, the zip not particularly straight, it looked to me quite perfect and the sort of thing I'd seen in small shops in Brighton where I could only afford to browse. I had only the fiddly hem to fix in place, the scalloped edges of it to sort out and it was done. On Friday afternoon, I sat in my room and undid the hem three times. It would not hang right. Exasperated, I knew it needed someone else's eye to pin it in place for me. My mother was somewhere in the house. She'd been in the kitchen earlier, sorting out cups that weren't cracked to use with the B and B guests. I darted up to the living room with armfuls of pink dress then realised she must be in The Upstairs Room, putting the final touches to the place. The door at the top of the attic stairs had been closed for so many months that it was strange to see it wide open now. I thought I heard voices or a noise at least coming from the room and wondered whether the wedding party B and B people had arrived early. I went slowly up the narrow staircase, peering cautiously when I got to the top, around the corner and into the room.

My mother was sitting on the bed, her hands covering her face, sobbing.

There was a sodden white handkerchief on the floor by her feet, another scrunched up into one hand. I had never seen my mother cry and for a moment felt both panic and confusion at the sight. Then I realised that she was talking. Or not so much speaking clearly as muttering words, sounding a name, through the clatter of her tears.

Fred, oh Fred, she said. And again and again, *Freddie… Fred.* I tried not to move, barely to breathe even, my precious pink dress still clasped in my arms, but suddenly, something made her look up. Perhaps a stair board creaked or a seagull screeched above the skylight and she glanced up and saw me. Her eyes were sunken and swollen from crying so that she hardly looked like herself and I found myself thinking instantly of the small woman on the doorstep that Saturday, those children's faces flattened against the car window.

And then I knew. I understood in a moment.

I turned and rushed downstairs, idiotically telling myself that my mother had not seen me or that at least she had not caught the awareness that must have shown in my face. I wanted to pretend that nothing had passed between us of any significance, desperately trying to squander the growing clarity and knowledge about my mother and Mr. Jarvis.

My mother, Ida Foster, and the late Fred Jarvis, our long-term lodger.

I shoved the pink dress back in my room, leaving it in a heap on the floor, grabbed my purse, my bag and went out. The Brighton bus was already at Beach Parade and there wouldn't be another for an hour. I ran madly across the road, darting between two cars and caught the eye of the bus driver who held on long enough for me to hurtle myself onto it. The conductor eyed me warily.

"Running away from home, love?" he said, and seemed relieved when I asked for a return ticket. Brighton was hectic. The summer crowds were thick on the beach and the pavements, eating ice creams, hot dogs, candy floss. I got jostled and shoved as I wandered without direction, trying to push out thoughts and ideas that insisted on chugging into my mind. But however much I tried to repress them, it was too easy to put pieces of the puzzle together, lock them into a landscape that kept growing, spreading back further into the past so that, uncover one clue and it connected instantly to the next. Like a treasure hunt with an unfortunate and very dark finale. A completed, highly cryptic crossword.

My mother and Mr. Fred Jarvis had been considerably more than landlady and lodger.

Something between them, an affair had been going on for months, years, in fact, ever since he'd moved into the attic room. Or possibly before. Perhaps he'd moved into the attic because they wanted to be under the same roof. And if Fred Jarvis hadn't gone and got himself killed, wrapped his car around a lamp post on a wet Friday night, it would still be going on now. In afternoons when I was at school and my father at work, perhaps, the two of them had been up there in the attic room he'd stolen from me. In between his varied hours at the college, his morning students and his early evening ones, allowing for my mother's occasional piano playing for the babies' ballet classes, they had been lovers. The reason for Miss Mackie's sudden departure from the house on the night of the play was suddenly obvious. She must have seen them together, stumbled across them while my father was out at his bridge class and I was flying around the boys' school stage in my fairy's costume, uttering blank verse. Her strange conversation in the library, her awkwardness, the way she had stared at me so oddly, suddenly made sense. I felt sick, light-headed, as the smell of onions from a hot dog stall snaked through the warm air already clogged with the suggestion of sugared donuts, chips, shrimps, cockles and whelks.

Perhaps I fainted. Or maybe I just tripped. I found myself on the hard pavement, anyway, my knees grazed, my arm bruised and aching from colliding with a low wall, one hand bleeding with the impact of trying to forestall my fall. An elderly lady looked concerned. A woman pushing a pram stopped to check then moved on once I assured her I was all right. Two small children with melting ice cream cones stopped and stared until their mother pulled them away towards the clockwork golf. I rubbed my knees, inspected bits of me for real damage. My head throbbed and I felt unsteady as if I had stepped suddenly from a rapid rollercoaster and could not stop the world rotating. Mad thoughts of rushing up to London and trying to find Eva flooded my mind. If I got to a phone box, I could try and find her number, ring Mrs. Mason even, and say I needed to reach her urgently. I could stay for a while on the floor of Eva's room and ask her what I should do next. But even as the ideas tumbled into my mind, I dismissed them as absurd. Eva was not now to me what she had once been. I no longer knew her the way I used to and was unable to predict what her reaction would be, whether she would even show any interest at all. Besides, drawing attention to my discovery by doing something as preposterous as running away seemed rash, foolishly impulsive.

I stayed late in Brighton. I caught the bus at seven and the long summer light meant that it was still as bright as midday when I got back to Sea View Parade. The bed and breakfast guests had arrived. I'd forgotten all about them. My mother had left my tea, a slice of corned beef, one of luncheon meat and some slices of cucumber on a plate on the kitchen table. My father, I could hear, was in the back garden, the lawn mower heaving up and down in regular, uniform lines. I ignored the corned beef, made myself a cheese sandwich, poured a glass of milk and carried it into my back bedroom. All afternoon, I had considered my next move. And when it came down to it, this meant either confronting my parents or choosing to sidestep my discovery out of cowardice. The idea of them having anything at all to do with sex was, in itself, repulsive, of course. But the prospect of an illicit, immoral relationship conducted by either one of them was too abhorrent even to contemplate. And where would I start if I set about a sort of interrogation? Force my mother into a confession, demand dates and details of this sordid affair when my own awareness of sexual matters at the age of sixteen was limited to what I'd picked up from school gossip and *Petticoat* magazine? Then there was the memory of my mother's distress, those appalling tears, and I was hauled back to the night of the policeman's visit, her conviction that he was bringing news of the wrong man. For after all, our Mr. Fred Jarvis, the Freddie she knew, was not married. There was no wife and two children in Croydon, but simply an elderly, dependent mother in Greenwich. For days, weeks even, my mother had been inconsolable and no wonder. For she had lost not only her lover (and I forced myself to face the reality of the word) but the very truth of who and what he was. And in spite of loathing her for her behaviour, for her despicable deception, I found the smallest shred of pity for her, for the way she had been used, her trust exploited for the gain of Fred Jarvis.

So I did what seemed easiest, behaved in the most ostrich-like of ways.

I decided to ignore what I knew. Dispatched the discovery

from my mind as best I could like I might a piece of sensational fiction I had read. After all, I just wanted our everyday lives to go on as before, the structure unthreatened, secure. For however bland and dull those lives were, they were normal, reliably ordinary, and the obverse seemed too precipitous even to consider.

My pink Leavers' Dance dress had been rescued from the floor of my bedroom where I'd abandoned it and carefully hung over the back of a chair. My mother, I could see, had neatly pinned up the awkward, scalloped hem, secured it for me with long, even tacks. All I had to do was to blind stitch it permanently, press it into place.

19

S he hands me Ida's rings.

"They just slip off her now," the care assistant says. "We thought it better to give them to you. She's not going to wear them again."

In my hand lie her wedding ring, a simple gold band, and another of semi-precious stones, amethyst and seed pearls in a circular setting. Her engagement ring has its own small box lined with velvet that is now thin, worn with age.

"Thank you," I say, and stare at them in the palm of my hand.

"It happens a lot," she goes on, almost apologetically. "They lose weight and nothing quite fits anymore."

I try each on the ring finger of my left hand. It's a job to nudge them over the knuckle, but they make it. I remove them, slip them into my bag. It seems to be the first thing I notice when I reach her room and see her sitting in her chair by the window. Her left hand, devoid of the rings with which I've grown so familiar that I haven't really noticed them for years. Now her hands look bare, as if she has just been the victim of a jewel thief. Nothing quite fits Ida any more. Her clothes are somehow inappropriate to her shapelessness. Cardigans sag from bony shoulders. Even slippers tend to hang, suspended. Gradually, her body seems to be shrinking away from the business of living, the obligations of eating and absorbing and renewing. It's wintering, withdrawing. It seems to have had enough. I take her hand in mine. She does nothing for several moments, still stares out of the window, then turns and smiles broadly, grasps my hand hard. Her eyes are watery. They often are these days and I never know whether there are tears or if they simply do not operate the way they should. I dab them with a tissue and she turns her head away, irritated. My mother used to take a handkerchief from her pocket, damp it with her tongue and rub a smudge, a crumb, a stray eye lash from my face when I was young and I always squirmed, resented the imposition. Now she is the one to protest.

Ida is spending more and more time in her room, these days, seems less willing to be downstairs, part of the group who sit together, but say little. The staff say she is increasingly troubled by too much noise or disturbance although the communal lounge is hardly a place of frenzied activity and fervent conversation.

"If she's happier alone with her thoughts, that's fine by us," one of the nurses has said to me in explanation. "Too much sensory input can be a bit too much at this stage."

But then Ida was never a particularly sociable woman. She had few friends; in fact, no close friends at all. There were only neighbours from the parade she'd speak to about essential matters. Unreliable milkmen, perhaps, or dustbins upended by marauding foxes. She'd mention the occasional name from the years in north London, someone she'd once worked with and with whom she'd failed to keep in touch. And it was not until I grew up that I realised how unusual this was. How unlike other people. No-one came to our house. My parents never invited anyone to a meal the way other people's parents apparently did. My mother did not sit at the kitchen table with a female friend, gossiping over cups of coffee, discussing their children, their husbands, their concerns. My father played his occasional bridge games, went to work at the tax office, but presumably chose to keep colleagues and acquaintances at arm's length. No-one could have called the Fosters a sociable, outgoing family. And perhaps this all stemmed from the covert nature of the arrangement with Mr. Jarvis. As if concealment had become a habit that, even once he was dead, survived into the way my parents conducted their lives. And now Jack is living alone he is still cautious, somewhat withdrawn, I find. He is wary of friendship as if not trusting motive. Suspicious of a level of intimacy that has no specified boundaries.

What do they want with inviting me into their place? he'll complain to me of his well-meaning neighbours. *Why would I want to eat my tea round their table when I've got a perfectly good one of my own?* As a result, his days are solitary on the whole. His company is limited to the safe confines of radio by day, television at night, his activities limited to the garden, reading his daily paper, some light local shopping. Yet Jack is a kind man, a thoughtful man and a gently gregarious life would have suited him if he'd so chosen it.

It's hard to remember when I first realised that Jack was aware of the arrangement with Mr. Jarvis. In fact, not so much aware as entirely complicit in allowing the affair to flourish. Or perhaps it is kinder to think of him as choosing not to act to prevent it which made him, in my eyes, equally culpable. What kind of man positively rubber-stamps his wife's adultery, remains agreeably blinkered to its narrative? No wonder I sidestepped the knowledge for so long, chose to see my father as the wronged victim of this immorality. After all, discovering that both your parents have behaved outrageously, each as deserving as the other of your loathing, is more reality than most of us are willing to face. So I think of the knowledge as creeping up on me surreptitiously, slowly sinking beneath my skin, a bit like the development of a chronic illness, symptoms stealthily accruing. Until one day, I let myself confront the fact.

My father had known all along about my mother and Fred Jarvis.

He had allowed Ida to engineer a situation, namely the big old house at 8, Sea View Parade, where we could all live in some astounding crucible of deception. At first, I'd imagined Ida negotiating quite openly for what she wanted. Laying her terms on the table, as it were, as a condition for the continuation of their marriage. But of course, it would have been nothing like that. Neither Ida nor Jack would have chosen to be so demonstratively antagonistic. It would have embarrassed them, offended their natural reticence. Instead, a suitable, plausible fiction had served the purpose. And my father, ever compliant, choosing to see only what suited him to see, abided by Ida's rules. He has always been a man only taking offence when it suits him. And it rarely does. Fred Jarvis, of course, was playing an entirely different game. If he had not been so foolish as to get himself killed one dark, wet Friday night, who knows how long he would have managed to go on deceiving so many so skilfully?

I wheel Ida outside into the neat garden. She seems uncertain whether she wants to go when I ask her, but her room is too stuffy and I've run out of conversation. At least outside I can make observations about the flower beds. I gather some windfall rose petals in my palm and offer them to her to smell. She smiles as I place some in her hand then lets them fall onto her lap and watches them lying there with the fascination of a small child.

"Go back," Ida says suddenly, "take me back." Her voice is clear today. Sometimes she only mumbles, a mass of sounds squabbling towards coherent words. But today she is precise.

"It's not lunch time yet," I say, anxious to stay outside. Preferring the fresh damp smell of weeded flower beds, the mild air of early June. Inside, there are only the inevitable stale smells of aging. Newborn babies have an aroma of exotic fruit, roasted barley sugar and all things sweet and verdant. Here there is only flesh in decline. Slowly, I push the wheelchair on, pass a frail elderly man on the arm of a middle-aged woman who coaxes him cautiously across the lawn. She and I exchange smiles.

"No, back!" Ida says suddenly, with more force than I have seen her express for a while. "Where we used... where I was... by the sea. There. Where all of us..." And she rests her head in her hands and I am afraid that she is crying. I put on the brake, kneel down next to her and try to uncover her face, slip my arm around her thin shoulders. I talk about the old house, about the sound of seagulls and Sea View Parade for I think it is what she wants to hear. I talk about the winter storms and the pebbles tossed over Beach Parade into the path of pedestrians. I remind her of her piano playing at the ballet classes. I wonder whether I should even pretend that it is still her home, enter into a kind of fantasy as if we are all there living out our lives in some kind of skewed harmony, for insisting on the truth, on tangible reality, seems cruel and without purpose. Gilded memories, perhaps, should be the landscape for Ida now. I look at her bent head, her bewildered expression, her too-thin fingers that discard her rings. The possibility of feeling and expressing passion seems so entirely remote from her that it is hard to believe she ever knew such a state. Ever, actively, sought it. Desire and longing appear alien and utterly incongruous. A husk of a thing, she is now, supported in her chair, yet her heart still beats and organs go on functioning in a way vaguely appropriate to the essentials of living. We've circumnavigated the garden at least three times. I've moved on to talking about other things in the past. The time she and Jack went to Scotland, all the way in a coach on some guided tour advertised in the local newspaper. Jack had wanted to pay extra to fly, but Ida had insisted on the slow, scenic route. They'd had a day and a night in Edinburgh, the castle, the Royal Mile, a shop selling all the tartans then were headed back south again along a multitude of motorways. Then there were a couple of day trips they'd made to France. Once I left home, Jack seemed intent on being more adventurous, enticing Ida abroad. No doubt he thought this would be a tentative introduction, with those early morning starts along the coast to Newhaven and a late return after a day inspecting the shops and wares of Dieppe. Ida brought me back a small jar of black cherry jam. On the second trip there was a portion of brie. I believe they went to Guernsey once. But she never really seemed to acclimatise herself to the fact that holidays were a legitimate activity, entirely normal and acceptable to most people and eventually Jack appeared to succumb to her reluctance to leave home. Perhaps he was disinclined to think too much about why she did not see holidays with him as something pleasurable. My father was, for Ida, functional. A practical, ideal asset. He provided adequate, unfailing support. I am not aware of them ever rowing. Nor can I remember Ida ever touching Jack spontaneously. A marriage of convenience, you could say, being cynical. Or a sensible, workable arrangement that sustains. It was what she saw for me with David, what she considered the ideal option if you were lucky enough for it to come your way. A cool wind picks up, the sun seems swallowed for the day. I head us back towards the house.

I have no idea how they met, Ida and Fred Jarvis. It's something I have increasingly wanted to know since I have allowed myself to grow curious about the man. Even before the letter arrived from his daughter, Eliza, I had begun to wonder about his children. About the order in which things had happened, Ida and Fred, Ida and Jack, Eliza, her sister and me. Over recent years, I have pictured the possibility of a confession of sorts. I have imagined a moment when my mother would turn to me, crave my understanding. She would seek to explain, justify even, the intrusion of Fred Jarvis and how he came to appear in our lives. Or I have confronted her at last, firmly, without embarrassment, demanding to know the entire story. But no such open exchange has ever taken place between us. The climate has never seemed right, propitious. And I wonder if we are particularly unusual in being a family who edge around conversations, rely on the banal to get us through our dealings with each other. We have never said anything at all, come to think of it, that could not be said to some chance acquaintance. An emptiness fills our dialogue that seems designed to disguise what we really want to say. And now it is nearly too late. It is certainly too late as far as Ida is concerned, who can only speak in distracted phrases, random snatches of conversation that seem to have little order or consistent train of thought. I can hardly play the interrogator with her now. And as for Jack, I finally face the fact that only distress can result from pursuing any revelation. He is living a sort of premature widowerhood, alone for the first time in over fifty years, training himself to make a single cup of tea each morning. Washing up one place setting each evening. Waking up alone in the middle of the night. And he sees, I imagine, only the bigger picture now. The years of mutual comforting and companionship. The solace of the sublimely ordinary moments that he and Ida must have shared. Regardless of the woeful shortcomings, it has been so much better, he might reason, being with her than being alone. He is a man who has always appeared to be grateful for less than he deserved and as a result has perhaps known a greater sense of happiness and contentment than most. After all, there is wonder to be found in the regularity of routine. Like the consolation of snowdrops in January. The pure light of evening skies in early spring. I have often wondered whether Ida ever recovered from the knowledge of Fred Jarvis' duplicity. There is a near physical pain in betrayal that unhinges, wounds in a way that is only ever partially knitted over, cobbled together piecemeal style. Perhaps Ida deserved it, for what she had preposterously set up and imagined that she could have. But I don't know. Fred Jarvis was having the last laugh all the time and for that, I can't help but feel maliciously gratified that he sliced into a lamp post at high speed one wet, slippery Friday night on his way, not to Greenwich as we supposed, but to his awaiting family in Croydon. Karma, as Miss Mackie said in the library that day over thirty-five years ago, his nemesis.

I fiddle with the blanket over Ida's knees. The last of the rose petals slips away. In the dining room the tables are set and I find her place, next to a woman who is very deaf. Ida looks up at me, as if confused suddenly by her surroundings.

"Home," she says too loudly, "not… no, not right," and she shakes her head and fiddles with the fork on the table. I pour her a tumbler of water that I know she will not drink. "I don't want… not here."

"Time for lunch," I say in a sing-song cheerful tone. "You must be hungry after the fresh air." I hope Felix is never so patronising. I hope he is never required to play the dutifully attentive adult child. But given the order of things it is perhaps inevitable. Each generation feels sure it is going to be the one to attain immortality, but it appears still to be eluding us. I told David, about Fred Jarvis. He is the only person I have ever told and his reaction was, naturally, very David. Bemusement, a tolerant sort of *well, who would have thought it* expression and a disinclination to delve deeper into the matter which hugely irritated me at the time. David is the sort of man who thinks psychological explorations at best an affectation; at worst, some sign of mental imbalance. In fact, I think he chose to forget the knowledge, bury it so that it would not confront him each time we saw Ida and Jack, his parents-in-law, and compromise his behaviour towards them.

Lunch is brought in. Meat and mushroom pie and creamed potato. Ida picks up a fork, but it slips out of her grasp. I rescue it from her lap, fold it into her hand more firmly and I quickly kiss her cheek.

"I must go," I say, backing away briskly. "I'll see you again soon. Promise. Look after yourself." I turn at the door to see she is staring at me, imploring. Her hand gestures towards me then falls away, as if not wanting to display her desperation.

★ ★ ★

I knew I would return to the letter. Otherwise, why not stuff it in the bin along with the teabags and pizza crusts and burnt toast the day it first arrived? Besides, Eliza Jarvis was obviously not going to give up at first or second attempt to grab my attention. One night when I couldn't sleep, I got up and retrieved it from the drawer where I'd stuffed it. Somehow doing such a thing at two in the morning, time set apart from normal living, exonerated me and I told myself I could forget the content by daybreak if I so chose. But I read it thoroughly this time with nit-picking attention. And I found myself getting to the end of it and starting again, searching and constructing and defining Eliza Jarvis out of the handwriting, the polite, careful phrasing. I imagined her small, slight, quietly spoken. Artistic, perhaps, like her father. I saw her as unthreatening, timid even, diffident and self-effacing. A figure most probably based upon my memory of her mother on the doorstep of 8, Sea View Parade one Saturday afternoon all those years ago. A memory based on the perceptions of a girl in her mid-teens and no doubt seriously distorted by time.

So when I decide the next evening not to prevaricate any longer with a written reply, but simply to pick up the phone and ring, I am taken aback by the voice that promptly answers.

"Hallo? Hallo, again? Anyone actually there?" The voice is assertive, insistent, and I've paused too long and alerted some suspicion. But perhaps I've dialled the wrong number. I ask to speak to Eliza Jarvis.

"Speaking," she replies, with the kind of authority that cowers. "Can I help you?"

I am about to cancel the call, but sense she'll ring back. This tone stems from a person not easily rebuffed. I sit down on the chair by the window in my bedroom, see the streaks of red in the mid-evening sky.

"You wrote to me," I say, somewhat feebly. "It's Mary Foster. And I was just wondering… I believe my father gave you my contact details." I state the obvious. I feel inexplicably wrong-footed, as if I have been the one initially to make the intrusion into Eliza Jarvis' life. A silence stretches out between my small terraced house in the urban south and Eliza's rural Lancashire village. I imagine dry stone walls out of her window. Sheep gently grazing.

"Well, thank you so much for ringing, it's quite a surprise, I must say. I really didn't expect to hear from you. It was just a shot in the dark, really, just a jab." There's nothing of Lancashire in her voice. And absolutely nothing of the woman I've conjured from the neat sheets of blue Basildon Bond. She sounds like someone who comes to my adult literature class, a formidable woman called Ursula who is alarmingly well read. I find myself fearing Ursula's interruptions each week as she seems to manage to quote German writers, cite French poets I've never heard of. Eliza Jarvis feels similarly undermining.

"Of course, it may all be a nonsense of mine," she goes on, "but I find I'm just too curious to leave things well alone.

And there's a certain ambiguity that is rather compelling. Fascinating, in fact."

Suddenly, this phone call seems a very bad idea. I can sense exactly where it is going and, although I may have allowed my own wild imaginings to drift in a similar direction in recent years, they have been simply that. Random thoughts and considerations not fit to bring to the forefront of any rational mind. I try to rein things in a little.

"I don't know why you contacted me after so many years." I try to sound assured. "I can't think that we have anything in particular to say to each other." Outside a man is putting out his bin for the following morning's collection. The neighbour's white cat stalks a sparrow from a distance.

"My mother died six months ago," Eliza Jarvis says, "a stroke. Very sudden. That's what prompted this, in fact, losing her. It's not something I could have done while she was still alive. And you're right, of course. There's absolutely no need for me to contact you. Call it pure selfishness, if you like. Or an insatiable curiosity that somehow grows as one ages."

"Why? I mean it's just something that happened in the past, surely. In very different times. A past belonging to our parents and very little to do with you and me."

There's a silence the other end. I'm hoping Eliza Jarvis is drawing the same conclusion. But she's not.

"I lost my father when I was six years old," she says. "That fact is forever in my present."

"I still can't see the relevance of you contacting me." I try to sound firm, definitive. But Eliza Jarvis has more to wield.

"You probably have more memory of my father than I do," she says. "I know of him mostly from my mother's point of view. Entirely, in fact, apart from the dimmest of recollections. A very few photographs. So, I suppose I'm groping around a bit, trying to find anything at all about him. Filling in the gaps, as it were."

I say something about doubting I can help, reminding her of how long ago it all was. At the same time, of course, recalling effortlessly his black jacket around the back of the kitchen chair. The smell of his cigarettes, his strong black instant coffee. And my mother, Ida, not frail and fragile in her wheelchair, her slippers hanging suspended from her feet, but neat and bustling and controlling. Meat and potato pie and a plate of rock buns set out on the kitchen table. Handkerchiefs and vests and tea towels neatly ironed into tidy squares. Eliza Jarvis suggests we might meet. She's coming to London for a conference later in the month, she says, she's giving a paper. I've shifted my viewpoint from someone artistic to a research scientist, possibly a criminal psychologist. An authority on community cohesion at a pinch. She says something about her husband that surprises me. I've thought of her as single, but she says she's always retained her maiden name, explains the awkwardness of her husband's surname of Egbert next to Eliza. I try to be suitably vague about dates, times, when she relates her London itinerary with the precision of someone consulting a diary, sidestep her attempt to pin me down to convenient days. Claim still to be equivocal about the idea of us meeting at all, but it's clear I'm hooked.

And no doubt she can tell.

For of course I'll turn up to meet Eliza Jarvis because the opportunity has presented itself and I'm too weak-willed to resist. Besides, she's the only possible source of reliable knowledge about Fred Jarvis.

About his possibly legacy.

I put down the phone and it rings again instantly. Too immediate even to be Eliza. It's Felix, apologetic, saying he'll be back a bit later than he's promised. I've not noticed the time.

The endless, unutterably beautiful long nights of midsummer are with us and nine o'clock seems more like midday.

In the kitchen I open the back door onto our long, narrow scratch of garden. Jack's given advice on the borders so that at least there's some busy lizzies, a bed of marigolds and night-scented stocks suggesting some attention. It eludes me, the garden. I intend always to learn how to sow it, plant it, feed it, so that it can be like other people's. Well-tended, seasonal, controlled. The mark of a stable, secure, middle-aged adulthood. That's how I see a neat garden, as something I should have grown into, carefully acquired. But it creeps up on me, my garden, overnight seemingly, so that a few hours spent weeding, tidying, are redundant. My narrow patch of land clearly knows of my ineptitude and is consequently as contrary as possible. David's a good gardener. When we were married, we had serried rows of annuals and perennials, regular, appropriate flowering that reflected David, celebrated his order, his sensible certainty. I bet Eliza Jarvis has an organised, substantial piece of land with a proper greenhouse and a garden seat and views of the Lancashire hills. She sounds like a woman who obtains what she sets out to achieve. The large tortoiseshell cat from next door sneaks in behind me, leaps up on the kitchen table, searching for scraps. It's taken to adopting us lately, although our own tabby is intolerant and will hiss mercilessly if she sees the intruder. Felix wants a dog. We're still in talks, negotiating. I'm yet to show my hand.

20

S usan and I went to the new Chinese restaurant in Bampton to celebrate my eighteenth birthday. I'd wanted a party. I wanted to hire the hall at the end of the parade where my mother played for the ballet classes and where a girl at school had celebrated her eighteenth in November. Anna's father had decorated the hall with fairy lights and her mother who was Italian had cooked huge bowls of bolognese and risotto and her uncle had provided ice cream from his shop in Brighton. The entire class had been invited. Anna had a boyfriend called Martin who worked in the estate agents in Bampton and there were rumours that they were secretly engaged. Girls in my Upper 6 history class said that she wore her single fake solitaire diamond ring on a string around her neck, a fact that somehow caused me to revere Anna's obvious worldliness. I'd spent Anna's party circling the room, hovering at the edge every time a slow number was played, half hoping and half fearing for the attentions of a fair-haired boy called Ralph. In the end, I'd seen him in a deep embrace with Madeleine during a Fleetwood Mac song that had ended the evening. Madeleine was captain of just about everything at school and heading off to read sociology at Kent in September. There was no way I could have competed with Madeleine. For a start, I still believed that the stigma of having transferred from the secondary modern to the grammar for the sixth form rendered me leprous. As if I was there under some sort of false pretence rather than as a right. I had spent the first year being as unobtrusive as I could, silent in lessons, impervious to the teachers' encouragements to join in discussions, voice opinions. Consequently, by the second year, Susan and I seemed to be viewed by most of the other girls as a dull duo that were best left to ourselves. We were, on the whole, happy to oblige their expectation of us.

In truth, it was only the idea of a party for my eighteenth that I craved, not the actual event, considering my inadequate circumstances. I lacked the material factors that Anna had, like her cosmopolitan sort of parents, her boyfriend and a circle of girlfriends who would wear the right clothes and grope the right kind of boys at the given, darkened moment. Eva was somewhere abroad. Switzerland, evidently, *Eva in Geneva*, her postcard said, but I think she was employing poetic licence for the rhyme. The last she'd told me was that she was au pairing with a French family near Strasbourg. *I'm getting expert at washing up,* she'd written in her Christmas card, *au pair girls are the bees' knees at the kitchen sink.* If Eva had been home, my eighteenth birthday may have been different. And I linked the reason for Eva's absence back to her time in Canada and the events we had never spoken about since that day in her kitchen. That broken zip on her split skirt, her mother's set, stern face, her angry voice.

So instead of an eighteenth birthday party at the hall like Anna Montenario, Susan and I sat with each other at the Hong Ying in between the cinema and the launderette and contemplated chopsticks.

"It tastes better if you eat it with these things," I said, "it takes longer too. We want the evening to last, don't we?"

Susan stared at the menu. I could see her eye gliding down towards the English Meals section. Chicken and Chips. Omelette and Chips. Scampi and Chips.

"Have you been here before?" she asked me.

"A few times," I lied, "quite a few." I'd been just once before with a girl called Sarah from school who was taking the same three subjects as me. Arty farty subjects, as Susan called them, with her head in her biology and maths and chemistry books. But Sarah had got herself a boyfriend from the boys' grammar at Christmas and that was the end of us spending any Saturday nights at the Hong Ying in Bampton.

"I think we should have the set meal for two," I said to Susan, showing her on the menu. The place was deserted. Four waiters hovered at the door to the kitchens, shifting from foot to foot. A couple sat waiting to collect a meal to take away, the man jingling car keys, the woman smoking a cigarette and talking to him in a low voice. One of the waiters served them tea in tiny china cups with a teapot that looked as if it came from a dolls' set. The woman lifted the lid, smelt and pulled a face. We ordered.

"Are we going to have a drink?" Susan said. "A proper drink so I can toast you. Sherry, perhaps, I don't mind sherry."

"You can't ask for sherry," I snapped. "That's so wrong. You'd get us laughed at."

"Then I'll just have lemonade," Susan said, and I was unsure whether I was more annoyed with her for such an inappropriate suggestion or for giving in so easily to my objection.

"I'm having vodka," I said, "with lime. You can try mine and see if you like it."

"No thanks," Susan said. "I know perfectly well what vodka tastes like. My mum drinks it with tonic and I don't like it at all."

Nor did I, of course. But Eva had introduced me to it when I'd stayed the weekend with her in London at the secretarial students' hostel. Splashing it sufficiently with lime conveniently drowned the taste and I was desperately keen to upstage Susan. Our drinks arrived and Susan solemnly chinked glasses and wished me well for the future. Then she produced a small box from her handbag and, a little embarrassed, pushed it across the white tablecloth.

"I can change it if you don't like it," she said, "or I can give you the receipt and you can get something you like better."

Inside was a silver chain with a small, single, cruciform-like shape suspended from it.

"It's an ankh," Susan said. "It's an Egyptian symbol of eternal life or something like that. It's meant to mean good fortune or freedom or possibly both, I think. I expect you've seen them on Egyptian statues in the British Museum."

Possibly I had, but unlike Susan I would have failed to remember or bothered to learn about them. I felt an extraordinary wave of gratitude to her, but at the same time guilt. I never thought of Susan as a best or particularly chosen friend, but as merely a convenient one. She was available. She was pliable. She was easily placated. My parents had not given me any presents for my eighteenth birthday. Not proper presents like other people had. There had been a card with a cheque, post-dated five months.

"It's for college," my mother had explained as I'd looked at it blankly. "You'll need to be buying things then, I expect, like books and possibly a kettle. There'll be a lot of expenses so you can cash the cheque in the summer holidays and spend the money then."

There had been a dictionary too. The pocket Oxford in a hardback edition.

"It's for the training college as well," my father had said, a touch apologetically. "Your mother insisted you'd be needing a new one then."

I fastened the ankh and its chain around my neck. It felt light yet notable.

"It's lovely, really special, Susan. It must have cost you the earth."

"Well, is a bit special, isn't it?" she said. "It's the beginning of us being grown up, after all. No good excusing ourselves as ignorant children any more. And now you get the vote at eighteen it makes you realise how we have to be responsible from now on." She shook out a white napkin onto her lap and watched as a waiter put small bowls of thin chicken and white mushroom soup in front of us. "This," she went on as she picked up her china spoon and sipped suspiciously, "is the start of us being adults." She swallowed and looked relieved. "It's all right, actually, doesn't taste of much. But it's better than it looks."

I swigged at my vodka and lime. I hadn't considered that I was supposed to feel different now I was eighteen. That it was the end of something benign and the start of something serious. As far as I could see Susan had been responsible and sensible and adult her entire life so that maturity seemed to be less to do with age and more with disposition. After all, I felt as if I were still the same girl who had spent dull Saturday afternoons coveting the Fairy Glen dolls' clothes at the back of Beaumont's. But then I thought of Eva. Eva had grown up. Or at least she had been catapulted into a sort of instant adulthood by becoming pregnant. Giving birth to a child. The overwhelming consequence of something that had stemmed, perhaps, from a moment of abstraction or casual curiosity. When I'd stayed with her in London at her student hostel, she'd certainly been different. Remote, a little distant, as if unable to trust herself anymore to be spontaneous. She was controlled, guarded, contained. Perhaps that was being grown up in the way Susan meant. I had been thinking of the next stage, leaving home and becoming a student, as being the opposite of responsible. I saw myself as being gloriously freed from the shackles of school and parental interference yet unyoked to the tiresome business of earning a living. Susan's view depressed me instantly. Arriving at eighteen suddenly seemed loaded with implication.

The door to the restaurant opened with a gulf of cold January air flooding in. Two men took a table across the room from us and ordered beer. A moment later, the couple who had been waiting for their take-away meal left, letting more arctic air in through the ill-fitting door. Susan fastened the buttons on her navy woollen cardigan.

"It's not the most popular place in town, is it," she said, "and it's not that warm in here either. I don't know why we didn't go to the new Chef and Brewer instead. That's certainly popular and they do prawn cocktails and Black Forest gateau there, you know."

"It gets really crowded here later," I said weakly, "when the cinema empties. And the pubs. You can hardly get a table then." At least that was what I'd heard girls at school say. Girls like Anna Montenario and Sarah Phillips who came here with their boyfriends on Friday nights. I'd heard them talk about the films they'd seen and how they'd drunk too much rum and sobered up on the egg fried rice. The waiter removed our bowls and loaded a warming tray with food. I spooned portions onto Susan's plate in a patronising manner that I wouldn't have dreamed of adopting with anyone else.

"Sweet and sour pork," I said, "in batter. You'll like those. And pancake roll. And rice, of course. And you don't have to use chopsticks if you don't want to," I added, thinking of the kindness of Susan, the silver chain and ankh hanging around my neck.

One of the men at the table across from us caught my eye. He smiled and I was appalled to feel myself blushing.

"So have you got your place?" Susan saved me. "At training college? You told me you'd had your interview."

"I heard yesterday," I said, digging a chopstick artlessly into the large pancake roll. "I got the letter confirming everything. So yes, it's sort of all settled." I had waited to feel excited, holding the letter with the training college crest in the top right-hand corner, grabbing the thick envelope off the hall mat as it had popped through the letterbox. Instead, there was only a dull sense of inevitability. I was doing what was expected of me, not particularly more or any less than that. I wanted to feel triumphant. Instead, I felt deflated. Susan nodded, forked another sweet and sour pork ball.

"It's nice to be settled, isn't it? I've got an interview next month," she said, "in London. I've changed my mind about training locally. There'll be better prospects at one of the London hospitals."

I was surprised. I hadn't pictured Susan forging her way in a new place, let alone London. I'd imagined her coming back each night to the flat above the fish and chip shop, changing out of her nurse's uniform and into overalls ready for the deep fat fryer.

"Prospects?" I said through mouthfuls of bean sprouts and the curious contents of my pancake roll. Nursing was surely nursing wherever you did it. Sick people on stretchers, blood and bandages and bed pans and plaster casts and bedside tables cluttered with barley water and grapes and get-well cards. However indifferent I felt about teachers' training college, there was nothing on earth that would have pushed me towards nursing. Susan spooned more rice onto the rash of bright orange sauce on her plate.

"It's a chance to get out and away from all this," she said, "the life I have here. I want something better than my mother's had, you know. She had no choice, of course, but I do and I want to make the most of it."

Susan had never spoken quite so stridently. Eva and I had always felt a bit sorry for her, with her plain, pasty-like complexion, her small, cramped flat and absent father. But we'd assumed she was indifferent to such circumstances rather than conspiring to change them. "And at a London hospital, I'll meet medical students," she went on, "lots of them, I expect. I'm bound to. Nurses always socialise with doctors, you know. So I'll be able to find one to marry. Doctors earn good money, everyone knows that, not riches, but a decent salary. It's a way of moving up in the world, that's how I see it."

I put my chopsticks down and drained the last of my vodka and lime.

"How can you be thinking like that already?" I said, inexplicably annoyed. "Thinking about the man you're going to marry, planning it all out. You might decide you don't want to get married, at all."

"Of course I want to get married. Everyone does. Don't you?" Susan spoke a little loudly so that the two men opposite looked up from their conversation. I saw one of them smirk, whisper something to the other. He laughed too and then signalled to the waiter to bring them more beer.

"Possibly," I said, "or possibly not. In fact, at the moment, marriage is actually the last thing I have in mind. Anyway, that's beside the point, Susan. You have to wait to see who you fall in love with first. Not just go around ordering any old doctor to collapse at your feet and propose."

Susan went on eating for a while, apparently taken with the sweet and sour pork. Eventually, she pushed her plate away. She folded her arms on the table, avoiding the stain I'd caused by slopping rice.

"You need a plan," she said, sounding as if she were talking to someone considerably younger, someone utterly clueless. "It's no good just expecting things to fall into your lap in life, Mary. And don't aim too high either. It's best to be realistic."

"What do you mean? We're only just eighteen. This is the time when we're supposed to dream and think that anything's possible. The moon, millionaires, princes, whatever we can think of. It's not the Victorian era, you know. We can wish for more than just a good marriage and a load of babies."

"Everything's a compromise, you know," Susan said. "No-one gets exactly what they want in life. That's just not how it is."

For a moment, I hated her for her sense, for sounding just a little too like my mother. And even more, I deeply resented her for the fact that, quite possibly, she was absolutely right.

"Only if you give in and make do with second best," I said, trying to rally an argument then immediately regretting it. I thought of the training college letter propped up on my desk, the acceptance slip awaiting my signature that soon I'd be signing and slipping into its return envelope.

"It's no good believing in fairy tales, Mary," Susan went on. "At least not for me. I have to be realistic about my chances."

"Chances?" I said sharply, then regretted it. Susan was a good, loyal friend, I reminded myself. Susan supplied what no-one else quite did. I tried hard to be nicer. "What do you mean?"

"Look at me, I'm hardly Miss World material, am I?" she said in her loud voice again. Fortunately, the two men opposite seemed involved in a dispute about football teams. Their voices out-shrilled Susan's with their Arsenal this and their Spurs that.

"But you're so clever, Susan, really brainy. You could go to university if you wanted." It was true. She'd got far better O level results than me and was always up for school prizes. But it was also true that Susan seemed indifferent to fashion and was at least two dress sizes larger than everyone else in the sixth form common room. She sat in the corner blithely eating half a packet of bourbon biscuits at break time, spilling crumbs over a biology text book while stick-thin creatures compared grapefruit and hardboiled egg diets. Living above a fish and chip shop on a limited income had had its toll too. "I'm not clever," Susan said, "I'm just hardworking. But thanks for calling me clever. No-one ever has. I just learn all the stuff in the books, you see. Spend hours learning, learning, learning. Because it can get me places, get me out. I'll never be able to rely on my face to do that for me."

"That's a very old-fashioned attitude," I said. "People don't think of women like that anymore."

"That's easy to say if you've got your face," Susan said placidly, "or your thighs. Mine are massive, you know." She glanced down at her legs under the tablecloth, clad in thick brown stretch nylon trousers.

"Useful on the wards, though, pushing all those beds and trolleys around," I said. The vodka had had some effect.

Susan giggled. It was so hard to offend her that she'd managed to avoid being the victim of bullying over the years by simply refusing to see it. Abuse ricocheted off Susan, boomeranged back to its perpetrator.

"Anyway," she said, "you'll be all right, Mary. I expect you'll be happy enough."

The waiter hovered with a pot of sweetly steaming jasmine tea. It was included in our set meal, I told Susan, so worth tolerating. She put two sugar lumps into the dainty china cup and sniffed it before sipping.

"I want more than that," I said, "more than happy enough. I want to be ecstatically happy. Have no regrets about anything. After all, we're only at the very beginning, aren't we? We've got a whole lifetime ahead of us." Yet even as I spoke I thought of Eva. Already Eva had a dark corner, a place unsafe for her to visit. And I saw the woman at the front door that Saturday afternoon and the two small children with their faces flattened against the glass. I thought of my mother's wild crying on the night we heard that Fred Jarvis was dead. And my father, forever diffident, undemonstrative, slipping into his jacket, taking us both down the road for a consoling bag of chips.

The truth was I was no longer quite sure where our lives actually began.

Probably years before we were even born, attached inextricably to past events and deeds so that we grew up unconsciously conditioned by them. Another cold blast of January air, this time spiced with sleet, reached our table as the restaurant door swung open again. The early evening showing at the Langham had just finished and several tables filled up.

★ ★ ★

Susan got her place at University College Hospital. We took our A levels in June and left school forever in July. Some girls cried. More got drunk on cider in the common room and someone called Francesca made a pass at the French teacher who was only twenty-two and straight out of Cambridge. We watched them leave school together in his Reliant Robin then Susan and I joined a crowd going down to the beach. It was unusually hot that day in a summer that had been at best cool and overcast. After initial end of exam exhilaration, I had felt strangely flat, set adrift from the routine of the past two years. The excuse of study had been a convenient shield, a justification for hours spent alone in my room. I'd got a holiday job at the library, but still there was too much time hanging on my hands just like the summer after O levels all over again. My mother tried to coerce me into helping with the bed and breakfast guests, but I recoiled at the idea of other people's used bed linen and claimed longer library hours than

I was actually working. We seemed to have grown out of the habit of talking, my mother, my father and I. It was surprising how easy it was to sidestep situations where conversation was required and I was not even sure whether they noticed that I was choosing to avoid them. But then I hardly ever saw the two of them together in the same room apart from mealtimes. My mother cleaned and washed and scrubbed endlessly and had taken to making her own jam to save on the expense of bought stuff. My father began to grow more vegetables and soft fruits so that the back garden was transformed into a veritable Dig for Victory thirty years too late. He'd got himself a second-hand bicycle too and took to taking long rides along the coast to Rottingdean and inland to Ditchling Beacon. Between the three of us lay a vacuum, a space vacant of clear emotion. I no longer knew what I felt about them and on the whole, tried to bury any consideration of the matter. Like a visitor to a terminal patient, I avoided the only subject that was really worthy of discussion.

Down on the beach, Gail bought the three of us sticks of pink candy floss. Gail Thomas had come with us from the secondary modern to the girls' grammar although had been a little more skilful in integrating. But now on the beach, after two years cramped together in the sixth form common room, there was still sense of some divide and we had drawn apart from the others. Gail was destined for a trainee job at the bank in Bampton. She'd wanted art school, but her parents thought art was for hobbies only and that art school was just an excuse for taking drugs and having sex. Susan had already been measured for her uniform and bought her black shoes and fob watch. I'd begun to summon some enthusiasm for teachers' training college. The others, the grammar girls, were scattering to Bristol and Kent, Leeds, Lancaster and Hull for Geography and History, English, Biological Sciences and French.

"We will all keep in touch, won't we?" Gail said, sounding hesitant. She always looked frail and insubstantial, with her thin face and large blue eyes and long fine flaxen hair that she resolutely refused to cut. She painted the strangest of pictures. Heads without bodies, bodies with tails and no heads. Cats with curlicue tails and one eye. She was particularly good at mermaids.

"Perhaps," Susan said, "although we can't be sure of that. We'll have to see where the next few years take us."

"Of course we'll keep in touch," I said, and the candy floss dissolved on my tongue, disappeared to nothing. "We'll write and arrange to meet up. In holiday times."

"We'll see," Susan said. "We'll make new friends, you know. We won't need each other in the same way."

Gail looked bleak.

"But new friends won't know about the person I've always been until now," she said. "They'll only know who I decide to become once I'm away from here."

She threw her stick of candy floss among the pebbles, scrounged in her pocket for the French cigarettes she liked to smoke.

"But you're only going as far as the bank in Bampton," Susan said bluntly, and Gail lit up her cigarette and blew her first inhale of smoke into Susan's face. "You're not even leaving here."

"You know what I mean," Gail said, tucking the hem of her long calico skirt into her waistband, discarding her sandals and wading knee-deep into the cold water. "We're all leaving who we are now. We're not schoolgirls any more, not tied to our parents' apron strings. We're growing up and we can become exactly who we want. Behave how we want." She was shouting into the sea breeze and we could hardly hear her. The mid-summer sun was still high in the sky and beamed down on her, illuminating her shape against the water. Straggles of her hair flew out around her, her bony shoulders protruding through her peasant blouse. I could imagine a strong wave coming and sweeping her up in its wake, stealing her away to some watery subterranean destiny. Susan shifted her position on the pebbles.

"She'll have to smarten herself up a bit for the bank, that's for sure. Black suit and 15 denier tights with no ladders in them. And proper shoes. You know, court shoes with little heels. That's what they'll want."

One of the others came over, lurching from the pain of pebbles on her bare feet. She peered down at us through large dark sunglasses.

"We're going back to my house," Lynette said. "My parents are out. You can come if you like, although it's probably a bit far from where you two live." Susan and I looked at each other. We'd never warmed to Lynette, a clever girl who managed to be rebellious and insolent whilst at the same time reaping school rewards through her calculated manipulation of staff. No doubt she'd do the same at Hull where she was heading to study English.

"Thank you very much, Lyn, but we've both got other plans," Susan said primly, picking herself up off the pebbles.

"Suit yourself," Lynette said, retreating before we had a chance to change our minds.

"Have we?" I said, "plans, I mean?"

Susan shook bits of shell and sand out of her sandals and did the same with her large white handbag.

"I don't know about you, Mary, but I'm on the mid-evening shift at the shop so I'd like to get back. No point hanging around any longer, I'd say."

Gail and I stayed on. She'd wanted to go back with Lynette and the others, but I managed to persuade her to stay by buying her cider and more cigarettes. Of all days, I loathed the thought of going home to Number 8, confronting the evasive conversations, my own cowardice in being part of the pretence in which the three of us now lived. We walked further down the beach and found a couple of old deckchairs that had been abandoned for the tide to claim.

"I don't think I want to grow up," I said, "if it means becoming like most of the adults I know."

Gail nodded. "Dull, you mean. Hopelessly conventional, like my parents. Stuck in their ways. Are your parents like that?"

"Not exactly," I said. "At least they are, but…" and I found myself unable to continue. Gail didn't seem to notice. She broke open her new packet of cigarettes.

"We're different, don't worry, Mary. Our generation is free and we break the rules rather than obey them. We're the lucky ones. I mean there's the Pill now and… I mean, what did our parents have? Glenn Miller? Vera Lynn and the white cliffs of bloody Dover? Whereas we've grown up on the Rolling Stones. The Who. John Lennon. That has to make a difference."

Gail was clearly going to be wasted at the National Provincial in Bampton. We sat astride our broken, sea-wrecked deckchairs, staring out ahead of us at the horizon, waiting for the sun to join the sea, hovering for just a moment before slipping irretrievably away.

"Blink and the moment's lost," Gail said, "unless you paint it. Then it's there forever."

"Is that why you do it? Painting, I mean. To hold on to things. To make the present last."

"Like a photograph. Except that photographs lie. Everyone can smile in them when really they are deeply unhappy. They just smile for the camera."

"And years later people look back at their albums and get all nostalgic. Whereas really it's all false. The past's full of lies." I thought of the few photos displayed around Number 8. My parents' wedding, the happy couple arm in arm. My christening, a small scrap swathed in a large blanket on my mother's lap.

"Possibly," Gail said, "but of course you can never be certain, can you? About what people are feeling. Anyway, it's all going to be great for us, you'll see."

She fumbled for a match to light her cigarette. I found the box of matches she'd dropped between pebbles and by the time we were settled on watch again it had gone. The sun had slipped down into the sea, the moment had passed.

21

It's a long time since I've thought of that conversation with Gail Thomas, watching the sun set at Beach Parade on our very last day of school, our eighteen-year-old selves perched on rotten deckchairs, on the cusp of futures that we foolishly imagined would be somehow astonishing. Extraordinary. Entirely in our control. In fact, Gail Thomas never even made it to the counter of the National Provincial in Bampton. In August of that year, she went on holiday to the west coast of Scotland where she met a man called Vic who made things out of driftwood. When the reason for her early morning sickness made itself clearly evident, they swiftly married and went to live on Skye. I believe they had five babies in as many years and possibly she and Vic still live there, although we lost touch after the fifth child. And Susan never found her doctor. Or if she did, she failed to entrap him along some hospital corridor. Instead, she married a non-conformist minister from Lyme Regis on her thirty-sixth birthday, a man she'd met through some church social club that she'd joined. Ever the pragmatist, Susan had appeared to adopt religion in order to procure a husband and became a steadfast, devoted wife of the manse. I went to their wedding, the bride in a huge white dress with a billowing veil looking placidly happy, her husband, conciliatory, excessively fond and devoted at her side. Three years later, still childless, they adopted beautiful twin girls from China. We keep in touch, the usual messages on Christmas cards with the genuine if unfulfilled intention to meet, the occasional email. We remember each other's birthdays with a card, a small gift, a kind of tradition that neither of us chooses to break.

Gail, of course, had been so wrong when she had assumed that my parents were as conventional and dully predictable as her own. Yet I could hardly explain their behaviour, insist that my mother's sexual transgressions could be seen as catching the zeitgeist of the moment, my father's tolerance simply a sign of the promiscuous times. After all, Ida was not Marianne Faithful or Jane Birkin. Jack was not Mick Jagger or Keith Moon. Their indiscretions were covert and clandestine and they wounded. They hurt. I remember wondering, on that late afternoon on the beach with Gail, how I could possibly explain to her my discovery: that the most ordinary of people behave in the most extraordinary of ways. And that the potential for deception is infinite.

★ ★ ★

I sit waiting for Eliza Jarvis in the reception of a hotel in Bloomsbury. It's one of those quiet, inconspicuous places just off Fitzroy Square that you can walk past a hundred times without noticing. 19th century red brick with a discreet brass plate and glass doors. I've arrived too early and, sitting awkwardly in the small reception area, have already scanned most of the free newspapers in the magazine rack. The date for our meeting has been changed twice already and I'm beginning to think the whole idea is better shelved. But she's insistent, apologetic when she has to postpone and immediately sets an alternative day. It's mid-July and London is overcast and humid. A thick blanket of still air seems to hang over the city, enervating and oppressive. My skirt sticks to my legs, my shoes rub and mark my bare feet. I wish I'd worn something else, something thinner and cooler. I've little real idea of the woman I've come to meet and with no photo am going to have to trust to instinct to recognise her. Inevitably, though, as people always do, I've built up a picture in my mind, a sort of photo fit from the scant evidence so far, very different from my original image of her. There's her dogged determination to make contact, our phone conversations, her attendance at this conference. Now I've got her down as neat, tall, trim and intimidating. Neutrally sartorial, carefully groomed. So when the doors of the hotel are pushed open rapidly and a large woman comes in, panting a little, pushing back untidy dark hair and adjusting a cardigan slipping from one shoulder over a blue and white floral summer dress, the sort of summer dress people were wearing thirty years ago, I assume she's not for me. I turn back to my newspaper. Scattered, thundery showers are expected by evening with the possibility of flash flooding in the south west. A heat wave in Eastern Europe. And then I'm aware that the woman has seen me and doesn't seem to be hesitating.

"Mary Foster? It must be you. I'm so sorry if I'm late. You never know with these seminars. They can overrun so, even the ones I'm conducting myself." She laughs very loudly, cheerfully, loops the white cardigan from off her shoulders and sits down on the black faux leather chair opposite mine. "Eliza Jarvis," she says, offering her hand. "Goodness, how strange to meet you after all these years!"

It's not how I imagined this would start. How I'd rehearsed it in my mind. I mutter something in greeting, take her hand, instantly at a loss. I notice that there's a man hovering close by and as if remembering him at the same moment, Eliza turns and waves him away. "Oh Tony, this really is no place for you, my love. Take yourself off for a couple of hours, there's a dear.

Amuse yourself, museums and galleries or something." The man, Tony, thinning dark hair turning gracefully grey, makes a mock sort of bow, acknowledges me with fleeting, kindly interest and then disappears back through the doors and out onto the street. "My husband," she clarifies, "Anthony Egbert. So rude of me not to introduce the two of you properly. But probably best not. He's such a dear, but no good in situations like this at all. Brilliant mind, you know, but hopeless when it comes to the human race and all its complexities." And she laughs again and tries to constrain her hair back with a large slide. I'm relieved as I'd not expected to meet her husband, this man called Tony or Anthony whom she's efficiently and speedily dispatched. She's on her feet again, gathering the awkward cardigan and shoving it into an oversized black bag that appears full of files and papers. "Come along, Mary, let's find ourselves somewhere a little less in the public eye. Ghastly places, these hotels."

"There's a coffee shop just up the street," I suggest. "I know it quite well and—"

"Ideal," she says. "I've only an hour or two at a stretch, but I'm sure that will do us. Lead the way."

And yet I feel she is the one leading both of us along the Bloomsbury pavement, past the second-hand bookshops, skirting the British Museum until we arrive at the café with green shutters next to a shop selling old maps. It's mid-afternoon and the place is quiet. We settle ourselves in a corner at a large wooden table, order pots of tea. Eliza adds a slice of carrot cake. She has a large, open face, the sort of face that is not at all attractive in a conventional sense, yet is nevertheless engaging. The kind of lively face people like to watch. There is a warmth about her, a softness in spite of her commanding manner. She props her elbows up on the table and studies me frankly.

"I have to tell you that my sister is appalled by what I'm doing. I spoke to her last night and she's pretty incensed. But then Dora won't even talk about the whole business. Never has."

"You can hardly blame her," I say cautiously. "I mean, acknowledging your father's infidelity so many years after the event may seem pretty pointless."

"But mother wanted us to know, believe you me. It wasn't a secret kept from us or anything like that. Dora and I are very different, though. Quite unalike in every way considering we're sisters. The past for her is simply that, ancient history that she can't be bothered with. Whereas I feel almost duty bound to delve into these rather murky waters. That's why I needed to meet you." Eliza speaks forcefully so that the girl bringing our pots of tea flinches, spills milk as she places the jug on the table. "And don't forget the cake!" Eliza calls after her. "I need something with a high calorific count to face the rest of the day."

For a moment I think she's referring to our conversation, but then realise she means her seminar. I am, after all, only a convenient and possibly vicariously entertaining interlude in her afternoon. She's given a paper earlier in the day and has a plenary session fixed for five. I feel a little overawed by this, but she speaks utterly without pretension or self-importance. The carrot cake arrives. I pour out pale tea.

"You probably know far more than me," I say, "your mother must have told you. Details about how long it went on, things like that. I only know that Fred Jarvis lodged in the attic of our house for a few years before… before he was killed. The rest I sort of worked out for myself. But only in very general terms. No specifics, you could say. No real facts."

I'm pleased the place is empty now, Eliza and I the only customers. It's not the sort of conversation you would wish to be overheard, after all. And I'm not sure how I'm going to react to what Eliza has to tell me. She breaks off large clumps of carrot cake with a fork, eats them quickly and picks up stray, sticky crumbs with her fingers.

"You can tell why I'm the size I am, can't you? I have the most dreadful sweet tooth. Quite the opposite of Tony, of course, who hardly eats a thing. But then he's got his own vices of a sort." Eliza finishes the cake, appears refuelled, pushes the plate to one side. She asks me whether I'm married, about children, career. About Ida's illness. And Jack, of course, she asks about him. I answer her briefly, more concerned to return her to the point. It's not, after all, the current Ida and Jack that are of interest, but the people they were when Fred Jarvis was alive. But Eliza seems to feel a need to delay for a while, reciprocating with such details about herself. No, she and Anthony have no children. They would have been hopeless parents, she tells me with a whooping laugh, far too self-obsessed, the two of them. Too dedicated to their work. Biochemists, she explains, then loses me in a description of what they actually do. She pours herself more tea, adds milk, ferrets for sweeteners in her bag and finally hauls herself back to where we've started.

"I don't remember a great deal about my father, of course," she says. "There are a few photographs, the odd impression in my mind that might be an entire fabrication of memory. I remember the odd incident. One day at the park when I dropped my ice cream – you know, one of those cornet things? And Daddy went straight over to the ice cream van and bought me another, bigger, more expensive one with a chocolate flake stuck in it which was the sort I'd wanted in the first place. I remember that. I must have been about five. I was wearing red sandals."

"You would have been very young when he died."

"Just six years old and Dora was four. So most of what I know is from what my mother chose to tell me in later years. Once I was old enough for her to… well, unburden herself a little. She seemed anxious to pass his story on, as it were. She didn't want Dora and me to be left with some false sentimental picture of our father, that's for sure. Although she was very clear that he loved us. Adored us, in fact, in his particular sort of way."

"It can't have been easy for your mother, left suddenly with two small children."

"Absolutely. But in some ways, I think that particular part of it was tolerable. In a purely practical sense. Obviously, there was a financial implication, but then my father was always unreliable where money was concerned. And as a young widow she found a lot of sympathy, everyone on her side, that sort of thing. Whereas simply as Freddie Jarvis' wife… well, I believe most people thought she only had herself to blame for marrying him."

"So he had a reputation?" I say. Eliza sits back in her chair. Her eyes are intensely dark, sharp, observant. The eyes of a clever, extraordinarily alert woman whose appearance is of too little importance to concern her. Absurdly, I try to relate her adult face to that of the small child pinned against the car window on a certain Saturday afternoon in Sea View Parade decades ago.

"My father was fifteen years older than my mother. Did you know that? No, of course you didn't, why would you? She was only twenty when she met him and she fell hopelessly in love with him. She told me that exactly, a *coup de foudre*, as she put it. It was a ridiculous marriage, of course, judged rationally."

"What do you mean?"

"My mother was a highly intelligent woman, most astute. She could have done anything, really. Medicine, scientific

296

research, she could have gone far. But then she met Fred Jarvis and the man simply charmed her. Well no, that's probably not quite fair. He did seem to have a natural charisma about him and evidently was awfully good-looking by the standards of the day. But she chose to abandon everything for him, including her university degree. It wasn't easy in those days to combine a career with marriage and children. Not for people like my parents. And I rather gather my father simply expected such devotion and sacrifice from her. Saw it as his unalienable, male right. He was the sort of man who assumes adoration. And on the whole, I suspect, tended to get it."

"And he was already an artist?"

"Oh aspiring, rather, to be something of the sort. He'd had some type of training although nothing as formal as a prestigious art school. I think he probably enjoyed cultivating the role as much as anything. People's lives could be so awfully dull then, after all, in that post-war decade or two, and he doesn't strike me as the sort of man who would have settled down comfortably to being a bank clerk or working for the local council."

I think of Jack, of my father's lifetime at the tax office, an obligation that went unconsidered. A necessity, no more nor less. Eliza goes on. "But he was feckless, really. My mother told me he was forever giving up jobs or was possibly sacked from them. He was working in a photographer's studio when they met, then he drifted briefly into advertising, I believe. It seemed he thought the 1960s was going to be his time to shine. An era far more suited to his temperament and talents. At least he convinced her of it, anyway. The big break was always just around the next corner, of course. And then when nothing really happened and he finally got the teaching job at the college on the south coast... well, the irony is that my mother told me she was initially delighted. She thought it meant he'd settled down at last, taking his responsibilities towards us seriously."

"Did he have real talent? As an artist, I mean?" I am trying to remember the picture with his scrawled signature at the bottom of the stairs of Number 8. I don't remember what happened to it. One day I was aware that it was no longer there yet I remember thinking that I'd simply got used to its absence rather than noting its abrupt removal. Eliza shrugs.

"Possibly more than some, less than others," she says. "A good amateur, I should imagine. Although I have to say that is my cynical view. I know so little about the art world. He certainly seemed to find it hard focusing on a particular discipline and developing that. There are examples of portraits, still life, landscapes, the lot, in fact, in various sketch books. But who knows whether he would have made something of a name for himself if he'd lived longer? My mother certainly considered him gifted and remained convinced of the fact. She kept all his work after his death."

"And did she remarry?"

"Years later, yes," Eliza says, "to a very kind man called Andrew. Again, he was considerably older than her. I can't say Dora and I ever really thought of him as a stepfather as we were both well into our teens by the time they married and he was more of an avuncular figure. But he adored our mother and he looked after her in every way. Financially, it made a huge difference to her."

"A practical, sensible choice, then, as far as your mother was concerned," I say and then instantly regret it. But Eliza's not offended. She nods, bats away a fly that's been hovering over her head.

"I am quite sure my mother didn't love Andrew. But she'd had that. Her *grande passion,* as it were. She and Andrew were companionable. They read similar books. Took pleasant holidays. Days out at National Trust houses together, that sort of thing."

I see Eliza glance at her watch. I'm beginning to wonder if this is all I am going to get, a limited account of Fred Jarvis' marriage to her mother. Perhaps it is enough, guarded, cautious. But all the same I sense there is far more for me to know. And for Eliza too. She may know of her father's affair with Ida, but she's given no hint that she's aware of his duplicity to my mother. To my father and me. The man appears to have been supreme in his operation of deception and I feel somehow that it's important for her to know that. I suggest more tea. Or coffee, perhaps. Eliza is enthusiastic and we call across the empty café and ask for two lattes. The girl looks up from her magazine and produces them with some enthusiasm as if relieved to break the boredom of her shift. A couple of customers wander in to buy take-away drinks, complain about the humidity, complain about the threatened Tube strike. Eliza checks her phone, laughs loudly and raps out a swift text message.

"Just Tony," she says, "just checking up that things are going all right between us. I think he was anxious about what I was getting myself into, meeting you."

Later, going home on the train, shoving my key in the front door and gathering up the junk mail from the mat, I remember that this was the moment when I could have retreated. When I could have diverted the conversation and remained blithely unaware of the pool of possibilities we unearthed.

But of course, I didn't. I pushed on instead.

"Have you any idea when Ida and Fred met," I ask, "or how? I mean, all of a sudden, he's living in our house and I've no clue where he came from. It's a part of the story that's a complete muddle to me."

Eliza shakes her head.

"Not really. But I gather my father had never been a faithful man. According to my mother he seemed immune to the idea of fidelity and was very easily flattered. Really, she had very little idea of how many women had caught his attention over the years. Both before and after their marriage."

"Was she very bitter about that?"

"I don't know what effect it would have had on their marriage if he hadn't been killed, of course. But I think you could say she always hoped and believed he'd grow out of it. Like an adolescent eventually leaving teenage angst behind. Or something of the sort. And by the time we were old enough for her to talk about him frankly, so many years had elapsed that any bitterness and resentment had probably gone. Death has a wonderful way of removing the negative, you know. The unpleasant facts about a person become more like amusing idiosyncrasies that can be viewed almost fondly. I think my mother was fortunate in being able to... well, shall we say readjust her memory of Freddie and therefore go on loving him." Eliza is grovelling around in her large bag, pulling up random scraps of paper, receipts, scrunched tissues that she pushes back down into the chaotic pit. Eventually, she pulls out a sketch book, lays it carefully on the table in front of me. It's old, battered and the binding is partly ripped. "I found a lot of these when I was clearing out my mother's things after her death. She was quite a hoarder and I threw masses away. But some I kept. And this one may be of interest to you, Mary. I think you should have it."

She leans over, flicks the sketch book open and thumbs through a few pages. Pen and ink drawings, some complete, some seemingly abandoned or crossed out. They are all dated, the earliest shown as October 1953, the final one May 1955. Some even have an indication of place or occasion. Many have names attached. *Kew Gardens,* for example, *woman with child,*

Hyde Park, Hampstead Heath, an old man. They are all sketches of people, some full face, others in profile, the occasional full figure standing against an abstract background. I thumb through rapidly until I find what I sense I'm looking for. *Ida,* it says, *Richmond Park.* Then a page or two later, *Ida, Putney Heath.* Then, *Ida, The Serpentine; Ida, Kenwood; Ida, Little Venice.* A few are simply titled, *Ida.* The dates span the spring, summer and autumn of 1954.

"Are they good likenesses?" Eliza asks after a while. I peer deep into the sketches, the angular chin they catch, the marked cheekbones and neat, bobbed hair.

"I'm not sure," I say. "After all, they were all drawn just before I was born."

I walk back to the hotel with Eliza. Tony is waiting for her outside, anxiously scanning his watch. She gives him an affectionate hug, gently mocks his attention to time. He looks at me suspiciously as if I have been subverting his wife's attentions for devious reasons. The sketch book is in my bag, wedged between a wallet and a paperback novel. I have no idea what I am going to do with it. Litter bins are now scarce in London, objects of suspicion rather than convenience; otherwise, it could already have been dispatched. Eliza places a hand on my shoulder.

"I would like us to keep in touch, Mary," she says, "but it's entirely up to you. I am quite sure there's more for us to find out about this whole matter." She gestures vaguely in the direction of the sketch book nestled in my bag. "You might want us to pursue it for greater clarification. On the other hand, you may just choose to dismiss it all as pure coincidence. The name, the dates, all of that. You may prefer to leave the past well alone."

"I don't know," I say. "I have no idea at the moment what I think. What I want to do."

Tony's impatience is clearly growing. Eliza laughs at him, takes my hand in hers for a moment. It's a surprisingly comforting gesture.

"Forgive me my selfishness for dragging you into all this. You might agree with my sister, Dora. She likes to detach herself from our parents' lives as much as possible. Has no interest in understanding them. Whereas I find I can't resist the hooks. Those cryptic clues. Now they're both gone in a physical sense, I feel more need than ever to secure something of them. I hope you understand."

And she's gone, drawn up the steps and into the hotel by her solicitous husband, switching rapidly into talking about the conference twilight session and delegates and dinner.

I find myself walking down the street, past the bus stops, ignoring the Tube station, walking on instead, through the thickening early rush hour crowds, pushing past the groups of tourists flashing cameras, past the small pools of people gathering on pavements outside pubs, glasses in hand. I cut through Covent Garden and down into the Strand, reach Trafalgar Square then switch south towards the Embankment. In the Embankment gardens I find the only spare seat on a bench and sit down next to a young woman with bright orange hair having a loud and angry phone conversation. She seems oblivious of me and carries on, cursing and swearing at the person the other end. A man, by the sound of things, a boyfriend, a partner, perhaps. When a pigeon hovers near her feet, she verbally assaults the bird as well. I sip from the bottle of water I've bought at a sandwich bar. I flick mindlessly through the evening paper left on the bench, trying to focus on national news, celebrity gossip. Cricket scores, even. On something impersonal and utterly unrelated to myself and the events of the afternoon. Suddenly, I feel utterly exhausted. Even the prospect of the short journey home seems too wearying. My bag bulges with Fred Jarvis' sketch book, like an unwanted, tasteless gift. But I know I will take it home. It contains too much to discard thoughtlessly and the idea of simply jettisoning it along with the city's empty drinks cans, cigarette stubs and discarded sandwich crusts seems intolerable.

But I have no notion of how to respond to it.

To the enormity or, alternatively, the insignificance of its contents, depending on your point of view. It's not that I'm doubting the identity of *Ida,* as portrayed in these pen and ink lines. When I think about it, there's a certain similarity to the photos of her taken around this time. Something about her cheekbones, the wide set-apart eyes, the jaw line even, are those I've seen in the few small snapshots taken just after my birth. And the likelihood of Fred Jarvis stumbling across another woman called Ida with similar features and choosing to draw her is implausible. Then there's my father's tuberculosis. He was ill some time before I was born. It's a fact I've always known in vague, rather unspecified terms, his isolation for many months in a sanatorium somewhere in Middlesex as it was then called, Harefield, I think, common treatment in that post-war period. My mother used to talk about it and a few times over the years my father has referred to it. There has never been the need or interest to demand from them exact details. Precise dates. Along with polio, TB, after all, was something that used to happen to people. It happened to my father. Before my lifetime and therefore always of limited curiosity.

Until now.

Until sketches of my mother hitch her to places, to dates and times that accurately anticipate my birth.

But perhaps it's all of no consequence whatsoever.

Even discovering that Fred Jarvis rather than Jack Foster may be my biological father could be seen as a technicality. The brash fact could be seen as just that and it would be easy to push it away, out of sight, if the man had not returned to our lives. If my mother had not engineered our move to 8, Sea View Parade, lodging her lover in the attic and placing us all so cosily around the table in that basement kitchen. Suddenly, I am seventeen again, sickened by my knowledge, by my proximity to these adults embroiled in their sexual entanglement. And now it seems my very existence may make me complicit, a catalyst, as it were, in the whole extraordinary story. Ida would never have married a man like Fred Jarvis with his precarious financial state, his lack of a secure, reliable occupation. Jack Foster was the man for that, a pragmatic selection, a considered choice. A man most anxious always to avoid rocking the boat, disturbing an apparent calm. And into the bargain, Jack loved her and remains devoted and caring as she declines, slides further and further away from the sentient human being who behaved with such bewildering audacity. In finding Jack, Ida certainly chose well. I have to give her that. But the bargain she struck in moving Fred Jarvis into the attic at Number 8 was based on an entire misconception. Served her right, you could say. I wonder, if she'd known, if Fred Jarvis had happened to let slip about the wife and two small children in Croydon, whether she would still have done the same thing.

The young woman next to me has changed her tone, stopped shouting and roaring into her phone. She seems to have forgiven whatever wrong-doing or mischief she's been berating for the past quarter of an hour. She even sounds affectionate, not exactly sweet-talking the man, but being patently flirtatious. She has plans for them at the weekend, she says. A party, someone from work, she's promised they'll go. Then she laughs loudly and shrilly and the early evening occupants of the Embankment gardens flinch, shift their attention more fixedly to their books, their newspapers.

Felix is sprawled across his bedroom floor when I get home. I tap on his door, open it a fraction and promise him dinner within half an hour. I ask about his day. Naturally, he won't ask about mine. Occasionally, the absence of social manners in adolescents is a gift. I push together some semblance of a meal, load Felix's plate, spare mine, but splash more wine into my glass. Tonight is not a time for sensible, healthy restraint. Lolling later in front of the television, Felix manipulating the remote control with such impressive speed that I only catch split seconds of potential programmes before they're fielded away, I take a risk.

"I heard something disturbing today," I say, "or at least something very surprising. I think another man might be my father. I think your grandmother had an affair with a man called Fred Jarvis and the affair resulted in me. It's possible people like your grandma and grandpa have been covering this fact up all their lives. And, of course, that means that this man, Fred Jarvis, who died years ago might be, biologically, your maternal grandfather."

Felix stops his channel switching for a moment. He turns towards me, his large eyes narrowed, a look of utter incomprehension on his face. It is a look with which I have grown increasingly familiar in recent years.

"What?" he says. "Did you say something?" He pulls one earphone out and I hear music pulsing from it, as it lies in his hand.

"Nothing important," I say. "Don't worry, it's absolutely nothing of any consequence."

22

David's at the front door.

"He's going to be late, sorry. Their match didn't start on time, the other team couldn't find the pitch or something."

He follows me into the kitchen, settles himself down at the table and I fill the kettle.

"It's no problem, we've got the whole day. Whatever are they doing playing football in the middle of July?"

I shrug.

"They just seem to carry on these days. No 'off' season in the way my father used to talk about."

"Felix should be playing cricket in the summer, not football," David says. It's what David always says, reliably, every summer. Foolishly, it never fails to annoy me.

"Why?" I snap. "Felix doesn't play cricket, you know that, he's never played."

There's a pause. I turn to the coffee mugs and spoons. David and I often start like this, sniping, scrapping, scoring with petulant remarks. But we move on always. It's as if some display of petty irritation is required to remind us of the reason for our divorce before we can resume genial conversation.

"Anyway, what are you two going to do today? Any ideas?"

David picks up the Saturday paper that's lying amongst a load of other clutter on the table, glances through the front page.

"Not really. It was easy when he was small, wasn't it? Deciding how to spend time together, I mean. The zoo, a film, even a pizza used to be exciting when he was eight."

"And now anything you suggest is just…"

"Boring," David says.

"He doesn't really mean it, he's just being his age. Just being normal. Showing real enthusiasm would seem too childish to Felix right now."

"I know," David says and sips his coffee, "but I miss it."

"Me too," I agree.

"At least in a couple of years or so I can start teaching him to drive. That'll give us something new to do together."

"No!" I say. "It will be too soon for that."

"Well, he'll be the right age," David says reasonably. And I sink down on the chair next to him and contemplate the prospect of the next maternal anxiety to face. No-one warns you beforehand that motherhood is a life sentence of worrying, constantly fearing the worst outcome of every event. Safely over one hurdle and the next simply rears ever higher and more precipitous ahead.

"Anyway, we'll probably find somewhere to have lunch," David sensibly leaves the driving subject, "just spend some time together. Whatever he wants."

I'd not intended to tell David about my meeting with Eliza Jarvis. But he's here sitting in my kitchen waiting for Felix and it's the only thing on my mind. The only thing I find I want to talk about. I start cautiously, tell him about the arrival of her letters, half expecting him to change the subject, get up, walk into the garden and advise me to cut the grass. But he doesn't. So I go on, describe our meeting and eventually go upstairs and fetch the sketch book from the back room and clear a space for it on the kitchen table. David drains his coffee mug. I get up, pour him more. He looks slowly through the pages, pushing my hand away when I try to hurry him towards the relevant ones. And when he sees the pictures of *Ida* he looks at them closely, intently, before closing the book in front of him. He looks up at me and smiles his very benevolent David kind of smile that I used to find an irritant and now view as mildly endearing.

"Poor old Mary, you've really dug up a lot of stuff here, haven't you? But why? I mean it's all so long ago. What can it possibly matter now?"

"You mean even if this shows that Fred Jarvis was my father and not Jack?" I sound melodramatic as if I am speaking a line out of a sentimental Victorian play.

"You have no proof of that, Mary, no clear idea of anything other than the fact that your mother and this... this Fred fellow knew each other years ago before you were born. You're reading so much into this."

"I know, but there's a possibility. A very real one. After all, that was hardly the end of things, some friendship between the two of them never referred to again. Fred Jarvis lived with us. We moved to Sea View Parade because of him. So that he and my mother could be together. Maybe even so that he could get to know me."

"Or so you say. You're choosing to put a particular slant on all of this, Mary. It's one way of reading the facts, certainly, but by no means necessarily the only way. You can't even be sure they were having an affair."

"Oh come on!" I say sharply. David's fair-mindedness can often sound like sheer perversity to me. "I was there. I lived in the middle of it all. And when Fred Jarvis died my mother was heartbroken. She cried. I saw her cry for the first and only time."

"Parents didn't cry in front of their children then. Just wasn't done."

"Therefore, it's all the clearer what was going on between them. She couldn't help herself."

"And your father? How did he react?"

"I'm not sure. Shocked, obviously. There was all the business about Jarvis being married, remember, the wife and children we didn't know anything about."

"And Ida? You're sure she had no idea that he was married?"

I nod. It's one of the few certainties I have about her.

"I've often wondered whether her grief was more about that than his death. It must have been a pretty devastating way of finding out he'd lied to her for years."

I've forgotten to drink my mug of coffee. I get up from the table, chuck the cold contents down the sink. Flecks of coffee grains pattern the white enamel. "I didn't tell Eliza Jarvis about that. The fact that he'd lied to all of us. I was tempted to, as a silly sort of defence for my mother. As if that made her sound less immoral, if you like. But then it made her father all the more culpable and it's hardly for me to point out that Fred Jarvis chose to keep his beloved family hidden in order to advance his situation."

"So you're happy to perpetuate that particular secret whilst at the same time trying to unearth all this other stuff and get it out in the open? I just don't see the point, Mary."

I turn and face David. His hair is now quite grey, I notice with something of a shock, although clearly it must have been subtly changing over years and I've simply failed to see. Felix has his height, a leaner, angular, fresher version. His eyes, though, a mix of hazel and dark muddy river brown, are mine. David's are the blue of moonstones. I go on.

"I want to understand Ida. Why she did what she did. How she felt she had the right," I say.

And the words sound futile, the sentiments extraordinarily foolish and ingenuous.

David stands up, pushes open the doors to the garden. The whirring sound of a lawnmower from down the terrace reaches us, the cry of the new baby from a couple of doors down, two small girls in the next-door garden squabbling over their swing. We listen to the noises as if grateful for their ordinariness. Their normality.

"Perhaps it was something she never understood herself. Maybe it was just an idea that grew then got out of hand, this Fred Jarvis business," David says eventually.

I shake my head.

"That wasn't Ida's way. She was always in control, always the one to make the plans."

"That's how she seemed to you. From the outside that's the way you saw her as her daughter and how she intended you to see her. Anyway, does it matter now? How much knowledge do we need about each other? To live reasonably contented alongside, I mean? Jack seems to have done all right. He's never struck me as an unhappy man."

"My father would say you have to think of the bigger picture. It's one of his favourite phrases."

"He's right. Some things are probably best left untouched, you know, Mary. Perhaps not all stories need to be told."

"You mean some truths are more important than others?"

David looks uncertain.

"Possibly. Yes, I think that's true. On the whole."

"You know, I think I always believed that one day Ida would talk about it all. And I've never been sure whether I was longing for that conversation or dreading it. Part of me has always felt indignant not to know all the sordid details whilst at the same time… perhaps if I had that kind of knowledge it would undo too much of the past."

"Undo your memories of a happy childhood, you mean?"

David's description doesn't seem to fit my own memories. Yet my childhood was certainly not blatantly unhappy.

"I knew I was loved," I say finally. "Does that define a happy childhood? I suppose I never doubted that. It just seemed very… joyless. As if my mother steered us towards a uniform kind of dullness that couldn't let us down. A sort of lowering of expectations, you could say."

And I realise that what I have really wanted to know all these years is whether my mother loved my father at all. Or if, for her, anything without Fred Jarvis was simply second best. An indifferent kind of life. A patch up and mend sort of existence best lived in a utilitarian way. Dying so soon, so dramatically, would have mythologised Fred conveniently for her too. Perhaps, over the years, she began to censor the truth by blotting out her knowledge of his wife, his two small children. Perhaps she is still doing it, sitting in her care home, grappling with ever increasing decline, thinking only of the man she loved, believing the narrative he chose to tell her, holding on to the last time she saw him, driving away too fast, too rashly on that wet, winter's night.

David puts his arm loosely around my shoulder. We walk down the narrow garden to the old bench stuck immovably against the back wall.

"Do you ever water those flower beds?" he says, casting a concerned eye at my attempts at summer bedding plants.

"Yes," I say swiftly, then concede, "but not as regularly as I should. I just forget. Anyway, it rained the other day."

"Get Felix to do it for you. Every evening at this time of year."

"Yes, good idea, I will," I say, knowing I won't. David knows this too, but we go along with the comfortable charade.

"So if you're asking my advice, which I don't suppose you are," he says, pulling us away from parched soil, "you'll just forget all about this business and do no more meeting of strange women in London hotels."

"You make it sound highly illicit. I assure you there's nothing strange about Eliza Jarvis."

"Even so, Mary." David places his hand on my knee. I am tempted to put my hand over his, but resist. "Just leave well alone if you've any sense. What's to be gained by all this, after all? And don't say that you need to find out who your father is. That's Jack in any real sense of the word and you know it."

"Of course I do. I'm not saying that." The side gate bangs and Felix appears, sweaty and muddy, football boots in hand.

"Well, look who's deigned to turn up at last!" David sounds relieved. He's coped exceptionally well with a subject so potent with emotion.

"I've been ringing the front door for hours," Felix says. "Why didn't one of you hear me?"

"We were talking," David says, standing up, "passing the time pleasantly until you came home. Did you win?"

"Lost 10-2. But the others are top of the league and at least two of their players should be in the older age group."

"We'll have them reported to the FA. Now go and have a shower and make yourself respectable so we can go out and leave your mother in peace."

Felix drops his boots, disappears through the back door into the house.

"Thanks for listening," I say. "I hadn't intended to burden you with it all. Blame Felix for being late."

We walk back towards the house.

"I think you expect too many answers, Mary. And it's too late for that. It's too late in the day now."

David's probably right. There was a time when I should have asked Eva explicitly about the birth of her only son and confronted Jean Mason's silence. A time when Ida and Jack were still young and strong enough to field an interrogation of sorts. But not now. Lives move on so that events, seemingly of huge significance at the time, become simply half-remembered moments. Partially-recalled stories. It's probably the only way to live and survive blithely alongside our mistakes and stupidities. There's consolation, after all, to be found in Jack's bigger picture.

Felix comes running down the stairs, hair still wet from the shower, sits on the bottom step to shove his feet into huge trainers.

"Where are we going, Dad? I'm starving. I really need to eat."

David opens the front door, car keys in hand.

"Lunch first, of course. And then… well, it's up to you, Felix. But I wonder if it might be a good day for the zoo."

David catches my eye. Felix starts to object then stops himself.

"Okay, whatever," he says, working hard at suppressing a smile. "The snow leopard's awesome."

★ ★ ★

Eva's here. By the best of coincidences, she's over from Boston with her daughters and manages to leave them for the afternoon. I'm so grateful. It's hardly, after all, an occasion that most would make an effort to attend.

"They're happy to be shopping," she says when she turns up just before two o'clock on the mid-October day. "They've got Don's credit card so don't worry about them. Really, I was just pleased the way things worked out. Thought it might help to swell the numbers for you."

Surprisingly, there are more people than I expect. For a woman who did not make friends easily, who, by nature,

313

tended to deflect company, Ida has a decent number at her funeral. My father, bereft, desolate at my side, takes note.

"People are kind," he says. "The letters I've had. You wouldn't believe." He stares ahead of him, awaits the inevitable, appalling procedure. He looks awkward, frail in his old dark suit that now swamps his thin frame. I'd suggested a church. Somehow, I thought there would be comfort in the orderliness of neat pews, choir stalls, that faint smell of dry air. The softness of slanting light through stained glass. To everything, after all, there has to be a season. But when I'd asked Jack what my mother had wanted, he'd looked at me, blankly.

"We never talked about it," he'd said.

"Surely, you must have done. At some point. Didn't you write something down? In wills, or somewhere?"

Jack had shaken his head.

"No. I don't think it really occurred to us. Should we have done?"

I'd hugged him, told him it was all right, that there were no particular laws or rules about this sort of thing. And I was reminded of when Felix was born. The maternity ward had been full of expectant women talking about their birth plans and I'd felt inadequate because I'd failed to make one. Birth and death equally, it seems, are supposed to have plans these days. As if these outposts are the bits we can control, leaving the expanse of life in between in free fall. Open to happenstance. Jack had looked relieved.

"That's all right, then. I wouldn't want to think I was doing the wrong thing. Just no fuss," he'd said, "your mother wouldn't have wanted too much fuss. You know how she was."

So there is no church and little fuss although we manage to choose a hymn between us, agree to a bible reading. Jack endures it all. I sit on one side of him, Felix the other, but he seems entirely alone. He holds the hymn book when we stand to sing, but forgets to open it, lets the rest of us struggle tunelessly through *Dear Lord and Father of Mankind, forgive our foolish ways.* It's only when we bow our heads in prayer that I notice his eyes are drenched with tears. In her last few days, Ida had been calm and subdued as if acquiescent to the idea of dying. Throughout September she'd been sleeping for more hours than she'd been awake, eating less, responding rarely to our voices. She seemed to be detaching herself from us, losing the instinct even to grasp our hands as if we had become an irrelevance to her. Tedious and tiresome with our entrenched insistence upon living. Daily, she grew more remote. Our voices, gestures, even our affections could not reach her.

And now the service is over and Jack shakes endless hands with people whose names he can't remember or doesn't even know. Neighbours of theirs, staff from the nursing home, one or two friends of mine who have so kindly come in support. David is here and stands next to Jack, quietly helping him as he flounders in his grief. Everyone seems to know a different Ida. I'm confused to hear a woman talk of her warmth, another of her practicality, even her patience and resourcefulness. It is not the woman I knew. My mother is being claimed by them all as if they want a part of her, to stake their own importance in her life. I can imagine Ida being unimpressed. Eva's at my side. She's wearing a beautiful pale grey suit, grey leather gloves and her heels are at least two inches high. She is clearly the smartest dressed mourner among us. I can see some people sneaking glances at her as if suspicious that she's turned up for the wrong funeral. I'd forgotten to plan what to wear and had opened my wardrobe only hours before and found a long green paisley dress that seemed suitable, but now manages to feel both drab and too casual at the same time.

"How are you?" Eva says and I grab the chance to move away from the kind couple living next door to Jack who are concerned that he refuses their offers to shop for him. Eva's company, even for a snatched moment, is so welcome. "It's never easy," she goes on, "losing a parent. Even though it's expected and inevitable and everyone keeps talking about it being a blessing. Whatever that's supposed to mean."

"I'm not sure what I'm feeling," I say. "I'm confused a bit about feelings right now."

"That's what I mean," Eva says and gives me a hug. "It takes time to absorb such a loss."

I agree with Eva even though it's not what I mean.

"Of course, I didn't really know your mother," she goes on, "not properly. But I remember her as very correct. Very upright and moral, I suppose. I think I was always a bit shy of her."

"No," I say, "you didn't know her at all, did you?"

Eva glances across at Jack.

"I remember your father as such a kind man. Gentle, almost. He looks so lost without her. I can't imagine what it must be like, to lose someone after a lifetime of togetherness. It's quite a testament to marriage, isn't it?"

"They certainly endured, if that's what you mean."

"All those years. Was it love, do you think, or just habit? I mean how can a choice made so long ago, presumably on the basis of passion, still be relevant? When you've grown old and ill and... well, so different to how you were. Do you think they still really loved each other?"

People are beginning to disperse, get into cars, waving away Jack's tepid suggestion that they go back to his house. They sense his reluctance to turn the afternoon into the semblance of a party. I'm relieved. I can't bear the thought of endless teacups and vacant conversations. I catch David's eye. The plan is to take Jack back home with me and Felix to stay for a few days if I can persuade him. Eva still seems to be waiting for an answer.

"I hardly think I'm the expert on marriage," I say dismissively. "David and I only managed three years or so. You'd know more about enduring love between husbands and wives than me, Eva."

The matron from Ida's nursing home comes over to shake hands.

"We'll miss her, you know," she says in a lilting Irish accent. "It always leaves a gap when we lose one of our little community. And your mother was such a pleasure to care for, never any trouble for sure."

I wonder how many times a month she has to go to such services, offer similar platitudes. As if families need to know their elderly relatives have been biddable and submissive at the last. No raging against the dying of the light seems to be the conduct deemed appropriate by homes for the elderly. David's having a hard time with Jack. He comes over as the Irish matron moves swiftly to her car and drives away.

"He's refusing to come back with you," he says, "wants to be in his own bed tonight, he tells me, alone with his own thoughts." I start to protest and he shrugs. "Just relaying his words, Mary, can't deny him what he wants to do, you know."

Eva taps David on the shoulder. He looks at her blankly then remembers. He's always a little strained with any friends of mine, as if wary that I might have filled their heads with negative tales of my former husband.

"You're looking older, David, and you've clearly forgotten me," Eva chastises him, "but then it's probably about ten years or more since we've met." He's obviously straining to recall her husband's name, her children, groping for anything appropriate to say so I rescue him, send him back to Jack, tell him to bundle him and Felix into his car. The four of us can, at least, drive somewhere together and drink tea. Then, if he insists, we'll drive Jack home and leave him to those thoughts. Eva's talking about trains. She's called a taxi to take her to the station. I hate to see her go, yearn to have her come home and sit her at my kitchen table to talk. But she has her two girls waiting for her at their London hotel, their tales of shopping excesses to share. She has somewhere more important to get to, people far more relevant to be with than an old friend who wants to confide in her, spill the story of Ida Foster and Fred Jarvis.

"I'm not sure it matters, anyway," I say to her as she searches in her bag for one of the grey gloves she thinks she's dropped. "I mean about whether it's really love or simply habit that keeps people together for years and years. As long as there's consolation there. That's probably what matters most. Being sure of finding consolation."

"Someone with whom to share the darkness, you mean," Eva says, "someone comfortably known."

"Something like that," I say and spot her glove on the ground by Felix's feet. There's a taxi turning into the car park and she goes over to say goodbye to Jack, takes his hand in both of hers then kisses him on one cheek. He seems hardly to notice.

"I'll ring before we go back," she promises me, "we've another few days. You must be busy, though, and…"

"You too," I say.

"Yes, it's quite a packed schedule. But if not this trip then next time, definitely." Felix produces the grey glove. He and David walk slowly with Jack to the car, ease him into the front seat.

"It's funny," I say, "I thought I was prepared to lose her. My mother. But now I feel as if I didn't make enough effort to know her. As if I let her down in some way by refusing to get close enough for her confidences."

Eva shrugs.

"Allow a person a bit of privacy, Mary," she says. "There's no reason why your mother should have confessed her deepest and darkest secrets to you, particularly to you, in fact, her daughter."

Eva's taxi man is getting impatient. He opens the back door of the car, looks at his watch.

"You're right," I say. "Come back soon, won't you? You're good for me."

And she's off down the driveway, waving out of the back window of the taxi, checking her phone for messages, shifting herself onto the next part of her day. Her family, her girls. Felix calls over to me.

"Sorry," I say, moving towards David's car where the three of them are waiting for me. "Sorry for holding you up. Let's go and find somewhere to have tea."

23

I sit down at my desk, switch on the computer and begin to type.

Dear Eliza,

It's over three months since we met. I've needed that time to let me consider whether I want to take things on to the next stage or simply forget that we ever made contact. My mother died two weeks ago. Although her last few days were peaceful, she did have a period when she seemed very disturbed by certain memories and, on one occasion, Ida kept murmuring your father's name, over and over again. Fred, Fred Jarvis, Fred. Freddie. Oh Fred. I was alone with her at the time and I sensed that there was something she wished to share with me. Her capacity for language, however, had mostly eluded her by this stage and she could only look into my face, grope for my hand, and repeat his name in little more than a whisper.

I think, therefore, Eliza, I'd like us to meet again soon. I've always thought I was content with the idea of being an only child, but now the prospect of possibly discovering two half-sisters is simply too much to resist. It would, after all, be so easy to find out for sure. And I am tired of secrets and concealed truths. If I am a legacy of Freddie Jarvis' relationship with my mother, I would like to know.

I print out the letter, put it to one side. Click on *Word* to start a new document.

Dear Eliza,

I am sorry that I have not been in touch since our brief meeting in the summer. My mother died a fortnight ago and as you can imagine my time has been very occupied both dealing with the logistical business of her death and coping with my grief and that of my dear father. Jack was devoted to Ida. They spent a lifetime together and I shall always be grateful to them for the love and support they showed me. No child could ask for more dutiful parents.

I see no point in us meeting again and would be obliged if you did not contact me at any point in the future. I am returning your father's sketch book under separate cover. Clearly, Fred Jarvis was a talented artist and his untimely death was a cruel loss to your family. Best wishes to you and your sister.

The two letters, typed and hand signed at the bottom, sit side by side on my desk. I read each one through several times. Outside, the neighbour's shed door is banging in the wind that has picked up over the past hour. The sound of a siren, police or ambulance, grows more insistent for a few moments before retreating. I look at the letters once again, then, suddenly entirely resolute, pick one up, pop the single sheet into an envelope and address it clearly to Eliza Jarvis. The other letter is discarded, torn up into several pieces, thrown into the wastepaper bin. I find a stamp.

Later, when Felix goes out to the park, I hand him the letter, ask him to slip it into the post box at the end of the road as he goes past.